W9-BIG-083

Imagine Me and You

for Joan,
Thank you for coming
along on this ride!

[signature]

NONFICTION BY BILLY MERNIT

Writing the Romantic Comedy

Imagine
Me and You

a novel

Billy Mernit

Shaye Areheart Books

NEW YORK

Published in the United States by Shaye Areheart Books, an imprint of the Crown Publishing Group, a division of Random House, Inc., New York.
www.crownpublishing.com

Shaye Areheart Books with colophon is a registered trademark of Random House, Inc.

Library of Congress Cataloging-in-Publication Data

Mernit, Billy.
Imagine me and you : a novel / Billy Mernit.—1st ed.
p. cm.
1. Married people—Fiction. 2. Imaginary companions—Fiction.
3. Jealousy—Fiction. 4. Man-woman relationships—Fiction.
5. Los Angeles (Calif.)—Fiction. I. Title.

PS3613.E76I63 2008
813'.6—dc22   2007024730

ISBN 978-0-307-39537-5

Printed in the United States of America

Design by Lynne Amft

1 3 5 7 9 10 8 6 4 2

First Edition

To Dee-Ann and Dick,
the original romantics

From what realm,
When your beloved appears,
Do you take the future?

RAINER MARIA RILKE

Contents

Imagine Me and You

1

Setup

A scene or sequence that identifies "what's wrong with this picture" in a protagonist's status quo; in romantic comedy, it implies that what's missing in the protagonist's life is likely to be fulfilled by a potential mate.

*O*n my third night alone since Isabella left, our home feels so haunted that I can't stand to stay inside, so I bolt through the garden gate and go stalking the empty street, crazed and aimless, only to realize I'm also keyless—I've locked myself out.

Even as I curse I have to laugh. Nothing is the way I want it to be, so it's only perversely logical that I'm forced to return to our place to stomp around the garden, peering helplessly at the barred windows. Such nice bars, too, with their hip, zigzaggy shape, befitting this perfect little Venice Beach apartment, a sweet one-unit bungalow, its only drawback (formerly an asset) being that you can't break in.

And such a beautiful night! The kind of beauty you only get when you're desolate, when it's all gone wrong. Everything painfully clear—indifferent stars twinkling through the dark branches swaying in the wind, a rainbow-ringed silver moon for me to howl at. The extra key isn't hidden where it's supposed to be, in the dirt of the potted olive tree by the back steps. I should rustle up a pickaxe, a battering ram. Instead I stand staring at the door, wondering: Did romantic comedies ruin me, or was I born a sucker for such myths?

I could blame Cary Grant, him and a whole seductive slew of movies I saw in my youth, which imprinted me with a formula for *how it's supposed to go.* I could blame my parents, sixty-somethings, who on the afternoon of the forty-seventh anniversary of their love-at-first-sight–ignited marriage were found rolling around on a couch, giggling and making out. No matter. Either way, I'm warped. I'm a writer who writes romantic comedy, a cinema studies teacher who teaches it, and I have so much faith in the standard beats of the successful courtship story that being left by the love of my life has me totally discombobulated.

Those beats weren't cooked up in some mad movie scientist's lab— it's a codified structure that replicates what happens when people fall in love in so-called real life: Setup (dueling personal histories) is followed by a Cute Meet (sparks fly) and a Complication (romance mucks up everything else that's going on). Further on comes the Hook (the sex is good). Then this thing that could be love gets tested, there's a Swivel, or turning point before a big commitment is made, and then one or both of the lovers hits that Dark Moment where they seriously consider bailing. But inevitably they have a clinch-and-kiss Resolution, and the audience leaves the theater with warm and fuzzy feelings, or merely feeling horny.

Well, we had all that, me and Isabella. After four years of marriage I thought we were living the reasonably happy ending. So the only way I can make sense of her leaving now is to rethink the structure of our story. I thought we were in Resolution, our Dark Moment having been back before the wedding when she had second thoughts about living here in Los Angeles, but that wasn't it, no, we must've been in a prolonged Swivel, questioning our decision. Now we're in a *real* Dark Moment— the crisis/climax preceding the finale, where she'll realize she was meant to be with me all along and the marriage is worth saving. So what I've got to figure out is how to move from sixth beat to seventh, from boy *loses* girl to *gets*. Not a simple task when your wife has already left the country.

First, though, I really ought to find that key.

Isabella used it last, having locked herself out a few months ago, and when she said she'd found a good place for it, I forgot to ask her where. I'm tempted to call her in Rome, where it's morning, except being the last person in Los Angeles who doesn't own a cell phone, I'd have to be inside to do this, inside the home that's so horribly silent and empty precisely because Isabella is on the other side of the world.

I walk to Joe's, the one neighborhood place still open this late on a weeknight, get my vodka and tonic and claim a corner of the bar. The new waitress I like with the round, kindly face sits a few stools down, done with her shift, blowing on a bowl of soup.

"So who had the affair?" she wants to know.

"Neither of us," I tell her. "It wasn't about that. Isabella was loathing Los Angeles. She didn't like the rest of America much, either. She missed Italy and her family, and she couldn't get her career restarted over here, and then, there's, you know . . ." A cavernous hole to step over, where the bad feelings live, born of my part in all this: how my struggle to find screenwriting work had made me cranky and only made her feel more insecure, and . . . "The usual stuff you run up against in any relationship," I say. "It all finally got to her, and . . . she left."

"Did she take the dog?"

I nod. The waitress tactfully sips her soup. I know what she's thinking, but still, there's a closet full of clothes and everything else Isabella's left behind. To look at the mess, you'd think she just went round the corner to get cigarette papers. And isn't *mercurial* the very definition of her nature? Oh, hope! Hope is the thing that does you in. But what's the thing that will bring Isabella back?

The waitress sighs. "She's so beautiful, your wife."

Isabella on the beach, pale cheeks reddened by the sun, windblown bangs in her brown Modigliani eyes, squinting at the small group of people standing on the bluff above her. After every gallery she'd approached in town had rejected her work, she'd invited her friends here to face the ocean, watching her use a stick as a brush, drawing in the wet sand only yards from the water's edge, an improvised series stretching down the beach: minotaur, mermaid, a child's face made of stars. Isabella called this self-curated exhibit *"Non Esiste,"* her tribute to all the work, made by human hands or by nature, that didn't exist in the eyes of the professional art world. I knew she thought she was the one who didn't exist, the invisible foreigner in an insensitive city. Later, when the rest of the group was gone, I sat with her watching the tide splash up over an angel and recede, erasing the lines of its wings.

"*Bella* Isabella," I say, agreeing with the waitress. "And still my wife. It's only a separation."

"Maybe you should go to Italy."

Don't even think about it, she'd said, when I was thinking of nothing else. When I threatened to fly over there, Isabella claimed she'd leave town to avoid me, the point being . . . "She needs some time alone."

The waitress nods while I think, How *much* time? The longer she's gone, the scarier this gets. It's scary enough already. I have a sense of how the waitress sees me: I'm the teacher-sometimes-writer from around the corner who's got the gorgeous Italian artist wife and the fabulous dog. If Isabella steps out of the frame, who really is that guy left in the picture?

"You think she might see other people?" she asks.

"I hope not."

She looks down the bar, and I follow her gaze to where a svelte dark-haired woman in black velvet sits paying her bill. "Maybe *you* should," says the waitress.

"What?"

"Date someone. If you want to get her back. If she's the jealous kind . . ."

The night we came home from the beach after *"Non Esiste"* was worse than bad opera. Isabella lit into me about a buxom blond friend of a friend who'd come to the show, someone I'd talked to for a few minutes.

"I'm surprised you saw anything I did, you were so busy staring at her. That's what you like, eh, those big American breasts!"

"You're being ridiculous."

"I'm ridiculous? You were the *bavoso*, like a dog with his tongue out!"

When Isabella loses it, her decibel level gets high enough to break glass, which was what I did then, finally, in an attempt to out-mad the madwoman. Figuring the only way to shut her down was to be more crazed than she was, I rammed my fist into a framed painting on the wall. And this did terminate my wife's hysteria, turning it to concern at the sight of my bloody knuckle and cut thumb, the tiny glass shards she picked out of my pants cuffs, and then, huddling with me on the bathroom floor, she erupted in gales of laughter, throwing her arms around my neck, apologizing for her accusations, and predictably we ended up making love with a ferocity that had been missing for a while, so . . .

"The jealous kind? Yeah," I say. "You could say that."

The brunette down the bar glances at me, appraises me quickly, then looks away. She's pretty, but wounded as I am, the prospect of even attempting to get close to another living, breathing female human being frightens and exhausts me. All that time and energy invested in trying to fit together two disparate psychologies, when I'll only end up confronting my newly defined shortcomings? I wasn't even able to muster the semblance of a smile when she looked my way, but let's just imagine, against all odds, I got lucky. *My place? Well, actually I'm locked out of my apartment because my runaway wife misplaced the extra key, and I'm only interested in a quick fling to make her jealous, anyway, so . . . how about yours?*

"Thing is, I'm not good dating material," I tell the waitress, and ask for my check.

Air. I hit the pavement, Abbot Kinney Boulevard all but deserted, the full moon looming larger now in the sky, wind rocking the palm-tree tops. It's the time of night I'd usually be out walking Maxi. I remember my last glimpse of the old mutt, in his carrier case at the airport as an attendant wheeled it away: his black-tipped nose poking out between the bars, one front paw rhythmically tapping at the door with the persistence of a prisoner demanding a call to his lawyer.

Memories like this are just what I need to keep at bay, but too late— the worst of the bad feelings are back. Ever since Isabella left, the fact of it has been gripping me physically. It's like the veil of daily life has been ripped away to reveal nothing but an enormous emptiness at the center of me, a hollowness so heavy it threatens to pull me right through the pavement.

I really should've ordered a second drink.

Ahead is a cluster of people on the sidewalk, bruisingly young and hip, muffled techno music emanating from a club. I'd consider braving it, for want of any other destination, but I'm as up for such revelry right now as I am for root canal work, so I keep walking. I stop short when I get to the corner of San Juan. Here is Stroh's, the best deli in the neighborhood, full of European gourmet foods. I'd rejoiced when they opened a few years back, excitedly ushering Isabella in there to see the chains of Italian sausages, the stacks of cheeses, the pile of brightly wrapped amaretto cookies imported from Rome. But their wares hadn't been enough to keep her here.

I peer through the window into the dark depths of Stroh's. Fluorescent lights in the fridges and display cases bathe soda bottles and pasta salads in a ghostly glow. A mound of blood oranges gleams on a countertop, casting a long shadow. The inanimate world is speaking to me, now that I have the time to listen. *I'm abandonment,* says the emptied salad bowl. *Here's loneliness,* whispers a solitary lime.

I'm listening. I understand. But though it will take more than a better imported mozzarella to manage it, I am going to get my wife back. I am. I just need to find that thing, the thing that will turn her around. Like I need to find that key. Realizing that there are only so many places she could have hidden it, praying that I won't have to deal with trying to find my landlord or a locksmith at this hour, I trudge homeward.

Turning the corner onto my block, I see the dim figure of a man sitting against the curb in front of my building, long legs stretched out on the asphalt. A black man, skin-and-bones thin, his clothes ragged, pants split almost all the way up to his hip on the right side. He smiles at me as if I'm a friend arriving just in time for an appointment.

"Well," he says. "Here we are."

I nod. The man's gaze is clear, his expression amiable. He's holding an unlit filterless cigarette in one hand, and as I watch, he brings it to his lips, inhales, eyes briefly closing in pleasure, and then drops his hand again, exhaling a cloud of invisible smoke.

"Need a match?"

The man shakes his head. "Nope, but I could use a little cash. Got a hundred dollars?"

I laugh. He jerks a thumb over his shoulder. "You live here?" I nod. "Then you gotta be doin' all right." He assesses me. "You not an actor. What, a writer?"

"Actually, yeah. I write."

"Anything I mighta seen?"

"No," I say, then add, a reflex: "But I did just sell something."

He nods. "Could be all you need, get it green-lit. Who picked it up, Paramount? DreamWorks?"

"A producer named Rumer Hawke."

The man gives a low whistle. "You workin' for Rumer Hawke, that's like Spielberg money."

"Nah, not yet," I tell him. "He optioned a novel I wrote. The big money only comes if he actually makes the movie."

"So you a novelist."

"No, I just wrote the one."

"And that's it? That's all you wrote?"

Amazing, the force of the culture here. Even in the pit of your darkest despair, you feel compelled to present your credits. "No—New Line optioned it seven years ago. I came out from New York to do the adaptation, but by the time that didn't happen, I'd already got the screenwriting bug, so I've kept at it. I've gotten a few things optioned," I hasten to assure him. "Just haven't gotten one *made* yet."

The man nods, takes a drag of his cigarette, exhales air. "So's Rumer Hawke gonna make this?"

"Well," I say, "in the one minute I spent with him when we met, he sounded enthusiastic."

"What'd he say?"

I remember exactly what he said, having mentally replayed this minute innumerable times since. It's been a little gold talisman to fondle amidst a myriad of daily Los Angeles anxieties, though lately it's lost its luster. "He said he was 'tremendously excited' about us working together, and that no one else besides the original author could possibly have a better grasp of the material."

"No shit."

"Of course, that was two months ago," I admit. "He's still holding on to the draft I did when I first moved here, and I haven't gotten any feedback yet."

"Typical," says the man.

"Totally," I agree.

Wind riffles the palm-tree tops. He looks me over. "What are you, thirty-something?"

I bristle, being a precarious thirty-nine. "Yup."

"Sounds like you got lucky just in time. Yeah, a writer hits forty in this town . . ." He shakes his head. "Put a fork in ya, you done."

I nod, reminded that having taken a sabbatical from teaching writing so that I'd have time to write, I'm writing nothing these days. I'm talking to a homeless person in front of a home I can't get into. I pull the change from my pocket and hold it out. "Well . . . Here you go."

He climbs easily to his feet and takes the money. "Much obliged," he says, cigarette dangling from his lip.

"Hope you find a light."

"Nuh-uh. Lasts longer this way," says the man. "Tastes better, too."

"Enjoy it." I step up on the curb.

He nods, walking away. "See ya at the movies."

"Thanks," I say, and open my garden gate as he fades into the night.

Once it's closed behind me, I survey the yard. I have some digging in the dark to do. Maybe Isabella hid the key near her studio. I walk through the garden to the former garage space with its padlocked studio door. Piled by it are paint cans, vases, shipping boxes—but nothing I turn over yields a key.

I go back and skulk around the periphery of the bungalow. Beneath the side window I stand on tiptoes, peering inside at the kitchen I fled in horror only an hour ago. Now the warm-lit interior beckons so invitingly. I'm like a Dickens orphan on Christmas Eve. Inside I see my bicycle headlight out on the counter. I was putting in new batteries earlier this evening, and the screwdriver I was using is still sitting next to it.

A tool! If I unscrew the screws on Isabella's studio-door lock, get in there and climb up through the ceiling trapdoor that goes to the attic crawl space that leads to the trapdoor above my apartment's hallway and drop down to the floor without breaking my neck . . . But how to get the screwdriver? The kitchen window's not locked. I could pull down the screen, reach through the bars—that is, if I had the arms of Elastic Man.

I return from the front of Isabella's studio with a yardstick and a mailing tube. I take off the screen, push the window up, but can't see what the hell I'm doing. I go get the trash can, plop it upside down in the underbrush—crippling one of Isabella's beloved plants, *scuzi!*—then climb up and set to work.

Window up, I maneuver stick and tube between the bars, pincer-like, closing in on the screwdriver. I get a grip on its handle and slide it back slowly, but the tube knocks the bicycle light off the counter. I wince as I hear it bust open against the formica floor.

Put a fork in ya . . .

Teeth clenched, I pull. Here comes the screwdriver, rubber handle bouncing across the formica. I pull out the stick and tube and let them drop. Face smushed against the bars, I reach down, fingers flailing. Then I've got the damn thing clutched tight in my fist.

I march triumphantly back to the studio door. Scary second when I think the screw heads are too small for the Phillips I've just rescued, but no, the first screw gives way. I've got the lock off and the door open in two minutes.

When I flick on the track lights, I'm hit with Isabella's inner world writ large—canvas on easel, drawings on walls, project-in-progress strewn over desk, a familiar smell of acrylics and oils. I force my gaze past it all, walk quick to the rear, and peer up at the ceiling trapdoor. I'll have to move a ton of things, and the stepladder isn't high enough. How the hell do I get up there? I'm scouring the clutter in desperation when I catch a glint of silver amidst an ashtray filled with pushpins. There lie the keys on their familiar heart-shaped locket and chain.

Ah, Isabella, the engineer who once perfectly reconstructed the fallen nest of a wounded sparrow—also the mystic who can't keep the quotidian details of key-keeping in her head. I leave the studio door shut but lock-less. I don't think a crackhead thief will have any more luck selling Isabella's artwork than she has, so the door repair can wait till morning. I trot up my front steps nearly as fast as I dashed down them when I left.

Once I'm inside, I'm greeted by the same crushing silence I was so desperate to escape. And no room within this spooky abode is safe. Step into the kitchen and I confront the specter of Isabella, a whirl of warmth and color in the crook of stove and counter, the night a young family living out of their van on our block got robbed and she whipped up a tuna-and-salmon pasta for them at midnight . . .

Walk instead into the makeshift office alcove between the kitchen and the back door, and there's the desk ingenious Isabella created out of wooden shelves we found on the street, she who measured everything and showed me where to pound the nails just so. . . .

Can't hang out in the living room: I'm suddenly reliving the first dinner party we ever threw here, for my folks in from out of town and six other friends she'd never met before—thinking about the guts it took to face them all for the first time, to play vivacious hostess when she'd barely moved in and was still struggling with the language. . . .

I take refuge in the bedroom, but that's where the worst of all this lies in wait. There'd be sound-track music, if this were a romantic comedy—the new single from the latest young melancholic Brit, acoustic guitars bathed in echo, the ache of bass and pound of snare, something noble in the choked minor-chord yearning of it all—but that's something they never really get right, do they? No. Your real Dark Moments are silent.

Not entirely, though. There's this bird who took up residence in the tipu tree when Isabella and I courted, singing at the top of its tiny lungs night after night, a real artist with a prodigious range, his aria the score for our own athletic ecstasies, just as impassioned and unceasing. We called him the King of Birds, fantasizing that he'd flown here from the Land of Love, drawn by our romantic energy. He's shown up every fall since, the renowned avian tenor returning to the scene of his debut triumph, and tonight, when I'm ready to hit myself over the head with the nearest blunt object to bring on the sleep that's been eluding me . . .

He's back. I hear him outside the bedroom window, doing his scales. And I want to welcome his presence as a sign, a divine message from the kingdom of the ineffable, heralding Isabella's inevitable return, a magical proof that our love really is eternal, but in the current circumstance his once-virtuosic scales sound crazed and desperate. He's like some berserk child's toy left outside, kicked into gear to run out its batteries, a midget madman reading from a sundial by moonlight, telling the wrong time to nobody who's asked.

Not the lullaby I need as I fall onto my appallingly wide and vacant bed.

Jordan,

Your message really shook me. This truly is a deplorable state of affairs, and my heart goes out to you.

It wasn't long ago that I lost a lung, a rib, and various other miscellaneous pieces that had been with me a long time and to which I had grown quite fond and attached. That's something I've almost gotten used to. But I imagine that were I to lose my wife (an event that I can't, in fact, imagine), I would truly be undone.

Still, as you say, the story isn't over yet, and this may well be the rift that seeds a greater bond for the two of you. Given your penchant for romantic comedy, it's hard to believe your saga will have a tragic denouement.

My own mental health is relatively good, thanks, probably a sign of denial. The last CT scan wasn't bad; we're waiting for the report from pathology on some fluid they took. . . .

Oh, I get tired even telling you about it. The good news is I'm still mobile. By all means, let's get together. Next week may be good. It's good, from my perspective, that there is a next week. Until then, hang in there.

Leo

I've been meaning to see Leo for months, and his early-morning e-mail evokes him whole—the professor, bearded, bald, and bespectacled, holding up a wizened forefinger as he asks, "Are you familiar with . . . ?," a mentor's wonderfully polite way of testing the parameters of his colleague's breadth of knowledge. He's a man who smells the binding of the book before he reads it, and one night, drinking port in Leo and Estelle's home on the Pacific Coast Highway with its picture-window view of the ocean, waves crashing against the deck pilings below, we agreed that one of the most beautiful sounds in life is that of an old-fashioned fountain pen's nib scratching ink onto paper. Leo is the one person out here who knows that I, in my heart of hearts, still aspire to greatness, to write something that will *mean* something to the world. "So why," Leo teases me on occasion, "are you trying to find work in the moo-vies?"—drawing out the syllables with an archly raised eyebrow.

A few years previous, Leo fought lung cancer and only won a partial victory. Recently he's been in seclusion after a bout of trips to specialists. The last time I called, Estelle explained that the cancer has returned, contained only by chemo, and though Leo's in a temporary grace period, his future is not looking rosy.

Feeling chastened (like *I've* got problems?), I reply to his e-mail immediately, promising a visit in the following week. But message sent, I'm contemplating the void again. Now what? I think to call Moony in

New York, but he's off shooting some indie pic. There's no one else I would want to talk to, and that silence looms.

Staring at the computer screen, I can't help thinking of what I'd ordinarily be doing on such a beautiful morning. It's just the kind of weather that would send Isabella and me pedaling up the coast for a brunch at one of our favorite spots, Back on the Beach.

Tables set out in the sand, far from the town that drove you crazy with its insidious promises. Isabella browsing through a yoga book, me correcting a student screenplay, Maxi underneath the table, facing the ocean and barking at the gulls. Talking to Carlos, the gay Argentinian waiter with the wide, wicked smile, about his countryman Julio Cortàzar, my favorite writer. And after, telling Isabella about the feeling Cortàzar gave you, the sense of another time and space, a dark mirror world seeping into the edges of this one, so that the idea that you're living a dream becomes scarily believable, Isabella now sketching on her ever-present pad and nodding. And when I ran out of words, she slid the pad over for me to see, and there it was: a drawing of us on the beach that made us look both contemporary and ancient, archetypes straddling two eras—the essence of what I'd been saying casually realized with her fluid mischievousness in the curve of every line. Leaning over to admire it, I rested my head against hers, feeling a blissful little pause in time, as if we'd arrived at our predestined place to be.

"Poor *amore,*" she'd said. "You work so hard to support this art of mine, and it's not even the work you want to be doing. Can you really be happy?"

I was, I told her, and it was true then, with sunshine on the silvery sea, castle-like clouds and seagulls, a child racing the tide up the beach. Maxi snapped up the bits of bacon I slipped him. Isabella wanted to take him down to the water, only to be stopped short by a sign at the sand's edge touting Santa Monica's list of ordinances and laws: DOGS NOT PERMITTED ON THE BEACH. NO DRESSING OR UNDRESSING. NO ALCOHOLIC BEVERAGES. NO LOITERING UNDERNEATH THE PIER. NO PLAYING OF AUDIO OR ELECTRONIC DEVICES BEFORE 8 A.M. OR AFTER 10 P.M. . . .

It wasn't enough that in this ridiculous pretend city the restaurants closed their kitchens at ten each night (the hour most Roman eateries were just beginning to fill), that you could not find a real tomato. Across the sea her friends were lounging, tanned and topless, in the sand of Orvieto, drinks and cigarettes in hand, blasters blaring, their Italian dogs bounding into the waves to retrieve balls and sticks.

Basta, as my wife would say. I pull open the blinds so that the morning sun wipes the memory from my eyes, and log onto *The Onion's* site in search of at least a laugh. Next to the masthead, a vivacious young cutie smiles invitingly from an ad for a matchmaking service. "The worst lie I've told is that I never tell lies," says Pixiehead. I contemplate her unblemished, carefree face. This can't be where my future lies, can it? Desperately courting Pixieheads?

The phone rings as I'm considering this, so loudly and unexpectedly on the desk beside me that I jerk back in my chair and the cup at my elbow flies into the air. I grab for it, twisting, the chair topples, one wheel smacking into my ankle, and in a desperate move to free it from the falling metal, I smash my bare toes into a couch leg.

Ow, I keep saying, ow, like a character in a cartoon, ow!, as if this is a magic word that can take the place of the actual pain. But no, hell, it really hurts. And the phone keeps ringing.

I snatch up the receiver. "Yeah?" is all I manage to croak into it, busy grabbing at my mangled toes, bright red, one bleeding. Amidst the crackle of long distance comes Isabella's voice. I can sense from the way she speaks my name that I've startled her, but I can only repeat myself. "Yeah?" The big toe isn't broken, I can wiggle it, though the next one is bleeding pretty good.

"Are you there?" she asks.

"Uh-huh, I'm just . . . What's up?"

"What's up?" she echoes, and I can hear the confused wariness in her, because shouldn't I at least be glad she's called? I am, of course I am, but I'm also huddled in the grip of hurt, hugging my poor foot and wanting, if such a thing were possible, to jam my toe into my mouth and suck it like a thumb.

"Well, everything is up. And down," Isabella says with a rueful laugh. "Rome is beautiful but it's freezing. I'm glad to be back but I'm devastated from leaving . . ." She pauses, hearing only silence from my end. "Hello? Still in the room?"

"Yes, I'm . . . Go ahead," I say.

"You're on the computer."

Isabella's near-psychic ability has always unnerved me. I believe she's somehow able to see through a telephone receiver. She can certainly see through any but the most firmly constructed falsehood. "No," I say, turning my back to Pixiehead. "I'm listening."

But I haven't hit the necessary pitch of readiness, to listen the way I'm supposed to listen. I'm in the recently familiar role of the disappointing husband. "Maybe this is not a good time," she says.

"No, it's okay." What I need is to get up and get some ice. "I'm just in a little pain right now," I tell her.

"I know," says Isabella. "We're both in pain, Jordan. But I was hoping you might talk with me—"

"Isabella," I begin.

"—because even though we're apart, we could help each other—"

"Wait!" It comes out as a yelp, due to the mistake I've made of trying to stand up. I have to hold on to the couch as flames of pain surge greedily up my leg.

"I'm sorry," she says. "I'm being a little selfish. It's not fair that I ask you to spend your time—"

"I stubbed my toe," I interrupt, aware of how ridiculous this sounds.

"Your toe?" said Isabella.

"Actually, I'm bleeding."

"*Madonna!* What happen?"

The couch, I explain, and ice, she commands, instantly becoming the solicitous wife. Can I bend it?

"Don't worry," I tell her, hobbling into the kitchen for paper towels. Despite the persistent throbbing, I enjoy a moment of martyr-like nobility in downplaying my injury. It's good to have full justification for suppressing a hurt, as opposed to my ongoing program of denial, in which the inability to confront my feelings is not, I know, exactly heroic. "Tell me. What's going on?"

A long sigh. "It hasn't been easy," she says, "the coming back. Nothing about this situation is simple. I think Maxi wonders where you are. He won't eat his food. And for me, too, it feels strange to wake up here alone. The thing is—"

I hear a buzzing sound, the muffled, throaty call of Isabella's mother, Isabella's rapid Italian in response. "Jordan, I'm sorry. My mother is here, she's early, we go to the gym. But I wanted to talk, to tell you my thoughts. And to see how you are . . ."

"Not great," I say.

"I know. This is so hard for both of us . . . *uffa*. But I have to call you back."

"All right." Toe wrapped, I open the freezer.

"Amore?"

"Sì," I say quickly, surprised to hear her use her old term of endearment for me.

"I wanted to ask you . . ." Equally unexpected is the uncertainty in her voice as she continues: "I spoke with Daniela on the phone yesterday, she says she's seen you in a restaurant, with some pretty woman . . ."

I think. "Oh, yeah, Lisa Myers from school. We traded curriculums for—"

"The conference you do each year," Isabella says. "Ah. She's the one who has the English boyfriend. Steven. And they're still together?"

"So far as I know," I say, struck again by how nothing gets by that ever-vigilant mind of hers. I've met the man a number of times and can never remember his name.

"So I guess you're finding ways to keep yourself busy without me."

"Come on, she's just a friend."

"Jordan, it's strange, but . . . Oh, I miss you. If I am allowed to say that . . . I have to go. I send you kisses." Kisses? *"Ciao."*

"Ciao," I say, and hang up perplexed. What is going on over there? From the tone in her voice, it sounds as though—*the jealous kind.* Well, how silly, if just the report of me being at a restaurant—

And suddenly I'm remembering that night of *"Non Esiste"* again, the broken shards of glass in my cuff and the dark, wet blur of her lips against my chest, and then, like a crazed bolt from the deep blue of despair, comes an idea.

It's a ridiculous idea.

Under a blank slate sky so empty there could be a "Your Sky Here" ad plastered across it, I point my battered little Nash Metropolitan toward Dutton's bookstore, intending to find a book for Leo as a sickbed gift (he's partial to the Eastern Europeans, so I'll look for Rilke, Handke, or some other dark heavy with a *k* in there) and wonder: Could I actually go through with it?

The concept is funny in a crazed sort of way, worthy of a romantic comedy pitch: Guy can't bring himself to date a real woman to make his wife jealous, so he dates an unreal one. A make-believe mistress.

Paused at a stoplight, I'm beside the storefront of a rare and second-hand bookstore I've driven by countless times: Wm. Arnold's. Venetian blinds are closed in the picture window by the entrance, but a small sign tucked in one corner says OPEN. An empty parking space beckons. On impulse, I pull over.

But could I, really? Lie and then keep lying, to *my* wife? Come up with the sort of inspired detail work that could withstand her laser-like scrutiny?

Yeah, I could. I can't let Isabella settle into her hometown. Every day she's away from me is another damning click of a dark hand moving down the dial toward the midnight of our marriage.

I open Mr. Arnold's door. Inside lies a silent, dimly lit mini-city of books. It's a vast labyrinth of bookshelves, tops grazing the ceiling, their towering wooden structures forming a byzantine geometry that obscures the inner reaches from view.

My sense of having stepped into some cracked emperor's kingdom of used bookery is borne out by the presence of a lone man seated at a desk tucked between two bookcases near the entrance: rotund, white-haired, and Ben Franklin–spectacled, wearing a dark suit jacket and a wine-colored cravat that accentuates the pallor of his jowls. As I approach the desk, he's copying figures from an open ledger onto filing cards in microscopic handwriting. "Yes?" he says, the terse syllable conveying the depths of his annoyance at being interrupted.

I tell him I want Eastern European literature. Ben Franklin's scary twin purses his thin lips, a gourmet chef who's just been asked for cooking tips by a customer who's wont to barbecue dog. He flicks his eyebrows to his right. "Aisle H," he says.

I enter the maze, following a polished wooden floor path, my mind trotting ahead of me, back on the Isabella track.

So who, then? Who would I supposedly be going out with?

Some aisles are shorter, others go off at diagonals, and soon I'm lost. The system isn't exactly alphabetical. Ethnic Studies leads me round a corner to Eastern Philosophy, then Ethics. I turn away from Ethics, needing to get my bearings. I dread going back to the forbidding gatekeeper for directions, not that I could find him.

Somebody I already know? Or someone entirely imaginary?

Deep in the thickets of this literary metropolis, without a breadcrumb trail to indicate my point of entry, I realize that a faint scent like incense or rosewater has been leading me, subliminally, to this spot. Peering down the passageway ahead, I'm surprised to see movement, a flash of color in the shadows. It hadn't occurred to me that I might not be alone. Optimism tweaked, I walk down the aisle. Maybe whoever it is can help me find Literature.

Someone who's not around now, but who I can use as a model, a template . . .

A rustling draws me round another corner. Now I see, through a narrow opening at the meeting of two sections, a cascade of dark hair topped by the triangle of a deep blue-green kerchief, the sliver of a figure standing . . . where, exactly, it's hard to tell, since I've come to a dead-end corner and can't gauge the distance from here to there. I see a pale finger tap at the binding of one slim volume on a shelf and then withdraw. I retrace my steps, thinking that the noise I'm making might flush her out.

When I get to where, by my best estimate, the woman had been, it's as if the floor itself has somehow disappeared her. But the perfume is more present here in Drama. Probably an actress looking for a how-to book, and unlike me, she knows her way around the place and has simply headed out. The scent she's left in her wake is oddly evocative, though, and as I picture again that hair and that kerchief—

It's as if someone has stepped right up beside me, forgotten until this moment but marvelously familiar, her face turned to mine with an expression of delighted interest. I recognize in this memory the exceptionally attractive student whose luminous green eyes fastened on mine for an entire halcyon summer quarter two years ago when I was teaching "Writing the Character-Driven Screenplay." Naomi.

Naomi Dussart, a promising writer here from France for a year to study screenwriting. Witty, knowing, walking across campus beside me in her casually chic clothes, those perpetually pursed lips smiling sideways at something I said. I'd glimpsed a freckle on the upper slope of one—the right, or was it the left?—of her breasts, and looked up to find her eyes meeting mine with open interest. I would stand at the head of the class listening to her read her work and feeling her feel my gaze upon her, and think, Not for me, with a sense of genuine relief, despite the titillation, secure in the passionate bonds of my marriage. On the last night of class, I noticed that she'd dressed up for the occasion. And a little frightened when I found her lingering in the hall afterward, I'd complimented her on her scarf and fled like a blushing schoolboy.

I remember the bright green scarf setting off the red highlights in her silken auburn hair, envision her staring after my retreating figure, her expression wistful. Naomi who is back in Lyon, living her Lyonese life.

Safe across the sea, oblivious to me realizing an imaginary version of her here . . .

I pace down the row of books, mind already awhirl with the fantastical logistics.

So: I might run into Naomi, for example, but how?

The volumes my fellow book-hunter had been perusing are mostly hardcover, wrapped in protective plastic. I scan the shelf, noting Artaud, Egri . . .

Say she's finished the screenplay she began in my class. Maybe gotten it financed. Why would she come back here?

Right under my nose are two books whose bindings, twisted inward at an angle, suggest the presence of a third pushed back behind them due to too-tight shelving. I suspend my Naomi musings to pry the books apart and a tiny thud rewards my suspicion. I reach into the recesses behind, my hand finding the contours of the fallen volume. I ease out a weathered copy of *The Art of Dramatic Interpretation* by J. Samovitch Alexi.

I flip it open, my interest tempered by the sight of cramped, near-gothic type, dense text. The page edges are yellowed, and the book holds a faint scent of mildew. It falls open as I riffle the pages to one that, judging by the stains in its margins, has been studied in earnest.

"One must begin, then," the voice of Alexi in translation says,

> *with the ground beneath one's feet. And what do the feet themselves reveal about the nature of personality? Salome stands before you barefoot. But on close inspection, would she not have adorned her toes with rings, bejeweled and belled? The soft leathered shoes of King Lear are not the tough soldier's boots that belong to Macbeth. Once more, the issue of singularity, of specificity, must inform the actor's choices, even in—especially in—the imagining of one's assigned character.*

I read on, intrigued. This exercise, created to help an actor bring a role to life, can also be used if the actor lacks a rehearsal partner and needs to imagine one in the other part. Alexi is presenting a virtual recipe for inventing someone, and having them pass for real.

How weird is that?

I snap the book shut, expelling a burst of dust. As I stride down the aisle with Alexi's tome, clearly some sort of cosmic validation for my screwy plan, I return to the model with whom I'll enact it.

Say Naomi's made her movie already, she's doing the final cut in L.A. and—this makes perfect sense—she wants my opinion on it, before locking it up. Just the two of us, in a little editing cubicle . . .

I still the image there. So far, so good. I think I hear the sound of murmuring voices ahead, a low lilting laughter as I approach the opening in the labyrinth of shelves that leads to the proprietor's desk. There he sits, still absorbed in his accounting. To my puzzlement, there's no sign of any companion. The man silently accepts the book from me, looking it over dubiously, as if I'm responsible for its shabby condition. "Busy day, huh," I say.

The bookstore troll looks at me blankly. I hand him a twenty. He punches buttons in his pre-WWII cash register, ringing me up with a loud mechanical curtness that says, *That'll be enough out of you.* I emerge into the bright gray light of day with my obscure but timely find in a bag, and my fantasy cast and ready to be scripted.

What I don't have is a book for Leo. I'll look for that in a store that's less . . . curious. Unlocking the car, I glance back at Wm. Arnold's, thinking that it might have vanished, mirage-like, from between the other nondescript facades. But its blind-drawn windows remain, indifferent to the likes of me and my concerns.

And now that it's all about Naomi, I'm obsessed. I rush home to settle down on the couch with a dead Russian.

Alexi has the mordant, wryly cranky tone I love in Slavic writers. His insights take Stanislavsky a step further. If your character has supposedly gotten a haircut, you go to the barber, you inhale the scent of balsam pow-der and talc, you figure out the right tip for the man, you check yourself out in every window on the way home, you shower to get the itchy hairs off your back. Only then can you call upon the experience when you show up onstage, freshly shorn and tailored for that important business meeting scene in Act Two. Obviously when playing Raskolnikov you can't murder your landlady in real life, much as you might want to, but you can take an object you associate with her, and beat it to pieces with a mallet. And then guiltily dispose of the corpse.

Okay, so: Say I've made up a new Naomi. I should actually *meet* her, right?

I think back to how I met Isabella: a Cute Meet right out of one of the rom-coms I teach. I'd shown up late for a party, a picnic in the Holly-wood Hills. And when I reached into a bowl to claim the one large, lus-cious strawberry left, my fingers met hers. We tussled over this prize, a natural flirtation. Isabella was the one who offered the compromise, bit-ing off half of it with lips as red and ripe-looking as the berry, smiling at me as I enjoyed my half, drinking in her every slow and sensuous chew . . .

I have to stop myself from remembering further, from fixating on the sweet taste of Isabella herself. If I'm ever going to savor those lips again, Naomi and I need to re-meet cute. First, I need to envision who exactly I'll be meeting. Alexi suggests a kind of guided meditation for his exercise, preparing the senses through the use of quiet music, dimmed light, perhaps incense. It actually sounds very L.A. yoga.

I locate a CD Isabella bought, her beloved Swami Girinanda's sanc-tioned recording of Tibetan "golden bowls," the resonating gongs of what sound like massive metal balls. I rummage in a kitchen drawer to find her cache of incense: Jungle Musk (no), Rainwater (too New Age), Temple Bells (clashes with golden bowls), and settle on Blue Nile, also the name of a favorite band that Isabella tried hard to love for my sake but couldn't. My Naomi will be a Blue Nile virgin. I can turn her onto them on our first date.

I put the bowls on, light the incense and a large floor candle, draw the shades. I sit down on the floor with Alexi, my back against the couch, knowing that if any of my old cronies in New York City could see me now, they'd laugh themselves hoarse. But the epigraph I read at the front of the book quiets those distant guffaws:

Purity of heart is to will one thing.

That's Alexi quoting Kierkegaard, who was no jokester, and while Alexi probably put it there as a prompt for aspiring actors to maintain focus, for me the quote actually inspires a seriousness of purpose. This is no crackpot chicanery. My heart's pure desire is to win back my wife. So here goes.

I turn to the passage I skimmed in the store and begin. I close my eyes for a visualization of Naomi's feet, then read the next bit from Alexi, who in my mind's ear has acquired a Karloff-Lugosian accent and timbre, and slowly work my way up the body. I have vivid memories of what Naomi Dussart looked like to help my process. I get briefly stuck in what feels like the parody of a "design your dream date" article in a men's magazine (though I know it's wrong to want this, Naomi was a bit hippy, and I want my girl to be slimmer). But this Frankensteinian erotic surgery is beside the point. The body, Alexi reminds me, is the home for the soul. How does the character's physical being express what dwells within?

This brings me at last to the face, which, as Alexi acknowledges, is the real challenge. I close my eyes again and concentrate. One has to imagine with the eyes of a painter, a psychologist, a spiritualist-photographer. The shape of the skull beneath the skin. The planes of the cheeks, the size of the nose. The eyes . . . A sketch and a memory hovers before me, shifting in and out of focus as if being adjusted through a finely calibrated lens. For an instant the softly tolling bells, the scent of the Nile-tinged incense, the words of a long-dead Russian guru come together to help me conjure the whole of her, and at last standing before me is a Naomi close to the one I remember.

But almost as soon as I can see her whole, the image evaporates, and my eyes flick open. The candle's sputtering. My back is sore and my right foot's asleep. And I'm as alone as I've been for days.

I don't have her yet, because all I've been dealing with is memory. And simply focusing on the image of Naomi won't give me the material I need to furnish the details that will convince Isabella that she has a rival. No, what I need to do—just as I would to research a female character in a story and make her experience real to me—is to walk with that character in my here and now. In Alexi's parlance, I need to go see the barber.

The sidewalk in front of the Academy theater is busy with industry folk as dusk falls, darkness dusting the gathering with a light veneer of casual glamour, the men in suits and the women in heels simply doing what they're supposed to be doing, in the town they own. A screening. I'd nearly tossed the mailed invite, a new Nicholson comedy, but now I'm glad I held on to it. This is exactly the right event, the right place, for what I have in mind. Not that my mind's made up. I've worked out most of it in the car on my way over, figuring I'll improvise additional details once I'm launched, but if it gets dicey in there, well, launch could be aborted at any stage.

Then an odd serendipity suggests that conditions are favorable. After having my name checked off the list at the table inside the front doors, I run into Albert Pistler. Pistler, of unkempt hair and morose air, his unseasonal flannel shirt's top button buttoned, wants me to attend an indie festival screening of his first feature. I tell him I'll definitely try to make it ("definitely try" being the favored Los Angelesian phrase of noncommitment), and move on. I have no intention of seeing his film again, having spent an exhaustive night in the filmmaker's apartment last year going over the final edit with him, but I realize that once again, fate seems to be in collusion with me here, because Pistler has just provided a key component for my evening's agenda, should I choose to activate it.

Seized with a new, nervous eagerness, I quicken my pace. There's a number of shiny women and self-involved execs trolling the lobby, cell phones ubiquitous. I stride past them, up the staircase to the lobby outside the auditorium's entry doors, an in-house gallery of vintage movie posters. While the general flow of traffic continues onward, going inside to claim seats, I pause on the threshold to survey the space, noting a few couples admiring the framed artwork. If I'm going to do it, now's the time, and this is the place where I'm least likely to be observed while I'm impersonating a psychotic.

Purity of the heart. I don't know what the ruling would be on a pure act achieved through impure, duplicitous means, but Mr. Kierkegaard isn't on the reservation list tonight. I'm on my own. And isn't that the very problem that needs be solved? I sidle past a splendidly inked Valentino profile, moving toward an empty corner, take a nervous breath, close my eyes, and start with . . . the feet.

Sandals. A woman in sandals, nice legs, standing with her back to me, motionless, emanating calm. The baby blue cashmere sweater I remember from class, maybe worn over a dark skirt that's slit up one side . . . but I'm being silly, that's not her style. Instead I imagine a simple, sheer white dress. That's more fitting, so I put her in it.

I return my eyes to the poster, as I would, naturally, and so, not looking to my left as I step leftward, bump shoulders with the woman who's just then moving right. We turn to face each other, and I see my own surprise mirrored in her expression, both Naomi Dussart and I starting to speak at the same time, laughing, and *"Oh my God,"* she says. *"This is too amazing! I was going to call you!"*

The poster in front of me is Barrymore and Lombard—perfect, so that's the tone, then: fast and light, let's zip right through all the necessary exposition, her *"—only flew in yesterday"* and my *"Did you ever finish that screenplay?"* and her *"Not only that, I've got it here, with me, the first rough cut."* And then, in a sudden flash of inspiration, I add a great plant for later. She means this literally, as she has a DVD of the rough cut in her shoulder bag—she's carrying it around with her, she admits, charmingly embarrassed. This will enable her to hand it over to me at the night's end, right then and there, when I agree to take a look. But I'm getting ahead of myself. Finish the setup.

"No, I'm here alone," she says. *"My friend Suzanne had the invite but couldn't come. She's who I'm staying with——"* in Santa Monica (in the apartment that's really Albert Pistler's, a Westside duplex north of Wilshire, arrested collegiate aesthetic with its fold-out couch covered in cat hair from Albert's obscenely fat tabby, and this is the perfect detail to fix the whole place in memory for me when Isabella asks, "Where is she staying?"). *"I took the bus here,"* she's saying (because she hasn't yet rented a car, trying to save money, I decide), *"the Blue bus"* (she knows all about it from her summer here two years ago). And of course we'll sit together inside. Not only that, forget the bus home, I'll give her a lift, not at all out of my way . . .

It's time to leave the screwball comedy poster, so I screw up my courage to continue this in the midst of a crowd. *"I guess we should go in."* I'm murmuring all this dialogue under my breath, but when I turn to go inside, it occurs to me that it's unnatural to join the flow of people passing through the doors without continuing the conversation, so I slow for a moment and revise—not a late bus home: Suzanne is due to pick Naomi up at the screening's end, except gentlemanly me has just urged her to call Suzanne and tell her not to bother. And so, with my imaginary companion chatting to her friend on her cell phone in French beside me, I'm able to walk silently down the aisle, fantasy intact.

The few people who look my way must be doing so because of Naomi's distinctive beauty. Good fortune provides two seats on the aisle about halfway down. I give Naomi the aisle seat, and we people-watch in silence. The auditorium is nearly filled. I spot a writer acquaintance, but he's far enough away so that a nod and smile suffice.

Just as the lights began to dim, a frazzled-looking man snapping his cell phone shut stops by Naomi's seat. "Is this taken?" he asks. Maybe it's the merest hint of hesitation he hears in my voice when I say "Yeah," but he gives me a peeved and slightly disbelieving look. He lingers, scanning the surrounding rows in desperation. I watch him reluctantly head down the aisle, radiating annoyance, finding the only available seat in one of the front rows nearest the screen. I settle in, fight an impulse to put my arm around the back of the seat beside me. Too presumptuous.

The movie is middling, an aging star stuck with fitfully lively material. Halfway in I realize I've forgotten I'm supposedly not alone. So I close my eyes to reassert the presence of my date and then, with a nervous glance around me, turn to look at her, hoping that darkness will cover what may appear to be quite deranged. I make a "so-so" gesture at Naomi, and she nods. She tilts her head toward the exit with a questioning look, but I shrug as if to say, *We might as well see the rest of it,* and she nods again, turning back to face the screen. I sit back, too, my arm on the armrest between us.

A small wave of laughter crests and breaks though the audience. A lulling sound. It's pleasant to sit here, the scent of her so close (a fragrance like rosewater), and as if this thought has been transmitted, I feel the light touch of her hand. Not quite a caress, but the soft skin of her fingers grazes mine on the armrest in the dark, a touch so perfectly casual as to be accidental, yet . . . Her hand rests there next to mine. I watch the tumult of Riviera color on the screen and feel her hand move away. I make sure to keep my eyes forward, not wanting to acknowledge that anything out of the ordinary has just occurred.

When the movie ends to scattered applause, I have Naomi say she's going to the restroom and hurry off to beat the crowd. I sit watching the end credits roll, relaxing for a moment in a giddy sense of accomplishment at having pulled this thing off. Then the frazzled man from before comes walking up the aisle and slows as he approaches, seeing the still-empty seat beside me. He glares at me and I keep my eyes on the screen. I wait for him to move on, but he stops beside the empty seat, pointedly ignoring the people who have to walk around him. "What's your problem?" he asks.

I look up at him, a short, stocky man crammed into a leather jacket and tight jeans. "My problem?"

"Yeah," the man says. "Kind of precious about your personal space, huh?"

"Not really."

The couple next to me wants out. I'm forced to rise and step back against my seat to let them pass, along with a woman choosing to exit on this side. The short guy stands his ground. "Something about me bothers you? I smell funny or something?"

"Not at all," I say. It's a strain to keep up my expression of innocent bewilderment as the guy glowers at me, assessing my size and weight. I'm aware of some lingering moviegoers taking in this after-screening sideshow. I have the sensation of having left my stomach in the seat behind me, of my throat and tongue turning to metal. I took six months of Tae Kwon Do once, but when was the last time I was in a real fight, grade school?

"Oh," the guy says, and juts out his chin. "So what's your deal?"

"No deal," I say. "Someone was sitting here. She's gone to the bathroom."

"I didn't see anyone," he says. "I think you're just an asshole."

It's the dawning of the imaginary girlfriend downside. I swallow, considering the heft of the guy. "*I* don't think so," I say. "I think you may need glasses."

The guy's eyes widen. "That's what you think?" His eyes flick right and left, seeing if he has allies among the witnesses. Then he emits a sharp bark of a laugh. "That's rich," he says.

I shrug. For a second I feel myself being seen as the snobbish indie type who won't rub elbows with the hoi polloi, and have to blink the image away.

The guy shakes his head. "Glasses," he repeats, then finally turns and starts up the aisle. He pauses once to stare back at me, then shaking his head again, moves on.

I stay where I am, waiting until the short guy is out of sight and the rest of my own body parts realign, the high-pitched hum of adrenaline abating.

Besides, Naomi probably needs a few more minutes in the Ladies'.

Flushed and sweaty, feeling I've barely escaped public exposure as a complete and utter nutjob, I'm relieved to be back in my car, to be by myself again after the crowd in the theater. I know I'm supposed to continue on, to install my phantom companion in the seat beside me, but for the moment I'm too suffused with incredulity at what I've just done to keep up the charade. *Oh, just doing some research for a project*—that's what I would have said if anyone I knew had caught me in the act, but right now I'm amazed that I've actually stooped to such absurdity.

Paused at the light to turn west on Wilshire, I un-hunch my shoulders, aware of how strained and rigid my neck is. I can't help but remember how sometimes Isabella rests her hand on the back of my neck as I drive, fingers caressing me lightly there for minutes at a time. It makes me go limp like a kitten picked up by its neck and carried in a mother cat's mouth. Right now I miss this more keenly than anything.

In the next car over, a woman driver sits talking to someone who isn't there. Handless cell phone. I watch her for a moment, one hand on the wheel, the other gesticulating wildly in the air. I remind myself once more of the reason I came out here tonight, of exactly what I hope to win by doing this. And when the light changes, Naomi is in the seat beside me.

She sits, serene and at ease, enjoying the cool night breeze from the open window, tapping her foot to the soft jazz on the radio. Because I keep my eyes on the road, it's easy enough to keep her there. I decide to ask her how she liked the movie, and hear the slightly throaty timbre of her voice in response, her accent so different from Isabella's. (*"It was no great piece of work, but of course he's always worth seeing."*) She also enjoyed seeing the South of France. Her family has a summer home by a lake not far from where those scenes had been shot.

I pull up by a driveway near Albert's and get out, going round to open her door before I realize she could easily misinterpret this as an intention to come inside, uninvited. But there I am, standing by as she climbs out of the car, so I do my best to cover this snafu: *"A gentleman would walk you to your door, but it's only yards away, and I think you're safe in this neighborhood."*

She smiles, looking me over as though she understands what lies beneath what I'm saying. The moon is working its way through a fleecy veil of clouds above the palm trees, and I'm struck by the whiteness of her teeth, the most prominent part I can see of her in the shadows. *"Thank you," she says, "for the company, the lift . . ."*

Here I remember to quickly insert the payoff I'd set up earlier, Naomi asking if I'll be willing to look at the cut, the DVD in her shoulder bag, now in my hand, so: *"Thank you," she says, "for the company, the lift . . . and especially for your critique to come. I hope you'll be kind. But honest!" she insists.* I nod. *"I don't know if Suzanne is at home," she says,* looking toward Albert's. *"I would ask you in, for a glass of wine or something, though actually—"*

It comes to me in a flash, so perfectly logical: She offers to take me out to dinner in return for my watching her film. *"Do you like sushi? My favorite place is Yamashiro."* I protest, knowing how expensive such a meal would be. Naomi counters by offering to cook for us. I'm delighted. When I assure her that I'll watch the film tomorrow, her face lights up at my evident interest. *"Really! So soon? Then can I cook tomorrow night?"* Both of us laugh knowingly; when someone you respect is seeing your work, you want the feedback *rapidamente* (wait, that's Italian, so what's the French for *immediately?* No matter). And she insists on cooking, especially since it's so hard to find a really good restaurant in her neighborhood (in this, I think, she sounds too Isabella-esque, so Naomi immediately corrects herself, laughing), not that she's really looked, it's just a thing any Frenchwoman who cooks feels honor-bound to say (this flash of self-awareness and deprecation is endearing). So we have a date.

"I just hope you don't hate it," she says.

"The food or the film?"

"The film!" she cries, laughing. "Absolutely no one hates my cooking."

I realize that what I'm really invoking in Naomi is my love for Isabella's pasta. Naomi, I suppose, should make us coq au vin. We stand at a loss, both smiling.

Did I tell her about Isabella's departure? I decide there was a moment outside the Academy: the prospect of going out for a drink, Naomi wondering if I had to get home, leading to my slightly embarrassed admission of my wife's estrangement. Sympathy and a hint of interest from Naomi, perhaps a comparable backstory of her own (problematic on-and-off relationship with a musician from Lyonne that's going nowhere, the boy is too young . . .). All right, then: I put out a hand to shake hers.

Naomi moves to kiss my cheeks, one and then the other, and then . . . She gazes at me for an intoxicating moment. Then we draw apart, she's walking quickly down the pavement, and I watch her retreat, tantalized by the ambiguities we've just unleashed, and with a little wave, she disappears up the driveway to Suzanne's.

Back behind the wheel of my Metropolitan, I exhale a shaky breath in the dark. I sit for a moment with my hand on the clutch, unable to shift my mental gears. She's gone, but I can't quite let go of her. For an instant I'm tempted to run after her, invite myself up for a glass of wine. I can see the apartment door opened by Albert Pistler, peering out at me in bewilderment.

"Madness," I mutter aloud in the quiet of the car. For the second time tonight, I'm seared by a burning sense of humiliation. I'm one large ache of a fool in the midst of folly. Alone as I've been since I woke this morning, ears still ringing from the door that slammed behind Isabella. She, I remember again, is the reason I'm sitting in a car on a quiet street in Santa Monica at ten o'clock in the evening like a flasher who's been opening his raincoat at phantoms.

I start the engine and turn on my headlights. A silver-gray cat sits in the street in front of the car, eyes gleaming green in the bright beams. I wait while the cat looks at me as if I'm the evening's entertainment. Finally I put the car into gear. When I turn the wheel, the cat gets up, ambles over to the curb and hops it, gray tail disappearing into the night as I pull onto the road.

Now the hollowness looms, a behemoth. Throwing things at it—a movie to watch, a book to read—is like heaving pebbles at King Kong.

I'm a hapless victim clutched in the monster's paw, a small snack to be devoured before bedtime. I drive. That's all you can do in this town. You drive.

Onto the freeway. I speed, the radio blasting some rock 'n' roll I'm not familiar with but it doesn't matter, there's enough melodic thrashing and banging and screeching "yeahs" and soon I'm screaming, screaming with all my strength, AAAAAAH!!! throat ripping, hands gripping the wheel at ten and two so tight I could lift it off its hub, windows open and outside, Los Angeles early to bed and gone into its dark homes and silent streets while I scream, face stretched, tired tears leaking out the sides of my eyes, AAAAAAAAAAAAAAAAAH!!! until the song ends.

This sort of helps, kind of. But then there's the silence.

2

Cute Meet

An inciting incident, or catalyst, that brings man and woman together and into conflict: often an amusing, inventive but credible contrivance that establishes the nature of their dynamic and sets the tone for the action to come.

"*I*s Jordan Moore in for Rumer Hawke?"

The assistant's phone voice is so cheery, she might be announcing a sweepstakes win. Bolting upright, I splash cereal milk over my kitchen table, assuring her that I'm in, and then I'm put on hold. The surprise arrival of this all-important call, first thing Friday morning, is miraculous, but my excitement's edged with anxiety. I haven't done any work on the project since our meeting, though technically I'm on Rumer's clock, with most of the small advance money already spent. What if he wants to hear some new ideas? I don't have an idea in my head, other than my bizarre plan to win back Isabella.

I rise to my feet as the Muzak's interrupted, but it's not Rumer, it's Yuko, Rumer's new personal assistant. Also inordinately happy to have found me at home, in the tone of a hostess who's pulled herself away from the cocktail party of a lifetime, she apologizes for Rumer's absence. He's had to take another call, but—sorry for the short notice—could I swing a two-fifteen appointment this afternoon? Considering how many people are presently clamoring for a few moments of Rumer's time, there's no way I'll be coyly unavailable. I'm quick to say it can be swung.

Once off the phone, I pace in a mad circle. Just as I woke up thinking Maxi needed to be walked, only to re-remember that Maxi was gone,

I have to stifle my natural impulse to rush next door to Isabella's studio and share my good news. She of all people knows what the activation of the project signifies. In fact, wait a second . . .

Suddenly all of yesterday's weird machinations seem less nutty. An imaginary girlfriend, that's only part of the equation, but add in a big career break, and won't my wife start seeing a new, improved Jordan— bigger, stronger, infinitely more attractive? Naomi and Rumer: Here could be my magic yardstick and mailing tube, to work, pincer-like, at lifting the delicate organ of Isabella's heart out of the city of Rome and back into my loving hands again. I'll call her now.

Not yet. Not yet. I brew coffee, fire up the computer, eager to immerse myself in the long-neglected Rumer notes. I go to change into my Pep Boys T-shirt, a good-luck talisman for all my writing work, but can't find it. I think to look in the storage bins Isabella uses as a bureau in the closet, open the top drawer and stop short at the sight of her leopard skin–patterned panties, suddenly remembering that morning I made fun of them and Isabella, her hands clenched comically into claws, crawled up the bedside, bare haunches gleaming, to rip the bedcovers off me with a deep-throated yowl . . .

As if sucker-punched, I stand unsteady, about to sink into a deep, fathomless well of sadness that's got the pull of a whirlpool. If I don't back out of the closet immediately, the waters will close over my head. I remain transfixed, hand clutching at my wife's underwear, realizing that all I know of her, all these intimacies, could already be lost to me for good. Already gone.

I get the drawer shut and the closet door closed. I walk now as a man pushing step by step against an undertow, the shore still far out of reach. When I reach the desk again, having grabbed an old Sex Pistols T-shirt and pulled it on, anxiety overcomes me. What do I think I'm playing with, inventing a lover, gambling with my marriage's fate? The thing could backfire, end up alienating Isabella altogether. I'm an idiot en route to becoming an imbecile. Well, it isn't too late to abandon the cockamamie Plan. I'll ditch Naomi and keep what I did last night to myself. If I want to win my wife back, I'll do it with the force of honesty, soul-baring, begging . . .

Like some radio-controlled automaton, I move to the phone, dial the endless string of international digits, wait impatiently as the foreign beeping sounds in my ear. Then I'm being talked at by Isabella's recorded voice in Italian, telling me to leave a message. She says it again in English—and I'm pathetically cheered by this, the idea that perhaps she's done this for my sake, just as my heart aches when I hear that she's kept my last name, following hers as usual, on the outgoing message. She hasn't even been gone a week, nothing's been decided, the dreaded word *separation* has yet to be invoked, and she's not yet declared herself an independent woman—all of this feeds my hope.

Nonetheless, she's out somewhere in Rome doing who knows what, and with whom?

When I hear the beep, I'm speechless. "I want to know how Maxi is," I finally blurt into her machine. Then I force a more upbeat tone. "And I wanted to tell you I'm having another meeting with Rumer, finally. So call when you can. *Ciao, bella,*" I say, and hang up.

The panel in the elevator up to Rumer's isn't where you expect, and it's hard to tell which buttons are for pushing and which are just decoration. It's a super-smooth ride, so noiseless that the doors appear to slide open on the same floor I've gotten on at as if I haven't moved at all. Two vacant corridors bank out wing-like from a reception area bereft of a receptionist.

I step onto a plush-carpeted straightaway, remembering from my one prior visit to head for the small nexus of offices in the distance. When I'm within the bustling half-circle of brightly lit desks manned by good-looking twenty-somethings with matching Mac computers, a lean Asian woman in black jeans and a cashmere sweater carrying a bottle of

Smart Water introduces herself as Yuko. She takes me round another bend, knocks on a nondescript door, and ushers me into the outer room of the Rumer inner sanctum.

Within, a vista of greenery fills the frame of a wall-length picture window. Rumer's offices are atop a building nestled in the Hollywood foothills. I was wowed last time by the impressively park-like view and the sleek *Jetsons*-styled desk that sits before it, but this time I'm distracted by the sound of breaking glass and screams to my left. A huge flat screen dominates this wall, and on it a sexily disheveled Korean woman cowers in the corner of a closet, covering her mouth with a bloodied hand while an unseen monstrous intruder hacks at the door above her with a hatchet.

Three teenaged girls sit rapt on a black leather couch before the imminent Technicolor carnage on the screen, pawing at a small vat of popcorn in the middle of a low glass table. To their right, a young man sits in a chair facing me, hands poised over a laptop. His black button-down shirt and Levi's, close-cropped hair, and requisite phone device covering his left ear say: office assistant. "Dead meat," calls one of the girls, indicating the cowering woman on the screen, and the other two giggle. I note the assistant attentively typing in response.

"Joely Hawke," Yuko murmurs at my ear.

"Ah," I say, recognizing the teen's bright mop of orange-streaked hair from magazine photos. Rumer's daughter, paparazzi bait since she began dating the son of a prominent actor while still in high school, pauses in mid–popcorn munch to glance briefly in my direction, then away. "I can't watch," she says.

"I'd be peeing," says the girl beside her. The assistant types again.

"Something we're looking into as a remake," says Yuko.

I nod, finding something peculiarly familiar in the tableau of closet-trapped heroine and splintering wood as the assailant grunts and heavy-breathes, closing in. "It's like *Halloween*," I say.

"It is *Halloween*," says Yuko. "Tsuo Jung's version. He's very hot."

Which means the potential project that Rumer is test-screening, with his daughter and her friends as focus group, is to be an American remake of a Korean remake of an American movie. Yuko straightens suddenly, saying "Okay" with a smile in response to a summons from her earpiece. "Rumer's ready for you now," she tells me, and indicates a doorway to an adjoining office. I steel myself for what waits within.

There are two things people who've met Rumer Hawke know about the man. One is that he possesses a megawatt charisma of uncanny seductive power. It isn't just the prematurely silver mane of hair swept back from a prominent forehead, the piercing blue eyes that could qualify him as a movie star. It's some near-mystical glow that emanates from Rumer when he talks to you. You feel that you, not he, are the most fascinating human being on the planet, and thus the time he is spending in speaking to you is infinitely precious to him.

The other thing about Rumer is that he suffers from Tourette's. The peculiarity of his particular syndrome is that he doesn't yell obscenities and bizarre non sequitors. He releases at unpredictable intervals the strangled squawks, hackings, and cries of what sounds like a large winged predator in pain. In town there are two cliques of belief regarding this. Some believe that Tourette's is God's way of evening the balance in Rumer, given the unfair advantage of his looks and intelligence. But others believe the disease to be pure fabrication—that Rumer has chosen this feigned handicap as a diabolical means of manipulation. It's certainly true that no routine yelling or shoe-pounding on desks can match Hawke's high-pitched, sputtering shrieks in their power to intimidate. One prominent studio president is rumored to have signed off on a deal favoring Rumer because he couldn't bear to spend another minute in the meeting with him. But no one has ever determined the veracity of Rumer's affliction, one way or the other.

Armed with this foreknowledge, I'm still nervous when Yuko opens the door for me, knowing that whatever perks and perils might lie in having an audience with the great man, my project's fate hangs in the balance.

"Jordan," says Rumer. "How goes it?"

I'm in a blond wood–paneled conference room, which is empty but for a long table edged with chairs. In the center of that table sits a misshapen oval of metallic-black webbing, resembling an egg laid by a computer, and it is from this object that Rumer's question has emanated.

"Fine, thanks," I address the speakerphone and remain standing, aware of Yuko discreetly withdrawing and shutting the door behind her. "And yourself?"

"Could not be better," says Rumer, his voice resonating richly from wherever he is. "Jordan, your story."

"Yes?"

"Captivating. We've been immersed in it, and if anything, its possibilities only become more and more intriguing."

I wonder if Rumer is using the royal *we,* or who, exactly, has been immersed in the work with him, but this warm praise sweeps aside such moot questions. "Well, thanks," I begin, "I'm glad—"

"No, Jordan." Rumer is chuckling. "I'm thanking you. For providing us with such an extraordinary wealth of material. It's Rabelaisian, really . . ."

Have I read any Rabelais? I can't remember, and have only a vague sense of what this adjective connotes—bewigged lechers and saucy maids with their skirts up?

"There's enough there to seed a franchise, which is why it's so important for us to get the thing right from the start."

Franchise? "Of course," I say.

"And it's your vision, Jordan, which is why we're determined to let you have your way with this. You're the man."

I recognize this brand of nonsense, pure hyperbole, from other meetings with other players in the past, but it's always fun to be so nicely buttered up. "Well . . ."

"Most of my colleagues wouldn't go this route," Rumer goes on. "They'd bring in Scott Frank or Bill Goldman to doctor the thing, Nathan Colt"—the mention of golden boy screenwriter Colt sends a brisk swipe of ice down the line of my spine—"but I have faith in your vision. There *is* a story there, and it *is* filmic, and you're the right writer to dig it out for us."

"I appreciate that."

"You know this story. You've got an innate sense of the structure of it, which is the most important thing."

"It is," I agree happily. "And my vision," I say, lapsing into his movie meeting–speak, but that's just as well, as it's a good moment to pitch my new ideas, "what I've been thinking lately is, maybe we can go even a little edgier than what I—"

"Ack!" says Rumer. "Ack-ack-AAAAR-kss-kss-AWK!"

Stunned into silence, I can only stare at the speakerphone, involuntarily taking a few steps back from it, and wait for the shriekings of the wounded pterodactyl to subside. As a part of me detaches and floats upward, watching me watch the squawking computer egg on the table, I have a vivid, lacerating ache for the presence of Isabella, the one person who would comprehend just how strange it is to be inside my skin. But this job, I remind myself, it's part of the Plan. And the Plan will bring her back.

"Actually," says Rumer, after a pause, "there's really only one hurdle. We need a new ending. So we've written up some notes."

Yuko materializes behind me, another woman beside her. Tall and long-faced, wearing a dark burgundy suit that certifies serious executive status, she holds out a pile of pages that looks phone-book thick. Reeling from the revelation that Rumer wants a new ending (how? what?), I take it from her, realizing it's my draft, riddled with underlining, highlighting, and scrawlings in the margins, atop another thick sheaf of papers.

"This is Dana Morton," says Rumer, "the best development person in the West, or as I like to call her, my right hand."

Dana extends her own right hand, smiling broadly while her clear gray eyes exude shrewd, don't-fuck-with-me intelligence. I juggle the page stack for a handshake that's alarmingly firm. "I'm a huge fan," she says, and nods at the draft. "Fabulous work."

"Oh. Thanks," I murmur.

"Dana's going to be with you, all the way," Rumer continues. "What do you think of Johnny D'Arc?"

"D'Arc?" I echo, thrown. This director, the Tarantino of the moment, is about as hot a commodity as exists in the business, but what does he—

"Because he's interested in the project," says Rumer. "And we have a window, a small one, before Johnny begins his next movie."

"Wow." I've just said "wow" to Rumer Hawke, a choice I'll replay as an Idiot Moment for weeks to come, but the surreality of the conversation has unmanned me.

"And that's why we'd like to proceed with all due haste, Jordan. I know you're fast," he adds. "That's one of the things we like about you."

I try to come back with some of the breezy playfulness I hear in Rumer's voice. "We're not talking the end of next month, right?"

Rumer laughs, a warm, robust, fruity sound. He's delighted. I'm delighted. Smiling Dana is, too. "Hell, no!" says Rumer. "By the end of next week."

Yikes. I want to be this fast, wise, visionary writer Rumer sees me as, and I'll do my best to be him, but even as I say, "No problem," I'm reeling, trying to reassess now all those bright new ideas I wanted to pitch. "So," I continue, "I do have a couple of thoughts—well, more like questions to run by you—"

"You read over the notes—they're just a few suggestions for the direction we want to go in. Come up with an ending we're all happy with, and we'll talk about the next steps, all right? Good."

"Right," I say. "And as for the rest of the draft?"

"AWWWRK! Kack-kack! ARRR-KSS-AWK!"

Yuko, with an eloquent smile that seems to speak for everyone present, is already graciously opening the door for me.

The ending is no small thing, given that it was largely the point of the book I wrote in the first place, and though I'd like to think this won't pose a problem, I carry Rumer's draft-and-notes stack as if it's a letter bomb as I walk in my front door and set it down carefully on the desk. The phone rings.

"Jor–dan!"

There's a certain way only Isabella has of pronouncing my name, a musical figure comprised of two notes, the first higher than the second, with an accent on the first note, which gives that first syllable a special emphasis, and the slight thickness of her tongue on its consonants and the timbre of her voice combine to strike a harmonic vibration in the ribs around my heart. This afternoon, even as I'm instinctively cheered to hear the favorite melody, I feel myself stiffen, hand tightening on the phone, a sailor steadying the ship's wheel to resist a siren's song. *"Ciao, bella."*

"I got your message, about Rumer Hawke. This is amazing!"

"Yeah," I say. "About time, huh."

"Yes, and you deserve good news! What does he say about your script?"

"He likes it. I just have to do a quick revision."

"Really!" I can hear the caution in her enthusiasm. She's used to disappointment when it comes to my writing career, and wary of my own unhappiness around it. "So you are starting to write?"

"It's more thinking than writing," I tell her, which is mostly true, though I'm stepping nimbly past my own anxieties about what I've been asked to do. "But yeah, I'm already getting started."

"Fantastic," says Isabella. "Wait—*momento, scuzi*—" I hear muffled voices, and in the pause, reflect that at least one part of the Plan is already having good effect. Then she's back. "I give you a big, big hug from my mama."

"Oh? Tell her I say thanks."

"What, you think that because of what goes on with us, my parents should abandon you? No, they are good, they love you, Jordan. And they have been so good to me! Oh, I can't tell you how wonderful it is to be with them, to eat my father's cooking . . . You don't know how much I miss this."

"I do know," I remind her, with a wince of guilt. It grew, her need to reclaim her family, her city, her world. But I still can remember when neither of us needed more than each other—it wasn't so long ago. That rush of wanting to get home as soon as possible, to be with each other again, simply because there was nobody else in the world we'd rather be alone with. Then the ordinary machinery of the everyday had worn down our romance in its meshes. If I'd been able to afford to fly us over there twice a year, would what had stayed strong have lasted longer? "You sound good," I acknowledge.

"I'm happy for *you*," she says. "And yes, happy to be here, where I've needed to be—for so long! I realize this now. But then there is my other home, my home with you all the way over there . . . I'm confused. I get lonely, especially in the nights . . . So last night I went to dance, a disco in Trastevere."

Funny, how these few words sound the alarm. *A disco in Trastevere.* She's out dancing in discos with who knows who—

"What about you? Rumer's writer! What have you been doing?"

Can I say it? Will I? She's disco-dancing, yes, but still affectionate. The sense that Isabella is teetering on a thin line between being with me and without me is what finally compels me to take a breath and take the plunge. "Well, I saw some movies. A new Jack Nicholson comedy, not bad . . . and an independent film," I tell her. "A first feature one of my former students directed."

"Really? You hate seeing student films."

"Well, I ran into her at the screening and she was so insistent . . ." I feign vexation at my too-generous nature. "She practically pleaded with me to take a look."

"And then you'll complain that you don't have enough time for your own work," says Isabella. "She must be talented."

"I think so. It wasn't bad, actually. Needs a little work, but . . ."

"She's lucky to have your interest. Did she pay you for a consult?"

"No. I'm letting her make me dinner."

There's a considered pause. I can hear the rapid Italian of Isabella's mother in the next room, talking back to her TV. "She has a name, this student?"

"Why?"

"I'd like to know the name, if you're dating somebody."

"I'm not dating," I say.

"You're having dinner."

"Yeah, but that doesn't mean dating."

"You're not attracted to her. She looks like a bag of old socks?"

"No, she's attractive," I say. "I'm just not . . . What is this? I'm not allowed to have meals unless I'm by myself?" My indignation is heightened by feelings of guilt that are very real. Alexi would be proud.

"So you're doing fine without me," says Isabella. "You have plenty of company, I shouldn't be worried about you, apparently."

"Wait a second! You were the one who talked about seeing other people."

"Talking, *sì*, but I'm not doing it! You haven't wasted any time."

"I'm not seeing people," I say. "I saw a movie, I'm having a dinner—"

"Bravo," says Isabella. "And she's very young, I suppose."

"No," I say quickly. How old is Naomi? "Well, not *very*. Maybe twenty-six."

"Of course. The perfect age. And the perfect figure, I'm sure."

"I don't know. Listen—"

"You don't know? Oh, that's right, you were only looking at her *movie*. Which is about what?"

I have no idea. My carefully constructed fantasy is already toppling. "It's—it's about . . ." Flailing, I lunge into defensive mode. "What's the difference? Isabella," I say, "you left. What am I supposed to do every night, sit home alone by the telephone, waiting for you to call?"

Silence on the other end. I think for a moment that we've lost the connection. Then she speaks, her voice subdued, repentant. "I know. I know," she repeats, a little tremulous. "But Jordan, to hear you talk to me like this, with your voice so cold . . ."

For an instant, incongruously, elation bubbles up in me that really is cruel. I can tell that I've gotten to her. It's working! Then in the next moment I feel horrible. The temptation to soothe her is nearly over-whelming. All I want is for her to come home—but this is exactly what I can't say if I'm really going to follow this through.

"Isabella," I say, "you're the one who went away. And you told me all the many good reasons for it! I'm not being cold, I'm trying to be practi-cal. You're taking care of yourself, so I'm just trying to do the same." Amazing, how reasonable I sound, how controlled, this imaginary Jordan who has imaginary dates.

And apparently the revised Jordan is effective because she sighs, then gives a rueful little laugh. "*Sì*, practical. While your crazy wife the painter is only wishing that we could stop time, stop the world spinning . . . because I need time, Jordan, you know? I'm here to take time to think, to understand what is the right thing to do. I'm not sure about anything anymore." She pauses. "I know I still love you," she says.

I know what she's asking for, the extent of the affirmation she needs, but I forcibly limit myself to the minimum. "That's . . . good to hear."

"Ah," she says. "Mr. Less-Is-More." There's another pause, pregnant with the unspoken. My withholding wins. "Well, if you need to go out, just to have a little fun, I can understand that," she allows. "But promise me, if something happens . . ."

"Something?"

"If you start to have feelings, real feelings for someone . . . We always said we would tell each other the truth, even when it's painful. Didn't we?"

"You're right," I allow. *"Hai raggione."*

"Hai raggione," she echoes wryly. "So you haven't already forgotten your Italian. Even with all these . . . distractions."

"No. Of course not."

We're tender with each other in parting, and there's a sweet wistful-ness in her voice that I haven't heard in ages. Off the phone, I'm a bit shook up, but I believe . . . It worked.

Though if I'm really going to bring this off, I need to do more research.

~   ~   ~

Some physical object—that's what's called for here, like that driver's cap I wore when I was writing Jake Rydell, the hero of my novel, or the cyclist's jersey I bought for the heroine, Margo. I want a touchstone that will instantly evoke Naomi Dussart, to keep her as real and present as possible. And emerging from the supermarket in the Marina mall with a bag of groceries, I spy just the thing.

It's got a tiny violet sewn in between its white silk breast cups. A slip of green fabric in there suggests the flower's stalk—maybe that's what hooks me as I pass the European lingerie shop window. I double back, eyes fixed on the bustier or camisole or whatever it is, because it's just what a married man having a rebound affair would buy for his mistress. I can imagine Naomi in it, draped on my couch like an odalisque, the tiny flower in her cleavage with its green to match her eyes. These, I realize, are the kinds of details I need to stock up on if I don't want to stumble into another cul-de-sac in the middle of my next phone conversation with Isabella.

Inside I'm bombarded by more purple, pink, and puce than any reasonable man could stand. This and a scent of lilac designate the area as a no-male zone, along with a well-lit cleanliness that suggests a harmless, utilitarian application for the bewildering variety of lingerie on display (Sex? Who's thinking about having sex?). Luckily I know what I want, and here's a saleswoman, smiling sunnily. "How are you today?"

I tell her I'm fine, and point out "that thing" in the window.

"The lace bustier." She nods approval. "That's from our French couture line. It's really beautiful. What's her size?"

Size. I picture Naomi, unsure: Medium? Small? "I think . . ."

"Slim or full-bodied?" She's used to this, the brute ignorance of the male.

"Slim."

She's leading me toward a display rack. "About your height, or . . . ?"

"I'm a little taller, I guess."

"Well, then she's a small. I don't suppose you know the bra size?"

This one stops me cold, not only because I lack such information but because fingering one of the bustiers on the rack, I've encountered the price tag. This would be the moment to bail, to thank her and say I'm "just looking."

My saleswoman interprets the look on my face as confusion. "It's because of the cups," she explains, holding up the bustier. "She may be a small, which is about a thirty-four on these, but she might need a 34C as opposed to a B . . . ?"

"C being . . ."

"Bigger. D's the biggest we carry."

Now she's got me going. What I'm really being offered is a rewrite. Do I want her to have bigger breasts? I opt for accuracy, best as I can remember. "Well, she's kind of . . ." I cup my hands in front of my chest. No, that's way too far out. I adjust—

"Maybe you'd like to call her." Smiling, the saleswoman proffers a cell phone.

"Oh, no," I say.

"It's a surprise," she offers.

"That's right."

So we figure the details out between ourselves, the saleswoman and I, and soon I depart with my imported-lace-and-satin bustier: the happy crackpot fantasist, hard at work.

I'm hanging my purchase on a solitary hook in the closet, placed where my lover would be apt to leave it and I'll be sure to see it on a daily basis, when the phone rings in the other room. Isabella again? Calling back to talk about getting on the next plane home, having come to her senses, dissolving the need for any Naomis and turning our life back into the cheery resolution of a congenial romantic comedy again? I snatch up the receiver, but what I hear is an indistinct, unfamiliar woman's voice, muffled. I recognize Japanese. "Hello?" I repeat, and I'm ready to disconnect when the voice abruptly switches to loud and pleasant English.

"Yes, this is Yamashiro. We confirm your reservation for tonight."

"My reservation?"

"Seven-thirty," she says brightly. "We see you then!"

Gone. I put the phone down, confused, musing that somewhere in L.A. some poor schnook is still wondering if his dinner reservation has been confirmed. Funny, though, because didn't someone just recently propose going to Yamashiro—

The hairs on the back of my neck are prickling. I know who I was talking to, who loved Yamashiro: a woman who wasn't really there. Now, that *is* odd, one of life's more bizarre random coincidences.

I'm staring at the stack of Rumer pages, seeing that even my title is encircled in red, confirming that nothing is sacred. This stings, but these are good problems, I remind myself. I'm in the game again, Isabella may be coming around . . . a celebratory dinner at Yamashiro only feels appropriate. Hell, it was my imaginary Naomi's idea in the first place—so long as I've got a reservation, why not meet her there?

The night is spectacularly clear when I reach the hilltop's circular drive. The white-gloved Asian valet smiles ambiguously at my weathered Metropolitan as I take the ticket from him. Below, shimmering lights sprawl to the horizon, impersonating a cosmopolitan city. Above me looms Yamashiro, a Hollywood version of a Japanese country inn crossed with a faux-palace, curved black eaves capping each white story, its architectural flourishes summoning visions of samurai. I stride up its wide steps and through the oversized doors.

The Asian hostess smiles a welcome. "Do you have a reservation?"

"I'm not sure," I tell her. "I might."

"Shall we pretend you do?" I shoot her a look. She smiles. "Jo-dan."

"Yes, Jordan," I say, startled. "Jordan Moore, for seven-thirty?"

"Jo-dan," she repeats. "Joking." As she checks her book, another woman, wearing a high-collared, green silk Mandarin outfit, glides to the hostess's side, murmurs in her ear, and steps back out to bow and smile at me, indicating I'm to follow her. A misunderstanding? I want to pull that book round and have a look, but the hostess is already turning the page over, and the second woman's walking inside the restaurant.

I'm confused. Either there's really going to be a mystery date awaiting me inside, or I'm going to make one up who'll join me. In any event my only real concern should be landing a decent table.

The woman sweeps us through the archway, moving us into the central courtyard, a Japanese garden surrounding a pond, giant orange koi fish zigzagging like neon mini-submarines through its lily pad–laden water. Lanterns sway below the open roof and night sky: a properly romantic setting for a make-believe meet.

We're nearing the end of the corridor, though, and the woman is quickening her steps. Puzzled, I follow her up a flight of wooden stairs at the far end. This is a level of Yamashiro I've never visited before. I'm ushered into a candlelit, paper-screened room filled with diners at a dozen black-lacquered tables. There's a sweet smell of jasmine and the sound of koto music. My guide deposits me at the sole empty table in the corner and disappears the moment she's tucked me in. Seeing people call to each other across the room, and sensing the festivity in the air, I gather that a private party is in progress. Is this where I'm supposed to be?

A full-blown old-style geisha materializes by my side. She's dressed in an ornate, intricately embroidered and brocaded kimono robe, its fine aquamarine silk glowing in the candlelight. A peacock comb twinkles from the crest of her raven-dark hair, exquisitely arranged to form a perfect oval frame for a face paled by subtly applied white makeup. "You would like something to drink?"

"Well, I'm waiting for someone . . ."

"Some sake?" Vibrant red lips smiling.

"Sure," I say. "That sounds good."

She bows, turns. I watch her poised elegance recede amid the more raucous guests. At the table across from me, another geisha stands talking to a seated Asian man with a ponytail and braided beard. As she laughs, adjusting the paper flower in the midst of her hugely inflated hair, the bearded man pulls her into his lap, tilting her wig to one side. Not a waitress, and not, I realize, hearing her curse playfully at him in English, a real geisha. To my left, a trio of schoolgirls in plaid skirts and navy blazers over white blouses clink bottles of Sapporo. Next to them, a rowdy table of blue- and green-haired Tokyo punkettes with boyfriends in American fifties biker attire pass around a plate of tempura.

Evidently I've crashed a costume party. I'm glad I dressed in simple black and that no one's taking any notice of me. A waitress in modern dress arrives with a small steaming sake vase and cup. Before she's gone my geisha rematerializes. She kneels beside the table to pour, and I can see that she's no pretend geisha, for her every gesture bespeaks a practiced grace. There's a fluid beauty to the way she leans in, the depths of her long sleeve offering a brief glimpse of pale flesh in mid-pour, and the gesture seems subtly intended for my appreciation. *"Dozo,"* she murmurs. Please.

I gingerly lift the cup to my lips and sip. As the hot tartness expands on my tongue, she produces a lighter from the fold of her kimono and lights the candle beside my chopsticks. The flame flares, brightly illuminating her face as I set down the cup, licking my lips, and . . . odd, but there's something so familiar in the look of her.

"From the house reserve. Our best, for our very special guests," she says, adding, the trace of another accent now unmistakable, "You like?"

Naomi?

I stare, uncomprehending. I'm recognizing the Naomi I remember from last night's imagining, realizing that the extra lengthening at the corners of her eyes is mascara, noting that the shape and personality of her features is anything but Asian. She doesn't move but holds my gaze, the start of a smile hovering around her carefully outlined lips, offering me this moment as she'd proffer another cup of sake, as though allowing me the leisure to discover that the impossible has just become real.

But no—it *is* impossible. I decide she's simply a woman who *looks* like Naomi, and that house reserve sake has a higher alcohol content than most.

As if to confirm this, she betrays not a hint of recognition. She's encouraging my attention, sure, but she's only being professionally flirtatious. She's picked up on my interest in her, is all, and—perhaps because I amuse her, or she's bored, or she's reflexively jacking up her tip—she's shifting into high geisha mode.

"I like it very much," I tell her.

"I'm so glad." She smiles at me, her infinitely attractive customer rising in her estimation because of his good taste. "Menu?" she asks.

The resemblance is still there, uncanny, and the coincidence of it truly strange, but clearly my woman of mystery in geisha masquerade won't be joining me for a date. "I'll have whatever you think is good," I tell her.

Joy dances across her face, flavored with a note of self-awareness that makes her performance arch within an inch of parody. "Wise man," she says, and in these two syllables and a flick of her eyelashes, I get the picture: how special I am to be so discerning, and what a total tool I am, to be such putty in her hands. "It will be my pleasure," she adds. Bowing again, she backs away from the table, managing the feat of only turning when she's a part of the shadows, so that her image lingers in my mind's eye after she's vanished from sight.

She couldn't be Naomi Dussart—the concept of a French geisha strikes me as oxymoronic—nor the figment-of-my-imagination Naomi because she's real, in flesh and blood. But how is it possible that a woman so . . . Naomi-ish should show up here, tonight of all nights, and what was with this random reservation?

Who knows? Downing a second cup of sake, listening to the koto player perform a pretty good cover of Tom Petty's "Stop Draggin' My Heart Around," I decide to let such questions slide. Instead I take mental notes for my next conversation with Isabella, revising and reconstructing the experience for maximum effect. *Well, she insisted on going to Yamashiro, I'll say, and I know they put on a big show up there, but the sushi is actually quite fresh.* When my faux-Japanese not-Naomi returns to serve the meal, I give myself over to being the solo audience for her elaborate offerings of sashimi, sake, and tea. And for the first time since Isabella's desertion, my angst and anxiety are quelled.

There's real power in this woman, I see. Because I've been spooked by the idea that by losing someone you can become *a loser,* I welcome the feeling that I'm no loser tonight. According to this woman, whoever she may be, I'm an attractive bachelor out on the town. And sitting there, enthralled by each whisper of silk and glimpse of pale skin, I become simply this and nothing more.

Senses gratified, stomach satisfied, feeling as pampered and revered as a sovereign, I'm swallowing the last of my green-tea ice cream on its bed of sugared rice wafer ringed with orange slices, when a loud clinking of glasses sounds across the room.

A man in Hokusai-like fisherman's garb, complete with broad-brimmed hat, is on his feet, addressing the gathering in rapid-fire Japanese. He raises a glass, leading countless other glasses to be held around him on all sides. I take a sip from my own cup as a woman at the table beside him rises. She speaks only a few words, but there's laughter, and then the man at the next table gets up. These toasts are going clockwise round the room, headed in my direction. Even now, two of the punkettes at the table next to mine are clambering to their feet to speak. I have no idea who or what is being celebrated, and now my intrusion's going to be exposed to ridicule or worse. It's too late to slink hurriedly from the room. To say nothing will seem more than rude.

Fortunately, my geisha has returned, deftly setting down the check. "You can tell I really hated it," I say quietly, indicating my empty dessert plate.

She smiles. "Oh, no. Absolutely no one hates our cooking," she says, and as if in reaction to the bemused look on my face—because where have I heard that line before?—she adds, "Jordan."

My own smile freezes. The line's familiar because I came up with it. *Absolutely no one hates my cooking* is what my imaginary Naomi told me last night, when we were flirting around the idea of dinner. And I could swear that the geisha's spoken my name—she who's just executed a brisk ballet of table-cleaning, leaving only the sake cup, the last drops of sake freshly poured. I'm restraining myself from arresting her arm as she withdraws when the punkette duo to my right, done trading sentences, hoist their Sapporos high to applause. I look up to find a roomful of expectant faces fixed upon me.

The geisha who may be Naomi has retreated into the shadows, but she's pausing to watch as I push back my seat and stand. Sake cup in hand, I clear my throat and say the first words that come into my mind. "I drink to beauty," I say. "To the . . . loveliness in women that inspires every man."

For a moment the room is silent. Has anyone understood a word? In the next instant hearty applause breaks out, cups raised all around me. Flushed, I down the last of my sake and seek out the geisha, who smiles at me with ambiguous satisfaction, gives a little bow, and turns away. It's a bow of good-bye, I can feel it, but now I'm determined to get to the bottom of this. I pull cash from my pocket and throw it on the check as she disappears through the curtain at the far end of the room. I hurry round my table and other guests cheer me on, as if I'm an actor leaving the stage after a fine show.

Outside the private dining room lies a dark hallway. I see the woman's retreating figure vanish round a corner. I start race-walking. I reach the end of the hall to catch a flash of that peacock hair comb disappearing down a flight of stairs.

The steps are narrow, full of sharp turns, and my inner sea of sake pitches as I hurry down after her, clutching the banister for support. I keep the midnight blue butterfly obi at the back of her kimono as the buoy to center me. At the bottom of the stairs, a muffled clanking, a chatter of voices, and the smell of frying seafood indicate that the kitchen's close. Her figure glides down the corridor. I'm a mere few yards behind her, almost close enough to tap her on one brocaded shoulder, when she's through a door and it swings shut in my face. I grab at the doorknob, yank the door open again, and barely have enough presence of mind to avoid tumbling down the three steps beyond it. I'm outside the building, in the near pitch-blackness of cool autumnal night, standing at the service entrance to the restaurant. The geisha is nowhere to be seen.

I peer into the dark, looking in vain for that gleaming butterfly. I'm alone, though not entirely—across the courtyard, two Asian kitchen staffers in white aprons slouch against the wall, smoking. They look on with idle curiosity as I follow the gravel path under the eaves round the side of the building.

I trudge up the sloping drive to Yamashiro's front entrance, more bewildered than ever, trying to reconstruct what just happened. Did I hear her right? I remember now the confusion at the hostess's station when I arrived. "Jo-dan," the woman had said, adding, "Joking." So maybe it wasn't my name the geisha spoke, but merely Japanese for making a funny. At any rate, there's no geisha among the cluster of dressed-up diners waiting by the valet station. I join them, bereft, and hand my ticket to the valet. The night's still clear, while my woozy mind is anything but, and I plod over with all the energy of a shelved puppet as my Metropolitan putters to a stop down the drive.

When I key the engine, a burst of frenetic Dixieland fills the car, the work of a valet who likes KJAZZ. I turn it down as an impatient driver pulls around me, and I glimpse a vintage pink-and-white convertible, a flash of red lips smiling in my direction—I crane my neck, peering through the windshield, now only seeing the back of her head, covered in a turquoise scarf—but somehow I know it has to be her. The convertible's taillights blink merrily at me, pausing as if to say, *What are you waiting for?* Then the car zooms out of sight down the long driveway.

I bolt down the hill, keeping an excited eye on her blue-green scarf. Jockeying through the lanes, I have a feeling that she's letting me keep pace. So she's just a playful waitress continuing a flirtation, or she's . . . what? I flash on the memory of riding home from the screening with my made-up Naomi sitting beside me, and suddenly I remember what I'd finally succeeded in briefly forgetting: Isabella. With a stab of guilt, I feel the ghost of her hand on the back of my neck. But isn't she the one who's always suggesting that I "go in deep," that I not be afraid to get in touch with my spirituality?

Here I go.

We've reached the crest of one of the city's steepest hills, La Cienega and Sunset, where all the sparkling lights stretch out before my windshield, a sea of costume jewelry on velvet. The geisha's car plummets. I dive after it into the glittering dark lowlands, swooping and darting to keep pace with her in the shifting currents, and much in the way I've driven in dreams, I feel like I'm a few feet above the ground. All the traffic lights turn green before us, and we cut a serpentine swath through the lanes, accelerating south. She's taking me back to my part of town.

On the freeway I lose her, regain her, the shrill radio saxophones bleating and mooing with manic glee beneath the roar of wind and car noise. At the Fourth Street exit I finally close the distance and pull up directly behind her. I'm about to toot my horn, hoping to meet her eyes in her rearview, when a gust of wind lifts the edges of the scarf she's been idly fussing with, and it flies loose as she makes her turn. The turquoise square leaps up and shoots back, flapping flat against my windshield. Straining to keep my foot on the brake, I grab at it, catch the colorful silk, and pull it inside. The convertible's gone.

I turn, peer anxiously into the lanes ahead. No . . . Still, she was headed right for my place . . . Fueled by faith, with the kerchief, soft and fragrant, tucked into my lap, I speed on. But when I get to my block and search the lines of cars on both sides of the street, there are no convertible fins in sight. The place is deserted.

Of course it is. For a while there I thought I was William Powell chasing Carole Lombard in a 1930s screwball, but it's all been sake-infused fantasy.

There's an open parking space opposite my house, small consolation, and I pull into it, inwardly deflating as the engine dies. I climb out of the car, moving slow, then stand there, contemplating the night light shining through the trees. I don't want to cross the empty street, knowing what awaits me inside: my own personal bar at the corner of Sad and Lonely, where everything I've been trying to avoid is set before me in a tall, chilled glass, a mixture of two parts grief to one part rage with a splash of longing, on the rocks.

Staring at the garden gate, it's as if I've looped back to the night before last: I'm once more keyless and forlorn, shut out of my own life. I can feel the ache of it all seeping out like a black fog from beneath the fence, enveloping me, and a silent howl of protest wells up in my chest.

This is not the life I want! I want . . . I want . . .

If purity of heart is to will one thing, for a moment I'm willing with all my heart for everything to change. Then, once again resigned, clutching keys and kerchief, I plod across the street and push on through, only to stop short as the gate creaks shut behind me. There's a pair of red high-heeled shoes perched on the bottom step.

I turn. A woman sits on the bench beneath the tipu tree in the garden, her bare feet propped up on the rattan table. There's nothing geisha-like about her. She wears a simple white dress that hugs her body like a second skin.

I stand by the steps, stunned, as she rises from the bench. Her bare feet make little noise on the soft gravel of the garden path. She blends with the shadows like a pale wraith, but with each step that brings her closer to me, she's more substantial, the soft curves of her body more pronounced, the glow from her eyes more intensely luminous. Her expression, in the dappled moonlight shining through the leaves, is more mischievous than demure. She's won the race, and her teasing eyes ask, *What took you so long?*

I have no reply but stand, jaw slackened, because . . . it is her, it's Naomi, there is no mistaking this face. But how? How has she appeared? How is it possible that my Naomi who doesn't exist, who'd only materialized through the concentrated effort of my conscious invocation, is here?

I close my eyes tight, seeing the dark rush of capillaries, tell myself I'm in the grips of a hallucination born of having recently spent too much time in my head. What did I do yesterday? I concentrated hard, so maybe the image got burned into some memory cells. But no, I'm feeling her presence, the way it feels when you're not alone. I try to imagine it differently because otherwise I am out of my fucking mind. I think empty: empty path, empty garden, Naomi in France, like Isabella in Italy, away, over there, gone. I'm alone by my house of loss and she's not here, not real . . . If I look and let this be, I've finally become a Californian.

I open my eyes at last. And I'm still looking at Naomi.

All right, I think. This is what happens: You mess with reality, and reality messes with you. Go too far, and the far strikes back. I have played with my mind too much and something's gone flooey.

Naomi's face looms before me, bright in moonlight. Can she be the real Naomi Dussart, somehow showing up on my doorstep in my moment of need, magically transported across the sea? No, I see that she's my imagined Naomi, dressed as she was when I first conjured her, a svelte beauty, hair the way I envisioned it, the same perfume . . .

I'm staring at her, trying to comprehend who or what I'm looking at, comparing my memories of the real Naomi with this one, and whether it's a trick of the light or God knows what, her visage shifts before my eyes, like an image being fine-tuned by a photo-shop technician, the green in her eyes deepening, lashes lengthening, cheekbones becoming more pronounced as some extra pounds disappear.

She speaks. "Have I got it right?"

I blink, take an involuntary step backward. Maybe I'm lucid dreaming. I'd like to answer her, but I can only gape.

"Well, aren't you going to invite me in?" She looks amused, apologetic, a bit pleased with herself, slightly wary—all of these emotions surface in an instant. "Though it's lovely out here," she adds.

I glance around me, seeing what's been my prison yard of sudden bachelorhood, decorated only by the absence of happiness. When I look back to Naomi, she's moved to my right, noiselessly, uncannily quick. She's closer, and my skin vibrates from her inexplicable nearness. She smiles, mischievous, bristling with energy. "You did want to see me, didn't you?"

"I . . . yes," I manage. "But . . . But not . . . like this."

She looks playfully puzzled. "This *is* how you wanted me. Oh—" She clears her throat, and when she speaks again, it's with a carefully calibrated French accent. "This *is* how you wanted me?"

"I don't understand," I say. An understatement. She's shifting her weight from foot to foot, flexing her hands, as if assessing the properties of a newly tried-on body. As I look back to her face, the whole of her seems to bob slightly in the air, as if her feet have briefly left the ground. But no, her bare feet are flat on the garden path, smartly displaying ten toes, nicely manicured and painted in a pinkish red.

"You called," she says. "I came."

I stare, my brain still stuck in stun. "But . . ."

Naomi frowns. "Don't tell me you're disappointed."

"No!" I say. "But . . ."

"But-but-but!" she teases. "What's the problem?"

"You're not real," I blurt.

Naomi raises an eyebrow. "I'm not?"

"You can't be." I take a step back as she comes up close to me again. "You think?"

I'm shaking my head, she's backing me across the walkway, and then my heel hits the foot of the steps. I'm stopped short, and with her face only inches from mine, I'm inhaling the scent of her, can feel her breath on my lips. "No?" she murmurs. My tongue lifts to echo that same syllable as protest, and before I can get it out, she kisses me.

Now there's no thought. Pure voluptuous sensation overpowers me, the sweet taste of her lips on mine, the warmth of her enfolding arms— even the tickling brush of her silken hair on my cheek is electric, and it's as if a flashbulb of ecstasy has flooded my mind and body with light. I nearly lose my balance and she giggles, breaking the kiss.

As I stare woozily into her smiling face, some last vestige of my former sanity prompts me to whisper, weakly, the word I'd been starting to say: "No . . ."

Naomi narrows her eyes. "Maybe you need a little time."

"Time?"

"To take it in."

I'm a man at sea. "Wait a second."

"I'll call," she says, slipping into her heels.

She'll call? "But . . . where are you going?"

"Oh, don't worry about that."

She's right. There are so many other things to worry about, like where she came from, what she's doing here—what she *is*. My mystery guest turns by the gate to smile at me again. *"Au revoir."*

I manage to muster a smile back. Then she's out the gate. I watch it creak shut, listen to her steps recede, then gaze around me, dazed and undone. There's no sign that anything has happened here. There's only distant traffic and a cautious two-note tweet from the King in his tipu tree.

3

Complication

A new development that raises story stakes, requiring the protagonist to commit to a decision that sets him at cross-purposes with his prospective mate, and/or sets his inner needs at odds with his ostensible goal.

Waking up in my bed, head throbbing, mind thrashing around in the dark, I grab at the thought that I must've imagined everything that happened after I came home last night. The idea that I had some kind of brief psychotic episode seems the lesser of evils. But when I pad into the bathroom for aspirin, wondering what new and interesting drugs they give hallucinating head cases these days, I find an erased world beyond my garden fence, the street disappearing into white, the edges of tree branches dissolving as if smudged into the pale gouache of a canvas. Am I still mad? No, an impenetrable fog has descended over Venice. When I open the front door, I have the relieving sense of a blank slate before me: Even the sounds outside are muted, as if reality has hit a pause button.

Then I look down to see the turquoise scarf lying on the bottom step. It's real, it's silk, and to my apprehensive sniffs it yields the scarily familiar scent of the woman who was in my arms last night. I need help.

Leo:

*I want to set the date for our get-together. After next weekend is wide
open for me—I'll go by your schedule, of course, although sooner is*

better than later, since, well, things are getting weird around here, and actually . . .

Do you believe in spirits? I know it sounds nuts, but I think my imagination is getting the better of me—it may have somehow conjured one into being, that is, manifested a spirit in human form, in this material plane. What's your take on such occurrences?

Just curious.

J.

Dear Jordan,

I'm on my way to chemo, so I won't make this long. I'm feeling okay, just tired. A week from Monday would be good. I may not have much stamina. They've got me dragging an oxygen tank around now, though hopefully it's not for long. Come to me around 4:30—that ought to work. But call ahead to confirm. Things are up and down.

Regarding your query, I can only tell you that I'm ready to believe in anything, any manifestation of any spirit, from any realm, be it astral or Aramaic. Shortly after my surgery, while in thoracic care, I became convinced that my dreaded Aunt Sue (dead for some years, thank goodness) had come to visit, and worse, was trying to disconnect my monitoring equipment. The nurse and I had quite a little row about it.

If you have indeed succeeded in manifesting a figment of your imagination in our material world, I can only say bravo. Ours is not to question or to comprehend such events. Maybe you've gotten in touch with one of the unconscious forces that are always at work, in the interstices of our day-to-day. We live our lives as if we know how we're living them, while underneath each step we take lie the phantom footprints of our truer, more real selves. Least, so it seems to me. . . .

Best always,

Leo

P.S. Did you know that "dreamt" is the only English word that ends in the letters "mt"?

Leo's view aside, the idea that my sanity might be drifting away from me, an untethered blimp floating into the ether with my helpless body left behind to gape after it, seems for the first time a real danger. Doubly spooked by the silence around here—still a sobering reminder of my Isabella-less life—I turn to the pile of pages sitting on my desk. They emit such a radioactive glow that I feel I should have on a Hazmat suit. But if anything's going to bring me back to the realm of the mundane, it's Rumer's formidable challenge.

A new ending. The task would be easier if I hadn't had a gun held to my head. Bring in Nathan Colt to doctor the thing, in between one of his weekly half-a-mil rewrites? Studio darling Colt, the young hack chameleon who's mainstreamed the interesting edges off every movie project I've ever coveted? Oh, Rumer knows how to get you where you live. But one look at the notes makes me want to crawl into bed and stay there for a week. Barely a sentence of my draft has escaped the withering scrutiny of his crony Dana Morton, and now I'm expected to whip it into shape and crown it with a perfect climax in one week. Or else. I can almost hear the ticking clock. But I'm also listening for a sound that's absent.

Naomi said she'd call. I don't know how this is possible. Instead of hoping for a call from my estranged wife, I can anticipate one from a woman who isn't supposed to exist. This isn't precisely a comfort. Hearing from her would signify that I've given up my already tenuous grip on reality. The phone lies on the desk with the hushed foreboding of an unmarked package that could contain a jack-in-the-box or anthrax. After fifteen minutes of masochistic note-perusal that yields not a single story resolution straw to grasp at, the telephone seems to tower over the other furniture. I'm slinking beneath its hulking shadow.

Inevitably, I'm sitting on the toilet when the thing finally goes off. I lurch to my feet, pants around my ankles, spastic-dance to the living room, stumble into the couch to grab it on the third ring, and gasp a "Hello?"

Crackle of cell noise. "Yo, dog, yo, son, yo, Moore-man!"

"Moony?"

"Come outside! I'm on my way."

"You're kidding," I say, but he's already hung up.

Out on the street, the fog has turned to mist, and from that mist, a black BMW emerges a few blocks down, headed toward me. A figure pops up through the sunroof, loses balance and drops out of sight, then emerges again, waving with both hands. Typical Moony to show up like this. He's hardwired to upset the status quo. He doesn't even know Isabella's gone, but he's one of the few people I won't have to don a mask to talk to. Actually, this feels like a perfect Moony moment.

The driver, a young guy in requisite baseball cap, exchanges nods with me as he pulls up the car. Moony climbs out wearing his WWII bomber jacket, his dirty blond hair disheveled, the shadow of a near-beard on his rugged chin and cheeks. Grinning piratical at me, he makes a peace sign. "He's due on the set in forty minutes," the driver says.

Moony slams the door shut, bats on the car hood with his fist. "Bugger off, dude! I'm in good hands!"

"All yours," the driver mutters, and drives away.

Moony advances on me, arms out, pulls me into a hug. Though his wild hair, which smells of patchouli, is getting in my eyes and Moony is holding on awfully tight, I have to give over to it because Moony won't let go. He's breathing heavily, and when he finally releases me and I step back, I see that his eyes are red-rimmed and teary.

"Hey, are you all right?"

"I'm good, I'm good!" Moony grins crookedly, sniffling. "It's just been too long, man, don't you think? When you coming back to New York City? Hey, look—" He brandishes a small, flat silver flask no bigger than the palm of his hand. "Beautiful, huh? It's a keychain! Check this out . . ." Moony unscrews the flask top, which does have a key ring attached, but no keys. He thrusts the opened flask into my hand. "Wakatake sake! Isn't that great? Hey, say it six times in a row, really fast."

"Um, Moony . . . ?"

"Do come on," he insists with a mock British accent. "With me, now: wakatake sake, wakatake sake . . ."

"Wakatake sake, wakatake sake . . ." I dutifully repeat, Moony chanting along loudly, palms beating on his chest and thighs in rhythm. He ends with a cry of *"Hai!,"* gesturing a "bottom's up" at the flask in my hand.

I shake my head, handing it back to Moony, who promptly downs a healthy swig. "Moony," I say. "It's eleven in the morning. You sure you're okay?"

"Better by the moment," he assures me, pocketing the flask. "And how's life treating you?"

"Well," I begin, "lately it hasn't exactly been a joyride."

"Yeah? Hit a little rocky patch myself recently. But I'm fine now, honest."

I want to get to my news, but Moony's insistence on all being well sounds suspect. "Rocky meaning what?"

Moony chuckles. "Ah, you'll never believe it." He looks around him furtively, as if not wanting to be overheard. "Kathleen. She had an affair."

"What?!"

"That's what I said! Among other things. But we're fine now, really, we're working it all out." He nods, smiling.

Kathleen's been Moony's faithful wife since college days, when we all first met. She is the rock to her husband's often gravity-less trajectories. Shocked, I can only say: "Unbelievable."

"It *is* unbelievable!" cries Moony. "Yeah, while I'm working eighteen-hour days on this crappy indie thing to make the money that supports us both, she's been fucking a semiotics professor from NYU. But we've had *talks,* we're really *communicating,* so everything's going to work out fine."

I was about to declare myself as the man in pain, the wife-abandoned one, but blindsided as I am, I feel for him. "Man, I'm so sorry."

"I don't even know what *semiotics* means."

"This is awful."

"Shit, yeah! We had the usual fight, the one we have every time I go on location," Moony rants on. "I never have time for her, my career's more important—and it doesn't help that my costar is a legendary slut. Next thing I know, I call from Toronto, and she's with this guy—but the worst is over," he interrupts himself, holding up a hand. "We'll be good as new, soon as I finish this shoot. I'm fine! I'm second stage, Jordo!" he crows with a forced grin. "Second stage!"

Brian Moon Hanson (whether his mother is really ten percent Cherokee or merely a one-hundred-percent hippie, still under debate) is referring to the four stages of being an actor. One, Who's Moony Hanson? Two, Get me Moony Hanson. Three, Get me a young Moony Hanson, and four, Who's Moony Hanson? "That's great," I say. "I mean, it's great you're working." He nods darkly, and I see the opening to share my own misfortune. "But hey," I begin, "I can relate. Because weirdly enough—"

"Man, is this thing still running?" Moony is staring, brow furrowed, at my Nash Metropolitan parked on the street, which has been pigeon-bombed overnight. Huge Pollock-like white blotches cover its maroon hood.

I give up. "I've been meaning to get it washed."

"Let's go," said Moony.

"Now?"

He shrugs. "We're in L.A. . . . . Car wash!" He uncaps his flask again and takes another swig.

As Mr. Feeling Fine guzzles sake, my concern for him grows, and my already strong urge to get away from my own dark home with its radio-active desk gets stronger. "Well, I'm supposed to be working, but I guess I could take a break."

Moony wipes his mouth with the back of his hand and smiles. "Excellent! Anyway, that's my headline: Bad times, but I'm feeling fine." He squints at me. "So, Jordo. What's up with you?"

~ ~ ~

The Marina Car Wash on Lincoln is crowded on a Saturday morning. Hispanic men in belted blue smocks swab at whitewalls and fenders, pile neatly folded rags on newly gleaming hoods, and whistle for drivers to collect their keys. Moony is too agitated to sit in one of the waiting area's orange plastic chairs. He paces the periphery of the auto rubdowns, wide-eyed with incredulity. "Terrible," he says. "That's terrible, man."

"Not knowing what's going to happen next makes it worse."

"Torture," he agrees. "She has to think it over, while you hang in the wind. You gonna go over there?"

I shake my head. "She's pretty adamant about wanting the time apart."

"You're Mr. Romance," Moony says. "Why not *move* to Italy?"

"Starving isn't so romantic," I say. "Especially when I won't even know how to say 'I'm starving.'"

Moony chuckles. "Yeah, but drink enough *vino*!" He raises his flask. "Besides, Rumer Hawke's going to make you rich."

"First I have to give him what he wants." I can feel the pull of that toxic paper pile on my desk. "Then the movie has to get green-lit—that's my payday."

"And then you can be bicontinental," Moony says.

"I just hope it's not too late." My Metropolitan has emerged, dripping, from the conveyer belt. The attendant parking it looks amused by its toy-like size. "I should've seen this coming," I tell Moony. "I know how hard it's been for her here, but . . ."

"Same with me," says Moony. "Same with any guy, right? We figure things'll work themselves out. Just one of the many things about men that make women crazy."

This said, as he takes another sip from his flask, I feel a flare of hostility toward Kathleen and Isabella. Moony couldn't have dealt with Kathleen's betrayal so quickly and easily, it's just not possible. His manic cheer must be masking major pain. Here's one argument for a make-believe girlfriend: She won't likely have a change of heart when you're not looking and annihilate you. "You sure the sake's a great idea today?" I ask

Moony. "I don't want to be reading 'Disaster on the Set' in *Entertainment Weekly.*"

Moony pats my shoulder, shaking his head. "You're the one who worries me. Looks like you lost a little weight, man."

"It's the sudden lack of pasta." Maybe it's neurotic, but I haven't been able to cook for myself since Isabella left—as if my taking over what's been largely her job would somehow jinx her coming back—and I've been subsisting on a diet of takeout. "Moony, ever think you'd be better off with a woman who isn't real?"

"With a what?"

"A . . . pretend woman," I say. "Someone you imagine, to keep you company."

"That might work," he says. "But even if she's an imaginary woman, she'd still give you imaginary grief. Hey, you know what you need? That. *That's* a car." He points at a pristine vintage cherry-red Mustang convertible with a black hood, early seventies from the look of it, that's getting toweled down next to the Metropolitan. A burst of hip-hop music emanates from his jeans pocket. Moony pulls out a cell phone and flips it open. "Yeah . . . What new pages?" He rolls his eyes at me and turns to have the conversation.

So much for broaching the topic of Naomi. Looking around, I see I'm the only person in the waiting area who isn't talking on a cell phone. It can't be this way everywhere, can it? There has to be a city left somewhere where people killing a little time can stand to talk to the people next to them, or not talk at all. But wait, here comes someone who isn't on the phone, a willowy young woman who oddly enough is looking my way, slowing in her stride and smiling, now changing course to head toward us, not that I have any idea who she is. "Moony!" she cries, and waves.

Done with his call, Moony turns to see her, registering generic congeniality, a flicker of alarm as he tries to place her, and then surprised recognition. Michelle, I soon learn, tends bar at one of Moony's hangouts in New York and turns out to be the owner of the red Mustang. Tired of bicoastal life, she's ready to be rid of it.

"You're going to sell that thing?" Moony asks her. "How much?"

"I'm asking six thou," Michelle says. "But for you . . ."

"Let's take it for a spin," says Moony.

I'm about to protest this inquiry on my behalf when I realize that Moony is interested in buying it for himself. Either that or he's interested in Michelle. In a minute he's ready to depart with his newfound friend. "Yo, Jordo, let's meet tonight, at this new place on Sunset where the whoosit used to be. Zanzibar, Zimbabwe . . ."

"Zulu?"

"That's it! Say eight o'clock," Moony says as Michelle takes the top down, then squints at me. "You gonna be all right?"

"Me?" I say. "Yeah, I'm all right."

"You're sure, man? Hang in there, okay?"

"Right. You too," I say.

"Oh, I'm good, man! It's all working out," Moony assures me.

Michelle has scooted over to the passenger seat and pats the wheel, smiling at Moony. He climbs in, guns the motor with a satisfying roar and grins at me, thumb up. I salute, calling: "Welcome to L.A."

Bemused, I watch Moony zoom out of the lot in the glistening car. Brokenhearted me has ended up hand-holding a guy who seems to be in worse shape than I am. It's brutal, what relationships do to you. But at least for Moony, Mustangs and Michelles materialize when he's needy. So what do I get?

The attendant holds up my keys. I trudge toward my clean car, aware that the one thing I have gotten, for better or worse, is Naomi.

The small package on my stoop bears Italian postage and a certain distinctive handwriting. I'm already tearing at the wrapping as I hurry through the door, too curious to know what Isabella could be sending me.

Having wrestled with her ultra-secure, ingenious packaging (she's an artist in everything), I behold a gift wrapped in an enigma. My wife has sent me a tube of Ebano & Ebano Moisturizing Shaving Balm—the kind

I like now, only available in Rome—nestled within two pairs of elegant dress socks, white: the kind I would never wear.

The aftershave cream isn't mysterious, and just the sight of the familiar gray tube makes my eyes tear, because I remember how the last one got used up only weeks ago. I'd been trying to squeeze the remaining drops of the Ebano & Ebano from its twisted-up tube and Isabella grabbed it, showing me how you really apply the pressure—and the precious goo had squirted, splat! against the bathroom mirror. And while I'd stood there glowering, pissed, she'd laughed, hugging me to her, and I'd seen the expression on her face in the mirror, the indulgent, adoring look in her eyes.

A glance at the postage tells me she sent this the day after she arrived in Italy, and my first impulse is to give this act—she paid extra for Priority!—the most positive interpretation: Yes, she left me, but see, she's been thinking of me, wanting to make me happy even on one of our Dark Moment's darkest days. With the white socks, though, I'm stumped. The accompanying card is a typical Isabellian drawing, elegantly sparse in line, wholly ambiguous: two doves in flight, either leaving or approaching a swatch of stars. Cast out of heaven? Coming into it anew? Is she giving me a gift to say, *Here's a balm for long after I'm gone,* or to indicate that there will be life for the two of us after Rome? I'll be trying to crack the code of this for days.

It's only now that I notice the blinking red light of the answering machine. Two messages. The first is Randy from the writing department, wanting me to know I have a full roster for my Romantic Comedy class, and that the handouts will be in my room this coming Tuesday night. That soon? Yup, this date is also on my calendar, the start of the first class after my scheduled hiatus. Oh, *there's* something to look forward to: pontificating on the rules of fictionalized flirtation while my marriage burns.

The second message is from Isabella. I listen to her twice, hope renewing. Because if I understand her correctly . . .

"*Ciao,* it's me," she says. "How are you? I'm looking at a beautiful Roman moon, and . . . doing a lot of thinking. I need to talk with you.

You should call me, so I can tell you . . . I need a favor from you—I'll explain—but if we maybe want to be together again . . . *Aiee,* this machine! I want to hear your voice. So call, whatever the time. Okay? I send you kisses. *Ciao.*"

Is she contemplating a flight home? Does she want me to come to Rome? I punch in the long string of digits. She picks up on the first ring.

"*Amore!*" There's unrestrained delight in these two syllables: a woman happy to hear the sound of her husband's voice, free of the bitterness I've been hearing from her lately. I feel a swell of longing to have back what used to be. I don't mind the noise around her that indicates she's out at a trattoria; my heart surges with the anticipation of having it again, all the love I've been denied. I'm patient while she moves from her table inside to the piazza, to get a more stable connection, both of us laughing over the interruptions, her friends arriving, Maxi barking. Then she settles, lighting up a cigarette, and I thank her for the gift. She's delighted the package came so soon. And the socks? "For the shoes! You know the ones."

Of course: the white Italian dress shoes, an early marital gift from Isabella now gathering dust in a corner of our closet. She'd bought them for me during one of our first trips over there, despite my protests that— phrased in more diplomatic language—I wouldn't be caught wearing them in my coffin. Now is not the time to re-address this worrisome predilection of hers to try dressing me up as someone I'm not, so I simply thank her for the matching socks, especially as her message sounded so positive and she's now so impatient to get to her business at hand.

"I want you to sell my easel."

This simple declarative sentence heaves a bolt of terror through my solar plexus. Her easel?! Her long-coveted Cavaletto da Studio easel, which set me back a small fortune only a year or so ago? To say she doesn't want it anymore is to say she doesn't want . . .

But Isabella is rushing on, misinterpreting my silence for consternation over logistics. "It won't be difficult, Jordan, you can go on that Web site, the letter one, the what-do-you-call-it, where you sell the things?"

"EBay?"

"*Sì!* You go on the eBay, you get a good price for it, and then I can have the money I need."

"To do what? Bella, you love that easel, you said it was the one you'd always wanted, the finest you'd ever owned——"

"I don't want you to be spending your money for this."

"But this is crazy. If you're talking about a plane ticket——"

And now I learn once more that there is no second-guessing the working of a woman's mind. The money she wants isn't for air travel. "It's a monastery," she explains, "in Todi, in the most beautiful medieval town. And the class, the . . . retrieve, you call it——"

"Retreat."

"Yes, the retreat, this happens only every two, three year, when Swami Girinanda visits this country—you know how important this man is to me, Jordan!"

I know, yes, but now? Isabella is saying that for her to achieve clarity, she needs to be in a monastery on a mountain, and I can't keep my voice from squeaking after she provides details. "Two weeks?"

"Yes, away from Rome, away from the rest of the world. One week, I visit my cousin Maria in Todi, then one week with Girinanda doing meditation, yoga—clearing my mind, feeding my spirit, making my body stronger—and I know you maybe think I'm only running away from problems——"

"Well, now that you mention it . . ."

"—but you're the one man in the world who can understood this: I do it for you, for us, as much as I do for me."

The one man in the world who understands gropes for a clue. "Because . . . ?"

"I want to take this time alone to learn something. To go in deep. To figure out if I should come back to America."

Now she's got me. "Really."

"To see if we can make things work. I can't promise," she says. "But I'm already thinking I might come for a visit——"

"A visit?"

"How can we predict anything? When I'm still so confused, and you are making your own choices about what to do with your time—"

"Isabella . . ."

"—who knows what may happen? But right now, for me, being away will help to make things clear."

"You're already away," I remind her.

"It's not the same. I need to nourish my soul. I want to find the good feelings I know I have. To understand maybe how I can come to be with you, in a better way."

The possibility of her return is such a beautiful carrot, dangling at the end of this Buddhistic stick. Both elated and frustrated, I cast about for that calm and controlled Jordan who'd handled our last conversation so deftly, but he's nowhere on the set.

"And you need the time to do your work," she's saying, "to concentrate, without difficult Isabella in your way. I know how important it is, this Rumer movie. If it goes well, and if I were to come back to Los Angeles, our life could be so much easier."

"I know." She's just read me a line from my own reconciliation script.

"Jordan, I tell you the truth, I had a dream about you, just last night. For the first time in weeks! And I woke up seeing your face and knowing everything, how I love you, knowing so much of what we have together, and crying . . ."

"The dream made you cry?"

"I was crying like a dog," she says. "Because I was missing you in that way, that way I never think I would feel again . . . and I have hope, you know?"

Hope! Wasn't I hoping ten minutes ago that I'd already won her back? Now, instead, a stalemate. True, the enormity of her proposed sacrifice is impressive (sell her *easel*?), offered in the service of saving our marriage, but two weeks? Still, she's talking about coming home, an idea that wasn't even on the table two days ago, so if I'm smart . . . Stick to the Plan. Capitulate for now, hold out for the big win.

"Jordan? Are you there?"

"Yes. I'm just thinking . . ." I'm searching for a role model, an image to fortify me, to help me suck it up. And suddenly I've got it, I see who I have to be: I'm Lloyd Dobler in *Say Anything,* standing defiant in the wet grass at dawn, arms holding a blaster raised high above my head, playing a song of unrequited passion—a man showing the woman he loves that he won't back down, he'll do anything to go the distance.

I say, "I'm not letting you sell your easel."

"No?" She's crestfallen.

"No. You're going to Todi, and I'll pay for it myself."

"You really love me," she cries. "You do!"

"You think?"

She laughs, and thanks me for believing in her, in the two of us, in the possibility of a new beginning, which this gift to her signifies. Once again, I'm the mature and caring provider who alone holds the keys to her happiness. *Thank you, Lloyd.*

"And maybe you should take some time to do the same," she adds pointedly.

"I should go find an ashram?"

"What I'm saying, maybe instead of . . . distracting yourself," she says carefully, and the specter of my unnamed distraction looms briefly on the phone line, "you could think to us. Then it's like we really do this thing together."

I hadn't meant to laugh, but I do. "You mean while we're even further apart."

"We're not so far apart as you think," she says, and for the first time since she left, I sense a plea behind her words.

"Maybe not," I allow, and for a brief moment I feel cravenly victorious.

"Well, it is up to you, too," she says, bristling. "You have the choice, to be with me in this moment . . . or to be with someone else."

It's the only card I have to play, so I keep it close. "I understand," I say carefully, and it's interesting, the quality of the silence between us. Then I hear her gather up her many feelings, retreating. *"D'accordo . . ."*

"I'll wire the money to your account," I assure her.

"*Grazie, amore.* I call you, when I come back from the bank."

"*Ciao, bella.*"

"*Ciao.*"

Alone again, I feel that hollowness at my core. She loves me. She says so, and I believe her. It's not unqualified love, though, and everything between us is still perilously unresolved. It's like she's leaving me a second time, and I feel a sharp ache of impotence. But as I stare out the window at my garden, I remember that I'm not so powerless after all.

How does one get hold of a phantom mistress?

I stare at the spot where she first appeared. I murmur her name. I close my eyes and try with all my might to picture exactly how she looked not in memory but last night, when her face loomed before me and her lips met mine. Yet when I open my eyes again, the garden's still empty. Evidently Naomi is now officially outside of my psychic reception area. Which means she is . . . where?

Or does it mean that she was never here?

If I hadn't gone to the Third Street Promenade to find the book I hadn't yet found for Leo, if I hadn't been caught by the swarm of shiny-toothed celebrity smiles covering the newsstand, causing me to loiter in the shade of the kiosk awning, I wouldn't have found myself face-to-face with what I briefly thought was another hallucination.

"Jordan Moore!" says Dana Morton.

"Dana Morton," I reply.

Rumer's right hand is the last person I feel like dealing with today, but I force a smile. She's dressed in slacks and a button-down shirt not unlike my own, and brandishes a few extreme-sports magazines. "Picking up some things for my beau," she says. "We're north of Montana. And you're a Venice boy, aren't you?"

"Yes," I say, "I'm an expatriate New Yorker, so I have to live near the beach, to justify my being here to my old friends."

She smiles, nods. "How's the work coming along?"

So much for chat. It's been barely twenty-four hours since our meeting, and it's a Saturday afternoon, but I don't want to be seen as *that wussy writer,* so I set my attitude on Wry But Upbeat as we fall into step headed north. "Going great. Though I did happen to notice that you guys gave me like one or two notes . . . ?"

Her smile widens. "Oh, I know we're note crazy," she says. "But don't let it get to you. I'm sure your new draft will deliver that champagne fizz."

Hearing this phrase, I look to Dana, startled, realizing she's been to my amazon.com page, the only place where my one, long-out-of-print book's early reviews are posted. There is the featured quote from *Kirkus Reviews* likening *Clinch* to "a box of chocolates," and that other one, from the small "Books in Brief" notice I earned in the *New York Times Book Review,* saying the plot "has a champagne-like fizz." I was delighted by such praises back then, in the first flush of publication, but now they don't sound the same trumpets and chimes. "Boy, you've done your homework," I say.

"I told you, I'm a fan," says Dana. "It really is a delicious read."

"Huh," I say.

"You sound a little dubious," says Dana.

"Well, it's not Tolstoy."

Dana laughs, a high-pitched cackle that suggests it's not so much what I said, but the surprise of being made to laugh. "Did you want it to be?"

What I wanted. I rarely let myself think about it, though it runs like a secret underground river beneath all my creative endeavors. I wanted to write like Chekhov, write like Conrad, I wanted to produce something of substance—something that would captivate and move people, the way my favorite books consumed and transformed me. And instead . . . This slippery slope leads to a Grand Canyon of bad feelings, so I pull back from the edge. "I always saw the book as kind of a lark," I say.

"Hey, we need larks," says Dana. "But I'm guessing . . . there's an opus grande in your past? The one that never was?"

"You're good."

"A big sprawl of a thing . . ."

"More like a swamp," I admit. "A murky morass of worthy intentions and tortured prose." I can still see the look of compassionate pity on my sophomore-year girlfriend Sarah Goldfarben's face as she struggled to find something good to say about the chapters she'd read, the look that finally made me give up on the book—and soon after, on Sarah Goldfarben.

"My unfinished novel's at the office in my file cabinet," she says.

I turn to face her. "You're kidding."

"No, I'm an English lit major with a hard-on for Hardy," she says. "Don't get me started on *Jude the Obscure*. So, okay, what led you into *Clinch*?"

I am going to have to reevaluate Dana Morton. "Well, I was working as a slush-pile reader at Cotillion Press, and they kept buying total trash for six figures. So one day I started this thing, just blowing off steam, almost as a dare. An homage to my favorite romantic comedies, really—"

"There's a lot of Howard Hawks in there."

"Exactly." I know she's stroking me, but still. "Point is, I wrote it quick, didn't take it seriously, so—"

"You were surprised you got it published."

I shrug. Dana's shaking her head. "Jordan, I don't have to tell you how serious comedy is at the core. I mean, you teach this stuff. Maybe you don't see it, because you've been so close to it for so long, but your book *is* about something."

"Well, I did try to do something a little different," I allow. "My leads don't get together in the end. And with the both of them being advertising executives, I'm making fun of that whole everything's-a-sell sensibility."

"It's about more than that." She pauses me outside the Barnes &

Noble windows. Nearby the resident Promenade mime, painted silver from top hat to boots, is frozen on his pedestal, a few skateboarders pitching pennies at his feet from their perch on the fountain across the way. "Your book is a satire on the culture of narcissism," says Dana. "And you're tweaking genre stereotypes to explore the nature of compatibility."

I laugh. "Yeah, what you said. I also threw in a car chase."

"Which is brilliant," she says, "because even though you used it as a parody of a movie-like ending, it really does give us a great set piece for the third act."

"Huh." I try Dana's version of me on for size, this super-savvy writer who's so commercially calculating. It doesn't quite stick, but it's certainly attractive.

"Anyway," she's continuing, "it's that self-loving/self-loathing subtext we want to go further with, really have fun with, which is why"—she flashes a triumphant grin—"we're talking to Chad Harley for Jake."

An alarm goes off in my head. Harley is a teen star. In his last movie he played a high-school senior. He's got to be early twenties at most. "Interesting!" I say, fending off panic. "That *is* young, especially if we're still going with a thirty-something Margo?"

"Isn't it scrumptious? Look, Jordan, I know that you were doing a Tracy-Hepburn, but my God, it's so much sexier with a young, wet-behind-the-ears hunk pushing the buttons of an older, still way-sexy pro—and it totally amps up your whole line-of-morality-keeps-shifting theme, don't you see?"

I see Jake zapped by a time machine's rays, pounds shedding, wrinkles smoothing out, salt-and-pepper hair turning surfer blond. It gives me an utsy feeling, which Dana evidently reads in my expression. "Come on, you'll have fun writing him young."

"I dunno, Dana," I hedge. "It's quite a shift."

"It even does a nice turn with your theme, Jordan—'cause they're not *physically* twins, it's hipper than that, we're saying they're perfect for each other *beneath* the skin, while we score big points with your adult date crowd."

"I guess . . ."

"I've already got the arc of the thing all graphed out for us," she says with an air of great significance that only makes me more uneasy. *Graphed?* Her cell phone's musicalizing. Dana pats my shoulder and starts backing away. "You'll make it work. You'll make it Rabelaisian. Think of the kicks you'll have coming up with zingers for Chad. And it'll make the chase scene totally rock!" I can only nod. Flipping open her phone, she hurries toward a black Mercedes parked in the no-parking red zone on Wilshire. "I'm glad we ran into each other," she calls. "Next Friday, sweetie!" Then she's on her call, climbing into her car, leaving me outside the bookstore. Played.

Approaching the line of cars at the valet station in front of Zulu, I'm a bit irritated at what Moony has roped me into. True, I've barely been out of my living room in the days since Isabella left, but I'm leery of a Saturday night to be spent at a trendy hot spot in the heart of Hollywood. I tell myself it'll be a welcome change from all the varieties of weirdness that have visited me at home—for it's just as well that Naomi didn't show up again. Now I can be a sane man living in the real world, relegating her outlandish arrival and disappearance to the realm of life's unsolved mysteries, and instead I can concentrate on, for instance, discovering why Moony would want to meet in a place like this.

Bamboo and feathers frame Zulu's entranceway. Inside the artfully darkened interior, leering painted masks and wooden shields hang above a mirror-topped bar that snakes its way round the dining room, jewelry and whitened teeth gleaming amidst the rattan. A tuxedoed man with a wire-thin mustache is rolling a quarter over his knuckles at the host's station. He consults the reservations list and points me in the direction of the booths lining the back of the narrow room. I head down the aisle of tables, aware of the vocal pyrotechnics of Yma Sumac wailing underneath the hubbub, the glances of models and industry folk brushing over me and away. There's Moony, waving from a booth.

"'Ay, mate, welcome to Africa!" He's freshly sunburned, unshaven, radiating nervous energy that suggests a chemical imbalance.

"Moony . . ." After sliding into the seat opposite, I lean forward to see if I'm seeing what I think I see. "Your nose?"

Moony blinks, wipes the thin line of white powder from his right nostril, and snorts it up from the end of his finger. "You're awfully eighties," I say as he gives me a mischievous grin.

"Have a taste," he says. "You could use a pick-me-up."

"No thanks." So in the space of a single day he's progressed from being *fine with everything* to being a textbook candidate for a twelve-step program.

"All right, then, what are you drinking?"

"Depends," I say, adding hopefully, "Are we on our own?"

"No way! My friend's got a friend. They've just slipped off to the powder room." He leans into me, grinning right past my apprehensive look. "Hey, listen: This'll be good for you! She's a D-girl at Miramax. Best-case scenario, you get laid *and* you get a development deal. Worst case, it's entertainment."

"Or torture." Miramax has passed on every project I've ever pitched them, including *Clinch.* "Jeez, Moony—I don't know how to talk to studio execs when I meet them in meetings, let alone on a blind date." Which sounds as inviting as a colonoscopy. "And what if this one's personally rejected everything I've written?"

"Aw, come on," he says. "This is what you need, a curvaceous distraction! Someone to take your mind off Isabella. And hey—" He gives me a sage nod. "Someone to keep Isabella thinking about you."

"I've already got one of those." It's popped out of me, just like that, and it's too late to backpedal as Moony brightens, excited.

"Dog! Who is she?"

"She's a young, gifted, beautiful . . . figment of my imagination," I tell him.

"Say what?"

"Remember me talking about making up a pretend woman to keep me company? Well . . . I'm dating one. At least that's what I told my wife."

Moony gapes. "Because . . . ?"

"Like you said. To rile her, to get her to come back."

"Bloody hell," he says. "Wouldn't it be easier to shag a local barmaid?"

"I'm not up for it," I say. "And I'm only going to keep talking to you if you drop that ridiculous accent."

"Hey, I'm Nigel, a homicidal safecracker from Manchester," says Moony. "At least till next week-*end. Act*-ing!" he crows, raising his beer bottle. "Got to do it, or it all means *bullocks*." He drinks, squints at me across the table. "So she's just in your head, this girl of yours? Your twisted, nut-job head?"

"Yep." Best to omit the detail that she left my head last night and morphed into something yet defined. The pretend-girl part is enough to wrinkle Moony's brow.

"Well, you may be onto something," he says. "No muss, no fuss with an imaginary girlfriend. She got a name?"

"Naomi."

"Good one! Sounds black, or Asian."

"She's French, actually."

"A frog? You're not getting your balls busted enough by an Italian?"

"The woman I based her on just happens to be French."

"Calling *Monsieur* Freud. Well, if it was *my* dream date?" Moony grins, sings: *"I wish they—all—could—be Cali-for-nia girls . . ."* He swigs his beer, bangs the bottle down. "Hey, y'know what we should do? High-tail it down to Bourbon Street. *'Take me to the Mar-di-Gras . . .'"*

We've been threatening to make this pilgrimage together for years. But after what's happened down there? Moony sees the look on my face. "Hey, they still have beignets. They still put chicory in the coffee." He brightens. "We'll go in my new wheels. Bring your friend!"

"You bought that car?"

Moony nods happily. "How could I not? So: top down, radio on—me, Daphne, you, Naomi—go tripping through the kudzu in the moonlight, man, those big-ass weeping willow trees . . ."

"Daphne?"

"From my show. She's the one who wanted to eat at this zoo, and—Hang on! Here they are now."

I turn in my seat. One of the two women coming toward us, with blond hair cut chicly short, wears the kind of shiny, body-hugging sheath only women in movies wear. She must be Daphne. The other, with long and immaculately coiffed brown hair, is dressed in a less flashy though still stylish blouse and skirt. She looks so well put-together that I immediately feel shabby. "You're in my seat," she says to me with a smile. I can't tell if this is meant to be flirtatious or if she's irked, so I get up quickly as Moony makes introductions. Daphne slides into the booth next to him and takes a sip of his beer in a way that telegraphs their intimacy. Madeline, my date, has a poise redolent of power lunches and a skin tone suggesting spa vacations. Mechanical Mozart rents the air as she sits. She reaches for her phone.

Nettled, I'm grateful our waitress is here and I can order a drink. I watch Madeline playing with the pearl on her earlobe as she talks. If I'm going to get through the evening without getting seriously cranky, I'll need to find a way to relate to this woman, but right now I'm at a loss. My romantic attentions are already being monopolized by one woman in Rome and another who's unreal. I don't want to have forced chitchat with this one, who's just snapped her cell closed. "Sorry," she says. "Babysitting a client. Colin Roberts, you know him?"

And here my anti-schmooze mechanism kicks in, the mouth working before the mind can exert control. "Not personally. But I know I hated his last movie."

Madeline's eyes widen. Moony's grinning at me, shaking his head as Daphne clears her throat. "That was Maddy's project," she says.

I look to Madeline, who's hard to read. "What did you hate about it?" she asks.

Oh, hell, might as well go for full-scale alienation. "Well, I'd say the violence was gratuitous, except the whole story was gratuitous."

To my surprise, she nods. "God, that's so true. Roberts is one of those posturing macho-dicks who think bloodshed is hip. You should have seen the first draft he brought in. There were heads exploding on every other page."

I'm honestly perplexed. "So you made the movie because . . . ?"

"He's one of Michael's boys. I just made it my business to clean it up and make it as palatable as I could." She shrugs. "Foreign was huge."

That's okay then, I want to say, *anything's justifiable so long as foreign is huge,* but Moony's leaning over the table. "Jordan's working on a project for Rumer Hawke."

"Really?" says Madeline. Her eyes brighten, and previously hidden smile lines show up at the corners of her lips.

I'm still incapable of playing nice. "What do you mean, 'Really'?" I ask. "Is that 'Really?' as in, am I really working for Rumer or just blowing smoke up everyone's butt?"

Madeline gives a low, throaty chuckle. Daphne and Moony are smiling, too. "One of my exes was a production exec on *Simple Complication,*" she says. "I understand Mr. Hawke is quite a character."

My date is now alert and engaged, and my martini has arrived. I take a sip, and with the cold flow of alcohol a renewed sense of well-being oozes through my body. She looks ready to hear something wonderful. "The Rumer rumors are all true," I tell her.

Madeline giggles. "The rampant Rumer rumors?"

I see her kind of bite back on the giggle with a flash of embarrassment, and suddenly understand something about her. She's the girl with the Coke bottle glasses I knew in high school, too bookish and too awkward to be popular. Only now she wears contacts, she's had some work done, she's learned how to dress, and she's thriving in a milieu where she's allowed to be smart, so she even feels a little sexy. There's the tell—a shy self-consciousness in her bright blue eyes, quickly darting away from mine. She's a dolphin trying to pass for a shark, and my heart gives a tiny clench of sympathy.

"So what's the project?"

Because she seems interested, I make a story of it, how I came out here to have three producers by turns turn my novel into something I barely recognized, and never got it made. How just when I was disenchanted enough with L.A. to be wondering why I was still here, the call had come from Rumer's office. I tell it wry, with the angst edited out, as though it's an anecdote about someone else. And Madeline's nodding— *Isn't that the way it always goes?*—she has war stories of her own involving novelists she's worked with who'd segued into screenwriting, including the one, she reveals as a new round of drinks arrives, who evidently took a chainsaw to her heart.

"Another one of those bad boys who thinks violence is sexy?" I surmise.

"Yes, when clearly I should have been meeting sensitive types like you."

"Sensitive types steer clear of studio executives."

"More the loss for all concerned," she says with a grin, and raises her glass.

It's odd, but no matter what I say, she's amused, whenever I go against the grain, she's entertained—to the point where I finally give up on trying not to belong to this club. I'm conscious of the proximity of real skin, real perfume emanating from it—an expensive scent—aware that a real, live woman is flirting with me. She wants me to bring her my next spec script. She's showing me her cleavage and her pointy-toed sparkly silver shoes, Giuseppe Zanotti—she's never spent so much money on a pair of heels in her life, don't hate her for it, and I don't. And by the time I've downed the rest of my second martini, this splendidly attractive woman intent on my every word, I am feeling at one with Zulu and the rest of its inhabitants.

Why shouldn't I be at home here? I'm a successful writer sitting in a good booth talking to an exec from a hot studio and my good friend, a rising actor (whose sexy costar is sweetly wiping fresh white traces from his nostrils), and here come beautifully displayed hors d'oeuvres on plates shaped like palm fronds, their actual food content indecipherable. Daphne is asking about the specials and the waitress is being witty, animated by the energy emanating from our group. Moony lifts his Corona in a salute to me across the table, then brightens, hailing someone over my shoulder. Two men, one tanned, suited, and smiling, the other dashingly disheveled and sober-faced, something familiar about him. The suit shakes Moony's hand. The other man knows Madeline, bends to air-kiss her cheek, and turns to me as she introduces him: Nathan Colt.

Hand outstretched, a complicit smile. Colt recognized my name. My wariness is defused by the star screenwriter's interest, however feigned, and I feel my stature elevating. A waiter is hailed to add chairs. Our party's enlarging. I examine Colt as he launches into a story, noting that he may be ten years younger than me, but I've got more hair. Though of course he's got one of those hip bed-head haircuts, and a suit I couldn't afford . . . Stop it. His anecdote, I realize, involves Rumer Hawke. When he's gotten his laugh, I briefly invoke my recent phone meet in the inner sanctum. Colt rolls his eyes.

"And I'm sure they're telling you they want it to be 'about something.'"

"Of course," I say.

"Please," says Colt. "They don't pay us enough for it to be about something. You know what it's about? Getting the next gig." He juts his chin at me. "Who's Rumer's wingman on this one?"

"I'm working with Dana Morton."

Colt nods. "You know how you recognize the development exec in a meeting? They're the one who, when you pitch them a remake of *Moby-Dick,* says: 'Great! . . . But does it have to be a dick?'"

We all laugh. An uncommon but welcome feeling of belonging swells in my breast.

"Speaking of dicks," Colt continues, addressing Madeline, "do I have to blow your boss to get him to sign off on this rewrite?" And though they start talking shop, Colt now ignoring me, I can sense people looking me over from the neighboring table, the volume of conversation in the room rising, cresting. And though now the name-dropping becomes nonstop, and the subtext of every subject is money—how much was made and who's getting more—and I'm actually participating in a debate on dog grooming that segues into talk of dog psychiatry (hey, I have a dog—overseas, sure, but he may well need a shrink by the time he gets back), I'm okay with it. When Nate gets up to greet someone at the next table, flashing an insincere smile as he goes, I smile back, magnanimous. Looking past Madeline, I see another man smiling at me, then with a jolt of surprise recognize myself in the smoked-mirror reflection. That's when I hear the voice at my ear.

"What are you doing?"

The husky whispered cadences are so loud and clear that I look up, bewildered to find no one beside me. "I mean, *really* . . ." the voice goes on. Luckily, Madeline's caught up in conversation with the next table now, so she misses the sight of me gawking at thin air in all directions, swiveling around like a long-necked goose. My gaze is drawn across the room, where a woman in a red dress sits on a high bar stool, spearing an olive in a martini glass and looking at me. I feel a shiver of vertigo as I make out the amused gleam in those distinctive green eyes.

I see her lips move. "What are you *doing*?" Naomi repeats, as present and distinct as if she were seated in my lap. It's crazy enough that she's materialized here. So why should I be surprised that she can throw her voice across a crowded room? Naomi brings the olive up to her lips. She flicks out her tongue and slips it into her mouth. Riveted, I watch her chew, swallow. I can hear each little pop of her moist lips meeting and parting.

I have to fight the impulse to leap up from my seat. I want to flee. I want to see her. I want to get her out of here. I had a feeling she wasn't a one-time-only hallucination, but I'm more alarmed than pleased to have my suspicions validated. Just how crazy am I?

Meanwhile Madeline's giving me a lightly contrite look that says she can't quite extricate herself from her conversation but will be back with me in a moment. I glance nervously at Moony, who's motor-mouthing about his and Daphne's movie to Suit Guy. I'm thinking I should be able to make a foray to the bar without anyone minding. But just as I look back again, I see Naomi coming down the aisle, headed right for me.

The tight red dress on that body, moving with a grace that would put your average runway model to shame, seems to draw all the spotlights in the shadowy room. I note darker eye shadow and longer lashes tonight, a subtle gleam of glitter on her cheekbones, streaks of color in her hair, worn half-pinned up with a cobalt blue barrette. Her bloodred nails, sharper than I remember, black net stockings, and improbably high heels make her look primed for illicit adventure, like the partner a Gallic gypsy would fling around the room in an Apache dance. There's only one thing wrong with the picture as she approaches, which is that this kind of vision should be turning every head in a heat-hungry crowd like Zulu's, but the only one watching her is me.

She looms over the table now, hovering so close to Madeline that Madeline must be aware of her. But clearly none of my companions see her there. "Hello, stranger," says Naomi, a mischievous gleam in her eye. All I can do is nod. Madeline smiles quizzically at me as her cell goes off again. Startled, I jump in my seat. Madeline picks up the call.

With a moue of amused annoyance at being ignored, Naomi leans over and blows at the curls of hair over Madeline's un–cell-phoned ear. Madeline smoothes her hair down. Naomi blows again.

"Stop that," I hiss.

Naomi rolls her eyes. Madeline glances at me, perplexed, tosses her hair, then says a quick good-bye to her caller and flips the phone shut. "Sorry," she says. "It's just, some of these people—"

Colt leans in from the next table. "Tell my friend Larry here how much you paid me to salvage that piece-of-shit thriller for you last summer," he demands. "He doesn't believe me."

As Madeline turns to Colt and his companions, I see Naomi reach for the phone on the table. "Everybody seems to be obsessed with these things," she says. "What's the big attraction?"

She picks up the phone and I make a grab for it. I have to reach up past Madeline to snatch it from her, glimpsing Moony, blinking at what must have looked like a self-propelled flying phone. "Hey!" Naomi says to me. I pray Moony will assume it's just really good coke, as Madeline turns back to see me holding her phone. "I— You don't mind, do you? I need to make a call."

Madeline finds my calisthenics a little strange, but shrugs assent. I get to my feet, turn briefly away from her to whisper at Naomi's ear. "Let's go to the bar."

"You're wound a little tight tonight," she says.

"Going to find a quiet spot," I tell Madeline, who nods, still caught up with Colt and co. Amidst the convivial hubbub, Moony's looking at me strangely. "Someone I have to talk to," I tell him.

I give Naomi a prod, and she precedes me down the aisle. The only person who pays us any mind is a frighteningly handsome blond waiter, whose butt Naomi reaches out and pinches in passing. I feel rather than see him straighten abruptly and stare after me, but I keep my flushed face forward as we come up to the bar. Naomi turns round against it to face me, smiling. "Miss me?" she asks.

Funny girl. But I'm aware that in her close proximity, my body hums like a struck tuning fork. For the benefit of the nearby bar patrons and the blond waiter, who hovers briefly in our vicinity with an insouciant grin, I make a show of holding the phone at my ear as I answer her. "So you weren't a dream."

Naomi cocks her head. "But you knew that."

She's right. "Okay," I say. "And the reason you've shown up again . . . ?"

"That's what I was asking you: What are you doing here?"

A simple enough question, but now, gazing into her smiling face, it's as if her words are dispelling an enchantment. I look around me. That expansive feeling of belonging has evaporated, and I see only, posing and pitching amidst the arch decor, the same strangers who alienated me when I first came in. "I'm not sure," I admit, gazing back at the booth. The person I saw in the mirror just minutes ago, aglow with a status I now understand was borrowed, ephemeral, is no longer there. I watch Moony channel Sid Vicious, laughing as he pummels his forehead with a beer bottle. Madeline's sucking up to Colt and his friends at the next table. Moments ago, I was afraid Naomi was going to disrupt my party. Now I'm starting to feel glad I've been rescued from it.

"If you'd rather get back to them . . ."

"No, it's okay," I tell her. "Though I'm a little worried about Moony."

"Oh, he'll be fine," says Naomi.

"You're probably right. I'm the one talking to someone that nobody else can see. Why is that, by the way?"

Naomi merely smiles and takes my hand. "Come on," she says.

"We're leaving?" She nods. I realize I can't abandon ship so smoothly. "Wait a minute," I tell her, and hurry back into the hubbub.

By the time I'm at the table, I've come up with a lame but borderline credible excuse. I'm banking on my date's love of dogs. "He wasn't feeling well all day and now he won't stop throwing up," I tell her, handing back the phone. "I've got medicine for him burrowed away somewhere, but my friend who's been dog-sitting can't find it . . ."

Madeline looks genuinely concerned and disappointed that I'm bailing, since there's been talk of going to another place after this. She presses her card into my hand and a lingering kiss on my cheek. Red-eyed Moony sees right through me, and is hugely amused. "Medicine for Maxi!" he crows. "God, you're a saint. Drive safe, though, Jordo, that's one bloody hell of a commute!"

I can feel him watching me as I return to the bar. Glancing back, I catch him craning his neck to see what I'm up to as I join Naomi, heading toward the exit. No luck there, mate. And it's a shame he can't check her out, because she really is the most stunning woman in the place.

~ ~ ~

I follow the red dress down the sidewalk. My two martinis wear less easily when I'm mobile, but I'm determined to get some answers, however wobbly I may be. "No, really, listen—why am I the only one who can see you?"

"You're the only one I'm here for," she says.

"And how is that?"

"How is what?"

"That you're here!"

Naomi laughs, and turns round to face me. "Well, we walked, silly—it wasn't very far." She's indicating a crowd outside the entrance to a club, where a hefty black doorman in a zoot suit isn't exerting much control over a cascade of revelers surging through the open doors. Before I can protest, Naomi scoots us past him.

Inside, a dark corridor booms with bass. We're jostled and carried along by clubbers, then spit out into an alcove that's purpled by black light where someone stamps a spider insignia on my wrist. The current bears us onward, and it's hard to keep track of Naomi. I've still got questions for her that really should get answered, but we've come upon the dance floor, where the DJ's playing the song I love from the first Arcade Fire CD at a volume that sends the beat caroming through the center of me. And when she darts beneath a mirror ball that's scattering silver bits over a group of people huddled at a bar holding drinks that glow bright green in the dark, all I can think is: Whatever those are, I want one.

I flag down the bartender and Naomi's beside me again, smiling, the silver light flecks swirling through her hair. "What are we doing here?" I shout into the music.

"You need to be out."

"I was already out."

"You need to be out of your mind."

Here's my glass of neon green. I drink, Naomi catching hold of my elbow, forcing me to down nearly the whole of it in one long, sharp, cold swallow. As it turns to a delicious heat in my belly and my head expands, she laughs, turns, and dives into the crowd of dancers. I finish the drink, lose the glass, and follow.

And I can't help moving to this beat, I'm dancing, my eyes on the flashes of her red dress as she snakes her way across the floor. Weaving and bobbing in her zigzagging wake, I watch her presence electrify the bodies as she passes, the men leaping higher where she lingers, the women undulating lower, and the energy buoys me higher and faster until I'm breathless and dizzy and we spin off the edges of the dance floor.

My ears are melting. I need water. We wait by the fountain for a goateed guy naked to the waist, painted from belly to pointed ears as Nijinsky's Faun, and his date, a blond mermaid with strands of Christmas lights blinking through her hair. When it's my turn, I drink a river before coming up for air.

"We have to talk," I tell Naomi.

She stretches her hands up to touch the low ceiling of the alcove, arches her back. "Have to?" she repeats, singsong.

An oval-faced girl who looks barely in her teens, an orange Glo Light halo in her dark hair, comes up beside her, unsteady on what could be her first pair of heels. She wants a drink of water, and I step out of the way. "You aren't the Naomi I thought up before," I say. "The one I fantasized."

"True. I'm not about fantasy," she says.

"You're not?"

The teen girl flashes me a smile, revealing translucent braces, and moves past us. Naomi leans in closer. "I'm about imagination."

"What's the difference?"

Naomi nods. "Yes," she says. "What's the difference?"

I'm utterly confused. Naomi's swaying to the techno-beat thump from the next ballroom, hair undone and falling over one eye. I lean in close to her. "If you're not really Naomi, why do you look like her?"

Naomi holds her arms out, hands up. "Isn't this what you wanted?"

"Yes, but . . ." I shake my head, thinking I can almost hear my brain rattle. "I just wish you'd explain—"

"I don't know if I'm explainable."

"Try me!" I plead.

Naomi's smile is radiant, affectionate. "Well, let's say that not long ago, you were a walking question." She runs her finger down the side of my sweaty face. "You were asking for something. From deep, deep down"—her finger descends to tap at the center of my chest—"in here. And what I am"—she rests her open palm there, generating heat—"is the answer, in a language you may be able to understand."

"The language of what?" I ask.

"No words," she says. "You really do need to learn to speak without them." As I'm trying to decipher this, she looks past me, her gaze narrowing. "For example . . ."

I turn to see a Glo Light halo in a shadowy stairwell down the hall. It belongs to the teen girl with the braces. She's with two men now, much older than she is, both of them muscular, in tight T-shirts and jeans. The bald one's dancing with her, very close. The second man, long-sideburned with weight lifter's forearms, has stepped behind her so that she's caught between them. The smile on her face falters as the other man begins to push his hips into hers. My giddiness turns to alarm. "Hey," I say.

"Exactly," says Naomi, and her hand gives a little push at my back.

I walk toward the group in the stairwell, aware that I'm slightly at a tilt. As I approach, the girl's trying to move out from between the two men, but the one behind has grabbed her arm, while the man in front grips her waist, holding her in place as he leans in to nuzzle her neck. The girl resists, pushing at him with her free hand, and in the next moment, my hand is on his shoulder.

The bald man stops moving against the girl, jerking back to glare at me. The girl wriggles loose of the weight lifter, sliding out from between the two men. There's too much of a din to hear what the bald man's saying, but the moment doesn't require language as both of them tower over me, the weight lifter tacitly blocking the girl's escape with his massive body. I try to indicate that she's with me, and as she slips to the left of the bald man, I reach around him, hoping to pull her free of the stairwell.

The man's hand strikes me flat in the center of my chest and I stumble back, nearly falling to the floor. Struggling to catch my breath, I come toward the two men unsteady but strangely focused. The weight lifter's advancing, yelling something I can't understand. The girl peers around the bald man, still not free and clear, and in the next moment—feeling unreal, as if I'm in some game or dance I'm trying on for the fun of it—I spin myself around in the one move I always liked most in those long-ago Tae Kwon Do classes, turning my back to the man as I kick out hard with my foot.

I've hit something. For an instant, startled adrenaline shoots through me, the crazy thought that I'm accomplishing my purpose. In the next moment I'm flailing in the air. What I've hit is the weight lifter's readied hand, which is now twisting my foot, and with an easy, almost lazy motion, he throws me into the wall. I smash shoulder, side of face, and knee, and crumple in a heap of pain, gasping. I struggle to right myself, ceiling tilted, walls swaying, and realize I'm most likely about to be ripped in two, like the phone books one sees bodybuilders decimate in those old ads.

The men are laughing. The weight lifter shakes his head, hands on hips. He's shouting a phrase that, ears ringing, I can't decipher but sounds like "Ooo-wee-hoo!" Neither of them makes a move toward me. I'm still trying to get to my feet. They just laugh, the bald man elbowing his friend and yelling that phrase in his ear. The weight lifter waves his forefinger at me, like a teacher reprimanding an errant schoolboy, and then, his attention distracted by someone down the hall, nudges his companion onward.

Still gasping for breath, I use the wall to get myself upright, conscious of the two men lumbering past me. It seems the mirror ball's above me again, tiny shiny stars flashing before my eyes. The teenster's at my side, her voice suddenly loud at my ear. "Are you okay?"

I nod, though I have no idea. "What was that guy saying?" I ask.

She grins. "He was calling you Bruce Lee Two."

I look to the ballroom doorway. There's a blurry cluster of people there now, drawn by the fight, if you can call it that. I think I see Naomi cheerily pumping her fist in the air, but I can't really tell, distracted by little explosions of pain and pulsation from various damaged parts of me. It's suddenly imperative that I stop trying to stand up. The dizziness swells, my stomach roiling, and I'm down on all fours again, crawling vaguely for Naomi when I gag and heave a splatter of neon green—not on the floor, exactly, but over the pointy toes of some oddly familiar silver sparkly shoes.

"Oh, hey, sorry," I tell Madeline of Miramax, who's standing there aghast with some folks from Zulu.

And it's like that scene in *The Lady Eve* where Henry Fonda's on the floor with dinner dumped all over his white suit, and he looks up at Barbara Stanwyck with this truly sick apologetic smile on his face that's in no way going to make up for the mess he's made. Only I don't look half as good as Henry Fonda.

Actually, that may be the least of my problems.

When I wake the next morning, ache-ridden in every muscle, it takes some effort to get my feet on the floor, which is strewn with last night's clothes. I dimly recall pulling them off before collapsing on the bed and passing out. Though I don't really expect her to be here, I listen for sounds of Naomi. There's a rustling outside the window. I raise the blind and meet the haughty yellow eyes of a gray cat pawing at a pile of leaves. I pull on my pajama bottoms, pad into the kitchen to put on the kettle. I gaze out the kitchen window to survey the garden and there she is.

An electrical charge zings through my wooziness. Naomi's seated on the bench, wearing the kind of saffron robe I've seen on Tibetan lamas, one shoulder bare, one knee tucked beneath her in half-lotus position, her eyes closed. As I gaze out at this portrait of feminine tranquillity, I realize I've become a stereo emoter—each feeling I have comes on with

its opposite in tow: Arousal accompanies dread, anticipation with appre-
hension.

Seeing Naomi is bringing flashes of last night back to me. I think I
was briefly on the fire escape of the club with her and the mermaid and
the faun, howling at the moon, but I might have dreamed that. The one
bit I do remember clearly makes me shudder. I'm quite sure that getting
into a fistfight and barfing on Madeline's Giussepe Zanottis was a most
effective way to kiss a lucrative development deal good-bye.

Regardless, here is Naomi again, doing some deep breathing. A
hummingbird whizzes past her head, pirouettes in the air and hangs
nearby, then zips away. I see the beginnings of a smile steal over her lips.
Either she's come to a particularly joyful moment in her meditation, or
she knows I'm watching her. I'm too hungover to worry about my sanity
or lack of it now. I decide to brew us some tea.

When the phone rings, I let the machine take it, and I'm not
entirely surprised when I hear Isabella's voice. I stride into the living
room and pick up.

"Amore!" She's pleased to be interrupted in mid-message.

"Ciao," I say. "How is it going?"

"Did I wake you?"

"No, I'm up."

"You sound strange."

Not surprising, but actually, I probably sound . . . not bad. Surreal as
it was, last night signified the first good time I've had since Isabella left.
Last night for a few hours in the midst of madness, the hollow got filled.
"What's strange?" I counter. "I'm fine."

"Is this a bad time?"

"Not at all." I steal a look outside. "Have you been to the bank?"

"Tomorrow, *grazie,* and I send you pictures of this ashram, Jordan,
it's so beautiful . . ."

Naomi is on her feet now, stretching. Watching her, I'm only half-
listening as Isabella describes the wonders of her upcoming intensive yoga

class under the swami. ". . . and listen that, I can already do a tree pose with the head totally back, relaxed," she is saying. "But I think with the swami I will really learn and understand some things . . ." Naomi, back arched, palms pressed together over her head, stretches up, up . . . I can't see her feet from here, but either her legs are growing, or she's actually leaving the ground.

"Jordan, are you there?"

I force myself to turn from the window. "Yes, I'm listening."

"You're up early."

"Uh-huh."

"But it's the weekend."

"Yeah." I feel her feelers probing. "So tell me more about what's going on with you," I say, trying for an earnest tone. "I want to know."

"Yes, I will," she says. "It's why I call you. But maybe . . ." She pauses, our silence underscored by global micro-conductor chatter, and it's as if the two of us are gazing at the same hiding place, my will to misdirect her only causing her to comprehend. There's an intake of breath from Isabella. "She's there, isn't she?"

My hesitation is confirmation, but I can't think of how to answer.

"That woman! I knew it."

"Isabella," I begin, not sure of what I'm about to say as I catch a movement in the window: the gleam of Naomi's ankle bracelet sparkling by. She's doing cartwheels.

"I thought we talked about this!" Isabella's voice is up an octave. "I thought we were taking time, this time to think, to try to understand, but instead— *Madonna, che parle!* I never should have called!"

"Isabella, *calma*," I exhort her. "You don't have to, to—"

"To what? To be upset? I shouldn't be upset, I find you fooling around with this . . . student? *Che pazzo!* No, it's fine, there's no reason to be excited," she fumes. "It's what I deserve, no? That's what you think."

"No!" I'm at the window. Naomi's disappeared. "Come on, I'd never say—"

"But it is my fault," she interrupts, abruptly adopting an ominously lower tone. "Of course, and who could blame a man . . ."

"But we discussed this, before you left. In those days when you and I weren't really being lovers. Didn't you say"—the words feel slippery in my mouth, but I bite down on them, self-righteous—"that I should do whatever I needed to do, that I should 'take care of myself,' if that was what—"

"We said many things. But I remember our last phone call, when we said this was a time to be serious! That we really look at each other and ourselves—"

"I am looking!" I insist. Naomi's upside-down face watches me from the top of the window. Good Lord, she's on the roof? As I gape at her, she retreats. I listen for footsteps overhead but hear nothing. Maybe she's hanging from a tree branch, and wouldn't that be a treat for the neighborhood, Naomi in the tipu tree—then I remember no one else can see her, and plunge back into the conversation. "You think I'm not thinking? I'm thinking about us all the time."

"Well, that must make things difficult," she snaps, "when you have some young girl in your bed." I'm silenced. To my surprise, she gives a little laugh. "I'm sorry," she says, "but this is too much. While I'm doing nothing, I'm a monk here, Jordan, I go to be living with monks. Not that I haven't had my opportunities, believe me!"

"Isabella," I say. "You left."

"Yes," she says quietly. "And evidently I did the right thing."

"If that's what you think, after all this time—when you're going away to get in touch with your 'higher self'—" I sigh, exasperated.

"Then what?" she demands.

"Then maybe you're right."

"Maybe so." In the pause that follows, I can see her pulling herself up, sense that Roman pride of hers settling into place, like a mantle of dignity round her shoulders. "You know, the first day I come back to Rome, I'm so relieved—to talk in my own language, to eat my family's food, to stay out late at night and answer to no one. It felt so good, not to think, not to worry—I convince myself I don't miss you, that I'm glad to be far away . . . And then I *do* miss you, I *do* begin to understand that what we have is so important—and here I am, working hard, trying to come into a good and positive place, not just for me, but for the two of us . . . It's ironic, don't you think?"

Through the back screen door, I can see Naomi again. She's pulled the robe's cowl over her head, and kneels on the back steps with her hands clasped in front of her as if in penitent prayer.

I turn away, walk out of the kitchen. What am I supposed to say? I'm tempted to deny any wrongdoing, but isn't this the very moment I've sought to achieve in the first place? Still, I know that in a sense I really have betrayed my wife. Though I haven't actually committed adultery with an apparition, my wild night with Naomi signifies a marital transgression. So there's no Method acting, no Alexi routine going on, the sweat on my palms and the shortness of my breath is truth, my anxiety running deep. "Isabella," I say. "When you left, all I wanted was for you to come back. For us to be together again. I practically begged you not to go."

"Yes, I remember. How fast those feelings disappear, eh?"

"No. I'm not saying I don't want to work things out between us. But you of all people should be able to understand having more than one feeling at a time."

"Feelings, maybe. More than one woman? I can't respect that."

"Well, I can't help having my own reactions to the choices you've made. Have you told me you're coming back? No, you've decided to go even farther away."

"I had good reason," she says. "I've been healing my heart and my soul. And I was hoping you would be doing the same. You maybe believe I'm thinking only of myself, but it's not true. I've prayed for you here, Jordan."

I pace across the room. "Everyone has reasons," I tell Isabella. "And maybe each of us needs to heal in our own way."

"*Sì*. And maybe a trip to Todi is not my answer. Maybe I should spend this money on some tango shoes, or a party dress. Well, we have many things to talk about, obviously. But this is not the time. You have company."

"Isabella . . ." The bitterness in her voice makes me all the more contrite. I long to fast-forward us through all this to a rosier future, or to be catapulted back into the past.

"You can call me—when you find a moment."

Her barb punctures my bubble of regret. "Come on," I begin.

"*Ciao*," she says, soft and sad. But the abrupt disconnection feels like a slap.

I stand staring at the dead phone in my hand, unable to move my eyes from its imperturbable black contours. The move has been made, the choice taken. I've fired this gun across the Atlantic. And you can't put a bullet back in its barrel—though there's a chance it may ricochet. I could call her back, but say what? Try to explain that "it's not what you think"? Even to an Italian this will sound like the most crippled of clichés. And then what? Apologize? What am I apologizing for? She was the one who set this whole mess of a mechanism in motion! She's the one who was so dissatisfied about so many things. And amazingly, even though she's the one who stomped over my heart on her way out the door, she's once again claiming that I've disappointed her.

I turn around and freeze, arrested by the sight of Naomi, who's somehow materialized within the living room, once more seated in lotus position on the wooden floor before the sunlit white wall, her cowl fallen from her disheveled hair. I think I'll find mockery in her upturned face. But her eyes are tranquil and trusting.

I'm not just Isabella's Jordan. I'm the man who merely hours ago was out of his mind and inside the moment. And here is another moment to savor, an antidote to all the angst and anger. The bright sunlight washes Naomi's skin to a glowing cream, white as the wall behind her, pearly as the teeth in her widening smile as she holds my gaze.

4

Hook

*A situation occurring at the story's midpoint
that irrevocably binds the male lead with the
female (the we're-in-this-together moment),
often while tweaking sexual tensions; it creates
deeper implications for the outcome of their
relationship.*

*W*ith the sun behind her, Isabella is a dark silhouette, so it's hard to see if she's really pointing it at me, that thing in her hand, but I'm nervously stepping out of her line of fire, shielding my eyes against the bright light, when it goes off, making a metallic noise—not a gun, but her cell phone, I realize . . . and my own phone's ring wakes me in an empty bed, morning sunlight whiting out my sight. "Hullo?"

"I have Stan Robertson for Jordan Moore."

"I'm here." Naked and asleep toward noon on a Monday. I stumble upright, my throat-clearing counterpoint to the smooth jazz Muzak. My agent is calling *me*?

"Jordan, my man." Stan's heartiness sounds forced. "How's every little thing?"

"Things are good," I say cautiously. "And yourself?"

"Excellent. Listen, Jordan, how's the Hawke movie coming along?"

"Great!" I have no ending. Maybe it's the residual Naomi fumes in the room, but I also have an odd conviction that I can power through what needs to be done.

"Well, good, that's good, I only ask because—you know we handle Nate Colt?" I know it well, but since when has Nathan become Nate? "Well, Phil had a brunch with Nate, and he was under the impression that the project might be up for grabs. Some talk of a feeler from Hawke's people—it's just smoke, but . . . Everything on track with you and the Rumer-man? He's happy with what you're doing?"

The situation demands that I use my Zelig-like tendency to come right back at Stan with his own brand of bogus bull. I take the philosophical approach. "Who knows what makes Rumer Hawke happy? All I know is I've got his notes and that his development exec's excited about the project."

"Good, good, but you might want to step on it. What's your delivery date?"

I make a show of getting to my calendar, but I know exactly, it's been circled in anxious red, and—hmmm!—it's now five days away. "I'll hit it, Stan, and actually—"

"Fabulous," Stan interrupts. "Look, Jordo, I've got to take another call, but if you can shave a few days off, all the better, you know? Go get 'em, son." With a chuckle that sounds more like choking, he's gone.

Huh. I fall back into my desk chair, exhausted by this bout of acting like Mr. Normal. Wouldn't that be just like *Nate,* to come on so fellow-writer friendly Saturday night, while lobbying to steal my project out from under me? I consider that pile of paper, gleaming in its desk corner. As difficult as revising the end of Jake and Margo's relationship may look, it's got to be easier than trying to rewrite my own. With a sigh, I reach across the desk to pick up my besieged draft, and it's then that my back seizes.

The spasm rocks my body. I'm stuck in a crippled pose half out of the chair, and it takes me a moment before I'm able, with a pained gasp, to sit upright on my butt again.

Not one of the truly horrific baddies, a put-you-on-the-floor-praying-to-unknown-gods attack. I can walk normally, albeit slowly; the disturbance has already abated. Experience tells me this is but a warning—the small tremor that could precede a Big One. The trick is to get help right after one of these minor spine quakes, and thankfully, I've caught a break: Martha is able to squeeze me in.

Considerable research long ago convinced me that Martha has the best hands in Venice. One of the great advantages of having found her, shortly after I first moved into the neighborhood, is that her place is within walking distance. She shares a small suite of offices with a Filipino acupuncturist in a building tucked into the odd no-man's-land south of Venice Boulevard, and when my back really goes out on me, rendering the mere act of driving impossible, I can walk down there, doing my best not to move so quickly that I'll spasm into Walter Brennan–like cripple mode.

Martha is happy to see me, as always. A Norwegian, big-boned, silver-haired woman who resembles a Viking vessel's figurehead, she has a lined face but her palms are remarkably soft. She alone has the power to soothe the smarting muscles at the base of my spine. It cheers me to be ushered into her womb-like workroom. I slide under the lemon-scented white sheets on her table with a sense of being safe in the house of healing.

I inquire after her project. Martha is embarked on a history of her family on her mother's side. Knowing that I teach, she always probes me for pointers on memoir craft while her hands seek the knotted hiding places of my body's pain. Today she asks about Isabella. She's saddened to hear about the separation. And when she asks how I'm coping with my loneliness, the slow, rhythmic kneading of her supple fingers on my back teases the whole story out of me, including the latest headline.

"But I don't understand," Martha says, her thumbs working concentric circles on the sides of my hips, a movement that melts me, that makes me want to coo with blessed relief. "You say you talk to this woman? This . . . Naomi?"

I'm too far within the pleasure zone of Martha-dom to edit, and there's a welcome feeling of release, too, to be able to tell someone the entire truth. "Yes," I say, the one syllable drawn out in sibilance from the lulling motion of her hands. "At first I imagined things, you know, that she might say, but now . . ." I shake my head in the basket of the table. "She just talks. She has a mind of her own, and she . . . surprises me."

"I see," Martha murmurs, and is silent. My eyes are closed. I know I won't sleep, but a delicious almost-slumber always sets in around the half-hour mark, and my inner clock recognizes its inviting approach. "And what do you two do together?"

"I meet her when I go out . . . or she comes over . . ."

Martha's hands grip my shoulders. Her voice is surprisingly loud by my ear, and my eyes blink open. "She's in your house?" she asks with an urgency as unsettling as the suddenly increased pressure above my shoulder blades. "She lives there?"

"Well, no," I say. "She sort of shows up and . . . then she goes away."

"What have you done . . ." Martha mutters. My head gives an involuntary jerk as her fingers, suddenly talon-like, dig into the flesh of my upper back.

"Um, Martha?"

She yanks me over on my side. I peer up to see that Martha's cheeks are reddened, her eyes a little wild. One of my arms lies twisted beneath me, and some serious pain shoots up my side. Martha pulls at the arm. In the next instant I'm flat on my back, Martha's massive hands pinning me to the table as she towers over me, breathing heavy.

"Jordan," she says. "You are playing with fire."

It's hard to catch my breath with the pressure of her palms flat on my chest. I gape up at her, shoulders throbbing, aware of the incongruous tinkling of temple chimes coming from the speakers above her head, and a cool draft of air raising goose bumps on my exposed haunches, the sheet having slipped below my waist. "Okay," I manage.

With one hand firm at the center of my chest, holding me in place, she runs the other through her disheveled hair, and speaks with a scary intensity. "You're like a child," she says. "You don't realize the consequences, the things that can happen when you toy with forces that a man shouldn't trifle with."

"Really."

"You've called a spirit into being. Do you believe you can control what may result? Don't be silly." Martha grips my jaw with her hands. I flinch as she holds my face rigid before hers, her expression calmer now, but with an ominous blaze still emanating from her eyes. "I've seen such things, in my country, I've seen what can happen when *un spoke* is summoned."

"*Spuh*-ka?" I echo.

"Yes, a changeling, a woman from the other side, we say. Now, you, you're a sweet man, a good man, but a little gullible, you know?" Martha lets go of my face and the back of my head thuds to the pillow. "Like a poet with his head in the clouds. *Un spoke* is like a bird of prey up there that can pick at your mind and carry it off." She taps a finger on my sternum. "Listen to me," she says. "You must send her away. You must rid your home of her. Do you understand?"

"Yeah," I say weakly, gladly taking on the role of penitent transgressor to get out from under her as quickly as possible.

"You thank her for the time she has spent with you, and you tell her, in simple language, that it's time for her to go. All right?"

I would agree to many things just now. I nod my head empathically, though I have little intention of following the advice of a woman who is clearly crackers.

"Good," says Martha. "Then no harm will come to you." She smiles, abruptly benign. "Now, over on your stomach."

I'm too rattled to disobey as she dispassionately draws the sheet up and tucks it in around my waist again. Her palms stroke patterns in my shoulder blades, her breathing settles, her touch as sure and gentle as it's always been, and as she works on me in silence, before long my lower back, at least, is quieted and contained.

Since I'm not really Martha's Jordan, a sweet cloud-headed poet, I also don't believe that Naomi is a malevolent spirit who needs be gotten rid of. In fact, I miss her antic presence as I anxiously chip away at my pile of Rumer notes. I'm trying to beat new sense into Jake and Margo with no

success, and meanwhile the telephone's silence is deafening. I'm not calling Isabella and she's not calling me. I keep telling myself this is all for the
best: I'm stoking the green flames beneath her feet.

By evening the temptation to leave the room is enormous. I want to
fly to Italy now. But one stays in the room—that's the job. I remind
myself that solving this script problem will be the ticket to making
Isabella fly home, and I trudge across the carpet to my desk to pick up the
draft's final scene. But the words are blurring in front of my tired eyes. I
need coffee. You're allowed to leave the room for coffee.

Out in the clear night air, still clutching the pages—I'll read them
over in the café round the corner, once I'm cranked up on espressos—I
have to remember to move at a reasonable speed, a twinge of warning
ache from my still-healing back slowing me outside my gate. I dig into
the base of my spine with my thumb, and as I stand there massaging, I
hear accordion music. It sounds live. Looking up the block to my right, I
locate the source, a white-haired guy seated on the edge of the deserted
patio of the Brickhouse restaurant, instrument in lap and an upturned hat
by his feet. A woman holding up one end of a diaphanous dress waltzes in
a lazy circle beneath the street lamp.

I was planning to go left, but now I'm pulled their way by the lilt of
the song, a sort of Django Reinhardt gypsy jazz, and the smile that illu-
minates a now-familiar face as the woman dances from sidewalk into
street, coming to greet me as if this date was prearranged. I should have
known she wouldn't stray far.

I suppose I should be apprehensive, as I walk to meet my madness.
But Naomi looks anything but malevolent as she slides her arm in mine
and I inhale a scent of sea air in her lustrous hair, some indefinable
warmth and sweetness, like fresh-baked bread, radiating from her skin.
Again it's clear to me that Martha has read Naomi wrong, and I'm nothing but pleased by her return. We pause, looking back at the lone accordion player. Then she nudges me in the direction of the corner opposite
and the long-way-round path to the café. We walk.

"What've you got there?" she asks.

I look down at the pages in my hand. "It's . . . my project. This script I'm working on, trying to fix the ending."

"And what is it about?"

"Well, it's a romantic comedy, about a man and a woman who are made for each other," I begin, the faint sound of the receding accordion music seeming to mock-underscore my words. "How much detail do you want?"

Naomi shrugs. "I'm sure you could do it in one sentence."

Of course I can. "All right," I tell her. "Two very well-matched rival advertising executives, chasing after an eccentric pop star to win his product endorsement, get into an escalating battle over the guy that nearly kills them both," I recite. "And the twist in the end is that they *don't* end up together, precisely because they're so alike."

"And this . . . ?" She indicates the pages.

"The ending I'm supposed to change, not that I want to." She opens her hand. "Really?" Naomi nods. Well, why not? I hand the sheaf of paper over to her. Naomi evens the creases, slowing her stride.

"It may not make a lot of sense on its own," I tell her, nervously qualifying, "but you'll get the gist of how it goes." We're standing beneath a broken streetlight, and as I wonder if she'll be able to read anything properly out here, she glances up and it flickers to life. Now we're standing in a pool of bright light. She reads and I follow her eyes, anticipating her arrival at the tricky dialogue exchange I'd finally gotten to land just so, making me—until Rumer's notes called the whole scene into question—inordinately pleased. Naomi turns the page, her expression opaque. Watching her, I realize I'm eager for her approval (any writer wants a good review, even if it's from a phantasm born of his own mind). My stomach clenches when I see her brow furrow.

"I don't understand." Naomi holds the last page before her as though the language has turned foreign under her narrowed gaze.

"Well, like I said, it's out of context. It's the last scene, after all—"

"It can't be," she says, thrusting it at me. "This can't be what you're doing."

Is it that bad? I take the pages back from her, more startled than affronted. "Well, it's only a draft," I begin.

"No, no," she says. "Where is your work?"

I'm stung to hear that it seems facile to her, after all the time I've put into it already. As I look at her in confusion, I grasp at a conciliatory straw. "It could be that you're not really . . . getting it, because you need to know the whole story."

Naomi looks incredulous. "You think I don't know what I've read?"

"No, but . . . Well, maybe you're just not familiar with the screenplay form?"

Naomi's gaze becomes Sphinx-like, atavistic, the kind of look that in ancient days turned men into stone. I'm x-rayed, flayed by the intensity of her eyes exploring mine. For a hallucinatory instant I can swear she's grown taller, my own form shriveled. Behind the outline of her dress lies the shimmering flatness of endless desert. Shaken, I steel myself for decimation by lightning bolt or rain of fire. But in the next moment, we're merely standing on the sidewalk again. She's reached out to cup my chin in her palm, a speedy succession of emotions—pity, vexation, compassion—flying across her face, and I dimly comprehend the vast breadth of what, according to Naomi, I do not understand.

"It *has* gotten started," she mutters, giving my chin a shake, then dropping her hand. "You just haven't grasped it yet."

"Grasped what?"

Naomi gives a groan of frustration. "I come when called," she says. "But what call are *you* answering to? Where are you, in all this compromise and camouflage?"

"I'm here!" I'm honestly bewildered. "I'm writing. I do have to make a living."

I didn't mean that to sound accusatory, but there's an ominous flash of fire in Naomi's eyes. "As opposed to what?"

"I just mean—I'm only doing my job, here."

"Your job?" she snaps. "I'm talking about your *work*."

"My work?"

"Yes! And it has little to do with . . . *this*!" She swats at the pages in my hand and they go flying.

"Hey—" I stoop to grab the papers before they blow away as the streetlight flickers out again. I have to dash into the street to catch one, and when I step back onto the sidewalk, clutching my maligned handiwork, Naomi's gone. Disappeared.

Stunned, I turn in the sudden darkness. "Wait a second!" I sputter. "You can't just . . ." But of course she can.

"Jordan?"

I reel around. Someone's calling me from the backseat of an old green Jaguar parked across the street, staring at me through the open window. I recognize the voice, and realize why the car looks oddly familiar. It's Leo.

At the moment, I'm too flabbergasted by Naomi's angry vanishing act to question his surprise appearance. I hurry across the street.

"I thought it was you," he says, his bald dome a half-moon gleam in the dark interior as he peers out at me.

I lean against the door. "What are you doing here?"

"We had dinner at Lilly's," Leo tells me, indicating the French place down the street. "Estelle's inside, wrapping things up with the Adlers."

I nod, unable to resist a quick glance back to the streetlight, thinking Naomi might have rematerialized. No luck.

"Our first night out in a while. I had to rest my eyes for a bit," Leo's saying. "Periodic naps are the norm when you're a one-lung man," he adds, smiling, as if he's indulging secret membership in some impressively illicit club. His face is gaunt and pale in the dim light, brow more deeply creased since I last saw him. He's shaved his beard, a new thin mottled layer of white hair bristling over cheeks and chin. He looks like a man who's been through battle.

"So you were asleep," I say hopefully.

"Not just now," says Leo. He's appraising me with the kind of

delighted anticipation he usually reserves for the inspection of a rare first
edition. "You seem upset."

"No, I'm just . . ." I shake my head. "I just can't believe . . ."

"Can't believe what?"

I exhale a shaky breath, incredulity shifting into outrage. "They're
lunatics. Whether they come from Europe or the great beyond, they're all
the same."

"Who?"

"Women! Females. 'The fairer sex'—that's a laugh, they ought to be
called the unfair sex."

"Bad news from Rome?"

"No, it's not her. It's . . ."

"You're seeing someone else?"

"No. I mean yes, but she's not 'someone,' she's . . ." I pause, exasperated, my gaze drawn across the street again.

"The one you were just talking to?"

I look at Leo, startled. "You saw her?"

"What I saw was you standing there talking to no one, and getting
fairly worked up about it. Then you threw those pages in the air"—he
taps his forefinger at the papers in my hand—"and then you scurried in a
circle picking them up, before looking wildly around you like a boy
whose toy had just been snatched. At which point I was compelled to
interrupt, before you ran into traffic or perhaps launched into an aria
from *I Pagliacci.*"

"Is that the one with the clown?"

"Precisely."

I look at Leo, who is probably the only person I know who may
understand this, and all my frustration spills out of me at once. "It's
that . . . spirit! The one I e-mailed you about. Only she wasn't a spirit
when I first thought her up, she was just a fantasy—someone I invented
to make Isabella jealous—but then she started showing up on her own.
And she's *real,* even though nobody else can see her, and now she's suddenly turned into a critic! Like she wants me to be doing something,

something else, as if I could know what that is when I don't even know what the hell *she* is!"

Amused interest gleams bright in Leo's owlish eyes. He nods in the direction of Lilly's. "They're being leisurely in there. Let's take a walk."

Climbing out, Leo employed the economical, carefully calibrated movements of a man who no longer trusts his body, and as we walk slowly, he stoops forward as if into a stiff wind. By the time we reach the corner, I've sketched it out for him as coherently as I'm able to right now, with that fire-and-brimstone look on Naomi's face still blazing in my mind and with me seeing red, myself. "I just can't believe that the imaginary girlfriend my wife is fighting with me over just went upside my head."

Leo chuckles. "At least she's helped you accomplish your mission. Wasn't that the idea—getting Isabella's goat?"

"Yes, but going out with some . . . troublemaking emanation from the spirit world wasn't part of the plan. I mean, how did that happen?"

"Hmm." Leo nods, folding his arms to hug his frail form as we walk on. "Well, evidently you expended a great deal of psychic energy in thinking up this companion for yourself, and you didn't know the extent of your own power. You were seeking something that was beyond this plane, and something responded."

"Looking like Naomi Dussart?"

"Mortals aren't capable of looking at gods, you know. It's said that angels disguise themselves in their visitations, so as not to blind people or strike them dumb. Sounds to me like your spirit chose to be rather accommodating. You wanted a Naomi, and she became one."

"To do what, though?"

"I suppose you'd have to ask your subconscious." Leo shrugs. "All men should be so lucky."

"Depends on who you ask," I tell him. "My masseuse just beat me up for inviting a *spuh*-ka into my house, and swears I've got to get rid of her."

"Really!" Leo's paused at the end of the block, where bushels of long reeds line the entranceway to an architectural firm's building on the corner. He takes one last long look down the sidewalk behind us, mutters, "This'll do," and starts up the short path to the front door.

I follow, puzzled. "Leo, they're not open."

He nods, turning around in the shadowy alcove. "Hold this a moment, will you?"

What he's thrusting into my hand is his pipe. I look askance from it to Leo, who's reached into his jacket pocket to produce a lighter. "What are you doing?"

"Medicinal," he tells me. I take a closer look at what's been tamped down in the pipe's bowl, and see a fat little bud of what's undoubtedly high-grade cannabis. "Estelle's been making me tea with the stuff," he continues, "but every now and then I've just got to have an actual puff. Oh, don't look at me like that." He motions for me to hand the pipe over. "It's bad enough that I haven't been able to smoke any tobacco in over a year now. Two inhales of this won't do me any harm."

"Got a cell phone on you?" I ask. "In case we have to call an ambulance?"

Leo's hands tremble as he holds the lighter's flame over the pipe bowl, face alight with anticipation. "Won't need one. Estelle would kill me before it got here."

With loving tenderness, he seems to kiss the end of the pipe stem and ever so slowly draws in a long, exquisitely modulated breath. I realize I'm holding my own breath as I watch, ready for him to burst into a chest-busting cough. Thankfully, he takes the stem from his mouth, eyes closed in an expression of concentrated rapture, and then, lips pursed, slowly exhales a steady stream of smoke. Only when he's done, and clears his throat instead of collapsing in paroxysms, do I breathe easily. "Here," he rasps, eyes hooded, and pushes the pipe at me.

I take a cursory puff to keep him company, Leo looking on with greedy, vicarious appreciation. "Perhaps she's Thalia," he murmurs. "A muse like Terpsichore, Calliope, Erato . . . Who knows who you've been spending time with? Could be a ghost. The ancient Japanese believed a living person was capable of sending an apparition out into the world."

I exhale, eyes watering. "Interesting. Good for them. But I've never believed in any of this stuff."

"Oh, me neither," says Leo, "though lately . . . Listen, if it'd make you feel better, I'll just say that you've simply lost your mind and gone completely delusional."

I stare at him. "You're really helping."

"My pleasure. Here, don't bogart it," he admonishes me, reaching for the pipe. "Two hits," he adds, forestalling any protest. "Two."

Once more the lighter flares, and again I watch uneasily as he takes a shorter puff and holds it for less time. This time he does cough, with a loud racking noise that bends him over, hawking and spitting into a nearby bush while I look on in alarm, a hand at his shoulder. "Are you all right?"

"Better than ever," he wheezes, fumbling a handkerchief at his lips.

"Jesus, Leo . . ."

"Oh, hush. I'm fine," he assures me. Straightening, he slips pipe and lighter back into his pocket, then peers around us, eyes glittering. "In fact, I'm fantastic. This is *such* good shit."

I nod. Even my one puff has brought on a healthy buzz. I'm aware for the first time that we're surrounded by brilliant red bougainvillea, as Leo, with the furtive satisfaction of a hooky-playing kid, leads us back to the sidewalk "And you say she's different every time," he muses.

"She's always her. But she sort of . . . evolves, from one visit to the next."

"Like a work in progress," says Leo. "Maybe that's what you've got on your hands, Jordan. First the spark of inspiration, then an inspired draft . . ."

"She's a piece of work, all right." Maybe his weed's mellowed me, but my outrage has abated. It's Naomi's smile I remember now, the impish grin she gave me in greeting before things got all darkly biblical. "I just hope she hasn't disappeared for good."

Leo makes a spluttering noise and I slow beside him, worried. But he's not coughing, he's laughing.

"What? What's so funny?"

He shakes his head, clearing his throat. "This is all just so Jordan of you."

"How so?"

"You're in another romantic comedy," he says. "Only this time, with some unidentified force from the beyond."

"Again: This is truly helpful stuff."

"Well, you can protest all you want . . ." I recognize the distinctive grin on his face as the announcement of a forthcoming bon mot that he's particularly pleased by. "But you're certainly not looking a gift force in the mouth."

"And what's that supposed to mean?"

"Come on—it's as clear as that glazed doughnut look on your face that you're a little infatuated."

"What? No, wait a second—"

Leo stops me with a hand on my arm. Just down the sidewalk ahead of us, Estelle stands by the Jaguar, looking anxiously in our direction. Leo gives her a jaunty wave, tightens his grip on me.

"All right," he says, "now don't start talking to invisible people again."

I look at him, thinking that if I can see the hint of red-eyed goofiness in his otherwise professorial expression, certainly Estelle will pick up on it. "No," I agree. "We wouldn't want her to think anyone here was, I dunno, *high.*"

Leo gives my elbow a shove and we walk onward. "We'll talk more about your adventures in the spirit realm," he murmurs, "when you come to visit."

"So looking forward to it," I say dryly, and we don our best game faces to greet his worried-looking wife.

~ ~ ~

Maybe it did need a little work. After exhaustedly revising my Naomi-maligned pages, I have to concede that the scene as I first showed it to her did read glib. Still—what was all that about? Though Naomi may not be a *spoke,* she spooked me. Leo likened her to a muse, but what kind of a muse disses your draft and throws it into the street?

And what kind of imaginary lover is no lover at all? Thinking back on all the times Naomi has appeared, I realize that our first kiss was the only kiss we've shared—and that one was only bestowed on me to prove a point. No, by now it's clear that she's playing a different role, its meaning known only to her. Is she Circe? La Belle Dame sans Merci? Holly Golightly? And who is that supposed to make me?

Unsettled to think that Naomi, whatever she may be, has some mysterious agenda of her own, I'm relieved to be left alone again. Though not entirely: Standing at my open window, smelling rain in the air, I'm aware that it's been a while since Isabella called.

Yesterday morning. Not a long silence by normal standards, but in marital time, with our future hanging in the balance, it seems quite a stretch. I've held tough, proving that two can play. If she's punishing me, okay, but by now I'm ready to resume the conversation, feeling strong enough to take it on. Has she gone off to that monastery? Even so, knowing her, she'll have her phone on. Midnight here is morning in Rome.

Isabella in the morning is a woman who usually wakes up happy to be alive, bright and ready for the day. We'd have morning cuddling, laughs, and sometimes, sleepy-sloppy sex. In the months preceding our marriage, Isabella back and forth between here and Italy, we had international phone sex, me going to bed sated and Isabella greeting her day with a wider smile.

But there's always been another, darker Isabella hidden inside the sunny one. I know that. The night I met her at that party, she gave me the address of the studio she'd rented for her brief stay in L.A. and invited me to see her work. When I showed up at the appointed time and knocked on the door, there was no response. Perplexed, I was ready to give up on this visit, when two doors down, Isabella happened to step out of her studio, a wastebasket in hand. She'd given me the wrong address. In the unguarded moment before her eyes found mine, I saw a sadness in her face that I didn't recognize from our first meeting. I sensed the troubled nature that came with her beauty, understood the force of it intuitively. In the next instant, as her expression brightened upon catching sight of me, I chose to forget what I'd seen because she was smiling at me, once more the cheerfully mischievous woman I'd enjoyed flirting with over a strawberry.

It's there, though. I've seen that sadness surface many times since— I've even come to love that darkness in her, so much a part of who she is. Wondering now which Isabella I'll find at the other end, I pick up the phone and call Rome. After three metallic rings, she answers. Her *"Pronto?"* indicates that she's already awake.

"It's me."

"Jordan! How are you?"

"I'm okay." I'm trying to decipher her tone, to decode her attitude.

"The work is going well?"

Not really. But I'm not about to admit that. "Yeah, I'm in the thick of it."

"That's good! You need to be at your best with this, I know. And me, I'm so busy, I decide to postpone the trip to Todi."

"Really?" I'm relieved but wary. Postpone till when?

"*Sì*, it's crazy here." And she goes on, an anecdote about having to help redecorate her family's apartment, all very bright, energetic. I stay in this mode with her, safely superficial, though meanwhile the huge mound of everything we aren't discussing sits on the oceanic table between us, smarting and simmering, radiating dark impatience, until I can't stand this for another moment and yank away its bulky wrapping.

"But you sound good," I say. "I'm surprised. The last time we spoke . . ."

"Yes, of course, Jordan, I'm feeling many things, but this morning there's good energy, and maybe I don't want to be always thinking about problems, problems . . ." Maxi is barking. Isabella shushes him. Picturing the dog, tongue hanging out of his black-gummed mouth, going blind but as feisty and cantankerous as an old boxer, I feel a surge of plaintive longing.

"Right," I allow. "I understand."

"And sometimes the thinking and the talking is not the point. Sometimes you just do something, you take an action, if you want to make a change."

"Hey, I'd be happy to jump on a plane. You're the one who said I shouldn't—"

"Who is asking you to do that?"

"You're talking about taking action—"

"Yes, but I'm speaking for myself. I'm taking care of myself, Jordan."

I'd been feeling, for the first time since she left, that I'd regained equilibrium and shed some neediness. But there's a red warning light flashing on the console of my consciousness, a sign some part of me is already assimilating while the rest of me struggles to catch up. An unfamiliar quality in her tone. "Meaning what?" I ask. "Isabella, what is going on with you?"

"Nothing is 'going on,'" she says, and pauses. There is a dark, dangerous place within this silence, I can feel the pull of it. She sighs. "Listen, this is not how I want to have this conversation."

"How else can we have it?"

Maxi's barking again. "I don't know, when there is peace, quiet . . ."

"With you, there isn't much of that," I say.

She makes a sound, an attempt at a rueful laugh, and I'm hoping I've breached the great divide, have started to shrink the distance between us. "Talk to me," I say.

"*Uffa . . .*" she murmurs. I wait. "This is all so difficult. I know that I hurt you, and I left you alone there . . . But I've been alone, too. I've been dealing with so much . . ."

"I know," I say.

"But you don't know," says Isabella. "And . . . *Madonna,* this is terrible, I don't know how to say these things to you . . ."

"Just tell me."

"But what was I to do?" It comes out in a keening cry. "The way things are between you and me—you're not the only one who's hurting, who has needs!"

"Isabella—"

"It's nothing I planned to happen! Jordan, I swear it to you, but . . ."

"What?" I demand.

"There is a man, and . . . I was with him, last night."

" 'With him'?"

"We had a night together. It's not serious," she says. "He's just a boy. It was one night! But *amore*—What did you expect?"

It only seems appropriate, when at last I hang up the phone, that rain is now pounding on the roof, that a cold wind is blowing through the open windows, the land of sunshine suddenly cast as a wintry blackened pit. I take the vodka from the freezer and down two shots in succession, but this seems to have little effect.

My mind still refuses to take in the phone call, while my body is left to register the damage—a muscle cramping in my thigh, the tightness hovering at my temples—as my eyes, like some computer program run amok, keep raking over every object in view with an accusatory glare—unclean, all of it, the photo of the two of us atop the refrigerator, tainted, the canvas of Isabella's hanging by the bedroom door, spoiled. Anything I look at is no longer what it was. She was mine, now she isn't, and our happy home's turning to mud before my eyes.

A night together. This doesn't have to mean what I dread it to mean, does it? But it does, I know it. No, she didn't exactly say— But of course it's true, why else . . . ?

My brain's become a caged squirrel, my heartbeat crazily rapid, while the wind and rain dutifully bat at the windowpanes, like a bad movie parody of anyone's dark night of the soul. In desperation I turn on the television, sink into the chair in the dark. What's on the screen is black and white and subterranean. I'm looking at big webbed claws emerging from steaming mounds of coal in an underground passageway, followed by the beady eyes of a black-faced, misshapen monster. With a jolt of primeval anxiety, I identify this scene, which had terrified me in my youth. It's from *The Mole People,* a Universal cheapie starring John Agar, in which an ancient race of horrible mole men—here's two of them now, clawing their way out of their coal pit—is found living far beneath the surface of the Earth. And here comes an unsuspecting crew member of the ill-fated anthropological expedition, whistling in the dark, unaware that out of the ground beneath his feet, monsters are arising to grab him and pull him under. Of course, the identification is complete: There I am, idiot innocent Jordan, thinking I've been walking on mere concrete and blacktop when really, mole-like monsters of my own creation have only been biding their time before wrapping their webbed hands around my thighs and dragging me—

I scramble for the remote, jab at the buttons, and the screen goes out with a quiet pop. Perfect. I will sit here in the utter darkness trying not to think of what Isabella is doing right now, across the sea, trying to keep flashes of those mole-man eyes, amphibian and unseeing, from monopolizing my mind. There's a scratching sound coming from somewhere beneath me, a soft shuffling. I sit very still. I know this sound. It can only be the possum, that horrific long-snouted beast that sometimes crawls and nests in the cellar. I have to be imagining it. I listen, frozen in the dark, hearing only the ringing in my ears, and then Isabella's voice on the phone, in that terrible tone she used—not a taunt, not in anger, more in pity—when she said, "But *amore,* what did you expect?"

Hugh Grant is taking me shopping to get the good clothes, better clothes I can afford now that he's going to play Jake in *Clinch.* "I can be younger!" he tells me happily, and even in the dream I know this is someone else's line from another movie, but it doesn't matter, he and his girlfriend—some beautiful actress, it seems, but she keeps avoiding me, it's as if I'm not allowed to see who she is—they're going to buy the rights to my new project for them to star in, only I haven't actually written it yet, this secret knowledge an undertow of unease I wade through as we enter the changing room.

"Right, here's the one for you," says Hugh, helping me into a suit that's made of mirrors, shiny, polished, exquisitely bright, but once inside it—the thing has a sort of hood, being more like a cloak—I can't see myself. "Brilliant," I hear Hugh say, "that's you all over," and I want to protest but my mouth's too thick to move properly, and now I can hear the girlfriend whispering and I realize, sickened, that it's Isabella—she's with Hugh Grant. I wasn't supposed to find out, but now that I know, I'm desperate to get out of this suit, and I'm furiously pulling at the hood—

I'm drooling, my face smushed into a leather crevice. I lurch to my feet and stumble to the bathroom, where the mirror exposes a face as deranged as I feel, mouth agape, hair flattened out in a halo from sleeping in a chair.

Now I'm wide-eyed and wired. Back in the living room, I peer at the pages I'd been reworking with such care. It's as if they were written by another man. This one here has no idea what to do with himself. And there are hours to go now until daylight.

"It's that simple," says Dana Morton.

But it isn't. Not even close. I realize I've been clutching the phone so tightly to my ear that I'm hurting myself. I switch ears, rubbing the sore edge as my mind turns right, then left, cornered like a bear in a cave. "I'm just not sure," I begin, "that if we go with your ending, we can keep the integrity of the original story intact."

Dana makes the barking sound that's her idea of a laugh. "The what of the original story? I'm sorry—that word—I don't know if I'm familiar . . ."

I feel my face reddening, know she's joking, but even so . . . "Dana," I say. "Is this really the movie we set out to make?"

"Maybe not. And is that a bad thing? Let me be necessarily blunt with you," Dana continues. "Who did you think you were writing this for? The forty-five people who actually read each issue of *Film Comment*? The people who only see movies at the Nuart? The Marxists at the *L.A. Weekly* and the *Village Voice*? Three or four of your writer friends, who by the way would run over their grandmothers to get a chance to be in business with Rumer Hawke?"

"No," I say. "But Rumer makes movies that have something *to* them. That's what got me excited about working with him. I mean, I want the movie to be entertaining, I know we have a mainstream audience in mind. But—"

"It'll have substance, and it'll be entertaining—it's going to be a freaking happy meal, Jordan. Wait'll you see the graph! Every beat is right where it should be now, except the ending . . ."

Dana and her graph. My head starts to pound. "But the original ending went *against* genre conventions, not—"

"You're afraid of a car chase!" she says. "Honey, I completely understand. You're worried that if we go too big in the climax, it becomes just another one of those Hollywood big-screen action-comedy things."

"Exactly." I'm relieved that I'm being heard.

"I totally get it. What could be worse? But Jordan—"

"I'm not even totally sold on the new Jake," I protest. "I mean . . . Chad Harley?"

"Unavailable," says Dana. "Now we're thinking some hot new unknown."

I sigh. Mid-afternoon, running on barely a few hours of sleep, it's all I can do to stay off the ropes. "Look, the whole idea of the original story was that even though Jake and Margo are so meant for each other, supposedly, that—"

"Meant for each other: You know, that's a better title. I mean, *Clinch* is good, but not everyone'll get it."

"Dana. The idea is that they're so much alike that they *can't* stay together in the end! That's the gag, that's the dark joke that makes this different from like a hundred other romantic comedies."

"I think we can have a sense of that," she says. "Right now I'm just lobbying for making a bigger set piece out of the car chase that gets Jake and Margo to that final beat."

"A car chase that was meant to be a *parody* of such set pieces."

"This is about trust," Dana says. "You have to trust Rumer's understanding of what works. Sometimes going too subtle is just the kind of choice that turns a hit into a tanker. It's ironic, really, because . . ." She chuckles. "You're being protective, and here I am looking out for you. I'm actually looking at your career, Jordan, I'm looking at the movie you get to write after this one."

I hear Nate Colt's words in my head, from that night in Zulu. *What's it about? It's about getting our next gig.* And suddenly I have the strange sensation that someone else is listening, like a third party on the line. I feel Naomi's attention tuning in from out there, somewhere. The ions of the air in the room are charged.

"I appreciate all you're telling me, Dana," I say cautiously. "But I don't see how making these changes in the third act—"

"Just see it," she says. "Sweetie, I'm seeing a movie that people will talk about, that they'll tell their friends to see, that will own not only the opening weekend but a month or more beyond that. A movie that will top the box office in Tokyo, Jordan. One of those clips you'll see in the montages they have on those AFI shows. A line of dialogue that people say to each other in bars and everyone laughs. I'm talking about your biggest problem, your most agonizing choice, being whether or not you decide to write the sequel yourself or farm it out to somebody else because you're about to direct, Jordan, your first feature, which you can call *The Story of Integrity* for all I care, and nobody will at that point because you will be able to do what-the-fuck-ever you want to do."

I manage a weak chuckle. "Right," I murmur.

"Damn right," says Dana. "What, you're too scared? You're saying you don't have the balls for this?"

I'm saying you're Satan, I want to tell her, but I'm struck mute. I'm seeing them, the people, those faces that scare me at airports, those regular, functioning, relatively well-adjusted humans I've never been able to understand, wearing the clothes I've never worn, speaking words from a vocabulary I've never spoken, unquestioningly living the responsible lives I've never dreamed of living, the people who own the world I live at the edge of. The dad, loading cardboard containers full of cheese-covered hot dogs and sodas at the concession stand, beside him a pimply-faced kid with a Game Boy in his hand and an older sister in a midriff-bearing halter top—they're the ones who really rule this land, while I, Periphery Man, stare down the narrow aisles of the Nuart Theatre with its sticky floor and bad lighting and empty row after empty row to see the one guy with the beard and glasses trying to read Derrida on the aisle seat, sipping at a latte. Do I really want to do the right thing for him?

That guy—and I struggle to put the best face on him, with his unkempt hair, the bad skin that rarely sees the light of day—he's as miserable as I was, before insidious good fortune smiled upon me. Isn't he the brother, though, the kindred soul, the one I want to give solace to? The one who recognizes what is of value, what is formulaic schlock, what might really make a difference in the realm of art and poetry and all that truly matters?

There is foam on his mustached lip, a permanent crease in his pockmarked brow. He'd probably loathe a romantic comedy, even a bleak, revisionist romantic dramedy. He wouldn't like the movie I originally wanted to write, he'd walk out on the damn thing. He's already frowning, impatient for the bad print of my indifferently received film to unspool, here at the end of its one-week-only run.

Meanwhile, in the fourth row of a packed theater in downtown Seoul on a Saturday night, a South Korean teenager, lips slathered with fake popcorn butter, gazes up at the screen, rapt in anticipation, nudging his best friend as the explosive finale to Dana's car chase, dubbed into Korean in digital, ear-busting Sensuround sound, comes on. They're seeing it for the third time.

I clear my throat. "Well . . ." I say.

"Good," says Dana. "Now, let's look at your transition on page eighty-nine."

When I'm finally off the phone, I can feel that my other listener is gone, too. If she was here, Naomi has left the building. And for a moment I'm bereft, as if some part of me is in the past now, some beloved old heirloom lost down a hole.

Evening ushers me into a new chamber of horror. The past Jordan, diabolical in his obliviousness to any future disaster, is to blame for the present me facing three hours of "Writing Romantic Comedy."

Though I usually enjoy teaching this course, the bright white horse I once rode in on, garlanded with roses, has been shot down under me in mid-gallop. I'm disillusioned and doleful tonight, but the show must go on. Students are pitching their projects. And for the first class, it's essential that I establish credibility and trust by being insightful on the spot. I gulp coffee to help simulate enthusiasm, and pace warily round the table of nervous aspiring screenwriters as they proceed to expose themselves.

Each pitch opens a window into a student's psyche, releasing a wish-fulfillment fantasy into the room. Some leave their authors some dignity, while others thrust their writers onto the tabletop in their underwear, baring birthmarks and cellulite. Tonight's first pitch pairs a greeting-card illustrator who's a pathological liar with a female boss who sounds more like a dominatrix than a romantic comedy heroine. It's delivered by Thomas, a beaten-down middle-aged guy with bifocals who looks like a greeting-card illustrator. I can see my own reaction mirrored in the faces of the other students as my request for feedback is met with silence. I lead with the necessary compliment (the story has a potentially funny milieu), then note that a male lead who always lies undercuts empathy. "We have to root for this guy to win the girl," I explain. "If we don't identify with him, we won't care if he gets her." As a few students nod sagely, I realize that by these standards, I am not an empathetic protagonist.

Keri with the cat's-eye glasses raises her hand. "Well, doesn't it seem like every other romantic comedy has characters using assumed identities?"

"It's been a genre plot staple since Shakespeare," I agree. "So why is entering into romance under false pretences the coin of the realm in seduction-land?"

Another hand goes up. "If men and women were totally honest with each other, about like, what they really thought, and who they really were—"

"Nobody would ever get laid," another student concludes.

"Well, they might have sex," I say, amidst laughter, "but they probably wouldn't be quite so quick to get married and have kids. Look, people do lie in romantic comedies, but ultimately they come clean. We're writing about 'happily ever after,' never-ending Big Love here."

Students jot down notes as I hear my words echo, like on a call to Rome, ringing hollow. My big love pledged herself, before God and her mother, to stick by her man through sickness and health, only to desert him because she couldn't find decent mozzarella in Los Angeles. And then slept with somebody else.

As soon as I did, supposedly. So what am I doing, encouraging these people to embrace romantic fantasy? My hypocritical stomach is turning. Looking round at their earnest faces, I remind myself that writers are professional liars. Fine, but that makes me doubly damned: I'm a duplicitous spouse, lying to a roomful of liars who are writing about lying lovers. My nose should be yards long by now. Instead, each falsity I utter makes me feel smaller. I'm shrinking. Soon I'll be a mouse-sized teacher. I see myself, jumping from one desk top to another across the now-huge crevasses, waving my tiny hands in the air, the student faces looming over me, wide-eyed, still rapt on each shrill little word. *He's awfully small,* they'll tell their colleagues later, *but brilliant.*

And who am I, really? A man who was lying to himself. I knew my limitations, my faults and weaknesses, but I willed myself into being the romantic ideal Isabella wanted to believe I might be. And Isabella had only seen what she wanted to see, in the throes of romance—romance, which blinded each of us to the realities of who we were . . .

Not that anyone's capable of truly seeing other people, whether they're in love or not. Look at everyone in this room! All the students have remodeled me according to their respective needs. They're seeing their own imagined versions of Jordan Moore. Michelle, for example, reacts to my mild suggestions about her pitch like a chastened child obeying an authoritarian father. Michael takes my comments in with a grinning brio that indicates he's sized me up as a potential drinking buddy who secretly hates women. Guy, the industry wannabe with eyebrows plucked, who's already asked about agents and whose pitch is predictably sharp and studio-attuned, sees me as . . . I don't want to think about it.

Whoever I am, I don't want to be here, impersonating a true believer, acting as a mobile screen for fifteen people's projections, but there isn't any escape. I force focus on the last student left. She's Rita, according to the folded card in front of her. I sense, from her tight halter top and air of nervous overstimulation, that she sees me as the next guy who'll sleep with her and dump her. She looks like trouble. And I'm already having an affair with a former student, in my way.

Her pitch is based on real life, Rita explains, telling a *When Harry Met Sally*–like anecdote about how her father had first set eyes on her mother when she walked into a bakery one afternoon, and he'd turned to his companion and said, "That's the woman I'm going to marry." There are a number of heartfelt "Aw!"s from around the table. And I, the man whose parents first caught sight of each other across a crowded room and have never stopped looking since, I'm the one who blurts, unable to keep the note of incredulity from my voice, "And they're still together?"

A few students look at me oddly, but my question passes for humor, and thankfully I can segue into the preprogrammed portion of our show, a genre history reel of clips. Hang in there. I move quickly to the monitor, powering it up, ask someone in the back to get the lights. Another student has a hand up. "In a lot of these movies, even after all the crazy stuff that happens, all the guy has to do is run after the girl in the last scene—"

"At the airport," someone interjects, to laughter.

"—and tell her how much he loves her, and all is forgiven. Are we really supposed to buy into that?"

Murmurs of agreement around the table. "Difference is, in a *good* romantic comedy," I say, "the guy's learned a lesson. And what we're seeing in the climax is proof that falling in love has had a real effect on him, that it's made him grow as a person."

My voice cracks on the word grow, as if to indicate that falling in love has only made me grow backward into a second adolescence. I nod at the student who's standing expectantly by the light switch, grab the remote for the VCR as the room is plunged into darkness, and press Play. "Okay," I say. "Let's take a look at the last seventy-five years of our genre."

I walk to the back of the room and take up a position against the wall by the classroom door. Here come those seven standard beats. Setup, from *The Philadelphia Story.* The pristine black-and-white gleam of Hepburn and Grant's profiles looks dim to me tonight. Cute Meet: But I find little joy in seeing Alvy Singer banter over white wine on the rooftop with Annie Hall, even as the scene's subtitles make the room fill with knowing laughter. I close my eyes, unable to watch this lockstepped dance of romance, and it occurs to me that I've gotten things wrong again in my own story. Isabella leaving wasn't our Dark Moment. *This* has to be it: her transatlantic wail of betrayal through the phone at my ear, my answering despair. But there's small satisfaction in such revisionist romantic history. I can only pray I'll find a way to get through the remaining two hours without that knot at the base of my neck blooming into a full-fledged head hammer.

Then I hear the quiet click and scrape of the door opening beside me, sense the accompanying current of air. In the next instant I feel the warm contours of another body slip behind mine. A familiar scent envelops me as two arms enfolded my chest.

She's come back. Naomi is here, and I can feel immediately in the strength of her embrace that she's forgiven me, she's set aside whatever trespass it was that made her rail at me and disappear. She's here to console me in my time of need, and I grasp her hands with a fervent squeeze of gratitude.

I open my eyes. All the students' faces are intent upon the screen, where a scene from Buster Keaton's *The Navigator* now flickers into motion. This is my cue to begin a narration. I clear my throat, gratefully luxuriating in the feel of Naomi fitting her curves to the line of my back. "As early as 1927," I say, "in this Keaton silent, we can see the basics of the form already in place."

Buster and his leading lady grapple on the rolling deck of a cruise ship, he trying to save her from falling overboard, she beating at him with her fists, thinking he's making a pass. Naomi's breath is warm on my shoulder. "He starts out a clueless wuss, but in trying to save the woman he loves, he's forced to become a functional man," I say. "This is the fundamental ethos of romantic comedy: love as a transformative force."

"And you?" Naomi whispers at my ear. "What have you been transformed into?"

Good question. I give a rueful chuckle. On the screen, the woman, now aware of the danger, clings to Keaton, clapping her hands over his eyes as the deck heaves and rolls, so that they nearly lurch right over the side together. There's laughter in the room.

Then Naomi's lips press into that sore spot at the base of my neck, and to the strains of silent-movie rinky-tink, the heat of her kiss dissolves the tension there and everywhere inside me. I push back, moving her toward the door, feel for the knob with my hand, and quietly, seeing the heads of my students all turned to the monitor, slip out into the hall.

Deserted at this hour, but well-lit—and now I see for the first time, as Naomi leans back against the wall, that she is wearing words. Her thin white dress is translucent, and two columns of small black print descend down the entire front of it. I blink, trying to decipher what looks like a page from a dictionary, shadowy lines of text rolling over her curves.

"Go on," she says. "Read me."

It's all I want now, to understand what strange missive she's brought me on her body. I'd like to take hold of the text with both hands and absorb the breadth of it through my skin, lose myself in this spiritual Braille, but the tiny letters look like Sanskrit, Cyrillic, Japanese, seeming to shift as I squint. I look up to her amused eyes.

"Old stories," she says. "You're a part of this"—Naomi sweeps one long-nailed hand down the undulating lines—"and you're more than all that," she adds, pointing back at the classroom.

"All what?"

"You're more than a formula, Jordan. And more than the sum of your regrets. Maybe you can't see it, in this moment. But you will."

I can see through the door's little window that my cue to stop the tape and go to live discussion has arrived. "Hold that thought," I implore her.

I step back through the door and pick up the remote, and as I turn round again to reach for the light switch, I see Naomi framed in the slim windowpane. She mouthes an *"Au revoir,"* and then she's gone.

Gone, but she's left me in a better place. I press Pause, turn on the lights, and face the expectant students. I'm aware that I'm smiling for the first time tonight as I return to the front of the room. I'm full-sized again, ready, at least for the moment, to take them on. "All right," I say. "Now let's see how love's effect on the central character drives the story."

The next morning, for the first time since the Isabella disaster, I'm able to face my own story, unresolved though it may be. I can read over the damn draft at least, not that its falling-in-love-is-such-great-fun sensibility says "hello" to me. By lunchtime I'm ready to pursue the ever-elusive great Jake and Margo ending again, but I'm also fending off an itchy compulsion to call Rome. I think it's wisest to get out of the house.

Soon I'm turning off the Pacific Coast Highway into a familiar parking lot. And there she awaits me, perched before a flock of seagulls in the sand opposite the entrance.

It's devious, I know, to have brunch with Naomi at the place I've always eaten with Isabella. But it's what I want to do. I haven't been back to Back on the Beach since she left America. Till now I've lacked the courage to go there and sit alone. But with my new companion, I can deal with it. This will be a sort of exorcism. I've never heard of bringing a spirit *to* an exorcism, and using a spirit to exorcise the memory of an actual living person is probably ass-backward, metaphysically speaking. But I want my pancakes and my side of bacon, and I'm happy to show the place to her.

It's not crowded. I get us one of the good tables at the far end of the outdoor area. I pull a chair out for Naomi, tuck her in. Her hair's Audrey Hepburn short today, with bangs and a ragged longer length on each side forming a dark helmet over her pale cheeks. She's wearing a sheer black silk blouse, worn over a skirt that appears to be comprised of peacock feathers, her brilliant turquoise toenails topping black-strapped sandals.

"Too much sun?" I ask. She shakes her head, and here comes Carlos the Argentine waiter, smiling, a single menu in hand. I take the menu and put it down in front of Naomi, murmuring that I already know what I want. I ask Carlos how he's doing. He's doing well. I tell him we'll start with coffee.

"Ah," says Carlos, "so your wife is joining you?"

I'm embarrassed for Naomi. "No," I say, "but bring two coffees, just the same."

Carlos cocks an eyebrow and moves off. Who knows what he thinks of this request? But by the light in his eye it's clear that anything is fine by him.

"It's a fine view," Naomi notes. The two of us enjoy it; there isn't any need for more conversation. A second waiter comes by with the coffees. I pat the tabletop in front of Naomi. "And another set of silverware," I request.

A little later Carlos returns, pad in hand. I feel a twinge as I remember the old ritual with Isabella, how she always laughs when I change my mind at the last minute. There'll be none of that today. "I'll have the pancakes and a side of bacon."

"Extra crisp," says Carlos. He remembers his part.

"Right," I say. "And my friend would like the fruit salad."

At this, Carlos does a marvelous thing. His gaze lingers over the extra set of silverware and the second cup of coffee, then he looks to the chair next to me. "Nothing else?" he asks Naomi. "You're sure that's enough for you?" And grins. He's enjoying what he takes to be a game. Or maybe he's read enough Cortàzar to accept the idea that not all realities are readily visible.

I turn to look at Naomi, who nods and smiles. Carlos smiles back. "Okay," he says, and with a dancer's grace, sweeps up the menu, spins round and strides away. I tap the edge of my mug against Naomi's, take a sip. It's a great cup of coffee.

We watch the waves break, the putter of a military helicopter low over the beachfront. I glance at Naomi, who is looking serene. "It's lovely here," she says.

Before long, Carlos returns. He makes sure to put the fruit salad down in front of Naomi, winks at me as he deposits my bacon.

The bacon is well done. Naomi makes no objections when I swipe a berry from her bowl. It's then I become conscious of a familiar voice talking loudly at a nearby table. I turn and see Stan Robertson, incongruous in a shirt and tie, sitting with the trades and the remains of an omelet, barking at the ether in front of him. My anxiety is briefly suspended by a surreal perplexity. Does my agent eat with imaginary companions? Then I realize that Stan is only on the phone, a Bluetooth dangling from his ear.

I quickly turn back to my pancakes. I lean over to Naomi and inform her, sotto voce, that I'm going to try to avoid someone. She nods, complicit, and just then, seeing the sun on her gleaming face, the wind whipping her hair, I feel a surge of giddy happiness. It's amazing that after the trauma of the past few days, I can be feeling so serene in this moment. I remember what Leo said about me being in another romantic comedy. Is it true? In the middle of my Dark Moment with Isabella, have I stumbled into a second story, with my make-believe mistress? If so, what beat are we in now?

Setup: I employed Naomi Dussart in my plan and imagined her here with me. Cute meet . . . would be that night after Yamashiro, when she took on a life of her own. Complication—I'd say that was when Isabella found her with me the other morning. Which means right about now, Naomi and I are in our Hook: the midpoint moment that irrevocably binds the two leads, implying that whatever happens from here on, they're in this thing together . . .

"So this is what a writer does." It's Stan's voice booming over my shoulder. I look up. "Tough life, huh," he says, "finding ways to spend your advance."

"Hey, Stan."

"Not even a laptop," says Stan. "Unbelievable."

Interesting. To Stan, who thinks creativity comes out of a can, I'm like a factory worker who's snuck out of his morning shift. I try to picture myself as one of those Colt-like technicians Stan's used to, but the image doesn't fit. "Even a writer has to eat," I say.

"Yeah, yeah," says Stan. "The feta cheese omelet here is amazing."

There's a pause as Stan takes in the place setting next to me. I'm thinking I don't really want Naomi to have to know Stan. But worse, at this moment, in this tranquil oasis, I loathe the idea of Stan having the power to challenge the spell, to shove my face in the dull pragmatic inanities of life as he understands it. This is wrong. I can't allow it to happen. Squinting into the glossy green spaces that hide Stan's eyes from view, I can sense the question he'll be asking in another second, and in this instant, I decide to close the breach. I embrace my reality with a new level of zeal.

"Stan, this is Naomi," I say. "Naomi, Stan. He represents my work."

Stan's usually smug visage creases in a half smile of confusion. I can feel my own face set into a calm mask of defiance. Isn't it your job, I think, to cater daily to the whims of high-paid, reality-challenged creative types all over Hollywood? So do it. *Deal with my world,* says my silence. *Deal with it, you fat fuck.*

Stan looks from me to the next chair and back again.

I'm crazed and I'm proud. I wait. Well, aren't you going to say something?

Behind his sunglasses a struggle flares and is quickly squelched. "Uh . . ." Stan says, with the slightest nod in the vague direction of Naomi. Then he forms his thumb and forefinger into an imaginary gun and points it at me. "Call me," he says, "when you've handed in that draft."

"You bet," I say. I watch the agent turn and trundle off, already busy with his BlackBerry. My heart's beating loud and fast. I take a breath, exhale, then turn back to Naomi. "I'm sorry," I say gently. "Stan's just naturally rude."

Naomi, radiantly composed, shrugs and regards me fondly. "You're happy to be with me," she says.

"Yes," I tell her. "Despite a few rocky moments." She raises an eyebrow. "You know . . ." In our little plateau of calm, it feels safe to bring this up: "Those pages I showed you, the other night—they did come out of hard work. Maybe the story doesn't appeal to you, but—"

"It's irrelevant, this script of yours," she says lightly. "It's you without me. It's beside the point."

I look at her, incredulous. "The point . . . ?"

"Of what matters." Naomi leans in close, runs her forefinger down my forehead, nose, and onto my chin, settling in the cleft. "Your potential's enormous, but you are a bit thick." This said with such evident warmth and affection that I can't be offended.

"I appreciate your vote of confidence," I say. "Not that I understand half of what you're talking about."

"You don't have to," she says. Naomi's finger glides up my face, taps gently on the space between my eyebrows. "For now you just have to feel that something has begun."

Gazing into her sparkling green eyes, I have that struck tuning-fork sensation again. "Well, *some* thing," I admit.

Naomi smiles. "And is it going well, the work you're doing now?"

"I haven't found what I'm looking for yet," I allow.

"Do you go as deep as you can go?"

"I think so," I say cautiously. "I mean . . ." I want to step away from what's been a volatile topic: "What I think is, I should keep hanging out with you."

"Smart fellow," she says, and gives my hand a squeeze. We listen to the ocean. "Maybe you shouldn't take it so seriously," she says. "Just let go."

"Let go?"

Naomi turns her face to the sky. "Like that." I follow her gaze. Down the beach a teenager has launched a purple dragon kite. I watch it paw a cloud, a fixed roar on its round ferocious face. Wind ripples its paper scales, completing the illusion of a live animal flying across a vast blue sea above our own sea. As I track its flight, dipping and rising like it's playfully swimming in the currents, the dragon's grimace looks more like a laugh to me. "Lethal creature," Naomi notes. "But awfully light on its feet."

Watching the kite dragon bob and dip, I'm suddenly seeing my tiger—roaring in his cage as Jake and Margo's cars zoom through the zoo, careening after runaway Daryl the pop star. Tiger not angry but laughing—instead of taking themselves so seriously, why can't rivals Jake and Margo be alive to the absurdity of the havoc they're wreaking, become united in their enjoyment of the chaos they've created?

"Wait a second," I murmur. "Keeping it light . . ."

Children's laughter. Pink and blond, two chubby tousle-haired twin cherubs in Hawaiian bathing trunks are playing by the low fence bordering the tables. They giggle and wave at Naomi. She turns round from looking at them, and as if having received a summons, rises from her seat. I gaze up at her in surprise. "You have your work to do," she says. "And you should take some time alone, to set your house in order."

"You're leaving?"

"Don't worry. I'll still be with you."

"All right," I say. Naomi's already walking away. She throws me a smile over her shoulder as she moves through the tables. I watch her step over the fence, headed for the ocean, and see the two kids trundle over the sand in her wake, as if catching up with their preoccupied mom. Who knows what business she has to attend to, in what dimension? Well, so long as she's coming back. Right now I'm busily running my images.

A gust of wind blows the tablecloth up, splashing my coffee. When I look to the beach again, Naomi and the children have vanished. But I catch the dark shadow of a dolphin arcing for an instant, out in the glimmering surf, surprisingly close to shore. It dives beneath the waves, and then two more dolphins jump and fall behind it, disappearing in the shiny sea.

Leo had it right. It seems so obvious to me now—now that a kamikaze attack of excited writing has yielded a sharper, truer-to-my-original-conception version of the movie's penultimate sequence than anything I've written all week. Like a fisherman who hoped to hook a trout but somehow dredged up a mermaid, in conjuring Naomi, I've summoned forth a muse.

Of course that's what she is. It all makes sense, all but the "how" of how she came to me—somehow one of those ephemeral beings that writers have been mooning about for centuries showed up in my yard. Hasn't she been proving inspirational? Her little flip-out of a few nights back must have been her trying to push me to do better work. And it's paid off, since the pages I've just finished are good—I can feel it—good enough, I'll bet, to make even Dana Morton happy. Now all I need is to nail down that crucial last bit: the final pages. And with Naomi on board, I'm bound to come up with something that will ultimately work.

Progress! Suffused with gratitude to the cosmos that's given me the gift of her, I pace circles in the living room, poring over each and every thing Naomi last said to me, trying to glean any yet unmined significance. *Set your house in order.* I think I know what she meant. If I'm going to do my best, most inspired work in the home stretch, I need to clear the decks. I've been worrying over and avoiding Isabella for too long, and it's time to confront whatever's next. Toward midnight in Rome. She could be home.

I dial, pacing through the kitchen, and end up in the little office alcove facing an oil painting of Isabella's, crammed snugly into the wall space between desk and shelves. Uneasily examining the abstract shapes on the canvas, I remember when she painted this.

Leo and Estelle were coming over for dinner. Isabella had been working on the painting all day and hadn't begun to cook, and considering all the rescheduling that had led up to this, after the many times they'd had us over for dinner, when she suggested I just order some takeout for the four of us, I did it but I fumed. I was embarrassed when our guests arrived, though I should have known Leo and Estelle would take it all in stride. They did, and despite my sulking, we turned near-disaster into a memorable evening, eating in the studio, cheering Isabella on while she finished the painting.

The canvas features dark teardrop shapes clustered in a beige oval, sienna-rimmed, making up the breast of a seagull. That's her, all right, in those teardrop shapes—this darkness flaring up at the heart of so much color. But looking at the glints of electric yellow adding a luminous glow to the painting's edges, I realize there's always this light, too—so much light in Isabella, who's apt to greet each morning with a smile. I'm pricked by guilt, remembering my bad behavior that night. Why would she want to live with a man who would blot out her light? It's true that my mind can get in my way, I *am* too much in my head, not enough in the moment with her and too controlling in general, and . . .

I can change. I can be Bright Guy, diffusing her darkness. That's what a marriage is about, isn't it? All those lovers I teach, like *Tootsie*'s testosterone-driven Michael Dorsey with soft, sweet Julie—the couples that work are the ones who learn to meet in the middle. She and I can do that!

Armed with this conviction, I'm hostility-free when Isabella answers the phone. At first we small-talk uneasily, like a pair of actors given last-minute rewrites on a scene, both trying to second-guess each other's feelings. She sounds contrite and vulnerable, and my resentment continues to ease, my affection for her resurfacing, when I make a direct inquiry about her Roman lover.

"Do I ask you for all the details, with your student?" she answers. "No, it's too embarrassing, the whole situation. I don't want you to have more pain."

"Don't spare me," I say. "If we have any hope of making things better between us, we can't be trying to protect each other, or ourselves, we have to, to—"

"To be honest with each other."

Oh, hell, there it is again: If I hadn't made up Naomi to begin with, I wouldn't be in this mess. For a mad moment, I consider telling Isabella what I really did. But what if this somehow causes Naomi to disappear? I can't chance that, not when I've just finally comprehended her true value. Besides, the damage is already done.

"Yes," I say. "Honesty is a good idea." And I can see the audience for this romantic comedy I'm starring in—some of them my own students—throwing tomatoes, leaving in droves. "The main thing is, it's over," I hurry onward, trying to get back on track. "You're not seeing this guy again."

There's a pause. "I'm not," she says finally. "At least I don't think so."

"You don't *think* so?!"

"You don't have to yell."

"I'm not yelling!"

"Well, Jordan—what about you? Are you still seeing *her*?"

"Isabella . . ." Just when I've been inflating with self-righteous anger—

"So you are?"

I can't believe she's turning this around on me. I can believe that steam is about to come out of my ears. My call-waiting beeps. I want to break the phone. "It's not the same," I manage. "*You* left *me*! None of this would have happened—"

"But this is another call, on your line."

"They can call back."

"What if it's your work? It could be important."

"*This* is important!"

"But Jordan, I don't want to be making a problem for you, when your energy and your focus, you need it for your project."

"I'm supposed to just forget about this?"

"*Coraggio,*" she says. "Life is testing us both. We need to be brave, *amore*. Listen, we talk later, when you have calm down."

Her composed and philosophical bent is only making me crazier. I realize I've been looking for the aggrieved, antagonistic Isabella to fight with, and my punches are landing in air. "Maybe we shouldn't talk at all for a while."

"I understand," she says, quiet and sad. "If that's what you wish . . ."

"I wish. *Ciao,*" I say, and slam down the phone.

Why is Isabella so understanding and rational now? Mr. Irrational wants to know. If life is testing me, maybe I'm failing a midterm, but so be it. She's the one who had to go out and give it up for the first likely prospect. Talk about nightmares: a young Italian. How young is "young"? She doesn't *think* she'll see him again . . . The phone's ringing. I yank it to my ear. "What!"

"Yo," says Moony. "You sound a little *agitato,* dog."

Bicycling south on Abbot Kinney, I see the vans lining the street up ahead, the cluster of LAPD motorcycles, the cop waving traffic along from the middle of the boulevard, and the small huddle of pedestrians on the corner. I recognize their glazed stare at the center of activity on the opposite sidewalk, the blaze of artificial light and crackle of walkie-talkies that indicate industrial dream-making. Locking my bike to a parking sign outside the periphery of the shoot, I steel myself for the hurdle ahead.

I doubt there's another group in America that could top the self-involvement of a movie crew on location in Los Angeles, whose members' peculiar air of entitlement comes from knowing that this city owes its very existence to their livelihood. Those who perhaps have only a court date, wedding, or cancer surgery to get to can wait in traffic with all the other flotsam while the cameras roll.

As I walk through the cluster of spectators hovering a few doors down from the kliegs and reflectors by the bar entrance, a young bearded crew guy in baseball cap and Nikes scuttles sideways to head me off, brandishing his walkie-talkie like an all-powerful fetish. I give my name and the crew guy puts his fetish to use. Waiting for clearance, I watch a man climb astride the camera on its crab-like metal throne, while attendant grips kneel before it, adjusting silver tracks laid down the sidewalk. Then a dreadlocked crew member arrives and announces that he'll take me onto the set. He weaves and darts at a near trot, cutting a path through the phalanx of busy crew members, then deposits me by a catering table in the parking lot behind the bar.

There Moony sits in a high chair, looking like he's done a header with heavy machinery. His left cheek is bruised and swollen beneath the eye, but before I can begin to be alarmed, I see that the young woman in designer sweats standing beside him is applying a prosthetic device the size of a large Band-Aid to his other cheek.

"Don't you look like a million bucks," I say.

"Bar fight scar," Moony tells me. "Jordan Moore, Maura from Makeup."

"Hey," says Maura, intent on her work. "Gonna be sexy," she informs Moony, affixing the scar piece along the line of his left cheekbone.

"I'm not already sexy?" Moony asks.

"Flex your jaw . . . okay, stop." She works a convincing blemish on the scar's edge with a brush, then steps back, squinting, looking from one cheek to the other. "It matches the real stuff . . . Okay," she says. "See me for blood before the next setup. For now let this dry. Which means do nothing."

"Yes, sir."

She shoulders her kit bag, turns to me. "Make sure he sits still for a bit?"

As she moves off, I step closer. "'The real stuff'?"

Moony gives a dismissive wave. "Little accident." I look at him. "The Mustang's in the shop," he allows, sheepish. "No big thing."

From close up, the bruise is wince-worthy. "Jesus, Moony."

"I know, I know. I had a few moments of . . . perspective loss. And it means I got written out of one scene. But I'm on the mend, all right?"

I'm not so sure. Moony immobile is an unnatural sight. I know that one half of his facial damage is makeup, but his gaze is glassy and he's talking at half-Moony speed. Oh, wait a second. "Percodan?" I ask.

Moony grins. "Vicodin," he says. "Hey, given what you told me on the phone, I'll be happy to break into my stash . . ."

"No thanks. Not that I'd mind the cushioning," I admit.

He squints at me as he gingerly feels the edge of his scar. "Think they've been talking, Isabella and Kathleen? They're part of some international feminist conspiracy?"

"Scary thought." I hesitate. "What do you hear from home, anyway?"

"We're negotiating the finer points, but the truce still holds."

"So you've forgiven and forgotten. You're ready to move on."

"I'm ready for make-up sex," says Moony. "That's the best." He's maneuvering himself out of the chair, and I'm startled to see him grab the handle of a cane that's hanging from its back. Moony catches my look. "Fucked up my knee a little is all. No big thing." I watch him limp slowly round the table, noting that the back of his left jeans leg is slit, evidently to accommodate the bulge of bandages around the knee. "Help yourself, man," Moony says, indicating the food.

I shake my head. "So how exactly did you get there?" I ask. "The forgiving and forgetting."

"Way-ell . . ." He surveys the cold cuts. "I considered the alternative . . ." He shrugs. "We've always had a good marriage, in spite of whatever, and when it works . . ."

"I'm not as far along as you are," I say.

"Not surprising," says Moony. "'Course, you *do* have an alternative. This . . . what is she, then—spirit? Sprite? Siren?"

"I don't know, exactly," I admit now. "She's more like a lucid dream."

"Is she here?" Moony reels round, wide-eyed.

I sigh. "No."

"So when do I get to meet her?"

"Moony . . ."

"I mean, you're getting serious about someone, I could at least weigh in with an opinion. You don't want her to meet your friends, it's a little suspect."

"I don't know if she's meet-able."

"Huh." Moony turns back to the table, grabs a bagel half, and begins manically slathering jelly over it. "So I guess you gotta weigh the pros and cons. Like, between what you had before with Isabella and what you have now? Say you give up the good fight." He's carving the bagel into little pieces. "You stay with this Naomi gal. So how's that work? Fact that she doesn't socialize with your friends, that's a con. The idea that she gives you plenty of space, that's a pro—"

"Moony," I try to interrupt, wanting to share my realization that Naomi's not so much a girlfriend as something more, but he's on a roll.

"Still, if she does move in with you, eventually one thing leads to another, and . . . You thought about kids?"

"Kids?"

"Get an imaginary wife knocked up and you get, what, a kid who's half-there? Maybe sometimes he's there and sometimes he's not," Moony muses. "Could save you some money on clothes and stuff, movie admissions—"

"Why are you so obsessed with my having children?"

Moony finishes chewing a bagel corner. "It's Kathleen," he says. "All she talks about, now that we're trying to save our marriage. The kids we could've been having." He takes a sip from an Evian bottle. "So it looks like we're gonna go for it now."

"Wow," I say.

"Yeah, wow," says Moony. "This show may have to be my last one for a while, 'cause she's not into me being an absentee dad. Part of the negotiations."

"But Moony," I protest, "you're second stage! After all the work you've done, to get to this." My incredulity is fueled by righteous indignation. "You're supposed to walk away from it, because she says so?"

Moony shrugs. "For a while. If that's what it takes."

"But this is the problem with real women," I say. "No matter how unreasonable their demands are, no matter what kind of heinous behavior *they're* guilty of—I mean, jeez, she's the one who stepped out on you, right?—you're supposed to just suck it up and do whatever they want you to do."

Moony's amused. "Are we still talking about my wife?"

"You know what's wrong with real women? They're totally unrealistic!"

"And this is news since like which century?"

"I'm just saying," I say, "what about what *you* want?"

"Well, that's the thing," says Moony. "I gotta have her, y' know?"

"Moony!" A short goateed man radiating authority bears down on us, followed by a string bean of a guy muttering into an earpiece. "Let's see the scar."

"He's looking at the barroom scar," reports the string bean.

Moony offers his cheek. "Good," says the short man.

"He likes the scar," says the string bean.

"Gary, this is Jordan Moore," Moony says. "Gary's directing this fiasco. Jordan's an excellent writer. Working on something for Rumer Hawke."

Still simmering, I manage a smile-and-nod. "Really!" says Gary. "My brother was first a.d. on *Simple Complication*." He turns back to Moony. "We're gonna work around the leg, but we need to rehearse it. You ready?"

"Ready 'n' steady."

"Great." Gary nods at me. "He doesn't entirely suck, your pal."

"Don't swell his head," I say.

"We're on our way," says the string bean as the duo hurries off.

Moony hobbles in their wake, and I walk with him. But I decline his invitation to stick around and watch. We say a quick good-bye and I make my way to the periphery of the set, brooding. Moony's going to junk all this, bail out of his career for Kathleen, because he has to have her. I'm supposed to forgive and forget because I have to have Isabella. And the justice in this can be found where?

I've emerged onto the sidewalk to face a crowd of staring faces. At first I think it's because of my undoubtedly twisted expression. Then I realize that they're thinking I might be somebody. For a moment I envision this other Jordan they're looking at, and wish I was him. But the feeling passes as quickly as their attention does. Behind me, the camera is rising on its crane.

I crave pizza. I want to gorge myself on thick cheese, spicy sausage, and hot hard crust, as if overloading my taste buds and olfactory nerves could blot out the incessant chatter of my brain, as if the greasy sauce could coat over and quiet the ache in my gut. I get on my bike and pedal furiously down to the pizza place, and while I wait impatiently for my two slices, I sip greedy swallows of sweet metallic Coke, pacing outside the storefront with can in hand, feeling unhinged, unfulfilled, un-everything.

Nearly burn my tongue but catch myself in time. Sit with the slices on the bench outside, glaring darkly at a happy gay couple with their giant dog, the mom with her too-pretty child in a stroller. They all have lives, lives with built-in meanings, while I'm living some senseless simulacrum of one. Thank God for pizza.

Now what? Full, but still empty, I toss my napkin in the can and get on my bike, remembering the pizza Isabella and I shared on Via Borghese, Roman pizzas all the more flavorful when you're laughing between bites, with the woman who loves you pushing the slice at your face. Now

I've had the pizza without the love, or at least . . . what kind of love do I have now? Was it ever really love, if it's been so easily corrupted? Look at Moony, for chrissake: drug-addled, then crippled, now abandoning a career. That's what love gets you. I don't even know what the word means anymore. *Fuck* love, anyway—

A cat darts across my path as I speed round the corner. I swerve, brake, nearly fall, wobbling madly, adrenaline surging. Blood pounds in my ears, I'm muttering curses as I pull over to the curb. The cat, half a block down, turns back to stare at me with vacant, coal-glitter eyes: What's *your* problem?

Score another one for the physical universe, determined to put me in my place. As I wait for my breathing to slow, I can hear the incongruous sound of laughter and a muffled electric guitar and bass. There's a knot of people smoking and hanging out by the open back door of Bing's, a former pool hall now gentrified into a hot spot for the martini set that's tucked into the curve of Abbot Kinney close to Venice Boulevard. Not a place I've ventured into for years. But the live music has a mean pulse that piques my curiosity. I lock the bike to a parking sign at the edge of the lot and walk over to have a look. Peering through the doorway, I find my resistance to merriment dissolving as the thump of the bass vibrates through my feet.

The band's just finishing a set as I take a seat by the wall at the end of the bar. I down the vodka on the rocks I order in two big swallows, and a new clarity descends over the welter of dark emotions I've been carrying, like the glass lid of a mason jar locking down, snapping its contents tight. It's over, isn't it? All of this craziness I've been up to has yielded what? If she really loved me, if she believed in our love as much as I do, I wouldn't be sitting here in what feels like the bottom of a deep, dark well, because face it: Isabella's already found another lover and she isn't coming back.

How is it possible, I wonder, after so many thousands of moments shared, of words exchanged, breaths mingled, every intimate inch of skin memorized, that it should come to this? I should feel a kind of grim liberation in the finality of this despair, but relief doesn't materialize. My mouth's sour, tongue dry. I order a beer, and Naomi slides onto the stool next to mine.

Tonight she has her hair up, wears a vintage fifties-styled leather jacket and short denim skirt. With her bright red lipstick and blue eye shadow, she might have just zoomed off the highway with a motorcycle gang. Actually, she looks sort of like Loretta Castorini from *Moonstruck*. At any rate I'm glad to see her, but long gone is that serenity and well-being that was with us on the beach.

Apparently she can read it right off my face. "Are we having a wake?" she asks.

I lack the spiritual strength to muster a smile. "You could say that," I mutter. "My marriage may be as good as dead."

Naomi props her chin in her hands. "You're giving up?"

I shrug, glum. "I think I'm the one who's being given up on."

"You sure about that?"

"No," I admit. "Have you come here to torture me with hope?" My beer arrives. I nod a thanks to the bartender and pull it close. "Because it's the not knowing what's going to happen—that's what's making me crazy."

Naomi looks me over. "And interfering with your work."

Come to think of it, yes. The joyful spurt of activity that followed our lunch on the beach already seems like a distant memory. "Work?" I ask, sardonic.

Naomi nods. "All right," she says, and rises from her stool. "Let's see what we can do." She moves around behind me and puts her hands on my shoulders. I see the two of us in the bar mirror behind the rows of whiskey and gin as she kneads the tense muscles at the back of my neck. Behind her, the guitarist is plugging in again, an amp buzzing. "It's morning, isn't it," she says, "in Rome."

I glance at the clock above our reflections. "That's right." I'm enjoying the feel of her fingers at work. I close my eyes.

"Good," she murmurs. "Keep them shut. We're going to . . . to the piazza."

"Which piazza?"

"You know the one. Near the church with the three Caravaggios. The place Isabella likes to sit in the early morning and do her sketching. At the café in the northern corner, with the bar man who has a nose like . . . that bird—"

"A condor," I tell her. "She calls him the Beakman." I should be surprised, for how could she know any of this? But she's Naomi, and her thumbs are generating a wonderful warmth at the base of my neck, and it's so vivid to me now: I can see the very place, the piazza in that early-morning light, the long shadows on the gray cobblestones. And I can feel the change in the air, smell that familiar Roman mixture of petrol and oven-baked bread, laced with tobacco smoke. Not too many people at this hour—the snap of a bedsheet being shaken by a woman in a slip on a balcony above the café—and here's the Beakman himself, carrying a check on a tray to where Isabella sits, smoking, her brown cape slung over her shoulders, her sketchpad open on the table, and underneath, Maxi, paws out, scratching the side of his long nose on the ground.

I rise involuntarily, my heart seizing at the sight of them both. I'm tempted to call out her name, but I feel Naomi move with me, the warmth of her hands ever-present at my neck, and hear the low murmur of her voice by my ear. "She can't hear you, or see you," she tells me. "Let's just watch for a little bit."

She's gotten some sun, Isabella, but she looks thin. She's had her usual two cappuccinos, I see, and she's laughing at something the Beakman says as he walks away, a comment on her drawing, I think. I walk nearer, wanting to get a look at it, but really wanting to drink in the sight of her from close by—alone at this hour in her normal routine, I'm heartened to see—but she's already shutting the cover on her pad, laying down the pen, the blue one with the super-fine point that I bought her only weeks ago, getting ready to pay the check. I hover anxiously as I watch her dig inside that overflowing canvas bag of hers to come up with her wallet. She removes the euro bill and puts it on the tray, ignoring the little wrapped candy there, goes to close the wallet and pauses, lingering over something, her eye caught. I think I know what this might be and I can't help it, I step right up to the table, halted only by the barking.

Maxi's up, head poking out from beneath the table and staring up at me, his little butt wiggling. "Maxi! *Madonna, cosa fai?*" He shifts his weight from side to side, the little dance he does when he wants biscotti, and grins a slacked-jaw grin. Gives me a sharp quick woof. I look to Isabella, who stares past us, frowning, toward the coo of the pigeons in the piazza, then slaps her thigh. *"Viene qui! Viene qui, Maxi . . . Uffa . . ."*

So it's like that, eh, this is your game? Maxi seems to be saying, tongue out, smiling. He shakes himself, collar jiggling, then sits back down at Isabella's feet, laughing to himself and keeping an eye on me. Isabella still has her wallet open, and now that the dog's settled, she pulls from its plastic sheaf the Polaroid: taken so long ago, before we were married, the two us at the kitchen table, Isabella seated in my lap, our faces smushed together, hers a bit blurry, mine fixed, both flushed with giddy joy. She stares at the photo, her expression so grave that my stomach tightens with dread.

"She's going to throw it away . . ."

"Shhh," Naomi whispers.

Isabella, intent, leans over the little square with its frayed and yellowing border. Her left forefinger darts out to carefully, gently, rub away a speck of something from our faces, and I notice the gleam of her wedding band as she slips the Polaroid back into its place at the front of her wallet, and snaps it shut.

Maxi barks again, impatient. *"Pazzo cane . . . !"*

"Come on," says Naomi, her hand pressing at my neck, and I let her take me then, around the two of them, toward the scattering pigeons and into a chair at a table across the way, her fingers giving a final squeeze to the hunch of my shoulders, the amplifier behind her crackling static again and I open my eyes. We're there in the bar mirror at the count-off, the click of drumsticks and the first chords of a blaring blues tune cutting through the smoky air. Naomi smiles, then slips out from around me and into the cluster of people in front of us on the small dance floor.

Beyond her, the guitarist, a sweat-drenched wiry Hispanic guy, wrestles with his hollow-bodied Gibson as if trying to wring the life out of it. Still trying to get my mind around where I just went and what I saw there, I watch the tattooed drummer and black bassist lock down that beat. Naomi turns slow and sinuous, arms above her head, moving with the churn of bass and snap of snare drum, and before long I can't help it, I start to rock on my stool, one hand keeping rhythm on the edge of the bar as the guitarist leans into the microphone, gold-toothed grimace right up against the mesh of its head, singing:

"Don't it feel so lonesome, sleeping by yourself . . ."

The chords shift, and he repeats the words as they always do, in this song and all the others, *"Don't it feel so lonesome / Sleeping by yourself . . . ,"* and I sing the words along with him, the truth of it filling me and lifting me, as we turn around the same old bend together, *". . . when the woman you love / Been out there lovin' someone else?"*

The bluesman bears down on the final turnaround, unleashing a brief flurry of bottleneck cries that climax in a single sustained note, wailed like a burst of fluid fire. Someone whistles, someone yelps, and everyone's clapping hard, the roomful of people becoming one giant amen, my own cry a bittersweet affirmation, because whether my trip to the piazza was real or imagined, that sweet poison has taken effect: Rekindled hope is coursing through my veins.

The band begins a subdued, slower blues, and some of the couples begin to slow-dance. The redhead seated on the next stool bobs along, smiling at me. Naomi, standing beside her, gives me an inviting look and gestures toward the floor. "You want to?" I ask her. Naomi nods and I rise from my seat, only to find the redhead smiling wider at me with a look of surprised delight.

"Sure," she says, and hops off her stool. She's unsteady on her feet, gripping my elbow briefly to get her balance as I look helplessly to Naomi.

"Go ahead," she murmurs in my ear. "Be good for both of you."

The redhead's tugging me onto the dance floor, so there's not much

I can do but go with this. I shoot Naomi an apologetic smile as I hold the woman lightly, keeping at a gentlemanly distance, one hand on her shoulder, the other at her waist. She's older than me, and a few drinks ahead. Wry smile lines crinkle at the corner of her dark eyes as she sways against me, staring past my face. I turn to see what she's looking at. On the TV set above the bar, a suntanned half-naked man and woman with matching perfect teeth cavort in the aquamarine foam of some Caribbean tide, a white sailfish moored down the beach behind them. As we watch, the couple goes into a clinch.

"Enjoy it while it lasts," says the redhead.

I laugh. "Roger that," I say.

"You know, years ago . . ." She talks over the music, eyes on the screen. "Before I got married the first time, when I used to jog on the beach, I'd always look to see if there was a white sail on the horizon. And there was always at least one."

Naomi watches from my stool, gives me a little wink.

"And it became a kind of symbol," my partner goes on. "As long as there was a white sail out there, it meant that me and my husband were going to be together. Like, for always. Now, when I look at that sail . . ." She looks back at to me. "You know what I think it symbolizes?" I shake my head. "A sailboat," she says.

"Ah," I say, and nodding, look to the TV again. "Sharks in the water."

She laughs. "And all of those ultraviolet rays . . ."

"An invite to skin cancer."

The redhead nods, holding my gaze with the signature intensity of the seriously inebriated. "Um-hmm," she says. "Ya know . . ." She gently prods my chest with her forefinger. "You may be the one other person in this room tonight who really . . . gets it."

"Maybe so." The song ends. Other couples are disengaging and applauding, but she stays pretty close. Although she could pass for my romance-disenchanted doppelgänger, I don't want to hang out with her in that dark, sardonic realm now. After my piazza visitation I'm too deep within my own quiet valley of cautiously renewed optimism. But I can see she's sizing me up for more than another dance.

Just as I'm wondering how to extricate myself without feelings getting hurt, Naomi comes up beside me, slides an arm around my waist, and nuzzles my cheek. And the redhead takes a step back, her expression gone peculiar.

"Huh," she says. "You're not really . . . on your own here, are you?"

I look back at her, startled. "What do you mean?"

Her eyes travel the outline of my face, sweep over Naomi, and come back again. "You got someone watchin' over you," she says.

"You think?"

She gives a slow nod. "I have an instinct for these things," she says, and smiles. "Well, thanks for the dance, partner. My next cocktail awaits." The redhead gives my arm a squeeze and slides past us, back to the bar.

Outside in the clear night air, strolling across the parking lot, I find I'm humming that old blues tune. Naomi waltzes round me, playing air guitar. "You seem a little less gloom and doom, cowboy," she says.

"Thanks to you," I tell her.

Naomi shrugs. "It's all in the service of clarity."

I look back at her as I unlock my bike. I picture Isabella again, and for an instant she's the one who seems unreal. She's part of a waking dream, the woman I'm involved with in another life. Here and now I'm with Naomi. She's the one who climbs up on the seat behind me as I straddle the bike and grip the handlebars, front wheel wobbling.

"Got your balance?" she asks.

"Barely."

Naomi chuckles softly. "Then drive."

Jake in one car, Margo in another, crazed Daryl leading them on at 120 miles per hour—they might as well be cruising in a circle, for all the progress I've made. I've got a serviceable climax on the page, but the resolution's uninspired. After my night with Naomi, I was ready to face my computer screen this morning. I only wish I'd had the presence of mind to ask her, point blank: What's my beautiful ending?

With the weekend deadline looming, panic takes the form of profound inertia. By noon I'm picking bits of lint and leaf off the carpet, and sharpening red pencils. When I find myself compulsively alphabetizing a bookshelf, I remember with a twinge of guilt that I still need to get a book for Leo. And I should call to see if we're still on for Monday.

The querulous "Halloo?" of Mrs. D the housekeeper responds to the second ring. I ask for Leo and after a sizable pause, a hoarse whisper gets on the line, the shell of a once-deep voice, asking me how I am.

I tell him I'm calling to confirm our upcoming date. Leo says he's looking forward to it. I'm startled by the barely-there rasp of his voice. He sounds like an ancient ghost, one who's caught a cold from haunting a drafty temple for decades. "We had a rough night, is all," he tells me. "The bronchitis is back."

"You sound terrible," I blurt. "I mean—are you all right?"

"Oh, I'll be fiiiiiiiine," rasps Leo.

I can envision the expression that accompanies this signature phrase of Leo's, his bushy eyebrows going up, forehead creased, the tight grin below his fat-bottomed nose. I'm a fool to think I can understand what he's up against.

"What are the doctors saying?" I ask.

"Nothing I want to hear," says Leo. "But tell me . . . how is your spirit?"

I'm about to tell him I'm just fine, certainly fine next to how he sounds, when I realize he must be asking about Naomi. "She's still at large," I say.

"I want to hear alllllllll about it," says Leo. "Tell me a story."

I wonder how much medication he's on. "Now?"

"Please."

"All right. Last night Naomi showed up at Bing's and somehow transported me to Rome for a minute—"

"For some manicotti?"

"No, she wanted me to see that Isabella still cares. So that I wouldn't go entirely off the deep end."

I hear a kind of breathy *heh-heh-heh* from Leo. "Such a loyal gal, this Naomi."

"You were right about your muse theory, I think. She's been helping me write."

"Aaaah," he intones. "So the gods have smiled. And how *is* your moo-vie?"

I consider. "I guess it's almost what it's supposed to be. It's better than it was. I mean, we can't all write something as great as *Groundhog Day,* but . . ." I look to my misshapen pile of pages. "I was hoping that with Rumer, I'd get to do something worth something. And it still doesn't feel like I've done that."

"You'll feel better when you've been paid."

"I guess," I say. "But I'm talking too much about me and you're talking too much, period. Can I bring you anything, when I come?"

"Bring me the head of Charlie Rose. I don't know how that man keeps his job."

"Seriously," I say. "Do you need something?"

There's a thoughtful pause. My cheeks grow hot as I consider the myriad implications of my casual question. "No," Leo wheezes. "Estelle is . . ." He clears his throat, making a horrible, choking noise.

"Save your voice for when I see you," I say. "I'll get off the phone."

After good-byes I linger by the open window, drinking in the deep orange of the calla lilies swaying underneath the sill and feeling sheepish about my own worries. I'm keenly aware of having all that Leo is denied: the sun in my face, the breathing in and out I've been doing without thinking until this moment. How much more than this does a relatively healthy man need?

The chastened screenwriter returns to his desk. But intimations of mortality are notoriously hard to keep hold of. No sooner have I checked my e-mails than I'm back in the thick of mundane drama: Dana Morton is expecting the draft tomorrow, Friday, so she can go over it before passing it on to Rumer for his weekend read.

Tomorrow. Friday.

Brain fatigue now gives way to paralysis. After a few minutes of watching the little cursor blink off and on, and off and on, the silence in this room is shouting in my ears again. I miss the melody of my name on Isabella's lips. Though I can hear those two notes distinctly in my mind, memory is a poor substitute for the real thing. I pick up the phone again, chest tight, fearing she won't be there as much as that she will.

"Pronto?"

"Ciao, bella, it's me."

"Jordan." And there it is—the magic musical figure. For a split second, all is right with my world again, even though I'm aware of a faint dissonance in the singer's tone that's tough to decipher. "I'm glad you call, because I've been wanting to call you, but somehow . . . I don't know." She gives a rueful little laugh. "I've been afraid."

"Io capito." I do understand. "Is this an okay time? I know it's late."

"But of course you can call, whenever you need. Are you okay?"

It's a simple question, but there's so much packed into it that the three words pierce right to the center of me. I was fearing coldness, defensiveness, but what I'm hearing is concern, genuine caring—love. And with a rush, my own neglected love for Isabella wells up in me, as if it was only waiting for such an invitation to be released. I have to clear my throat. "Maybe okay," I manage.

"Because I worry about you," she says. "I know we have been fighting, but I can't help it. I need to know that you're all right."

"That's . . . very sweet."

"I'm thinking that place, on the back of your neck, it needs a good rub, eh?"

Good Lord. I'm coming undone. What's really unraveling are the threads Naomi has spun, giving me the sense that I'm not alone, that I've been with a soul mate in a magical realm. While the real human being I want to be with has been so very far away . . .

"But maybe you don't need for me to take care of these things any-more," she continues. "There is someone else in my place."

This said gently, tenderly, with no undertone of bitterness or reproach. I can't stand it. After so many days of steely resolve, it only takes one tiny step over the invisible boundary, and before I can even think to question what I'm doing, I'm past it. "Look," I say. "Isabella, there is no someone else. I'm not seeing another woman."

"I don't understand."

"She's not a real woman!"

"What do you mean?"

"I wanted to make you jealous. I was thinking that if you heard I was seeing someone, maybe you'd reconsider leaving, you'd come back. But I couldn't stand the idea of actually getting involved with anybody, so I invented a woman—an imaginary person." It's such a relief to be saying this, it pours out of me like a stopper's suddenly come unplugged. "The truth is, I pretended to go out with her. The whole time we've been fighting over her, there hasn't been any 'her.'"

"No her?" echoes Isabella.

"I mean, there is a *woman,* but I made her up." Later I'll explain the stickier, stranger facts in the case of Naomi, but for now, I'm excited to tell her some of the truth at last—at least enough of the truth to set things right. "I never intended to be unfaithful, Isabella—I never was, not really! And the last thing I wanted was for you to go off with someone else. This whole thing has been one big messed-up . . . misunderstanding."

"Because there is no other woman."

"She was a figment of my imagination!"

There's silence at the other end.

"I know, it's a lot to take in," I say. "And I don't blame you if you're mad at me for putting you through all this, but—"

"Jordan," Isabella interrupts. "I suppose you mean to touch me, with this story, I should be moved because you want so much to make things better—"

"It's not a story, it's—"

"But I don't understand why you say such nonsense."

"It's the truth!"

"The truth?" The contempt-laced venom with which she spits these words is as potent as the honey she'd been pouring only a moment ago. "Then you tell me, who is this woman you are with, in the bar on Abbot Kinney?"

"What?"

"According to Flavia, who was there at Bing's Bar, she is quite the hot number. She was really turning heads!"

"But . . . that was . . ."

"A woman who doesn't exist? Flavia saw you dance with her, Jordan!"

My mind flounders. "But she, I . . ."

"*Sì,* you, her. For real!"

I'm flailing from my hoisted petard. "But if you mean the redhead—"

"*Madonna! Che parle?* You're dating more than one?"

"No! Isabella—"

"Listen, I'm tired, it's late, and to listen to any more of this, it's too much! Let's talk another time, when you really want to be honest with me, eh? *Ciao, buona notte.*" And she's gone.

When night falls, I'm seated on my front steps with head in hands. I've tried working, mindlessly kneading and poking at my stopgap ending, but I had to give it up. My marriage has been re-torpedoed, and I'm useless.

Purity of heart is to will one thing. That's where I'm screwed. According to Kierkegaard—I researched this online, in one of my many procrastination salvos—I'm the epitome of wrong: I'm the double-minded man. Attached to Naomi, while loving my wife. Wanting to live in another dimension, wanting to live my regular real life. My heart's about as pure as the driven slush.

"Difficult day?"

She's standing in my garden. And this time I'm more apprehensive than cheered to see her. Naomi's in a black dress that resembles Victorian underclothing, tight-bodiced, flaring out at the hips in long folds over her bare legs. Though I'm struck anew by her ageless beauty, by the classic lines of her face and figure, I'm in a black mood of my own, and something in me rebels at the sight of her. As if sensing this, she keeps a little distance. "Yeah, kind of gnarly," I tell her.

"And you're kind of looking forward to a restful night? I don't have to stay," she adds softly, "if you don't like me being here."

In the same way that Isabella's surprising gentleness unmanned me hours ago, looking into the warmth of Naomi's eyes, it's hard to hold on to my resentment. "I think . . ." I hesitate. "I don't know what to think," I admit.

"Thinking may not be the best approach." Naomi holds out her hand. "Come."

I hold my ground. "Where?"

"Jordan . . ." She's reproachful, disappointed. "When have I misled you?"

"It's where you lead me that worries me," I tell her.

"Come on," she says simply. "We'll spend a little time together, that's all. I'm sure you'll find it helpful."

Helpful? I can't sort it out anymore, the good or the bad in being with her. She was helping me win Isabella, now she's lost me Isabella . . . Her smile, promising secrets to be shared, is difficult to resist. Slowly, warily, I rise from the steps.

We walk west in silence. The not knowing what I'm in for is, I realize, part of the allure. A black dog, a collarless mutt, trots up beside Naomi as we reach the avenue. She gives the dog a pat on his head and he lopes away. I have the impression that they've had some kind of conversation, and I give her an inquisitive look.

"He wasn't lost," she tells me, "only looking for a friend who was here earlier."

I nod, starting to let go, a by-now-familiar muscle unclenching, the suspension of disbelief that always accompanies these visits settling inside me as she pauses at the curb to sniff the air, much like a dog herself.

"These winds have come from very, very far away," she reports, and glances up, tracing the trajectory of something invisible up there. "Ghosts," she murmurs.

I look for supernatural beings in the telephone wires but see nothing but sky.

The beach is deserted but for a few homeless people gathered in the shadows of the public bathroom structure near Brooks. There's a low murmur of voices, the red dot of a cigarette's glow as we walk past. A crescent moon sky, wisps of cloud scudding across the panoply of stars, the black waves a quiet crashing. Naomi and I walk side by side, sandals dangling from our hands. The sand is unexpectedly warm beneath my bare feet.

She pauses a few yards from the darkened circle that indicates the tide's last splash and sinks to her knees, the folds of her dress fanning out around her. Beyond her to the north lies the dim outline of the coast, the long glittering line of the Santa Monica Pier, with its tiny ferris wheel silently blinking pink and blue.

"You don't usually go to church, or to temple," she says. I shake my head. This has been an issue with Isabella, who takes her religious practice seriously. Naomi merely nods and looks out to sea. "But any place is a place of worship," she says. "Any place you show up, if you're a person with intention." She rummages in her bag, produces a silver pen and a scrolled piece of paper. She flattens its edges in her lap before handing both to me. "Write down what you hope for," she says. "Just that."

The pen's cold to my touch. I consider, thinking of her, Isabella, Rumer. I hold the paper down on my thigh, at a loss. Hours ago, I thought the sound of my name on my wife's lips was the key to regaining my equilibrium. Now I'm as uncentered as ever.

Naomi pads onto the darkened sand, gathering up the hem of her dress as she reaches the sputtering foam at the water's edge, a hunched shadow against the gray sea. Hope? A tricky thread to pull from such a convoluted pattern. I hope I can get my life back, my incomprehensible life. I still believe, even after all that's happened, that Isabella can help restore the sense of it, if she returns. If there's anything I hope to have, it's one clear idea of how it is that I am supposed to live. Clarity is what I want, and what I really hope for, on so many levels, but . . . Bending close over the page to track my handwriting in the darkness, I write the only word that makes sense for me to aspire to: *resolution*.

Naomi's returned. I look up, expecting she's brought back shells, a bit of driftwood. She's carrying a bright green Frisbee. She removes a small blue glass from her bag and places it in the center of the upturned disc. She retrieves a lighter, clicks it on, and I see that the glass holds a votive candle. She lights the candle, its flame flaring white and then blue in the recesses of the glass. She looks back at me. "Did you write your hope?"

I nod. Naomi drips wax on the center of the upturned Frisbee, settles the blue glass atop it, fixing it in place. She walks, bearing the Frisbee with its tiny-flamed center before her. I follow her to the water's edge and she turns to face me. "Go ahead," she says, indicating the paper in my hand. I dip one end into the flame, which licks hungrily up the sides, then quickly engulfs the whole of it. I let it fall, blackened and crumbling, into the Frisbee. In moments it's ash blown off in the night.

Naomi wades across the wet sand into the shallows. Her figure merges with the darker shadows of the sea and sky, the flickering flame held at her waist casting just enough light to illuminate the pale silhouette of her face as she leans over to nudge the Frisbee into the receding tide. The little blue flame dances. A shallow wave spins the plastic dish, pushing it back toward Naomi. She wades in deeper, wrapping the material of her dress around her waist. And when the next wave breaks, she pushes the Frisbee out farther, beyond the pull of the undertow. The candle bobs atop the wave's crest. The wind rises. The tiny dot of light recedes into the great blackness of the water.

Naomi wades backward, eyes fixed on the bit of blue riding the dark tide. She lets her dress down and the wind blows it round her legs. I won't be surprised if that wind lifts her up and sends her flying over the surf, blowing our ocean offering out to sea like a seraph from a medieval painting. But feet splashing up the wet sand, she joins me again and we stand in silence, looking for the blue light. I'm not sure I can see it now.

Naomi takes my arm, leading me back to the warm sand where we left her bag and shoes. She smoothes her hair, sits back on her haunches. She gives my hand a gentle squeeze, as if telling me not to worry, that everything is going to be all right. What can she be thinking? There's no way to guess. In spite of moments when it's uncanny how much she feels a part of me, she's still uncannily Other. Nonetheless, hand in hand with the riddle of her, I'm seized with a strange, powerful serenity. At least, just now, I'm with someone who doesn't require me to be anything other than I already am. It's tempting to just stay with her in this realm, like a mad monk with a madder nun, to defy the world I'm supposed to belong to.

"You know," I say, "I still don't have an ending—at least not one that's brilliant."

Naomi shrugs. "You'll do fine," she says. "You've got plenty of limitations to transcend, but the way I see it, you're essentially good to go."

I laugh. "Glad that's how you see it. But I'm talking about my project."

"Well, there's your *project*," she muses, "and there's the project that is *you*, Jordan. In both cases, the best ending would actually be a beginning."

"I'm sorry I asked."

Naomi laughs and gathers me closer. "Relax," she says. "Settle down."

I lie back in her embrace, so that my head rests against her breast and her arms enfold me as we both face the ocean. Her voice is a soft counterpoint to the sighing of the wind and the hissing of the tide. "Look up there." She points, and I shift my gaze from the pinpoints of light glittering on the waves to the sea of stars above. "Do you know what you're seeing?"

"Suns," I say. "Planets . . ."

"And souls," she says. "That's what some of those lights are—the souls of the dead, souls of the living, souls unborn . . ."

"Really."

"Um-hmm," she murmurs. "Some of them are parts of souls that have gone missing. They're keeping watch on this little planet, hoping someday they may come back here to live."

"It's like a celestial orphanage," I suggest.

"That's right," says Naomi, smoothing the hair back from my brow. "And what the missing part of a soul looks for is a certain kind of light. You see, every person's soul shines—you can see it in the eyes—but it's not always as powerful a light as it can be. Sometimes people have such a hard time of it, in this life, that their light grows dim. Or they get so distracted by what's outside themselves that their light loses luster."

I watch a small black shape break from the black shoreline. A dog darting in and out of the tide, with no owner in sight. Maybe it's the same one we met on the street.

"Once upon a time," Naomi continues, "there was a child who believed in all things magical and mysterious. The forces that exist beyond what you can see and hear. But as he grew up, he was so concerned with *being* grown-up, and being *like* the other grown-ups, that he stopped believing in what he used to imagine. He lost a lot of light—not so suddenly that he'd have noticed, but little by little it slipped away from him."

"Happens all the time, I bet." The dog, emerged from the water, trots up the beach. Shakes himself and bounds off down the sand again. I watch him with sleepy eyes.

"In this man's case," she goes on, "there came a day when he was feeling so confused, so deeply lost, that the light that was still left in him flared up like a beacon. And that was the signal, strong enough to be seen from the deepest, darkest regions of the night. The missing part of his soul recognized this light, as a call for her alone to hear. So she flew across the universe to join him."

"Leaving all her friends in the orphanage behind."

"Her fellow souls were very glad for her."

"Twinkling, merrily," I say, drowsy. "And did they live happily ever after?"

"It's not that simple," says Naomi. "He was a grown-up man, after all, and had forgotten a lot of what he used to know. He might not be able to hear the kinds of things she wanted to tell him."

"Like what?"

She whispers, but the words are as clear and loud as if they came from the center of my head. *"All the things that once were holy, I keep them for you."*

It's hard to keep my eyes open. "He'd hear that," I tell her.

"Who knows?" she says. "It's only a story."

The wind whistles. Naomi begins to hum, a melody I can almost place. Her hum merges with the whooshing repetition of the waves. In the place of my blue flame a thousand tips of sea-flame sparkle on the moonlit water, and fade slowly into the dark.

Then another flame rises in that darkness. It's a book of fiery pages, with a pageant of familiar figures dancing in its smoke. Oh, I know that story, I realize. And it's ready to be told. The burning pages flicker now in a sudden downpour of crystalline blue rain. And it's up to me to keep this fire in the rain from going out . . .

The rumble of a motor brings my head up. Headlights loom over the slopes of sand. I scramble to my feet. Naomi's shoes and bag are gone. I turn around, searching the shore as the beach patrol car slows, then passes on. I grab my sandals and begin trudging up the beach. In the distance, at the edge of the parking lot, Naomi's silhouette crouches on the curb's edge. She's talking with a pair of pigeons.

When the ringing comes in the middle of the night, I'm so confused that I slap the top of the telephone with my hand as though it's an alarm, and only in feeling the strange contours of the phone beneath my palm do I understand, hurriedly lifting the receiver to stop the noise. Naomi lies close beside me, deep in her own dream, if she does dream. I pull the phone to my ear and croak a hello.

"*Ciao,*" says Isabella. "I'm sorry I wake you."

"No, it's okay," I assure her, knowing it's morning in Rome and sensing from the timbre of her voice that something's up. It's strange anyway that she's calling now, since I'd imagined I'd be the one who'd have to call her to resume our fight. I wonder, apprehensive, if something's happened to Maxi or her mother.

"I know we're not supposed to be talking. But I had to speak with you."

"Uh-huh." I keep my voice down as I slip out from my side of the bed and fumble into my slippers in the dark.

"How are you?" asks Isabella.

Such a simple question seems so loaded. "Okay," I mutter.

"How is the writing? Have you finished what you need to do?"

"Pretty much. I hand it in tomorrow."

"This is wonderful, Jordan. I have good feelings about your project. You're going to have big success with this one, I can tell."

I murmur a thank-you, wondering how happy she'd be if she knew how much Naomi had to do with getting me through it, and her radar picks up on the signal.

"Is she there?"

By now I've walked into the living room, swinging the bedroom door quietly shut behind me, so the lie comes to my lips with an old equivocator's ease. It's a technicality—I am, after all, alone in the living room. "No," I tell her. Not that you should be asking this, I think, and again as if she's heard me, Isabella says:

"I know, it's not my business, but still . . ." She sighs.

I listen to the tiny echo of her transatlantic voice, fully awake now, wary. It's her call. And for once, my estranged wife is startlingly direct. "I've had enough of this," she says. "I want to see you. I'm coming home."

How long I've waited to hear these words! So long that I've nearly forgotten that these are the words, or the lack of them, that have predicated most of my existence for nearly two weeks now. It's almost too much to believe. The unreality of it creates an odd clench in my stomach, makes it a moment of joyous disbelief, makes my cautious breath catch on the verge. I can't quite let myself feel the exultant relief I've expected to feel. Her next words bring me, with the sharp, cold surge of adrenaline you get when you miss a stair step in the dark, to the reason why.

"On one condition," Isabella says.

Of course—there has to be a condition. I wait.

"You know what it is."

"Oh?"

"You have to stop seeing her."

Instinctively I turn toward the bedroom door, listening to the silence beyond it. Incredibly, I'm worrying that she'll overhear, worrying that I'll have to tell her this.

"Jordan?"

"Yeah."

"Am I asking so much? Because really, if you can't—"

"No," I say quickly, hearing the alarm in Isabella's voice. "I understand."

"Do you have to think about it?" It isn't merely a question, it's an edifice, a duplex, an entire condominium she is erecting in front of me, so many are the levels, the rooms, the hidden sub-basements of this sentence. If I wait another second, it's going to be as large as the Chrysler Building, its spire top poised to pierce me through the heart.

"Of course not," I tell her. "It's just . . ."

"I know," Isabella says. Does she? I'm not sure what I was about to say, myself. "And if you would rather that I don't come back . . ."

"No, no," I assure her. "I want you to come."

"So you'll do what you have to do," she says.

We don't stay on much longer. She's going to call again with flight numbers, logistics to discuss. It's only a matter of days.

When we hang up, I can't let go of the phone. I pace in a mad circle, clutching it until I stop short, dizzy with relief—I'd almost stopped imagining this was possible! I lie back on the living-room couch, head still whirling.

Then another thought wrenches my ferris-wheeling mind to a shuddering halt. I sit up in the dark, silent phone in my lap, staring at the bedroom door, staring so hard that colored sparks dance in the space before my gaze. I see again the flickering points of light on the black waves, dimly remember the glimpse of a fire, the blue rain, the tantalizing sense of another story, ready to be realized . . .

I'm realizing now that until tonight I hadn't allowed myself to think about giving up the habit of Naomi. It's a dark seep of uneasiness into my moment of shining victory, and though I know I have to face this task, I can't imagine how.

But I've won. I've won!

The next morning I put a last Naomi-inspired fix in my draft: The final dialogue between Jake and Margo ambiguously echoes the very lines they spoke when they first met, suggesting *an end that could be a beginning.* I like it. I freeze the I-can-live-with-this compromise ending. Then, dizzy with triumph, I'm out of the house and onto my bicycle, to pedal for Staples and the triumphant Xeroxing of the completed script.

Thing is, I have to keep moving. Because when I slow down, the sobering undercurrent of what I don't want to think about is exposed, glimmering steely gray beneath the bright blue sky. And I tell myself: You can't have it all.

She was gone from the apartment before I woke. Does she know? Who knows what she knows? Who knows what it'll feel like, when she's gone for good? Thinking about this drains the energy from my body as if I've been bled. And I need that energy. Haven't I earned the right to feel better about my life, to bask in legitimate hope for the future? I focus on being done with the draft, after a week of brain-busting. I hold on to this, hunched over the handlebars, and in the way you disparage what you can't have to rationalize not having it, I remind myself: Much as she may have inspired the best parts of the draft, Naomi has never cared much for my screenplay.

Then, striding into Staples, I'm thinking: Why can't I have everything? For a reckless moment I consider just telling Isabella that Naomi is gone, simple enough since in one sense she's never been here. Because what if Rumer needs more rewrites?

No. The idea reeks of bad faith on so many levels that my stomach curdles. I don't want to poison this morning, this unusually blessed morning, where inside the store, there's no line at the copy counter. And here is Dan the copy man, a lanky Texas Ranger–like guy who adores Isabella and considers me one of life's more confounding mysteries: a useless dolt who's inexplicably snared a world-class beauty as his mate. Though he's disappointed to hear Isabella is out of town, I tell him, "But she'll be back in a couple of days," enjoying the sensation of stating this out loud to someone for the first time. And Dan says that for Isabella's honey, the job will be ready in fifteen minutes.

Isabella's honey decides to visit the bedding store next door. Inside the cluttered shop lies a bewildering variety, and it takes me almost fifteen minutes to settle on a set that might befit Isabella's homecoming. The beige is close to the color of one of her favorite sweaters. The woman behind the register is an East Indian of massive girth, attired in an old-fashioned blouse, jacket, and matching skirt that has to have been custom-tailored. She gives me a complicit smile after looking over my purchase. "Very nice. A nice color."

"You think?" I'm delighted, having been validated, given permission to be proud. "It's a gift for my wife."

"Oh," she says, drawing out the vowel long in a singsong way that doesn't sound at all upbeat. "Then you should reconsider. These are very low in the count. Here, you see? Not soft. Not very soft at all."

I'm led back to the wall-length display and given a crash course in thread counts. Fingering some of the highest-grade fabrics, I have to agree that there's no comparison, though the costs are astronomical.

"This one sheet," I note with a smile, "is a hundred and ninety dollars." The bedding woman looks at me with a pitying sadness. This man, her gaze says, so typical of those poor creatures, knows nothing of the finer things in life, nor of how to please a woman. What kind of a pathetic person would balk at treating his beloved to years of silken bedding pleasure? I picture how Isabella, who delights in things of quality and calls them "treats," would damn my low-budget sheet purchase with faint praise, adding this folly to her gathering pile of marital disappointments.

Purchase of 600-thread-count, top-of-the-line sheets—there is no one in Los Angeles who will sleep in higher-count luxury—maxes out the one credit card I've sworn never to max out. So what? Isabella is coming home.

Next door to the bedding store is a phone store. I remember Isabella enduring the perpetual unreliability of her old cell phone and needing a new one. I go inside, a heretic entering the house of technology.

Twenty minutes later, though I've been treated with the indulgent deference one might accord the mentally challenged, I have a cell-phone contract and a sleek silver sci-fi pod that I know my wife will like the looks of. Dan the Man has disappeared, replaced by an acne-ridden kid who looks like he's been left minding the copy counter for his absent mom. After much searching he locates my job on the shelf directly below him. The copies are not on three-hole paper. When the copy kid, after an indifferent apology, estimates a two-hour wait to have the job redone, I invoke the politically correct term that has replaced the act of clubbing a troublesome tradesman over the head with a blunt instrument. "This is unacceptable," I say, and ask to see the manager. Within ten minutes, I'm back on my bicycle, the draft freshly copied, safe in my bicycle basket and nestled between the expensive sheets and the boxed cell phone.

I have every cause to celebrate, to be relieved, fulfilled, and all of that crap. Instead I ride the bike as if there's a small black cloud attached to the handlebars, blocking out the sunshine that's making all my happier Venetian neighbors beam. I have every reason to be afloat with renewed hope and excited anticipation, etc., and instead my heart lies heavy on my stomach like a slowly sinking stone. I expect to see the bicycle tires flattening beneath me as I pedal.

The black cloud stays with me, an inflated pendant of malaise bobbing from my car antennae as I drive into town, headed for Rumer's. I seek to counter my unease, which keeps rising up, an inner tide of disquietude, with thoughts of this coming Sunday. Soon I'll have a real woman in my bed—a living, breathing, human animal, with all her delicious impurities. And then she'll be joined by the animal I love, sniffing and barking and dancing for biscotti in the kitchen, filling our home with his doggy, peanuts-like smell, snoring in the corner of the bedroom.

And here is my draft in its manila envelope lying beside me on the car seat, like a silent passenger, like a friend who knows too much about all we've gone through together to say a word about it. The stark L.A. sunshine pours through the windshield, giving the envelope a golden sheen. It will never look so good again, emanating the beauty of promise, of unlimited possibility. Maybe it isn't as smart as I think it is, my draft, maybe it'll only go so far, like so many other young hopefuls being chauffeured around this town. But I've done all that I can with it, and though it's been made over from toenails to hair color, there's still some integrity at its core, Dana's cynicism aside.

I give over to reverie, allowing myself the fantasy of a future life I've been denied for so long. Life after the movie is a go: Throw money around, garage this old Metro, and get the convertible Isabella's always coveted. A rash of meetings, new projects dangled before me, a whole new strata of socializing. Dinners with name directors. Before long, Isabella and I will be what I sometimes see on a sunny L.A. day when I'm stopped at a light: that couple in the shiny new convertible, hair blowing in the wind, dog sitting in the back, good music blasting from the CD player, her hand ruffling the hair at the back of his neck. But not the

obnoxious kind, with the Bluetooths at their ears, that air of arrogant entitlement; no, the quirkier, sweet and funny sort, the left-of-center writer
and his beautiful Italian wife—genuine, interesting people. The real thing.

Basking in the glow of this vision, I drive north into the Hollywood
Hills, until the black cloud at last floats away, evaporating into the blue,
blue sky.

Approaching the LAX on-ramp, I slow down, casting a wary eye on my
companion. Moony, riding shotgun, is nearly falling out his window, trying to soak up his last L.A. ultraviolet rays. "Good-bye, Hollywood!" he
calls, shaking his mane in the wind. "Hollywood is not responding. Typical!" He looks over at me as we turn the final curve into the airport
proper. "It's the next one here. Don't you want to get into that lane?"

I shake my head. "The white zone is for the immediate loading and
unloading of passengers," I intone. "I'm coming in with you."

"You're a prince," he says. "But what's with the tribute to Johnny
Cash?"

I glance down. I have on a black shirt over my black denims, my
boots are black, but it wasn't a conscious choice. "I'm in mourning for
my wife."

We enter the parking structure. Moony's really giving me a look
now. "Joke," I say. "Theatrical reference. You know, opening line, top of
The Seagull—"

"Sure, but you said *wife*."

"Huh?"

"The line is, 'I'm in mourning for my life.' You said *wife*."

"No, I didn't," I say.

Moony shakes his head. "When's she due in?"

"Tomorrow afternoon." Saying the words gives me a pleasurably
unsettled feeling. Inside the terminal moments later, standing by while
Moony gets his boarding pass, I look around in surprised relief. The air-

port is only an airport now, no longer a dark symbol of grief and trauma. Tomorrow I'll be here again to welcome Isabella, and then it'll be the scene of a bright new beginning. I glance down at my black-on-blacks. Though I've been trying to block it from my consciousness, I keep imagining Naomi's face, the look I'll see in her green, green eyes when I tell her to *go away.*

Here comes Moony, ticket in hand, sans cane but still limping, his multidirectional hair and that black-and-blue bruise on his cheek completing the image of a man going home from a battlefront. "Hey, you know what's weird? When I got here, we were both a couple of bachelors. Now we're both married men again."

"Funny how life is," I say.

"Hilarious," says Moony. "So have you done the deed yet? Dumped Naomi?"

I shift uncomfortably. "Tonight, I hope."

"She'll pack her imaginary things, and poof?"

"That's the idea," I say. "Poof."

"Closure, there's nothing like it," says Moony, reaching into his bomber jacket. He pulls out his silver flask and unscrews the top. "You know what we are, man?"

"Lucky?"

"We're samurai, Jordo. Warriors of love." He takes a brisk swig and holds out the flask. "Gotta finish this off before I go to the gate. C'mon, dog. Drink to us."

I take the flask. "To our survival," I say, and dutifully drink. The sake is cold, a little bitter, but good. Moony nods approval and pockets the flask again.

We slow near the back end of the twin lines of travelers headed for security. "So," I say. "What's the fate of your Mustang convertible?"

"Still in the shop, out in Twenty-nine Palms. After which Maura in Makeup's gonna take it off my hands, for a cool thou and the cost of repairs."

"Huh." Moony is more bruised and battered than when he arrived, but he's also a little more grounded. "You know," I say, "it's prob'ly a good thing you're going home."

"As in, stayin' out of mischief?"

"Might be a nice change of pace."

Moony shrugs. "Sometimes you gotta go pretty far out to find your way back in again." He gives me a crooked grin. " 'Course, you wouldn't know anything about that."

I smile. "Me? No."

We stand looking at each other for a moment. Then Moony cocks his head, listening to the voice over the loudspeakers. "Hey, that's my ride," he says.

I hold out my hand. Moony ignores it and moves in on me, enfolding me in a tight hug. This time I relax into it, but Moony's already letting me go. I give his shoulder an awkward squeeze as he steps back. "Man," Moony says. "Isabella leaves you alone for a few days, and you turn into a marshmallow."

"Tell the pilot to drive carefully," I say. "And then go fuck yourself."

Moony chuckles. "Later." He points a finger at me. "New Orleans! Gris-gris gumbo ya-ya, dog—next time, on the bayou!"

I know it's rhetorical, like the "Next year in the Holy Land!" salutation that's said at the end of a Passover seder, but I nod, and watch him limp off to the security line, shouldering his carry-on. Then I turn around and head for the exit.

In twenty-four hours, I'll be here and coupled once more, but for now I'm alone again, truly, which is exactly what I need to sort out my feelings, to get my bearings, if I have any left. I'm passing the phones as I think this, noticing a green scarf over auburn hair—a woman hanging up a phone who turns, her face lighting up with recognition as she catches sight of me. "Jordan?"

Naomi, in another one of her getups. I should have known. There's a lurch in my gut as I steel myself for what has to come, though I'm glad, in a way, that she's shown up now instead of later. "Hey," I say, forcing a smile.

"Hey, yourself," she says. She's grinning, seems unusually excited to see me, and much as I've tried to get used to her ever-alternating appearance, I'm a little thrown by the fresh tan bringing out freckles over the bridge of her nose, a lighter hair color, and her well-lived-in leather pilot's jacket. "Isn't this something!" she says.

I glance at the ebb and flow of travelers. "Crossroads of the world," I say.

"But what are you doing here?"

"Gave Moony a lift. He's gone back East," I tell her. I'm thinking that this is as good a time and place as any for the big good-bye, if we can find a quiet corner in one of the cafés upstairs. Might as well get it over with.

"So you're not flying off somewhere?" she asks.

"Not today," I say. "Listen, what do you say we go upstairs for a drink?"

Naomi laughs. *"Mais oui,"* she says. "That sounds delightful. You're sure you have the time?"

"Naomi," I say, and I can't keep a note of wistfulness out of my voice, "when have I not had the time for you?"

She bats me a look that could only be described as coquettish. "And here I was beginning to wonder if you really remembered who I was."

"Funny," I say, rueful. "As if I'll ever be able to forget."

"Why, Jordan," she says, eyes widening. "What has happened to you?"

"You should know," I say. "Look, let's just go upstairs and—"

"Mademoiselle." A European-looking man in a business suit is accosting us. "Is that your bag, by the telephone?"

"Oh, yes, I'm sorry, is it in your way?"

"No, but you ought to keep an eye on it."

"Yes, you're right. *Merci,*" she says, and he's already moving off with a kindly nod, just an international passenger doing his duty, as Naomi turns back to smile at me again, unaware of the affect this perfectly mundane exchange—a couple of human beings being human—has had on the man who witnessed it.

The jolt of adrenaline coursing through my body might as well be a bullet train that has me locked in its high beams, as I finally comprehend that I'm looking into the now-unmistakable eyes of my flesh-and-blood former student, Naomi Dussart.

5

Swivel

Stakes reach their highest point as the romantic relationship's importance jeopardizes the protagonist's chance to achieve his goal—or vice versa; the decision made by the protagonist at this turning point determines how the rest of the story goes.

*T*he real Naomi—and this is what I have to call her in my head, so as not to confuse this one sitting across from me in the airport Starbucks with the other Naomi I'm about to break up with—the real Naomi is in a state. Having been anxious about the safety of an overseas flight and irked by the many security hassles, she's exhausted, conflicted, wary of America, and already missing home. And now that she is here, Naomi says, "It's so strange, Los Angeles. I thought I would be used to it but it's not a place to be used to."

I nod. I'm still in shock, but my companion's obliviousness to my inner life is a great help. She has no idea that I'm only pretending to participate in her discussion of world politics; I'm actually fixated on the simple act of sitting at a public restaurant table with a flesh-and-blood Naomi who has littered the tablecloth with ham and cheese croissant crumbs and is licking them off her greasy fingertips. A woolly-haired bearded guy at the next table is pretending to look through his knapsack while staring at her, a phenomenon that's always annoyed me when I'm out with Isabella—the way some men openly salivate at the woman you're with, assuming they're in no danger of you threatening to punch out their lights—but that I now find obscurely heartening. *Go ahead, look at her, because she is* here.

The overpowering here-ness of the real Naomi is additionally welcome because it was wobbly for a minute there, when she first approached me by the telephones. Though the evidence before my eyes told me this couldn't be *My* Naomi—she was too normal, too voluble, too thickly-accented French to pass for an ethereal being—it still took me a minute to wholly believe it. Only when she noted that she'd never seen me in a shirt other than my standard classroom powder-blue button-down and I recognized her coy, slightly leftward-tilting smile from class did I finally accept that she was who she appeared to be. And now, as she leans across our table to reach for a sugar packet, I can't help examining her cleavage, wondering whether I got the location of that freckle right, after all.

"To be here now," she's saying, with a roll of her eyes, "back in this country, where they changed for a while the name of 'French fries' . . ."

"I can imagine." I notice downy fuzz on the line of her jaw. This is news.

"With my project, I could have done everything over the Internet, I suppose, but I knew that I did have to come in person if I really wanted to make some progress."

I nod. "We do have the best post-production facilities."

"Post-production?" Her charming brow is furrowed.

"For your final cut."

"Mais non," Naomi says. "It's just a screenplay."

"Oh, right," I say quickly. "I was thinking . . . of your other film." She still looks confused. "The one you were working on . . . ?"

"Oh, in your class. No, we never got the financing. This one is written to be shot here, and for less. I meet tomorrow with a producer who is interested, it is why I'm here."

I nod again, flustered to realize that she said as much before, but I was too busy comparing the color of her hair to that of My Naomi to retain it.

"And what is completely devastating," Naomi goes on, indicating the public phones she's abandoned after three useless attempts to reach

Marie, her girlfriend who has the keys to the apartment where she's supposed to stay, "is that for now, at least, I have no place to go."

From the depths of what formerly untapped idiocy has my generous offer arisen, to give Naomi a lift into town? If I was smart, with one wife en route and one phantom lover still at large, I'd have already left her to her own devices. But who said I was smart?

I only know that the gods are messing with me, fucking me over good and proper. At this crucial juncture they have materialized not some random temptress, but *her,* the one her who can truly commandeer calamity. And these same perverse gods clearly know me well enough to have predicted that I would not, like a man who has a brain, run for the terminal exit and keep running. No, sure enough, I have welcomed this woman into my life, I am unlocking the door to my Nash Metropolitan for her in the LAX parking lot, and now I am really in for it.

I don't want to go into the details of my personal life with the real Naomi. I'm certainly not about to tell her about my need to end my unearthly affair with another version of her. But when she asks after Isabella, I have to provide an explanation for my wife's being out of town. Discombobulated by the presence of a real Naomi right beside me in the front seat, I do my best to sketch in the bold before-and-after strokes of my story, conscious of my need to leave out its all-important middle: I used *you,* Naomi—you're the reason my wife is coming back.

My unwitting accomplice is happy for me. "So all is forgiven," she says. "And this is wonderful. Not everyone would be so understanding."

Yes, I'm being understanding about Isabella leaving me and being unfaithful, and Isabella is being understanding about my having an affair that I only theoretically had. "Well," I say, "I guess that's what happens when it's real love."

"Real love," Naomi repeats. "I've heard of such a thing, I guess."

I glance over at my companion. She has one hand held outside her window, dipping and rising in the freeway wind. Fresh off an eleven-hour international flight, she looks, if anything, more spectacular than I remembered or fantasized. I force my eyes back to the road. "So, what, you've never been in a serious, a long-term relationship?"

"Long term, this is for parking, in America," she says. "Maybe you could say I'm a short-term parker. Oh, this song!"

She leans over to turn up the radio. So the real Naomi loves U2, I learn, while My Naomi thinks they suck.

It's barely five in the afternoon, but I'm declaring cocktail hour. Having deposited Naomi Dussart on the Promenade in Santa Monica, walking distance from the place where, she assured me, her friend is bound to show up soon, I head into Joe's for a much-needed head-cleaning, alone.

I'm almost paranoid enough to think that My Naomi, somehow prescient as well as all-powerful, has sent the real Naomi to muck up my life as a preemptive act of revenge for my imminent breaking up with her. But it's as antidote for such unhinged thought that God invented alcohol. And here's that kindly waitress, starting her shift with a friendly smile for me, tactful enough not to inquire after Isabella this time, and Hector the bartender with his excellent pouring hand, the bar not yet crowded this early in the evening. So I'm able to relish the delicious sensation, with the first icy swig of vodka boring a jolly Cossack's bridle path down my gullet, that I've removed myself from harm's way. It's on the second sip that things go south, as I glance through the doorway into the dining room and catch sight of a familiar figure seated at a little table for two in the corner, looking my way with an expectant air.

I take the drink with me to join My Naomi. It can only be her, since the real Naomi Dussart lacks this one's ability to whimsically transcend earthly boundaries of time and space. The lights are thankfully low in here. It's time for me to do the dreaded right thing, and it seems only appropriate that I should perform this crime under the cover of near-darkness.

Naomi's elegant in a black suit jacket and skirt, royal blue blouse, knee-high leather boots. She has a beaded handbag with her, and wears a chic black hat pulled rakishly over one eye. She looks like she's just alighted from Lubitsch's limousine, lit from within, possessing a preternatural glow that makes the real Naomi Dussart's beauty fade from my memory. I both do and don't want to prolong this moment, and uneasily finger the menu the waiter has left for me.

"Jordan," says Naomi, an eyebrow arching under the rim of her hat. "I can't describe this in a way that'll make sense to you, but your aura's reading radioactive."

For a moment, I wonder what I do look like to Naomi—one of those plastic see-through "Visible Man" models, with organs both physical and metaphysical exposed? So much for the light conversation and fumbling preambles I didn't want to have, anyway. I drink for fortitude, put the glass down firmly. "All right," I say. "Listen . . . This may seem kind of sudden. And strange, considering all we've been through. It's not easy, and I wouldn't even be doing this if I didn't have to, but I'm . . ." I shift in my seat. "I think it's time to . . . well—move on."

She cocks her head. "Move on?"

"I'm sure you know how much you mean to me, Naomi. But you also know how much my marriage means, and now—"

"Jordan . . ." Her smile is incredulous. "Are you trying to get rid of me?"

I clear my throat. "That's a cold way of putting it, but . . . Listen, the truth is . . ." The truth is I don't really want to be doing this at all. In truth, bad selfish human that I am, I'm already feeling uneasy about the work that may lie ahead of me—I'd like nothing more than to have my muse on tap, but . . . "Isabella has decided to come back," I announce reluctantly, "and . . ." She's laughing, a hand to her mouth. "What?"

"I'm sorry, it's just . . ." She shakes her head helplessly. "You really are the most stubborn, blockheaded human."

"Maybe so," I say. "But the point is, my wife—"

"You think this is about *her*?"

"Of course it is!" I say, exasperated. Some people have been seated at a nearby table, and a little boy in dress-up trousers and button-down shirt stands on a chair, staring at me, his indifferent mother caught up in conversation with friends. He has the curious gaze of one skeptically studying adulthood, and I don't blame him. I shift my own chair so that I can keep my back to him, down some more vodka, then speak more quietly. "I know we've gotten close, I never could have imagined how close, but the truth is, when I brought you here in the first place—"

"You're unbelievable," she says, and leans forward. "Honestly, Jordan. Aren't you astonished by what you've conjured?"

"Well, sure," I say, "but—"

Naomi draws herself up. "Am I not beautiful? Hasn't our time together been fruitful for you?"

"You are!" I say quickly. "And it has, and I'm . . . amazed, which is what makes this all the more difficult—"

"You're confused," she says gently. "I can see that, but we'll work through it." She smiles encouragingly. "The seeds have been planted. It's only a matter of time."

"I don't have any time," I say. "And you've been incredibly helpful, and supportive, and the last thing I want to do is to hurt your feelings, but . . ." I wince as I come out with it. "You really do have to go."

"Nonsense," says Naomi.

I open my mouth, shut it. She is a portrait of tranquillity. "No, really," I say. "I mean it. This is over, Naomi, because—"

"Not at all," she says. "You think I'll just disappear? Because you say so?"

"Well, *yes.*"

"Why?"

"Because I'm the one who made you appear in the first place!" The new arrivals are staring at me. I lower my voice, lean in closer to Naomi. "Look, I know why you came, and what you're doing here—"

"Do you?"

"Yes. You're a fabulous, inspiring creature, and it tears me up to have to push you away, but . . ."

She's studying me. Or looking through me. "Maybe it *would* be best," she murmurs thoughtfully. "Maybe being on your own might help."

"Yes!" I say.

"Yes," she echoes, nodding. "Some time to learn what you need to know."

"Sure," I say. "A learning experience. That's a way to look at it."

"And then we can begin the work in earnest."

"No," I say.

"No?"

"Naomi . . ." I rub my fingers at my now-throbbing temples. "We've always understood each other so well. And I'm sure we're going to *get* to an understanding, if you'd be willing to listen to me for a minute . . ."

She shakes her head again. "Jordan," she says. "I'm not just . . . yours. I also answer to so much more than you. As do *you*." She pats my hand. "We've barely begun. We've got so much further to go together . . ."

Maybe she's right. Why couldn't I live with Isabella and still have Naomi in my life? Say my wife wants to stay at home, holed up in her studio, painting, leaving me at odds. I could meet Naomi, get my creative fires stoked, then come home in time for a Prosecco with Isabella. Not that she'd ever agree to such an arrangement, which would mean more lying, more betrayal—

I have to do the toughen-up. I tell Naomi, "No, that's the point: I really, really have to be on my own now. That's what I want. It's what I need."

"As if you know," Naomi mutters, exasperated.

"I *do* know."

Naomi's eyes blaze green fire. "You know nothing," she whispers, and then she flares—like the bright negative afterimage in the wake of a camera's flash—and is gone.

The chair opposite me is empty. There is the table setting, undisturbed, the untouched water glass. Startled, I sit rooted in disbelief. Just like that? The sudden absence of her spreads across the table like spilled wine, seeping under my seat, and the emptiness chills me, undermining any sense of relief. I remind myself that this is what I had to do.

The waiter's back. I tell him I'm not eating after all, press too much cash for the drink into his hand, and get up, wobbly on my feet. The depth of what I've just given up weighs upon me as I walk across the room. I feel more like an acolyte expelled from his monastery than a man who's parted ways with a mistress.

I turn in the entranceway and look back. The place is filling up rapidly, people eating, talking, laughing. Nobody glances at the place I've vacated. But for an instant, I imagine that I am being watched—by the spirit-guides, the angels, the phantom doppelgängers hovering by all of the people in the room, their presences gleaming more luminously than their material companions as they shift their curious glances from Naomi's empty chair to stare accusingly at me.

I turn and quickly walk away, seeing nothing until I'm outside in the too-beautiful light of a coming sunset, where bored valets gaze past me as I hurry on, as if I'm not really there.

It's good to walk, though. And with every step—it's craven to think this, I know, but it's the truth—I'm feeling lighter. Yes, I'm shaken, I'm sad, but I can't deny that relief is the larger emotion flooding through my body. I'm back in the realm of the known and credible, instead of the un- and in-. I've made the necessary sacrifice that Isabella asked of me, I've cleared the way for what's to come. And by the time I reach the gate to my place, I've almost convinced myself that I'm on the proper path at last.

Then right inside my garden I stop short, heart hammering, and I open my mouth to protest the sight of Naomi, evidently even more stubborn than she said I am, standing in front of my door, when I realize it's not Naomi. It's not *My* Naomi, that is, but the real one, her roll-on baggage by her feet and a sweetly apologetic look on her tanned face.

"I'm sorry," she says. "But still there is no answer from Marie. I get bored and I wanted to go to the beach, so I took a taxi"—alarmed as I am, I'm nonetheless charmed by her accenting the second syllable in *taxi*—"and I thought, maybe if he is home, I could perhaps leave my things here . . . Or," she continues, with a bewitching smile, "perhaps, if you're not so busy, you would like to come with me to see the California sunset."

Peace, tranquillity, restful solitude would have been nice. Instead, here is the real Naomi, not quite the companion I would've chosen to take the edge off my having just broken up with the imaginary version of her. Nonetheless, she gives a frisson of new meaning to the word *distraction*. With that unerring feminine instinct for ferreting out whatever it is that a man doesn't want to talk about, she returns to the topic of men and women and the meaning of their relationships, as the sun begins its fiery descent. Love and the meaning of it refuses to leave our conversation, and the sky outdoes itself now, throwing in colors that rarely exist in nature as we walk barefoot in the hard damp sand a few yards from the water's edge.

"So real love means fidelity, I suppose," she says. "You were faithful throughout your marriage?" I nod. "And when she left . . . ?"

"I'm not saying I never looked at another woman," I say, thinking: It wasn't the real you I was with, so technically, I wasn't unfaithful, and besides, I never stopped loving Isabella—

"You looked but you didn't touch," Naomi says. "And this is virtue."

"Virtue, I dunno." A lone fat seagull scurries across our path, fixing me briefly in his stern black gaze before turning his back on the two of us and flapping skyward. "I'm just saying, you keep the faith, if you're with the right partner . . ."

"A soul mate," says Naomi, in the tone one might use when speaking of unicorns. "Still, there's human nature. And humans aren't necessarily monogamous."

"Maybe not," I say, "but if you're truly in love, you make a choice," I insist. "Once you know what's really important—"

"Which is?"

"Trust, for one thing. Honesty . . ."

"So real love means you're honest with each other," she says. "And what about being honest with yourself?"

She can't possibly know the extent of my multiple duplicities, and I try not to squirm. "I'm as honest as I'm able to be," I tell her.

"Admirable," she says, smiling at me, glowing an incandescent pink, the wind lifting and caressing her soft hair. Her back is to the setting sun, the tide's white foam pooling round her ankles, and all that's missing is the halo of a giant seashell to complete her transformation into Venus, newly risen from the sea.

"To me," she says, "it always seems we take turns. First I'm the one who leaves, the one who loves less. And then I am left, I am the one who loves more. There never is a perfect balance, don't you think?"

I consider. It's true that in my last relationship before Isabella, I was the dumper, not the dumpee. And after Isabella broke my heart, aren't I the one who just broke things off with My Naomi?

"I don't think," the real Naomi continues, "there is any absolute in love. Maybe love is only something we pass back and forth between us, and its shape is always changing." Another wave breaks behind her, the tide rushing up to splash the backs of her calves and then withdrawing. "Like that!" she calls over the noisy surf, and gestures at the whole of the ocean. "It's never the same, and nobody can own it."

The rolled cuffs of her jeans are dark with salt water. The swath of bare belly between her belt and her blouse gleams in the orange light. But Isabella, I tell myself, Isabella's coming back.

I incant this phrase later, like a mantra, when she leans close, steadying herself with a hand on my shoulder so she can put on her sandals, and

I catch the scent of her hair, her perfume, the fragrance formed of her sweat and the sea: *Isabella's coming back.*

We order wine at an outdoor café on the boardwalk and watch the sky slowly purple in the sun's wake. And maybe it's the calming effect of alcohol as the night comes on, but at last, when she begins to talk about her writing, I feel that my incantations have won out. Looking at the real Naomi across the table, I see once more how young she is. The imaginary Naomi didn't smoke, but waiting for our entrées, the real one lights up a sickly sweet-smelling clove cigarette, the kind I hate. As she talks on, waving it for emphasis, I inch my chair back a bit, and the distance that once lay between us falls back into place. I begin to relax, an old complacency returning. I am merely an avuncular mentor, the friendly teacher doing a former student a favor.

This false security lasts all of ten minutes, until I'm blindsided by her coming at me again with the thing I had forgotten.

"I always wondered, you know. About that last night of class." She keeps her eyes on the cigarette she's stubbing out in the ashtray, and I detect a little flush in her cheeks. "I was surprised you didn't ask me out for a drink, for a cup of coffee." Naomi looks up, smiling. "Was I so unattractive?"

"Oh, yeah. Horribly unattractive." I'm still feeling comfortable enough to tease her, and am rewarded with a full-throated laugh, the flash of her white and cutely crooked teeth. "Especially with that scarf."

"My green Hermès scarf," she says. "I thought you might like it."

"It was very effective," I allow. "But . . ." She raises an eyebrow, waiting. "You knew I was married."

"Certainly," she says. "But to go for a drink . . ."

The waiter chooses this moment to bring us her cappuccino, my espresso. In the silence that's suddenly awkward, I comprehend, stomach tightening, what now lies beneath the banter. And my interrogator presses on from this advantage, as soon as the waiter's gone. "You knew I was attracted to you," she says. "So what, you didn't want to give me . . . any encouragement?"

That was only the half of it, and I know she knows this. "I suppose."

"But I'm a big girl," says Naomi. "And you were—are—a married man." She shrugs. "Where would there be the harm?"

Her eyes are alight with archly feigned innocence. I can feel the cold teeth of the trap at my toes. "All right," I say. "I was being a little over-protective. Of myself."

"Ah. You didn't want to face any temptation. To test the limits of your faith."

"My faith," I echo.

"In love, in honesty, fidelity, in all those things you prize so highly. The things you talked to us about in class—the 'foundations of the suc-cessful relationship, be it in romantic comedy or drama.' Do I have that right?"

"You obviously took good notes."

"You thought I might try to seduce you?"

My espresso cup is trembling slightly in my hand, and I put it down. "No," I admit, "I'm not that vain."

"I didn't think so," she says. "So then?"

"Look," I say. "Nothing would've happened, so maybe it was silly of me, but . . ."

"*Mais non,* even to flirt a little, this is such a sin?"

I force a chuckle. "No, but a flirtation can be frustrating."

"Ummm," she muses. "But frustration is only truly painful when a strong desire is being suppressed."

I want to lean across the table and gently wipe that little line of cap-puccino foam from her upper lip with my finger. I want to slap it off with the flat of my hand. Both urges are equally strong, but instead I watch, with a kind of dread fascination, as the tip of her tongue flicks upward to lick her lip clean. *If you want to be as unfaithful as Isabella has been . . .*

I don't, though. "Yes, I'm a man, and men are hardwired to be hound dogs. But I love my wife," I tell her. "And when you believe in the vows you've taken, you don't break the contract."

"Even after all that's happened?" asks Naomi.

"Even now."

Naomi nods slowly, impressed. "That's how much you love her."

"Yes," I say. "I love her that much."

There. Amazingly, she is silenced, I can sense her retreat, feel her pull back her many forces from the front, and something like a state of grace envelops me. Just as the floodwaters rose, I called up a bridge that could lift me to higher ground, made of simple words, a truth: I love someone that much.

Another call to Marie, and still no answer. Naomi Dussart has no place to stay tonight. Feeling invincible after our conversation, I do the gentlemanly, gallant thing, and offer her the use of my couch. Naomi gratefully accepts.

The wind is colder at night, and her jet lag is kicking in as we walk back, talking fitfully of other things. Once inside my apartment, there is a swift and logical progression. I find clean bedding for her in the closet, and when she meets my obligatory offer of a nightcap with a loud, pro-longed yawn, we laugh, make quick good nights, and retire to our respec-tive sides of the living-room door.

Sanctuary! I've pulled it off, incredibly, and done the right thing. Well, it's a testament, really, to the power of love. I'm suddenly exhausted from this long, long day, the day of two Naomis, and though I'm acutely con-scious of this Naomi's movements, just audible through the walls, I hope that a little reading will have me nodding out in a matter of minutes. If I really can sleep. Sitting on the edge of my bed, I'm struck anew by the bizarreness of having Naomi as a houseguest. My Naomi, gone only mere hours ago, shifted in appearance from one encounter to the next, but how many times tonight have I been jarred by how different the real Naomi looks from my memory's reconstruction? It feels even stranger to be in such close proximity but so distanced—so nothing like the relationship I've been in, that it's as if both of us are pretending to be other people.

The sound of faucets tells me Naomi is in the bathroom between us. I get into my pajamas, wait until I hear her exit, then wait an extra minute before going in to brush my teeth.

When I open the bedroom door, the door to the living room is open as well, and just beyond it, Naomi stands by the sheet-covered couch, facing me, naked but for the pillow she instinctively clutches to her chest. I'm struck dumb as she stares back at me for a suspended moment. And then she puts the pillow down.

Pale light spilling from the bedroom behind me outlines the curve of one bare hip, the perfect oval of one full, firm breast. From the depths of my own shadow comes a husky murmur. "Jordan?" she asks. "How much is 'that much,' really?"

I've never believed in teleportation, but this is how it happens: One moment I'm standing a crucial couple of yards away from Naomi Dussart, and in the next, I'm holding her pliant perfumed nudity in my arms. Her heat, her smell, the wet hungry force of her lips flattening mine is so overwhelming that I'm truly mindless, like a man suddenly pushed, still clothed, into a bubbling Jacuzzi of sensuality. I need to breathe but have forgotten how. Then the feel of her nails raking the soft hair at the small of my back as she slides her hand under the elastic of my pajama bottoms jerks me up and out of this dizzying kiss and I'm looking down at her again, tilted, trembling, all too aware of her breasts pressed against me and the pained straining of—what do they call it in those romance novels?— my *hardness,* tent-poling my pajamas.

Naomi grins, her slightly crooked teeth a wicked gleam in the dim light as her other hand plays at the back of my head, fingers capturing and twisting my hair. I'm understanding in this instant how the Salem witch trials came about, comprehending the derivation of the term *unmanned,* while between my legs, that thing with its own mind is seeking—again, the Harlequin phrases I found in rom-com research blaze across my brain in lavender neon absurdity—*his hardness sought the liquid core of her*—

Ironically, it's this that saves me, the image of His Hardness. I'm picturing a little guy with a crown on his head *(Good morning, Your Hardness!*

Will His Hardness be taking a bath today?), and it's just enough to combat the spell. I actually push Naomi's shoulders away from me, taking a step back (don't look down, a closer angle on the Valley of the Freckle and I'm over the cliff edge for sure) and remembering, yes, that's how much I love my wonderful, coming-back-to-me Isabella, so much that I can even withstand this.

It's also true that as she withdraws her arms to face me in bemused defiance, a hand on each exquisite hip, I'm beholding the carnal, the mortal Naomi, who lacks the more ineffable wiles of My Naomi. Her charms are still considerable—so much so that I have to fasten my gaze on her forehead, avoiding her amused look as I mutter apologetic inanities about what can't be and what won't happen—but she isn't otherworldly, after all.

Nonetheless: Inside the bedroom, I wedge a chair back under the doorknob of my resolutely bolted door.

In the morning, up early to use the bathroom, I put my ear to the door, and hearing no activity in the other room, quietly remove the chair. Like a thief breaking into my own apartment, I slide the lock open with exaggerated care and tiptoe down the short corridor. Half-asleep, I give a start when I see the figure moving toward me in the picture glass on the wall. I know it's only my own reflection but it scares the hell out of me, all the same.

I allow myself a quick glance at the scarier reality lying beyond the doorway: There's the dark oval of Naomi Dussart's head, tendrils of wavy hair fanning out on her pillow. Then I slip into the bathroom, gently pull its door shut, and turn to contemplate the toilet. After a brief woozy debate I decide, as I'm already well within the realm of the ridiculous, to pee sitting down since it's less noisy. I don't even flush, but pull the lid over this breach of hygienic decorum, and when I run water in the sink to wash up, I take great pains—damn, but the hot-water handle squeaks—to allow only the softest trickle.

Hands dried, I ease the door open, and purposefully avoiding even a peripheral glance in the direction of the living room, hurriedly pad back to the safety of my room. Shut the door with a satisfyingly quiet click and feel my way to the bed in the shadows, slide under the covers, and nearly leap out of my skin as a pale form rises beside me.

"Bonjour," says Naomi Dussart, pouting prettily as I rear back against the wall, heart gone jackhammer crazy.

The collision of syllables in my mouth yields something like a "Bwah?!" sound as she sits up. Relieved to see she's at least put on a skimpy nightgown, I try again. "What are you doing?"

"It's not as if I am going to bite you," she says, smiling, "though I really would like to know what you taste like. But that couch, *mon Dieu!* I have such a . . . what is it you say, crack, right here . . ." With a pained expression, she stretches back her shoulders, kneading at the side of her neck with one hand.

I recognize this cue from decades of French farce but I shake my head, trying to free myself from the tangle of sheets and clamber out of this bed, telling her instead, "Hey, I'll be happy to take the couch," except that Naomi has already shifted her weight to trap one of my legs beneath hers and is laughing—laughing at me, sadist that she is.

"Oh, Jordan," she says, *"tais-toi!* Just stop. I am not going to take your bed away from you and put you on that couch."

"I like my couch," I insist, trying to ease myself out from under her.

"Liar," she says. "Stop wriggling like an eel, please, just lie back and forget about me, because I am going to sleep, and I will sleep much better here in this warm, soft bed, *d'accord?* Relax."

Right. I sigh. I nod. I'll give this a few minutes until she really is asleep again, and then escape into the other room. I shift my weight to warily lie at an angle shifted away from her, and Naomi at last slides her leg from over mine and turns as if to lie with her back to my back, then pauses, looking over her shoulder. "Why is it that you must always be so serious with me?" she murmurs.

"I'm not always."

"You are." She pokes my side with her forefinger.

"I am not."

She pokes me again. *"Oui, monsieur."*

And before I can open my mouth for another protest, she's pounced, both hands at my sides, tickling me. There's a brief paroxysm of hysteria, me twisting, she laughing, me laughing in spite of myself while determined to push her away—away from my writhing body with that supple flesh—until suddenly we're suspended, breathing heavily, my hands gripping her shoulder and forearm, and she glances down at my lap and giggles. For His Hardness has graced us with his presence, he's threatening to burst through my pajama fly in all his royal-rosy glory.

And now the phone rings on the bedside table. No one should be calling at this early hour. As I'm staring at the phone in startled perplexity Naomi pulls at the belt of my pajama pants with a mischievous grin. I arrest her hand and snatch up the receiver. "Hello?"

"Ciao, amore. It's me."

In this first moment of shock, the guilt of hearing my wife's voice so loud in my ear is outweighed by the relieving knowledge that she's thousands of miles away. *"Ciao,"* I manage, heart banging in my chest. Naomi is pulling at my pajama bottoms, trying to slide them down, and as I swat at her hands again, I'm so perilously distracted that at first I don't understand what Isabella is telling me. But then, as I grab hold of Naomi's wrists, I have the sensation, one I've only read about and never believed to be possible, of all the blood in my body running cold.

"I'm in the international terminal," Isabella says. "I'm just waiting for my bags."

It's as ridiculous a notion as the earth deciding to change the direction of its rotation, but due to the vagaries of Alitalia, she got herself onto an alternate connecting flight, and for once in her life, Isabella is early. She's calling me from LAX.

Because one cannot will a woman to leave a house faster than she feels like leaving (a rule of gender I long ago learned the hard way), I have to leave Naomi to get dressed and gather her belongings, with directions that'll send her on foot to the Rose Café, from where she'll try her friend again, or if all else fails, call a cab that will get her to a hotel. She's a good sport about it, and amused by my barely contained hysteria, assures me that it will be no imposition to change the bedding. I only have time for a two-minute shower and I scrub madly with a bar of soap, leaving myself red-skinned, and gargle enough mouthwash to nearly gag. But if anything, as I wait for the light to change on Lincoln, nervously sniffing at my armpits, I'm only suspiciously clean-smelling.

I drive. Sunday morning, blissfully traffic-free, so not much time to berate myself for getting into such a mess. I'm amazed at the disaster I've just dodged, and oddly guilt-stricken. Why? If I had succumbed, I'd have only been doing what I've already been tried and convicted for doing. After all, my wife has done the same. No blame! Then how to account for the lingering uneasiness, the queasy guilt that set in even before Isabella's phone call this morning? Now it hits me: It wasn't my wife I was nearly betraying first and foremost. It would have been the other woman: *My* Naomi.

Madness. She's gone. As for me, I'm rounding the curve to the long straightaway parallel to the airline runways. A Virgin 747 looms large over my lane, looking like it's about to land on the hood of my car. I try to empty my mind of all but what lies directly ahead. Isabella has come home (Isabella, a whirling blaze of color at the stove, smiling at me through the stream of fresh-cooked pasta) and this, I tell myself, is the only thing that matters.

Knowing Isabella, I expect complications at the terminal. She changed planes and went through customs in New York and has promised to meet me curbside, outside the baggage claim. Who knows what unforeseen drama might have unfolded? But amazingly, when I pull up before the crosswalk, there she is, a figure simultaneously familiar and not: Isabella, in a salmon-pink dress, thick-heeled shoes, her white Spanish shawl draped round her shoulders, a new, oversized bag dangling from one hand, hand-rolled cigarette in the other. She gives me a wave and a smile as I turn off the engine.

I climb out, struck by the look of her, a beautiful woman, curls of dark hair framing her lovely face, those soulful brown eyes, the soft, pale skin. She stomps out her cigarette as she hurries toward me, the two suitcases abandoned as I step up to meet her, and then her arms are flung round me, her lips nestled into the hollow of my neck. We cling to each other. I inhale her aroma, the feel of her fit against my body. She lifts her face to look at me, running her hands through my hair. I stare into her eyes, searching for what I know in them, searching for our past, for the loving look I need to see again. We both smile, realizing we're mirroring each other, and she brings her lips to mine.

The kiss reveals everything and nothing. I taste her, feel the rush and throb of my wanting to feel, but don't know what my emotions really are. The kiss is a question, and I press on into it, seeking an answer, but even as my tongue meets hers for an instant, she's pulling away. I see in her eyes some of my own confusion, though she's smiling, and I understand that we're in this ambiguous beginning together, sense that it's too soon to know more than that we're meeting. *"Ciao,"* she says.

"Ciao," I reply.

"Oh, but you wouldn't have believed it, the two of them," Isabella says. "This little blind girl and her brother—maybe seven, eight years old, but he was perfect, Jordan, perfect! Unwrapping the salad, putting on the salad dressing for her. The father slept, the brother, he did everything, and with a kindness . . . *Madonna,* your heart would break! She, the girl, with this patient smile . . ." Isabella shakes her head, picks a fleck of tobacco from her lip. "I was crying, just to look at them. All the things we take for granted . . . when this is what's important, eh? This is love, is what I thought."

I nod, eyes on the road. While Isabella smokes and talks beside me, her pile of bags creating a new cityscape in my rearview mirror, I pray that Naomi has done as she was told, noting that on this morning of all mornings, when with each turn of the wheel I yearn for time to slow down, there is no such thing as traffic in Los Angeles. No matter how I wish for a front tire to blow, hope for perhaps a hail of frogs, we sail over unclogged streets in record time to reach our soon-to-be-happy-again home.

"The weather is good, of course, still a little hot," she comments. "I was thinking to go to the beach, but I'm exhaust. I mean, exhausted!" She leans back in her seat, eyes closed. Maybe she's too jet-lagged to be in her usual near-psychic state of alertness, and my level of stress will seem only natural, given her surprise early arrival. Still, my shirt is soaked through with sweat as we pull up at our destination. TV parking awaits us: a perfect spot right in front of our gate. I peer at the door beyond it, closed, and see the window blinds drawn.

I get busy with unloading the suitcases, hoist one and roll the other through the gate while Isabella inspects the garden, checking to see that things are growing as well as they're supposed to with winter coming on. "You haven't been feeding them enough, my girls!" she cries, examining the potted lemon trees by the front door. I take a deep breath and unlock it. Stifle an impulse to call, "Hello?" I can sense the place is empty, though. I scan the living room, carrying in the bags. All looks as it should.

"You've kept it clean," she notes. "Still the neat guy." She's looking the living room over with the focused intensity of an NYPD detective. I tell myself that it's only because she's the mistress of a house, returning to it after a long absence. Naomi has done a good job. When I peek through the bedroom doorway, I see that the bed has been carefully remade with the new sheets I practically threw at her in my dash to the airport.

"Where does this come from?" Isabella is holding up the coffee coaster from my desktop, a kitsch painted photo of a Hawaiian hula dancer.

"I found it in a store on Main Street."

"Cute," she says, continuing her tour of the desk and its environs. It's hopeless. She will find me out, no matter how I, Naomi, or her own disorientation might conspire to save me. I can only hope that my inevitable fate will befall me simply and soon. Nonetheless, when I spy the glint of shiny metal on the end table by the couch, I move to shield it from Isabella's view. As she walks into the kitchen, I grab the thin silver bracelet that Naomi evidently removed from her wrist before bedtime and then forgot. I slip it deep into my pocket, adrenaline draining, and feel a surge of smug jubilation. Then the sound of a hand knocking on the garden gate kicks my heart rate back into overdrive.

I'm across the room so quickly that I nearly take a header over Isabella's larger suitcase, but manage to dance nimbly over it to the door, my wife looking on curiously as I bound down the front steps. It makes no sense for Naomi to be returning, unless she's more determinedly perverse than she appears—*wicked* is the word that comes to mind—but when I open the gate I'm looking, to my immense relief, at a complete stranger. She's a short blond woman with an angular face and shrewd small eyes, dressed in designer overalls, her hair up in a tight French flip, and she smiles at me as though my air of high anxiety is entirely expected. "Hi," she says brightly.

"Hi?" I'm aware that Isabella is peering through the screen door behind me. A stranger asking for directions? Someone with the wrong address?

"I'm Marie," she says, expecting but seeing no light of recognition dawn on my face.

"Yes?"

Marie leans in a bit closer. "Naomi's friend," she says quietly.

I stare at her, mute as my mind struggles with this anomaly. Naomi's friend is Suzanne, whom she called from the screening—no, that was the friend based on Albert Pistler. The real Naomi's friend is indeed named Marie. But the idea of another person acknowledging Naomi's existence—even though she does exist now—is so strange in this moment that I feel I've slipped into a dream. Behind me in the apartment, the phone rings. I turn around, panicked, fearing that, this being a dream, it might *be* Naomi on the phone. Isabella is already retreating from the doorway. "I'll get it," she calls.

I stare after her, heart thudding dully in my chest, Marie waiting patiently close by. "I'm sorry," I mutter to her, straining to hear the conversation within. Marie smiles. I hear Isabella's voice rise happily. She's speaking Italian, it's someone she knows.

"We're over at the Rose Café," Marie informs me. From the tacit complicity in her voice, I understand that she understands the situation. How much *does* she know? No matter. The music I've been subliminally aware of, some guttural rap music, is coming from the radio in the BMW convertible parked at the curb behind Marie, engine running.

"Oh," I say. Isabella has returned to the door and is gazing out at the two of us while she talks on the phone.

"She was wondering if you might have found something that belongs to her?" Marie's careful wording gives me the impression that she not only knows what's going on, she's enjoying her role. In Marie's movie, a light comedy-caper pic, she's the leading lady doing a best friend's naughty detective work.

"Oh!" I repeat, and dig my hand into my pocket, then stop. Isabella's speaking English now, something about her portfolio, but I'm sure she's watching me, so I can't possibly hand the bracelet over to Marie, just like that. What was it doing in my pocket? This is only the first of many questions my wife will naturally ask, and it could be even worse to pretend that I didn't snatch it off the couch this very morning, as if I've been carrying it around with me like some romantic keepsake.

"Huh," I say. I could make a show of going inside to look for the bracelet, and retrieve it from the place I supposedly stored it in readiness for such a pickup, but this is a dangerous proposition with Isabella close at hand. Stuck, I force what must be the smile of a fool onto my face, and venture, "Yes, I think I saw it somewhere in the house . . ." I gesture vaguely in the direction of the bungalow, Isabella at the door. "But . . ." I pause, helpless.

Marie is not the star of her espionage adventure for nothing. "You're busy right now," she says.

"Actually, yeah," I say. "Maybe . . ."

"Maybe some other time," offers Marie. "That's cool." Nodding, she backs away from the gate, hands slipping into her own pockets. I peer after her, rooted in the doorway, my elbow holding the gate open, as Marie turns round suddenly and steps back to me again, hand extended. "Thanks anyway," she says. "Nice to meet you."

"Right," I say. "Likewise." Taking her hand, I feel the hard edges of something in her palm, now in mine. A business card. Brilliant. I'm marveling at her technique as she turns back again, returning to her bass-pumping convertible. She's a natural. As if to acknowledge this, she gives me a little wave before opening her car door and disappearing within.

I'm able to slip the card into my pocket as I turn back to Isabella, shutting the gate behind me. She smiles, giving a roll of the eyes to signal some difficulty in getting off the phone. I smile back as I shuffle up the steps and join her inside. She hangs up, faces me. "Who was that?"

I look stupidly toward the door, as if I've already forgotten the encounter. "Some tourist, lost in Venice," I say. "Looking for Rialto."

She frowns, and I half-expect her to tell me to come up with a better one. Then she says, "Rialto, that's not here, that's by the post office."

"That's what I told them," I say, adding eagerly, "Should I put on some tea?"

"*Sì,*" she says. "Because I have to tell you what just happen!"

Full of guilty triumph for having gotten away with something, at least for the moment, I follow her into the kitchen. Isabella is wired from her phone call. A wonderful coincidence: Jennifer, the one gallery owner in town that she has a personal relationship with, calling today. "And she didn't even know I was gone!" she says, beaming. "She wants me to update my portfolio, which is fantastic, because I have things to show."

"That's wonderful news," I say, genuinely cheered.

"It's a good sign!"

"Yes, it's like Los Angeles welcoming you home."

"*Sì! Sì-sisimo,*" she jokes, hands up, palms spread, swaying back and forth. She twirls in the middle of the kitchen as I fill the kettle, then stops abruptly with a cry. "*Aiee!* But the car!"

"What about it?"

"My car is up at Flavia's, in Laurel Canyon, and Flavia is still not back here, and there is no way to get the keys—but tomorrow, Monday, I have to go to the gallerist—"

"I can take you."

She brightens. "Really? All the way there and back?"

"Oh, no," I say. "You have to walk back."

Isabella laughs, a musical peal of happiness, and I remember that this is one of my favorite things in life, making that sound happen. The parameters of our marriage are already reasserting themselves, and I welcome it, all of Isabella's intensity. It's as heartening to me as the dancing steps she takes from the living room into the kitchen, whirling round in excitement as I prepare a tea, telling me of the new drawings she's brought back, I have to see, and *belissima!,* how they're just the thing for the new portfolio—

She catches the look in my eyes as I stand drinking her in, and she slows for a moment, hovering by the stove, her eyes telling me that she feels my affection, feels some of the same herself. Still, it's too soon for either of us, especially me, to assume any security in this. Which is why, though we stand close, close enough for me to smell the scent of Italian sun on her newly tanned skin, to be tempted to pull her into my arms, to be enfolded in that warmth, I resist. Instead, like two dogs tentatively sniffing each other in a chance street encounter, we both maintain the small distance that makes all the difference. It's too soon to share intimate feelings, things are not that simple. I acknowledge the justness of this and she sees that I feel as she does, all of this conveyed in a quarter of a second.

I ask the one safe question that borders the unsafe territory. "How is Maxi?"

Isabella grins. "Oh, he is fat as a house! Mama feeds him pasta every day."

"That's not good."

"I know, it's ridiculous, and of course he *love* it . . ." She looks away, sobering, running a finger over the curve of the stove top, then glances up at me again. "I thought to wait, you know," she says. "We see how it goes here . . . before we bring him back."

"That's a good plan."

The teakettle is about to whistle. Isabella reaches past me quickly to shut the burner off. "You hate that sound," she says. "It drives you crazy." The affection I hear in this is balm on a wound, a long-sought ease soothing my anxiety.

At the table, she claims the chair that's been mine for a while now, but was hers before. We sit letting the tea steep. "Why don't you just take my car to the gallery? I don't need it tomorrow."

"No? But I couldn't. You don't like it when I drive your car."

"I'll like it fine."

"*Grazie, amore.* That would be great." We're smiling at each other. My relinquishing of control is the tacit beginning of a new contract. Things will be different.

"Oh!" I remember her homecoming surprise and fetch the new cell phone. I'm rewarded with appreciative oohs and thanks, but it turns out to be a bust.

"Don't you remember, Jordan—I picked up a new one, just before I leave? It's in the studio." I vaguely recall this now, a detail lost to me in the upheaval of her leave-taking. "But you should use this one. You really need it!"

New beginnings, sure, but this is taking things too far. Nonetheless, I make a show of putting the silver pod in my jacket pocket. Maybe I'll use it for emergencies.

Isabella's manic energy is swelling again. "We should go to the beach. To Back on the Beach! They stay open for dinner, and I've been missing it—the California water. Or maybe we drive up the coast, eh? To the seafood place, with all the bikers!"

"It's far," I note gently.

"Maybe too far, you're right. But the fish place, near Topanga! Not that I'm so very hungry—better to roll another cigarette, though *uffa!*"

She's rummaging through her pocketbook. "I'm already out of this good tobacco . . ."

"Wait." I rise and victoriously produce a little bag, a forgotten stash of hers, from the kitchen drawer.

"No!" She beams with pleasure. I am the smart husband. When the cigarette is rolled, I light it for her, gallant attendant. The phone rings.

I'm a little apprehensive in answering, and for good reason, as it turns out, because it's Dana Morton, sounding as manic as Isabella. No, Rumer hasn't read the script yet. This is about adjustments. Dana wants just a little adjustment here and there—the draft is good, really, it's so close to what they want, but still, before she hands it in to Rumer—who won't get to it until tomorrow morning . . . She knows it's a Sunday, and this is short notice, but couldn't I come by this afternoon? A few quick fixes and the draft will be perfect.

What fixes? Well, the ending. It's not landing the way we discussed it. My spirits sink as I comprehend that the story has to go under the knife for a final procedure. The carefully compromised ending has been my last holdout, my last defense to her assaults—I should've known it wouldn't hold. Now the blade's handle is being pressed into my hand, there is at least this courtesy—and I see what will emerge at the operation's end. Only minutes ago, the movie was my beautiful child, but now it'll be something helpless, forlorn, a baboon wearing the head of a princess.

Isabella is puttering around in the kitchen cabinets. She smiles at me as I come back in. *"Dodo,"* she says.

"Izzy," I reply. This experimental exchange of pet names is a test to see if the tradition will hold. Like everything else we've done together since her return, it has a tentative, unreal quality, as if we're under-rehearsed. "You're not going to like this," I begin.

But when I've explained the situation she's remarkably sanguine. "Of course, you have to do what needs to be done. I'll be fine here," she says. "There's some of the tuna I like. And beside, I probably take a nap."

"We can go to the fish place tomorrow night."

"Yes, and then they make your movie—"

"If it's still my movie."

"—and then we go to the Oscars." She grins. "Anything is possible!" she reminds me. "Let's be positive, eh? Maybe things will start right for us this time."

Didn't we start right before? A familiar defensiveness rises in me and I have to consciously hold it in check. We're balancing on a rope together, one thickened by the general novelty of us having been apart. The amount of what we haven't yet begun to discuss fills the thin air around this high wire, but maybe putting one foot after the other and not looking down is the smartest way to proceed. So I simply nod.

"Hopefully," I say, "I'll be back in a couple of hours."

Under a relentlessly blue sky, I park in front of Dana's Santa Monica home, a familiar L.A. facsimile of a Spanish mansion that looks like it yearns to be another house, a bigger one living in Bel Air. I walk up the slate path and ring the bell, steeling myself to save what I can of what matters to me, or go down fighting.

I hear a strange scurrying before the door opens, and a tiny rat-faced thing some might call a dog flies out to run circles round my feet. Dana is on her cell, dressed at home as she was at the office—I picture close variations of this slacks-blouse-and-jacket ensemble stretching back into the depths of a vast walk-in closet—and she waves me inside, snapping her fingers at her mini-mongrel.

The living room is immaculate, a large Hockney swimming pool painting hanging over an unused fireplace, a long brown leather couch. The Hockney isn't a print. Given that it might have cost as much as a real swimming pool, I think maybe Dana swims in it, before pretending to have a fire. I give out my best, amiably mimed "Don't worry about me" as she deals with her call, the dog-thing zipping past us to career down a hallway. From her tone, I sense a disagreement. "Tom," Dana keeps saying, "Tom . . . ," but whoever Tom is, he's not letting her get in more than that one syllable, which becomes increasingly loaded with an impressive gamut of emotions by Dana. I hear a cajoling "Tom," an offended "Tom," and after Dana disappears briefly into the kitchen, then reemerges to heave a small bottle of Smart Water at me, a repressed-rage-laced-with-wounded-fearfulness "Tom," before she barks, "Fine," and snaps the cell phone shut.

I look up at her from my seat on the couch, water bottle perched atop the briefcase in my lap. Dana is smiling, composed. "You brought your laptop?"

"In case we decide to print out the pages here," I say, leading with my subtext for the day: We're making easy, little quick-fixes, right?

Dana nods. "Let's go into my office," she says.

Soon my characters are fighting for their lives again. Dana has sniffed out all my many equivocations, places in the third act where I've met her halfway but haven't really gone *her way.* The movie in her mind has gained force while my vision's faded, as if my inner projector's bulb has burned out. But I'm desperate to protect my new Naomi-influenced ending, which at least preserves the intent of the original story. After Jake and Margo emerge bruised and battered from the fiasco that nearly destroys both their careers, the audience expects them to come to their senses, stop fighting and embrace, since they're so clearly a perfect match. Instead, they walk away from each other amused, thinking, God—that's the last person in the world I could ever be involved with!

I've finessed it so the audience can entertain the *possibility* that they might hook up again. But Dana is lobbying for an ending that makes this a foregone conclusion. Okay, we've made her older woman/younger man dynamic work, and maybe my comedic take on her car-chase finale does suggest big-screen entertainment, but I'm determined to tie down the one thematic thread that keeps the story from seeming brain-dead. Within half an hour Dana and I are duking it out over every other line.

I'm retyping, she's pacing, the rat-dog occasionally making an hysterical run around the office desk, when the sound of someone unlocking the front door comes from down the hall. Dana excuses herself. I listen to the rapid tat of her heels on the parquet floor. According to the incongruous Felix the Cat clock in the corner, whose round black eyes keep shifting right and left as its plastic tail wags back and forth, I've been here an hour. We've gotten through three pages of the final twenty.

I'm a truant student stuck in detention. The blinds behind me throw a pattern of bars on the floor. I rise and peek through them. I'm facing a hedge, and beyond it I see the open second-floor window of a neighboring English Tudor. Within, a rotund white-haired woman stands rocking a swaddled infant in her arms. I can hear her babbling nonsense syllables at it. Why do people always do that? If Isabella and I ever have a child, I'm going to talk to it like an adult. For a moment, this fantasy offspring hovers in the air before me, faintly see-through like the imaginary child Moony suggested I have with Naomi. My Naomi, looking up at me from under the brim of her hat, then gone. Gone for good? To the furthest, deepest regions of the nighttime sky?

I was an idiot to tell her to leave. If I've ever needed inspiration . . .

I turn away from the window. I have to get my focus back.

From elsewhere in the house comes the bang of a slammed door, the muffled sound of raised voices. The draft's beleaguered page blazes before me on the little screen, accusatory cursor blinking, but Marie's business card has been burning a hole in my shirt pocket. I know I have to call about returning Naomi's bracelet, and it'll be good to get the necessary closure there: Thank you for a night to remember, and if things were different, but they aren't, and where can I drop this off for you?

No Naomi. I get Marie's machine. I'm momentarily stymied. "Hi, this is a message for Naomi. It's Jordan," I begin, and pause. *That was quite a visit,* I consider saying, but this sounds wrong, so . . . what? I'm leaving an absurdly long silence on the machine. "I hope everything's good with you," I venture, lamely. "And I hope we can get together, but . . . I'm not home, so I'll try to find you later. Actually, I should be home tonight, though—" Once again I stop. How to say, *But don't call me, I'll call you,* without making the situation sound even more blatantly dicey than it already is? An impatient beep sounds in my ear. So much for coherence and cool. I hang up and stand, receiver in hand, uneasily reconsidering my last words. I said I'd be home tonight, which could be misinterpreted. She wouldn't call me at home—except she might. Gut dropping, I realize I'll have to compound my lack of cool by calling the machine again.

The dog is back, and here comes Dana, remarkably calm for a woman who's been shouting behind closed doors for fifteen minutes. "So where were we?" she asks.

The next time I lift my head, we're ten pages further along, many a bloody skirmish behind us. A number of times I've suggested that I go back home and work on the rest of it, but Dana isn't having that. She brings in fruit salad, takes and makes cell calls, flipping through a pile of scripts and pacing behind me when she's not looking over the latest printed page. She doesn't leave the room until the still-unseen man upstairs (Tom, is my bet) calls to her from down the hall.

I'm alone again but for the dog, who's guarding the office by peeking round the doorjamb, running off and coming back again. But if I try to walk out of the office now, alarms will sound, some *Star Wars* force field is likely to smack me down. Next Dana's face will appear on a floating screen, a cyber–Wicked Witch of the West, demanding that I keep my fingers moving over the keyboard. According to Felix, it's been way over an hour since my call to Marie. What if Naomi has already gotten the message?

Marie's machine picks up again. Where are *les femmes*? I leave no message.

Fending off panic, I consider a jailbreak. Maybe I can't get out on my own, but if Isabella calls here, say with a domestic emergency . . . Gingerly, I retrieve the shiny new cell phone from my jacket, flip it open, and dial home with shaky fingers, only to hear my own obnoxiously cheery outgoing message. "*Ciao,* Isabella," I say. "I'm trying to wrap things up here, finally, but it's not easy, so . . ." Where is Isabella, sleeping? "I'll try you at the studio."

I disconnect, and do just that, but this time it's Isabella's bilingual outgoing message I hear. All the women I know have been replaced by digital devices at this crucial moment, except for one, who, as I finish saying, "I hope you'll pick up this message, because I really need to get out of here," appears in the office doorway again.

"I'm sorry," Dana says. "It's kind of a . . . crazy day. Look," she says brightly. "We're doing really well. And if Rumer wasn't breathing down my neck to read this thing, I'd say let's come back to it later. But we need to push to the finish line, okay?" I nod. "You need a quick break? Want to sit out on the patio?"

"Let's keep going."

"Great," says Dana, crossing to a closet. She yanks the door open, and her voice emanates from its depths as she rummages within. "We're up to the dialogue between Margo and Jake, just before the chase takes off."

"Right. And you want to add a few lines—"

"To underscore how into him she is." Dana emerges from the closet with a suitcase, depositing it on the floor with an emphatic clunk. "No matter how much she's screwed him over, no matter that she practically murdered him to get to this moment, she really does care about him. There's real love there."

"Couldn't we just get that in a look? Before they each go—"

"No," Dana says, and slams the closet door shut. "Trust me, even if we get Julia for this, *especially* if we get Julia, she's going to want a line."

"I just think we risk overplaying—"

"I'm not saying they have to *kiss* each other," Dana says, furiously unzipping the suitcase at her feet. "But the audience has got to believe"—zip!—"she loves the guy!" Zip! "Even if *he's* not willing to own up to it!" She flips the suitcase top, which hits the floor. "She's the one who'll take the rap for this mess"—Dana grabs a folded poncho from within the suitcase and tosses it onto the chair beside the desk—"because she's a professional, and even if he chooses to just walk away, *she—is—loyal!*" Pounding her palm with a fist on each word. "*That's* the kind of heroine she is.

C'mon," she says. "You're great with characters, Jordan, you can make it play."

Next she's going to tell me it should be Rabelaisian and I'll have to ask her what the hell she means by that and she won't know, not that she'll admit it, and this'll all go downhill even faster than it's going. But what she actually says is almost as bad. "Go for a gag if you don't want to be too on the nose, do a Billy Wilder—but give it a shot, okay?"

Oh, hell. I'd love to pull Billy Wilder out of her closet right now, the way Woody Allen produced Marshall McLuhan in *Annie Hall,* to tell Dana, *You know nothing of my work!* in that tart Germanic accent of his, except Wilder's dead, I'm not Woody, and—

A phone is ringing elsewhere. Dana abandons her suitcase and stalks off down the hall. The dog remains, skittering back and forth across the doorway. I watch it, yearning for a small handgun. If only I had the power to make up a better Dana—now, there's a character worth rewriting. Oh, how have I ended up here, behind this desk, under this thumb? I was happier, wasn't I, far away from all this, back in Manhattan—what ever made me think this was the work I should be doing? What does any of this linguistic butchery mean or signify? I hear Leo's voice in my head gently admonishing me for betraying my calling. I think of literature, of poetry, of my own words and no one else's, words unprostituted, pure and aglow with meaning, and again a craving for My Naomi seizes me. But no, I think bitterly, I'm on my own. Lost. Sighing, I pick up the phone and dial one more time.

Marie greets me like an old chum. She assures me that Naomi has gotten my message. "So you'll probably be seeing her anytime now," she says cheerily.

"What do you mean?"

"Well, you said you'd be home tonight, and I think she was maybe planning to stop by."

What I need now is a helicopter, a rocket pack. I have to dial my own number twice because my fingers fumble over the buttons. Machine again. I stand staring at the alien pod in my hand, seeing Naomi and

Isabella at my kitchen table, chatting amiably over espressos while Isabella retrieves knives from the drawer, selecting the proper length and serrated edge to be used for carving up a husband.

From the back of the house comes the sound of breaking glass. The dog flees. I have the same impulse and stand up from the desk, but the noise of heavy steps approaching puts me back in the chair, eyeing my watch. It's nearing six o'clock.

The man who leans in the office doorway is barefoot, wears tight, perfectly faded blue jeans and a white T-shirt, and can't be more than twenty. He has the chick-melting features of a teen idol, complete with sexily disheveled sandy-blond hair, the hooded eyes and thick lips of a crooner. He has to be an actor. I wonder if he's Dana's son.

"Hey," he says.

"Hey," I reply. The guy is focused on the suitcase. He steps inside the office and, shaking his head, wheels it back to the closet, as the frantic nattering of the dog's nails grows louder, a counterpoint to Dana's martial heels in the hall.

"What are you doing with that?" Dana indicates the suitcase.

"What's it look like?" He retracts its long handle. "I've got mine."

"That's not enough," she says.

"Babe, it's only a five-day show."

"It's *freezing* in Canada," Dana snaps. "Just because you're playing another Mr. Macho doesn't mean you can't catch a cold." She grabs the handle, pulling it out again.

"Babe . . ." The guy jumps back as she wheels it past him, nearly running over his bare foot. Then he's following Dana as she marches out the door with it.

I listen to their muffled voices in the hall, the loud whir of suitcase wheels reverberating, and the room tilts. I'm reeling from that "babe" and my comprehension of who *Made for Each Other* is about now, of why Dana insisted that the role of Jake be played by a sexy young unknown. Then she's back, face flushed, smiling tightly.

"Sorry, sorry," she says. "How did you do?"

"I didn't," I admit. "Look, Dana—"

"Maybe if we read the scene out loud," she says, shutting the door behind her. The dog, as alarmed as I am by this, darts under the desk and back out again. Dana cocks her head, listening to movement overhead. Things thrown on the floor.

"Maybe," I say. "But the thing is, I really think we'd do much better if I could finish this up at home. I can e-mail you the last—"

"There's no time," she says sharply.

"Then let's go with the draft as it is." I'm humiliated by the quaver in my voice.

"Look!" Dana advances on me to briskly riffle through a stack of pages on the desk, and I can't help pulling back in alarm as she bats a sheaf of them to the chair and then pulls one sheet out, brandishes it at me, triumphant. "It's all *here,*" she announces.

She shoves the page in front of my face. It takes me a moment and then I get it, only I wish I didn't. Because this must be Dana's infamous graph: a thick, jagged line of red Magic Marker that looks like a cross between a crazed kindergartener's scrawl and a stock market chart, emblazoned on a piece of actual graph paper. There's a slightly thinner blue line that loops over and around and through the red one, and though the thing might have had some meaning, say, to Jean-Michel Basquiat on a bender, I haven't got a clue.

"Every beat in the thing is where it's supposed to be," she declaims, like a lecturer trying to speak loud enough for the people in the back to hear. "This one! This one!" She's thwacking the point of each red spike with thumb and forefinger. "They all line up! Except . . . *there*!" And she jabs her finger toward the end of the line. "You see?"

I see plenty, all right: Dana's reddened face, wide eyes, flared nostrils, I see a medicine cabinet lined with prescription bottles, a small, white padded room. But what the meaning of the shaky squiggle at the red line's end might be, I can only guess. "It . . . goes down," I venture.

"Yes!" she cries. "Where it needs to go up! *Up!*" She's thrusting the graph into my eyes, as if perhaps to imprint it across my face, and instinctively, defensively, I take the piece of paper from her and lay it flat on the desktop, finding it easier to look at than at Dana, who's breathing heavily, towering over my chair.

"Well," I say, nodding. "Well." And I nod some more. "But this *blue* line here, *it* seems to be going in the right direction . . ."

"This isn't helpful."

I look up. Dana's turned steely. She's got the poncho bunched in both hands now and she's squeezing it into a tight ball. I clear my throat. "I'm just thinking, Rumer should be okay with this draft, if we tell him that the end of the movie isn't frozen yet—"

The sudden thumping of loud hip-hop bass above brings both our heads up. Then Dana turns her glare on me again. "Like you know anything about what Rumer is or isn't okay with," Dana snarls, "you little—" Her hands rise and I flash on My Naomi beneath the streetlight, about to thunderbolt me in her rage over my pages, though Dana wields only a bunched-up poncho as she completes her sentence: "—fuck!" The poncho projectile flies past as I step aside, the *thwap* of it hitting home behind me followed by a high-pitched howl. The dog leaps at Dana's feet, yipping hysterically.

"You fucking . . . *writer!*" Dana throws open the door, grimaces at the ceiling and stalks into the hall. "You want out of this project?" she tosses over her shoulder. "Fine. I don't have a problem with that. You're out."

I stare after her, a gust of horror blowing through me. But in the next instant I remember what I have to do, if I don't want to be out of a marriage. Briefcase in hand, I'm out the front door in a New York minute.

I drive like a fiend, holding my watch up to the passing streetlights as if it's a talisman against disaster. After an intolerable wait behind a moving van—of course there has to be a moving van, large as a locomotive, blocking the traffic on my street in both directions, with no way round it, at ten to seven on this particular Sunday night—I'm finally able to park in front of my gate. I pause outside the fence, peer through the trellis and see, with a jolt, the shape of two silhouettes on the kitchen window blinds.

Too late! A nightmare come true, then: Isabella and Naomi Dussart, sharpening claws as they wait for me to stroll inside? I fight an impulse to turn tail and run. Run where? Clutching my briefcase like preserver and shield, I push through the gate, stride up the steps, and unlock the door. Swallowing the metallic taste of fear on my tongue, I enter my home.

I smell tobacco and hear Italian over the burbling funk on the stereo. Braving the kitchen doorway, I find my wife at the table with Flavia. Isabella smiles when she sees me, and I'm at her side in two strides, enveloping her in a hug. "*Madonna!*" says Flavia, laughing. "He really is glad to have you back."

"*Amore,*" says Isabella.

I breathe in the pungent mix of cigarettes, Opium perfume, hennaed hair, and sweet Isabella sweat, then let go of her, giddy with relief. I smile at my wife's friend, a sparrow-like wisp of a woman with tiny features and translucent skin. "Flavia, *come stai?*"

"*Bene, grazie.*" We buss cheeks.

"Flavia brought my car," says Isabella. "So I can go myself, tomorrow."

"Excellent, excellent," I say. "So we'll drive you home, when it's time?"

"*No necesito, grazie,*" Flavia says. "I'm only waiting for—"

Three toots of a horn outside interrupt her, and the women laugh. "Claudio!"

There's a flurry of Italian, bag-gathering, hugs. I follow them out and wave a hello to Flavia's boyfriend, who sits smoking behind the wheel of a double-parked Fiat. As Isabella accompanies her friend to the car, I give the street a cursory once-over, but I don't really expect the specter of Naomi to pop out at me from the shadows. She'd call first, wouldn't she? I hurry back inside. The answering machine is message-free.

"I'm back!" Isabella bounces inside, turns up the music. She dances around the periphery of the living room, idly rearranging the clutter on tabletops, reclaiming her territory. "You had a productive meeting?"

"It was . . ." *Great, but for the minor detail that I think I just got fired,* I could say, but no way. I don't want to alarm her right now about the seeming loss of my livelihood, nor raise my own anxiety level again. Later on, when I've figured out how to fix this, I fervently hope I can tell her all the details and we'll have a good laugh. "Well, it was difficult," I say. "But I think we got the job done."

"*Molto buono!* You know how to make these people happy, I'm sure. So many candles," she adds, looking at the cluster of them in the corner by my desk.

The ghost of My Naomi ripples through the air, and I blink it away as I rise to face her. "Can't have too many candles," I say. Isabella rests her palms on my shoulders, swaying to the beat.

"I worry about Flavia," she says. "Things with Claudio are not so good. She looks terrible, don't you think? She lose too much weight."

"*Sì,*" I say, starting to move with Isabella. "She's thin as a rail."

"As a what?"

"As a rail."

"Which is what?" Isabella's eyes are widened, expectant.

"*A rail,*" I say, drawing out its vowel and emphasizing the *I,* "like the track that a train runs on." I hold my thumb and forefinger an inch apart, moving my hand in rhythm to the music. "The two long, thin metal lines on the ground—that's a railroad track."

"Of course! A rail." She's delighted, imitating my gestures. For Isabella, learning a new English phrase is like opening a present. She especially loves words that sound like what they mean, and any one inputted in her computer-like brain becomes operative immediately—I'm certain to hear her using it in conversation. She grins, chin bobbing, shoulders swiveling, and chants: "Thin as a rail, thin as a rail, thin-thin-thin—"

"—as a mouse's tail."

"*Bravo!*" she cries, clapping her hands. We're moving across the room together now, me mimicking her moves. "Thin as a rail, as a mouse's tail . . ."

"Envelope thin, like a piece of mail?"

She laughs, bumping her hip to mine. *"Bravissimo!"* Teeth flashing, eyes alight, she swivels round against me, and we bump hips again. "Thin as rail, thin as a tail, thin as a piece of a mouse's mail . . ."

This is the woman I've missed so much. Pursing her lips and flapping her wrists, hands flat, walking like an Egyptian, eyes sidling sideways to look at me, impish, then turning again, rolling her belly, serpentine, laughing as I try to do the same and purposely make a mess of it. She gets me, is the thing, just as I get her, and I revel in how a strand of hair catches in the corner of her smile, how her supple shoulders bend, mirroring mine, every gesture both foreign and familiar, all of it alluring.

I'm so grateful to have her back, tonight of all nights, her dancing figure diminishing my day's waking nightmare. I yearn to get lost in her. I put my palms to hers and she pushes back, her breasts brushing my chest, eyes holding my eyes. We dip together, an old move I remember well, both of us smiling as we come up again, and I slide my arm around her, pulling her closer, though the music's beginning to fade. Her skin's so smooth, shining and flushed, I can't resist leaning in to kiss her as she turns slightly, so my lips land awkwardly on her nose and cheek. She smiles and moves her lips to mine. I savor the flavors of cheese and tomato, laced with tobacco, on her tongue. She gently pulls away, then rests her face in the hollow of my neck. The music's over, and we both go still in the silent room.

There's been a quake, with all its unforeseen upheavals, precious things have been broken and irretrievably lost, and we listen for the creaks and rustles of an aftershock. Once the floor has given way, it can never feel quite so solid. But she's holding on to me, and our bodies, so long estranged, are already alert with a familiar tingling of erotic awareness. A tightening in my groin announces the primal pull, away from the world and all its worries. I lick my lips. "Someone didn't wait for dinner," I say.

"Flavia bought a pizza. We were starving."

"I thought you might cook." I'm caressing her side, beneath her breast, and from the way she settles in my arms, I can tell I'm not alone in my arousal.

"I will," she says. "Soon, I promise. I own you."

I draw back in mock wariness. "You own me?"

"No?" She looks up at me, biting down on her lower lip.

"Well, maybe you do," I muse. "But I think you mean—"

"Owe you!" she corrects. "I owe you a meal."

I kiss her forehead. *"Sì, senora."*

She smiles. "There's some slices left, I heat them up. First, I need to change these clothes." She disengages but runs her fingers playfully down my chest. "Put on something else, okay? Something good." She nods toward the stereo.

I flip quickly through the CDs as she disappears into the bedroom, and pop in a Keith Jarrett I know she likes. There's a Bordeaux I've been saving in the kitchen, and I hurry in to open it. This is the best way, my excited body tells me: into the bed, into the makeup sex that Moony rightly touted, and work out everything else that needs to be worked out after that. If we don't talk but touch, don't stop to dwell on the follies that came between the last time and now, surrender to what our lips and tongues remember . . .

I uncork the bottle, pour both glasses, and start in on one, seated at the kitchen table, when I realize that there's no noise, other than Keith Jarrett moaning over an arpeggio, coming from the rest of the apartment.

Isabella is sprawled on her back on the bed, eyes closed, closet open, clothes strewn around her feet. "I'm sorry," she murmurs. "I sat down for just a moment, and the jet lag . . ."

I sag, but understand. Maybe it's just as well. I help her out of her skirt, Isabella slumped against me like a toy unwound. The glimpse of her underwear, the curve of her stomach and ridge of ribs I've kissed a thousand times pierces me, a sweet ache lingering as I tuck her in beneath the covers, lean over to kiss her forehead. She's already deep in slumber. Looking down upon her, I feel like I've returned a recovered treasure to a safe.

A sense of unreal peace steals over me. It's easy to love a woman while she sleeps. Her expression is untroubled, she looks far from any care as she snores softly, evenly, legs wrapped around a pillow beneath the sheets. Now it's Isabella who, as intimately as I know her, seems a beautiful and tantalizing unknown.

I know one thing about her, though: If she wakes up tomorrow to find out I've blown the Rumer job, I'm fucked.

The bedroom door shut quietly behind me, I pace the living room, all the anxieties I've suppressed for the past twenty minutes whirling round my head again like the misshapen fanged and winged creatures from a Bosch painting. The night's still young, I can still save my butt, salvage the end of the draft by e-mailing new pages to Dana—that is, if I can figure out what the hell to put on them. But nothing's coming to mind, nothing that will act as a sop to what she wants (a more conventional happy ending) while remaining true to what I need (a fresher and more real life–like ending I can live with).

The car chase ends with Jake and Margo losing the prize that both of them were after. Ironically in a way they've won, since they're alive, and after all, what they've really been chasing is each other. But how to bring them into a clinch that feels genuine, earned, not movie-movie glib? In my book, they just went their separate ways, and that still feels right to me, despite Dana's efforts to shove them together.

I've got the draft up on my computer again, cursor blinking smack in the middle of the dialogue where everything went sour hours ago, and all that's in my head is gobbledygook. I'm on my feet again, wearing a groove in the carpet as, shameless in my desperation, I troll the works of *real* writers for help, picking at the bones of Oscar Wilde, the pithy denouements of Tom Stoppard, and inevitably, the entire oeuvre of Adam Sandler. I'm back at my desk again, grimacing gargoyle-like at the implacable screen.

There's only one way out of this I can think of.

Outside in the cool night air, seated on my garden bench, I close my eyes. I need to sweep the bold typeface of Dana's revisions from the foreground of my forehead, as if clearing a bedspread of books and papers before lying down for a meditation, and try to quiet the siren swarm of all the day's voices, a murmuring counterpoint to the word I start silently chanting: *Naomi . . .*

I conjure. Start with the sandals. And the bits of her body come on, then her face, those eyes, and I put a good spin of willfulness on it, furiously *intend* her to show up again. *Naomi, Naomi . . .*

The mantra helps, calm stealing over me, the brain-chatter quelled. I'm being here now, aware of a distant seagull's caw, the faint scent of eucalyptus, the wind in my face. I'm far into this test of the emergency Naomi broadcasting system, her figure fixed brightly in the center of my mind, blossoming like a pale pink tulip amidst the darkness behind my eyes—and then the picture fades.

The wind rises and the garden gate squeaks. I look up. The electric negative afterimage of Naomi hovers briefly in the air, and though nobody is there, the gate hangs ajar a few inches, papery leaves scattering across the pavement underneath it. The hairs at the back of my neck prickle. But she doesn't appear.

Well, why should she, after I told her in no uncertain terms that I needed to get her out of my life? Nice work, Jordo. One more time I curse myself and then forgive myself for doing what had to be done, and then I tromp dejectedly back inside the house.

Isabella snores quietly. I set the alarm, reasoning that if I get up before she does, at the crack of dawn, maybe I'll have dreamed my way into a viable solution. With a yawn, I contemplate pulling down the blinds. No moon tonight, but strange, I see two tiny points of green glimmering in the leaves out there. I peer at the darkness, trying to comprehend what I'm looking at. Above us, stretched out on the lowest bough, is a long feline form, a shadow, leopard-sized, but no, the curves are human, feminine, and those two tiny green glimmers—

With a paranoid glance at Isabella, who emits a louder, whistling snore, I hurry stealthily to the window, and there she is: My Naomi, garbed in black leotards, resting her head sideways on her branch as if she's some waylaid performance artist commando settled in to watch a show.

I pull down the blinds with shaky hands, trying not to make a sound. Then quickly, quietly, I'm dashing through the apartment, out the back door and down the steps, aware of each soft crunch of gravel as I approach the tree.

"You came!"

Her only reaction to my hoarse whisper is a steady gaze, more cat-like than womanly. I glance at the darkened bedroom windows, only yards away, then step closer. "Can we talk?"

She murmurs something I can't hear from where I am, and I'm about to call up to her to repeat it when I catch myself, nervously glancing at the windows again. I hold up a forefinger to My Naomi and hurriedly fetch the folding chair by the garden bench. With the chair wedged against the trunk, I'm able to climb, and though there's a scary moment when I nearly lose my grip on the flaking bark, in another moment I'm up, I'm seated straddling the branch beside hers.

I take a second to catch my breath. "It's good to see you," I whisper.

"Really." She doesn't look like she shares the sentiment.

"Look, I know you're probably put out with me, and I don't blame you, but I wouldn't have asked if it wasn't important." Her expression remains imperturbable. "Naomi, it wasn't *my* idea to send you packing," I tell her. "And I guess I'm realizing now that I was a little too hasty in—"

"Jordan," My Naomi says. "What is it you wanted?"

The air of unconcealed impatience in her attitude makes me wonder suddenly what or who, exactly, I may have whisked her away from. Is she already seeing another writer? Is my muse not exclusive? But I can sense that now isn't the time to pose such questions. "I still don't have the ending," I confess. "Jake and Margo's final moment, when they get out of their cars and face each other. I don't want to do the obvious thing of them going into an embrace, though. That's not like either character, and it's too easy and too pat. But there needs to be a sense that they're still in this thing together, somehow. Otherwise, what's the whole climax about?"

"So," says My Naomi, "you've asked me here to help you make a car chase more meaningful."

Her tone is unmistakably withering, but what can I do? I nod.

Naomi gives a little sigh. She picks a fallen leaf from her hair and regards it, holding it out at arm's length, twirling the stem. "It's really a tree in microcosm," she murmurs. "One vein goes this way, one goes the other, but they're both attached at the bottom. Separate directions but still connected. You see?"

"Yeah," I say cautiously. Is she only here to play with and confuse me?

"It's the same way this branch wends its way east," she continues, stretching languidly, "while that one grows west. But they're still growing from the same trunk."

"Uh-huh," I say, wondering when she's going to get around to dealing with my question. I'm staring at the leaf, which she's waving slowly back and forth like the dangling stopwatch of a hypnotist. What the hell does a tree trunk have to do with—

That's when it hits me, a jolt of understanding that's as sharp and blinding as an electrical shock. "Wait a second!" I exclaim. I wobble on my perch as I guiltily steal a look at the closed blinds below, then turn back to her. "You're right," I whisper excitedly, my thoughts already whizzing ahead, seeing the way this scene could unfold. "Naomi, you're amazing—I think I've got an idea that's going to work."

She looks at me, the leaf fluttering from her hand, expression ever-inscrutable. "Do you?"

"Yes! Separate directions but still connected. That's— Thank you! I can't wait to get back to my draft to try this out."

Naomi lies there, saying nothing. I can tell I'm not off the hook with her, and that it seems criminally uncouth to simply pick her brain and then run for my computer. But I want to get this down on paper while I can see it all before me, while there's still time to mend bridges with Dana and forestall Isabella making an abrupt return flight. And given the situation, I can't very well invite her in for coffee. I grope for a diplomatic retreat. "So, Naomi—I'm just so grateful that you were able to . . . to come over like this."

My Naomi rolls her eyes. As I grope in frustration for an amenable peacemaking angle (what am I going to suggest, *Let's have lunch sometime?*), the headlights of a car turning up the alley illuminate the tree in stark relief, then blind me as they sweep by. I blink, and when I stare into the darkness of the branches, Naomi has disappeared again. There is no one, nothing there.

I climb down, scraping skin, muscles straining as I find a foothold on the chair. I tread softly through the garden and survey the tree boughs as I stand for a long moment on the stoop until my pulse slows. Then I hurry back inside the house.

It doesn't even take me an hour. All I had to do was pay off a setup that was always there, hiding in plain sight.

The entire time Jake and Margo have been competing to sign up unhinged pop star Daryl for their respective ad agencies, Daryl's comic-relief sidekick, a quirky airheaded little gnome of a rock guitarist named Zippy, has been becoming a star in his own right. It's finally occurred to me—as it now occurs independently to both Jake and Margo, on the next-to-last page of the movie—that even though Daryl has literally crashed and burned, Zippy will make a viable substitute for Daryl, if he can be persuaded.

Thus, as Daryl's carted off to the hospital, Margo and Jake say their bittersweet good-byes, with a handshake that lingers a beat too long and the kind of lengthy soulful look beloved by actors: It says they each realize what they're passing up here and just how deep a passion is being irrevocably denied. Then Jake gets into his Jaguar XK, Margo into her Porsche Boxster S, and they drive off in opposite directions. We leave a beat here for some poignant "movie's over" music to come up and for the audience to register disappointment: these two meant-for-each-others didn't end up together. Then Jake reaches for his cell phone and Margo reaches for hers.

Are they calling each other? No, they're both calling Zippy's management. Great minds think alike, and as Jake says, "I'll hold," with a grin, and Margo does the same with a matching smile, we realize this isn't the end of their relationship, but the beginning of round two. Once more, each of them is chasing after the same client.

The last visual I write in comes directly from My Naomi's *separate directions but still connected:* Jake wheels left, Margo turns right, and though they're on different roads, through the magic of split-screen, we see them zooming right toward each other, silhouetted against that golden late-afternoon sun. And just before their front fenders are about to kiss, FREEZE and—FADE OUT.

I type that in. I save the document. I do a nutty little victory dance around my desk, because though it took me ten days of head-banging to get here, this is the ending that can make everybody happy. It's no reinvention of the wheel, but it's not as on-the-nose sappy as what Dana was pushing for. Still, it gives her the happy ending she wanted, and it's low-key wry enough to make me feel it's true to the spirit of the original book. I e-mail the new pages to Dana with a diplomatic apology for my earlier departure. Then, suddenly exhausted, I shut down the computer and turn out the lights.

In the bedroom, I undress quietly to the sound of Isabella's slow and even breathing, then slip beneath the covers. Sitting up in bed beside her, I peer into the enveloping darkness. A myriad of shadow figures huddle around us in the room. There's the sorrowful Isabella as she was before she left two weeks ago, with a shell-shocked me beside her. There's My Naomi, timeless, with her fifty-fathoms gaze, the real Naomi Dussart with her insouciant smile—it's a wonder there's any room for the two of us on the bed. Turn left, I might bump into any one of these phantoms; turn right, and I might confront some unknown creatures from the depth of Isabella's dreams.

How many times have I fantasized this body back here, entwined with me beneath the sheets? It's still strange to lie next to her again, both of us the same and not the same. She shifts against me and tucks her cold feet beneath my calves and ankles. This is the gesture, the welcome I've been yearning for, and soothed by it, I carefully slide an arm round her head on the pillow, gently encircling her, and close my eyes.

Forced to choose between a woman made of star-shine and the soul mate in flesh and blood, this is what I swiveled toward in my Swivel. When love demanded a sacrifice at the turning point of my story with Isabella, there really wasn't any question.

When the Rumer check arrives, I'll buy that convertible. Maybe a Mini Cooper, ubiquitous in town. They come in so many color combos—light blue with a navy top, red with black. Here's a silver one, black-topped . . . a metallic gray with a cap of kelly green . . .

6

Dark Moment

A crisis/climax wherein the protagonist's "swivel" decision yields disaster: In a humiliating scene, explosive secrets are revealed, and consequently the relationship and/or the protagonist's goal is seemingly lost forever.

*T*he bike path at the beach is nearly deserted, so we're able to pedal side by side, Isabella with her broad-brimmed hat on, a blouse tied over her swimsuit. Los Angeles excels at these impossibly brilliant days, the sky a Technicolor hue, cloudless, the illusion of crisp, clean air when the wind comes up. Mid-October, and it's as warm as a summer morning. It's as if Venice is doing its own advertising for my wife, assuring the prodigal expatriate that she's made the right choice in coming back. Who would want to give this up?

"The seagulls!"

She points. I look. We smile. An unspoken agreement holds: We talk only of what is right in front of us.

An uneasy peace reigned at home today. Neither one of us was eager to engage in a summit meeting on the uncertain state of our reunion. During our first morning in the apartment together, we deported ourselves like friendly but slightly estranged roommates. After showering, Isabella emerged from the bathroom wrapped in towels and dressed behind the closed bedroom door, a tacit reminder of former intimacies now denied.

My disquieted state was somewhat alleviated by an e-mail reply to my new ending from Dana Morton: *Pages received, thanks.* This terse message can only be interpreted to be tacitly amenable. If I'd really been fired—and who's to say Dana actually has that power?—there'd have been no such acknowledgment, only ominous silence.

Isabella wanted to lie in the sand and soak up sun, do nothing until after lunch, when she'd drive up to the gallery. Having only the anxiety of waiting for word from Rumer on my schedule, I was fine with keeping her company. I seized the opportunity to make a certain phone call while she showered. Now on the bike path, I steal a look at my watch. As I predicted, Isabella wants to go to that spot she adopted, some months back, just a bit north of the Santa Monica Pier. We park, lock, and trek down to the water's edge. I shoulder her bag with its crammed-in towels, suntan lotion, water, and the pile of magazines she means to go through, my Tolstoy tucked in the bottom.

We settle on a place where the sand rises, one long sloping dune. Once Isabella is on her towel and lotioned, I pace by the tide, waiting for the approach of ten o'clock. When it's time, I come back to Isabella, who's on her back, eyes closed, and luckily she does it for me, there's no need for subterfuge. "You're restless," she says. "Why don't you ride further, if you want. I'll be fine here."

That's the idea. After making doubly sure that she has all she needs, I'm on my way again, hunched over my handlebars, pedaling furiously northward, the silver bracelet heavy in my pocket.

Back on the Beach isn't crowded on a Monday morning. I survey the tables, then go round to the entrance proper, where my Argentine friend is chatting up the female hostess. "Hey, Carlos. Just stopping in for a coffee," I tell him.

"Take any table you want."

I pick one in the semi-shade of the restaurant's eaves, facing the ocean. Carlos lopes over, grinning wide. "How many are you today, my friend?"

"Actually, someone will be joining me, but I don't know if she'll stay."

"Just the one coffee, then?"

I nod, but he leaves two place settings, nonetheless. I realize I should have brought along my book. But that might have aroused Isabella's suspicion. It was risky enough making the call to Marie's.

And here is Naomi Dussart, waving gaily from the entrance. I rise. She's wearing a brilliant white sundress and oversized sunglasses, already more tanned than yesterday. *"Bonjour,"* she calls, and hurries up to kiss me on both cheeks. Her heady perfume gives me a quick, vivid remembrance of those crooked white teeth smiling at me in the dark—it was inevitable that she would reek of seductive sensuality, with my wife a short seagull's flight from where she stands. It makes perfect sense that she should lean over to smell the one-flower centerpiece before she takes her seat, affording me a nice view of her black lace bra. If I was truly smart, I'd drop the bracelet on the table and run.

But here is the Argentine with my coffee and a menu. "Actually, I'm famished," Naomi says. "Do they make the omelets well here?"

Carlos assures her that they do, any way that she might like them. Naomi orders an avocado, cheese, and mushroom combo, a selection he happily endorses as he departs with the menu. I already have the bracelet in my hand as she turns back to face me. "Here," I say.

"Ah! Thank you so much," says Naomi, slipping it over her hand and clasping it with a tiny click. "I know it must seem silly of me, to be so intent on getting this back, but it belonged to my grandmama. I wear it always, and I've been feeling so naked without it." She pats her wrist, sits back in her chair, face upturned to soak in the sun. "It really is like a little Riviera here," she says, then shakes her head, smiling at me. "So. How does it go? Your wife is back at home, and you are happy?"

"*Happy* is a big word."

"Enormous."

"But yes, I'm glad she's back."

"So all is well. All is like it was before." Her eyes are intent on mine, not mocking, but amused.

"Nothing's the same," I say. "Still, I think we've got a good shot at working things out."

"*C'est bon,*" says Naomi.

"And you?"

"Oh, it's a lot of fun to be back in Los Angeles," she says. "And this week will be even better. My cousin has a chalet in Telluride, so I'm flying out there to spend a few days with her."

"How great. I've never been," I tell her. "I hear it's beautiful."

"It's too bad you can't come," Naomi says, touching my hand. "I had such a good time with you the other night."

I can endure the gentle stroke of her fingers on my skin. It's the breathy sincerity in her lowered voice that scores the direct hit. I uncross my legs, straighten in my seat. "Yes, that was . . . memorable," I say.

She gives a little sigh. "But so brief."

"Naomi . . ."

"I know," she says. "Still, I want you to know that it meant something to me."

"Me too." Pulling myself up from the depths of her wistful gaze takes no small amount of effort. "But actually, I should be getting back."

"*Mais non!*" she cries. "At least keep me company until my food arrives."

"All right."

"I'm going to the restroom. And when I come back, I'm going to give you my phone numbers and address in Paris. In case . . . you decide to visit. One never knows." She stands, runs a finger lightly down my arm. "Oh, but I wish I had my camera. Your face, it's something priceless."

I'm sure it is. I'm also reasonably certain that I will not, God willing, be paying Naomi Dussart a visit in Paris. What a life she's living, though—like a hummingbird darting among the blossoms of a big, international garden. Again I commend myself for having steered clear of any real entanglement there, as I catch myself watching her shapely calves recede in the distance, and squeeze my eyes shut. I open them again to behold Carlos returning with Naomi's café au lait. "She's even prettier than the last one," he tells me with a wink.

Funny man. I drum my fingers on the table, sip my coffee and check my watch, consider my attraction to Naomi Dussart, a woman I barely know. It was just physical, wasn't it? And youth and talent, sure, but next to Isabella . . . Isabella is a woman of real substance and soulfulness. Isabella is an artist.

Isabella is locking her bicycle next to mine on the bike rack. She straightens up now to look my way, a hand shading her eyes. In the time that I think to somersault out of my chair and crawl out of sight beneath the tables, she's found me, is lifting her beach hat and waving it at me, is happily hurrying around the hostess's desk and heading my way. I get to my feet before she reaches me, my panicked survey of the table assuring me that Naomi took her beach bag with her. "I was just having a coffee," I say.

"And I wanted a milk shake!" She kisses me on the cheek and moves toward the nearest chair.

"We can get it to go," I say.

"But you haven't finished," Isabella says, indicating Naomi's café au lait, and she slides into the seat, looking brightly around her. "Where is our friend?"

Here comes Carlos now, directly behind her, bearing an avocado, Swiss cheese, and mushroom omelete on his platter with the magnanimous air of a man delivering a gift and not a death warrant. He slows as he draws closer, taking in both the new arrival and me standing by the table with a look of alarm. His brow furrows briefly, then his mouth widens in a toothy grin as he recognizes Isabella.

"Hey, *señora!*"

Isabella turns. *"Buon giorno!"*

"Come stai?"

"Bene," Isabella tells him. "And how have you been?"

"Fabulous," says Carlos. "How can I complain, with this sun, and this ocean?"

"Yes, I've missed this place, and you—and your vanilla milk shakes."

"Aaah!" Carlos nods, taking the omelet plate from his tray.

"Here," I say, abruptly sitting down in Naomi's chair. The waiter's hand pauses. His gaze meets mine for a second of complicity before he deposits the plate in front of me.

"Jordan!" says Isabella in surprise.

"I was hungry."

"Really," she says. "Me too, a little."

"Would you like a menu?" asks Carlos.

"Sì, grazie."

"And you, my friend—some ketchup? Hot sauce?"

I shake my head. "No, I'm good, thanks."

Carlos nods and turns back to Isabella. "You want that shake?"

"Yes, I do—extra thick!"

"Of course, *señora,*" he says. "It's good to have you back."

"Thank you. Such a sweet guy," she adds to me. I watch Carlos walking away. He flashes a jaunty smile over his shoulder before disappearing inside.

"Yes." Odd, though I've seen and written variations on this scene so many times, a scene often featuring the frenetic opening and closing of half a dozen bedroom doors, I've never experienced it from this vantage point, with the bright blue sky above, the cheery yellow eggs steaming before me, the warm beige sand below. Beneath me, if only I could access it, lies a direct route to China, where I could stroll atop the Great Wall, perhaps, meeting only people who don't speak my language, thus enabling me to pass myself off as a nice man, an innocent fellow with no secret agendas beyond, say, a harmless desire to collect a couple of those neat Mao-era propaganda posters to hang on my refrigerator door back home. But I can feel the stubborn firmness of the ground underneath me, as now, following the inexorable logic of a nightmare, Naomi Dussart rounds the corner.

She's two steps down the path between the tables when she sees that I'm no longer alone. I've never attempted telepathy. But I give it my best shot now, willing her to understand, to find the right role, the appropriate attitude, the proper lines to say. The amount of willful concentration radiating from my eyes as I hold Naomi's gaze alerts my wife, who is just now stealing a fried potato from my plate with a mischievous smile. She turns to see what I'm looking at.

Naomi's gaze shifts uneasily from Isabella to me as she reaches the table. "Jordan?" she says, tentative.

"Hi," I say, and shoot to my feet, bumping the table and spilling au lait froth.

"I thought that might be you."

"Oh!" is what I manage, aware that Isabella's perplexed look has taken in the coffee spill, and that she's now studying Naomi's face.

"I was supposed to meet a friend here," she says. "But I'm very late, and I don't see her . . ." Here, she affects to scan the neighboring tables, and I feel a swooning admiration for her, which almost defuses the terror that's making every inch of my skin go slack. Isabella looks from Naomi to me, alert and expectant, as Naomi turns back to the two of us, eyeing my wife with open interest.

"Oh," I say. "This is—"

"Naomi," says Naomi, smiling.

"Isabella," I say. "My wife."

"Hi," says Isabella.

"Hello," Naomi answers.

I have to breach the cavernous pause. "Naomi took a class of mine, some time ago. Years ago."

"Ah," says Isabella.

Naomi looks to the omelet. "Well, I don't mean to interrupt . . ."

"Not at all," says Isabella. Her voice is so free of any significant inflection that I cling wildly to a far-fetched hope that she hasn't made the connection between Naomi and the unnamed student of our transatlantic conversations. One glance at my wife's face evaporates any such fantasy. The look in her eyes is feral, primeval as she assesses the other woman: Dispose of this creature after killing it, or eat it? She knows.

Naomi checks her watch, the silver bracelet clinking against the timepiece as she raises her wrist. "I'm sure I've missed her," she says. "I should go inside and try to call, if they have a phone."

"I'm sure they do," I say, glancing at Isabella, so ominously silent.

"Well." Naomi smiles again at my wife, and faces me. "*Tout va bien?* Everything good?"

"Great," I say. "You?"

"Just fine," she answers.

"Here," Isabella interjects pleasantly. She's holding out her cell phone. "Please," she adds as Naomi hesitates. "Go ahead."

"You're sure?" asks Naomi.

"Be my guest."

I pass the phone to Naomi, who says, "*Merci.* That's so kind." Isabella shrugs. Naomi slips into the chair on my right. I'm now the only one still standing, and seeing Carlos reappear, I sit back down between them.

"Here you go," says the waiter, plopping down the shake in front of Isabella.

"Yum," she says, and takes the menu he proffers. "*Grazie.*"

"Extra thick," he announces, and smiles at me, then Naomi. "Anything for you?" Naomi, absorbed in dialing the cell, shakes her head. "I'll be back for your order," he tells Isabella, and beaming at me, departs.

At least someone is having a good time. I steal a furtive look at my wife. She's perusing the menu with great absorption as she takes a prolonged, noisy slurp of milk shake through her straw. Is she biding her time, waiting to catch me in a look or a phrase that'll expose me?

On my other side, Naomi begins speaking a rapid, singsong French into Isabella's phone. I remember that I, too, have a cell phone now. But I have no one to call who can get me out of this. For that matter, no one has called me on it yet. True, I only gave the number to a few people, but I've progressed from being the last person in Los Angeles without one to being the only person whose cell phone doesn't ring.

My brain is babbling. In another moment, I might start saying stuff like this aloud, and then I'll really be in trouble. I focus on the omelet, marveling at the utter composure both women evince. But it's only natural: I'm the amateur here, outclassed by centuries of European sophistication, rube America in bib and high chair, a guest at the adults' table of Italy and France.

There is something terrible about their mutual ease in the midst of my peril. I have an insane urge to overturn the table. The impulse vanishes, replaced by a pang of searing loneliness in reaction to the odd collusion between the two women, one idly flipping over her menu, the other *uhr*-ing and *ooh*-ing to her unseen friend. I have a vision of myself in perpetual estrangement—deeply, completely alone as only a man dependent on a woman's love can be. I taste the emptiness of that solitude on my tongue.

I raise my eyes from the tabletop to the horizon. A figure silhouetted against the line of sea and sky walks down the beach toward me, a trio of seagulls scattering in her wake. She's dressed simply this time, in black jeans and a powder blue man-tailored shirt, a red kerchief knotted at her neck, hands thrust into her hip pockets, cowboy boots kicking up a little sand, the wind whipping her hair about her face. She saunters onward in a direct line toward my table, pausing to step, with a gunslinger's ease, over the low fence that makes up the dining area's boundary. She keeps coming, while Naomi Dussart chatters on in French and Isabella takes out her tobacco and papers, setting down the menu to roll a cigarette upon it.

I'm amazed that neither of them can hear my heartbeat, since it's so loud in my ears as My Naomi slows by the table across the aisle. She eases herself into the closest empty chair, straddling it backward to face me. She folds her arms over the chair back and rests her chin atop her hands, fixing her gaze on me with the faintest of smiles. Her expression says: *So. Now what?*

I knew she would be back. Now I turn with her to size up Naomi Dussart, still coddling the cell phone, absently twisting a curl of hair around her fingers, and I'm struck again by the difference in their appearances. The Frenchwoman's artful makeup, the willful pout in her ample lips, contrasts the frank, unadorned beauty in My Naomi's face. My Naomi is studying her with the slightly incredulous curiosity of someone examining candid photographs of her own foolhardy youth.

She shoots a glance at me, both wondering and reproachful, then looks left of me to examine Isabella, who carefully taps tobacco into her papers, deftly rolling up the little cylinder. She licks it shut and twists one end tight just so, ever the craftswoman, then looks up to meet my gaze, her deep brown eyes opaque.

The snap of the cell phone closing turns everyone's attention to Naomi Dussart. "She's already home, my friend," she says. "Just as I thought. *Merci,*" she adds, passing the phone back to Isabella.

"*Prego,*" says Isabella.

"It was nice to meet you," Naomi says, rising.

"*Sì,*" says Isabella. I get up as well. I'm alarmed to see My Naomi follow suit, rising from her chair. She'd been intently fixed on Isabella, but now both she and Isabella regard the younger woman, Isabella appraising her like a boxer sizing up an opponent.

Naomi Dussart appears oblivious. "I must come back here sometime, though," she says. "That omelet looks very good." She smiles at me. "Good to see you."

"Yes," I say.

"*Au revoir.*"

She shoulders her bag. My Naomi looks from her to me, eyebrows raised.

I jerk my head, indicating the area outside the restaurant.

"You're sure you're not too busy?" she murmurs.

Lips set tight, I pointedly roll my eyes in the same direction.

She gives me a grudging shrug. And as Naomi Dussart strides leftward down the aisle, one hand holding down the back of her skirt against the wind, My Naomi saunters off right, a mirror of her departing not-quite twin, toward the small playground area that lies beyond the periphery of the tables.

"Jordan," says Isabella. "Do you have a lighter?"

I nod, realizing I'm still on my feet. I sit, unzip my jacket pocket, and dig out the yellow Zippo I put back in there this morning in anticipation of such requests. I flip it open and roll the ridged wheel with my thumb. Isabella covers the flame with one hand as she bends over it. I steal a glance over my shoulder. My Naomi is seated in one of the swings, languidly stretching her legs, the tips of her boots pushing at the sand.

"*Grazie.*" Isabella sits back, exhaling, and looks at me. "Well," she says coolly. "Fate is so peculiar. She is the one, isn't she?"

Not exactly, I think, aware of My Naomi's eyes upon me. "Yes," I say, and steel myself for fireworks.

Isabella shrugs. "But it's over. It's all in the past, isn't that what you said?"

"Yes," I repeat uneasily, surprised by her continued calm.

"And actually, maybe it's good that I see her. Because I can't imagine anything serious with that one, anyway," Isabella says. "She's just a girl. A little puppet. She may be pretty, I guess, but . . ." She shakes her head. "If that's the best you could do . . ."

I open my mouth and shut it. I know that my irrational impulse to defend Naomi Dussart must be ignored. And the real best that I've been doing, someone neither girl nor puppet, waits for me a dozen yards away.

"I just hope nobody at the school, they find out. A teacher with a student—" Merry electronica rends the air. Her cell phone's ringing.

"A former student," I correct her.

Isabella holds up a finger. "*Momento,*" she says, answering the call. "*Prego? . . . Ciao, Roberta!*"

I rein in my irritation as she rattles on in Italian. I've been given the reprieve I need, and get up from my chair.

My Naomi, swaying left and right, digs her heels into the sand and stills the swing as I come up beside her. "You're a man of many interests," she says. "It's a wonder you get anything done at all."

As I look into her upturned face, I'm keenly aware of how much I've grown to depend on her presence, even as her mocking expression makes a familiar string of anxiety twang in my stomach. "I was hoping you'd show up again."

She shrugs. "I don't think I can be of much use, when you're so pre-occupied." Abruptly, she gets up from the swing. "I've given this my best shot, but I guess I should recognize a lost cause for what it is."

"A lost cause?"

"You're still not doing what you're supposed to do."

"Which is what?" It comes out as a yelp. The small group of seagulls who've been seated a few yards from the swings begin back-waddling away.

"I mean, really, it's bad enough that you've been wasting all your energy on this *movie* of yours, but to find you here giving your attentions to that, that silly . . . facsimile of a woman!" She sighs, and calls out to a departing pelican. "He's incorrigible!" The pelican gives his long-beaked head a shake in evident commiseration and struts onward.

"Naomi . . ." I reach out to her, but she steps back.

"And here I was ready to try again." Naomi smiles ruefully. "Well, you did ask me to leave, and I can see that's only right. You're too involved with other things."

"It's my life!" I tell her. "I'm trying to work out a way to make it better."

"But if you're ever going to become the you that you *could* be . . ." She stops, shaking her head. "No, it's useless," she says.

"You know," I say, "if you didn't only speak in riddles, maybe I'd be able—"

"Jordan, who are you talking to?"

Startled, I turn around. Isabella stands a few feet away, staring at me with a look of perplexed concern.

"Oh, dear," Naomi mutters.

"No, wait," I say.

"For what?" Isabella asks. "I've *been* waiting, Jordan, and now I find you here, acting like a crazy person."

Naomi shakes her head. "The other night you wanted a resolution."

"You mean, here on the beach?"

"Yes, we're at the beach," Isabella says, stepping closer, with real alarm on her face. "*Amore,* look at me."

"Just a second." I'm still looking at Naomi. "Go on."

"Jordan!" Isabella puts a hand on my shoulder. "Are you there?"

Naomi sighs. "You see? I can't work like this."

Isabella reaches up with both hands and turns my face to look at her. "*Amore,*" she repeats. "You take too much sun. Maybe you should sit down for a moment."

"I'm fine!" I twist around to see Naomi turning away.

"*Ho paura!*" Isabella says. "I think what you better do is be quiet for a moment and come with me." She takes my arm now, leading me back to our table. "We sit in the shade, have a drink of water . . ."

I steal another look behind me, seeing Naomi's empty swing sway slowly back and Naomi herself, head down, sauntering round the corner of the restaurant. For all I know, she's going-gone, for good. Isabella's signaling for Carlos. "*Acqua minerale, per favore,*" she calls, while her soft fingers caress my neck, as if she senses that I want to bolt. "Poor baby," she murmurs. "I think it's a very good thing that I come back when I did." Her phone chimes. "*Madonna!*"

Fate, toying with me, has tossed me a bone: Isabella's mother calling, which ought to keep Isabella in her own language and out of my way for a chunk of time, so I rise, miming that I'm restroom-bound, and back away from the table and my wife's dark-browed nodding as she motor-mouths with Mama.

The restrooms are set back from the patio by a low, vine-covered wall. Oddly enough, Naomi is emerging from the Women's behind it, and for a surreal moment as she comes into the light, I'm looking at Eve returning to the Garden, naked as creation, until I realize she's wearing some French designer's droll gag of a bikini, three sheer dabs of flesh-colored material— "Jordan!" cries the figure that is Naomi Dussart's, I realize, from the thickness of her accent, the stylishness of the scarf tied through her tresses, and the—whoa, little slippage in one of the dabs there, as she reaches for the string on her back that's come untied—"Can you help me with this?"

Not a sign of My Naomi. This one, beach-bound, girlishly awaits my manly assistance, so I slip behind the wall and nervously attend to re-knotting her top, Naomi smiling, leaning one voluptuous haunch into me, saying, "I don't know how everyone can live here and not *swim* in this ocean."

"There you go."

I give her back a chaste pat. Naomi turns around to face me, very close, holding my hand at her shoulder. "I wish you could come in."

"Jordan?"

At the sound of Isabella's voice I move without thought, pushing down. Naomi Dussart is suddenly on her knees in front of me, beneath the wall, out of sight, as Isabella's face appears around the back, the phone at her ear. *"Ascolte, Mama, momento—* Is everything okay, Jordan?"

"Yeah!" I call, Naomi's face in my thighs. "I'm just washing up."

"You're sure?"

Naomi Dussart blows out a soft raspberry of warm breath into my groin, pressing herself against my legs. "I'm fine, Bella—I'll be right out!"

And I steel myself for the inevitable—Isabella's outraged discovery and the end of everything I've been striving for, destroyed in an instant of absurd farce—but—

"All right. *Mama, va bene . . .*" To my awed disbelief, Isabella's too caught up in her conversation to investigate further. Her voice fades around the bend. I'm saved. And now, with a giggle, evil Naomi climbs up my body to get to her feet.

It's then that I see her, beyond my companion's teasing smile. My Naomi has reappeared at the edge of the parking lot to stare at us. As my eyes meet hers, even from this distance I can feel the heat. The sky starts darkening behind her and I sense an ominously familiar biblical cast taken on by the afternoon light.

"If you should change your mind," says Naomi Dussart, "Marie knows how to reach me." The wind is picking up. My Naomi's now just a few yards away, hands on hips, eyes crackling green from her dark silhouette as this Naomi hurriedly retrieves a towel from her beach bag. "*Putain,* it's a monsoon!"

She darts a quick good-bye kiss on my cheek and strides off, shielding her face with the bag against what's become a sandstorm-like hail of red bougainvillea bits blowing across the patio. I turn back, alone at last to confront My Naomi, but she's shaking her head, her unmistakable gaze of disappointment piercing me as her image shimmers like a mirage, a trick of the suddenly brightening light, and then she disappears.

And no matter how pressing my questions might be, I'm going to be left with them unanswered, because in this abrupt quiet as the wind dies down again, I'm sure I've just seen a look that said good-bye.

By the time we return to the bike path, pedaling home, I've convinced my wife that I'm not having a nervous breakdown. Overworked, we agreed, toiling too hard, under too much pressure. But though Isabella may be mollified now, I'm only feeling worse. Because as we bicycle down the shiny shore, I'm thinking, What have I done?

I had a muse. A confusing one, true, yet nonetheless my own. I thought at first she'd come to help me with Isabella, then realized she was helping me with my Rumer project—even though according to her, she was here to facilitate the creation of something else. What, I have no idea, and what's making my insides ache is the comprehension that I never will know. Whatever great work ("the new work," she kept saying) may have been seeded, it never got nurtured into being. Because I've sent her away, and now she's gone for good.

But how do you measure the loss of something when you don't know exactly what you had? I force myself to think instead about what I've managed to hold on to. Focusing on what's in front of me, I watch the lines of Isabella's body rise and fall as she pedals onward down the bicycle path, her curves shifting with each turn. This is why I did what I did. Let me not take for granted what's still here, what seems to have endured.

In fact, let me take some solace in the idea that I just averted a catastrophe with Naomi Dussart. Hard to believe, also unsettling, but Isabella has apparently taken the encounter in stride. The woman is inexhaustibly surprising. Now, as we turn from the path proper to cross the boardwalk, she's flushed and exhilarated. "I missed this crazy place," she tells me as I draw even with her, weaving our bikes through the cluster of peddlers with their incense, their spin-art paintings and T-shirts for sale. "Maybe when Rumer makes the movie," she says, "I can get a real studio, away from the house."

If Rumer makes the movie, if I've still got the gig . . . I fend off my fears. It helps to take refuge in Isabella's idle fantasy. "Maybe we can get a real house."

"Ours is real," she says. "Maybe a little *sur*-real. But if you want a new house . . ."

"Maxi would like it."

She grins. "Ah, well, if it's for *Maxi* . . ."

Uplifted by such fanciful conjectures, Isabella insists on racing me over the streets that lead from the beach to our block. She wins by a few bike lengths, and is laughing, breathless, as we walk the bikes up to the garden gate. "My lovely garden!" she exclaims as we enter. "I haven't had a moment . . ." I take hold of her bicycle as she hurries for the hose. While I wheel both bikes around to the back and lock them up, she waters the greenery up front, talking quietly to the plants as one might to household cats.

The clothesline I rigged for Isabella here came down some weeks ago. Now I retie the loose end to its tree branch. The talk of a future for us and this simple act of nesting pours a soothing coat of normalcy over my raw and jangled nerves. I tell myself I'll be able to do whatever script revisions Rumer may ask for on my own. I smile when I see Isabella come round with her watering can, ready to service the stray plants where the hose doesn't reach.

She stops short. "Oh, no!" She kneels by the potted olive tree.

"What?"

"You've practically killed it!" I look at the olive branches, drooping, a whole section of leaves an accusatory brown. "You're supposed to water it twice each week, I told you! What could be more simple?"

"I guess I missed a couple of times," I say sheepishly.

"I can't believe it!" she cries. She pulls, despairing, and a dozen dead leaves flutter to the ground. "This is just like you. It's you, exactly!"

"I'm a half-dead olive tree?"

"It's just like you to not even notice!"

"I'm sorry." And I am, feeling guilty now for a broad variety of betrayals. "But it's still alive, isn't it? We can save it."

"I don't know!" she says. "And I don't know how you could be so distracted." She straightens up from fussing with the lower branches to glare at me. "But I suppose a little cheap French perfume is all that it takes."

And we're off. The small safe haven of our homecoming was constructed of tinder, and it's blazing in seconds, the heavier logs soon rolling right into the fire, dry and crackling. All the accusations that haven't been aired are suddenly flaring, all the grievances ignited. No wonder she left me. I'm disconnected from all that really matters in life, my values are hopelessly corrupt, I have no idea how to love a woman properly, I am not the man she'd married—

"You're not the woman I married!" I fumble at the back-door lock. "Nobody can still be the person they were in the heat of passion! It's only natural in a marriage—"

"There's nothing natural about it!" Isabella stamps up the steps behind me. "Besides, how am I different, eh?"

"You're hysterical," I say, knowing this is gasoline, but unable to keep from throwing it on.

"Because I have feelings? Because I am in touch with them? Because I am not some repressed, cut-off American?"

"Oh, please." Banging our way into the house now.

"So this is what I came back for? To be abused?"

I pause at the threshold of the living room. I know why this has started, know what part of it is my own fault, know that a fight like this can never be won. I feel a chafing, almost palpable on my skin, as if someone is shoving a jacket over my frame that doesn't fit. I realize that the helplessness I'm feeling is learned behavior, a part in a particular play, and it's nothing that's natural to me. Whether I submit and appease Isabella or fight back, my self will shrink. There has to be a way to stop the fireworks without my disappearing altogether. I turned around to face Isabella, who has retrieved last night's pizza box from the fridge and bangs it down on the kitchen table. "Look," I say quietly. "No one's abusing anyone. We're just under a lot of stress. It's understandable, isn't it?"

"There are some things about you that I will never understand."

My peace wreath flutters to the floor. "Maybe we should just not talk."

"Maybe you're right."

I turn and walk across the room to the blinking answering machine, stab at the button. "You have one new message," the machine announces.

"What are you doing?" Isabella's in the doorway, outraged. I jab the button again, halting the machine.

"I'm getting the messages."

"But this is too much!" she cries. "In the middle of our conversation—"

"You agreed we shouldn't talk!"

"This is exactly what I mean. You have no feeling for what matters, you'll let a plant die while you're busy with your computer, you would rather listen to a machine than deal with a living person—"

"Isabella."

"I'm going to change my clothes," she says abruptly. "I'm going to the gallery, so you'll have plenty of quiet, soon enough."

I watch her stalk into the bedroom, hear the door yanked shut. What I wouldn't give just now for that erasing device Jim Carrey and Kate Winslet used in *Eternal Sunshine* to wipe both their minds clean of their tortured romantic past. Oh, to start over with a clean slate! But I've got no such technology, just this answering machine. The message is from

Moony. "Is 'John the Revelator' a Blind Willie Johnson or a Blind Lemon Jefferson song?" he wants to know. "And has anyone ever put out a compilation of all-blind blues songs? There ought to be one. Call it . . . *Love Is Blind: A Very Special Blues Collection*. Heh–heh–heh . . ." The sound of the bedroom door slamming open overrides Moony's laugh. I look up, startled by the heavy tread of Isabella stomping across the living-room floor and into the kitchen, head down. "So," Moony continues. "Just droppin' in to see what condition your condition is in." Sound of a kitchen drawer wrenched open, a clatter from in there—"As for Kathleen and me, let's say I'm cautiously optimistic . . ."

Isabella comes barreling through the living room again with a carving knife in her hand. I instinctively recoil as she marches past me, the wicked serrated edge glinting. "But I got one word for you and me, bro: *jambalaya*," Moony's saying. "Call me."

Bewildered, I stare after her, stop the machine, and hustle into the bedroom. When I come through the doorway I behold my wife standing by the open closet door, holding out a white silk bustier. I recognize, stomach sinking, my touchstone: the gift I bought to lend credence to my imaginary lover, back before My Naomi first appeared. Isabella stabs at its breast with the knife and slices it down the middle. The bustier comes apart with a loud tearing sound. With a frighteningly fixed absorption, she saws at a seam, then drops the knife on the bed. Isabella takes hold of the white fabric in both hands and rips one half in half. Only then does she glance in my direction.

"I hoped you would clean the house better than this," she says, holding up the decimated lingerie. "But if you are too lazy to take out your own garbage . . ." More tearing finishes her sentence for her.

"Isabella . . ." I begin.

"Lupe always needs some rags, when she comes in to clean." Isabella shrugs, then turns the full fire of her gaze upon me, brandishing the jagged square of silk with its one thin spaghetti strap dangling. "Or maybe you'd like to keep this under your pillow? Because obviously you still need to have her near you."

"Isabella," I repeat. "This is ridiculous. All it is——"

"Ridiculous?" she roars. I've waved a red flag at a bull. "I'm not the ridiculous one here!" She's furiously gathered the ripped material into a ball in her fist and now slams the closet shut. "Or yes, maybe I am, to come back here."

"Would you stop for a second?"

"I don't have to stay."

"Isabella . . ."

She advances on me, knife clutched in her other hand, and throws the ball of lingerie at my chest. I have to step back against the bedroom door as she storms past.

I follow her through the living room and into the kitchen again, where Isabella, having tossed the knife in the drawer and banged it shut, yanks her chair out from the table, wooden legs screeching on the Formica, and sits, grabbing her bag to pull out her tobacco and papers. The pizza box, I note, is overturned, open, on the floor.

"I can call Flavia," she says, fingers working at her cigarette. "Or maybe Marcello, he's closer."

I turn from fetching paper towels. "What are you talking about?"

"I don't have to stay here tonight."

"Come on! Will you calm down for a moment?"

"You think I am so, so . . . dependent, that I have no resources? You think I'm weak, maybe, because it seems I come running back to you. But I can buy another ticket, you know. You think I won't? Maybe I should put it under *my* pillow, to sleep with every night! How would you like that?"

Beneath her with sponge in hand, I sit back on my haunches. What's more pathetic than cold pizza on the floor? "Listen to me," I entreat her. "Isabella, it was a simple mistake! That thing you found, it was so unimportant that I forgot it was even there. It means nothing to me."

Rolled cigarette jammed in her mouth, she flicks her lighter once, twice, gives it a shake. Her lips are trembling. Compassion and exasperation knot in my chest. *"Amore,"* I say. "I'm sorry." I'm already in the supplicant's position. "You know I love you, you know I don't want you to go anywhere. Come on . . ."

Isabella turns her tear-filled eyes to me at last. "I do know," she murmurs. "And I'm trying to be good. I *want* to feel good about us . . ." The phone is ringing. She blinks back the tears, dabbing at one eye with her finger. "Aren't you going to answer?"

"The machine can get it."

She manages a crooked smile. "No, please. Answer it."

I recognize this as a truce offering, and hurry to the phone. It's Yuko, asking if I can possibly make a three o'clock meeting with Rumer. "Sorry about the short notice," she says cheerily. "But he's off to Toronto tomorrow, so if there's any way—"

"Of course," I tell her, heart hammering. The only thing on my calendar is the long-awaited visit with Leo, at five. "Three o'clock is perfect."

"He's at the Chateau Marmont today. Suite 542. See you there."

In this town good news travels fast and bad doesn't travel, period— when somebody passes, they simply disappear. So the speed of Rumer's response bodes well. Nervous elation enables me to brave the walk back into hostile territory.

Isabella looks up at me, eyes red. "That was Rumer's office," I begin.

"He wants to see you," she says. "That's good."

"Well, we'll see how it goes," I say. "But listen . . ."

"I know," Isabella says. We stare at each other for a long moment, as if allowing a silent traffic jam of emotions to subside. Then she stubs out her cigarette. "Look. You told to me you're sorry . . . and I'm sorry if I lose my head."

"No, I understand!" I'm relieved and thrown by this uncharacteristic apology. "It's only natural . . ."

She sighs. "Nothing is natural now. Go. Go to your meeting, and later . . ."

"We'll talk," I say.

"I'll say a prayer for good things to happen," says Isabella. I nod thanks, though I can see by how she busies herself with cleaning up the table that she's intent on keeping me at a distance. "And maybe you should do a meditation," she adds, "before you go. To center your energy."

It's surprising enough that she's calmed down so quickly. But since when has my Italian wife become so Californian?

I walk quickly through the lobby of the Chateau, where everybody looks like they're somebody and a few of them actually are. I dread seeing Dana face-to-face almost more than I'm excited to be in the same room with Rumer Hawke again. Maybe with Rumer present, she'll be on good behavior.

Maybe there'll be no Dana, the meeting just me and Rumer, writer and producer, mano a mano, the beginning of a more intimate relationship as the green-lit project acquires heat. Perhaps within weeks I'll be ensconced in a suite at the Chateau as the movie launches into frenetic pre-production, doing inspired midnight oil–burning dialogue revisions under Rumer's hands-on guidance, with a Johnny D'Arc or a Johnny Depp in tow. One of those Johnnies. Reading through the so-much-better pages, then driving down Sunset to the Viper Room to hear a Tex-Mex band, drink Mojitos, and unwind.

Once inside the elevator, I turn around to push the proper floor button and find myself facing Dana Morton. I shrink back against the wall as she steps inside, immaculately coiffed and suited, her face blank of any recognizable emotion. She makes no response to my nodded greeting, and as the door shudders noisily shut before us, I wonder if she's pretending not to know me. It's an old man of an elevator—small, slow-moving and slightly palsied. The two of us stand uncomfortably close, facing front, in a prickly silence that's interminable. I'm trying to formulate a diplomatic, casual way to pick up the shorn threads of what had been an ongoing conversation between us for nearly two weeks now, when she finally speaks.

"The pages you sent me will function for the moment," Dana says, her eyes on the trembling elevator door.

"That's what I figured," I venture.

"But once Rumer signs off on this, you'll have some heavy lifting to do. I've got notes," she adds ominously, and with a shudder and sigh, we're on the fifth floor.

I follow Dana down the carpeted hallway, surprised by how close and cramped it is in the nether regions of this legendary hotel. The door to 542 opens in response to Dana's knock and Yuko, murmuring into her headset, waves us inside.

Here, too, the rooms are small, but there are many, all in a confusion of activity. Directly in front of us a pair of twenty-something women in restaurant uniforms busily fill the living-room table with an assortment of sushi, salads, and fruit. A TV tuned to CNN monologues quietly in one corner. A Korean woman in a bright yellow smock exits a bathroom and crosses to a closed door, bearing a pile of smooth, steaming stones on a tray. I catch a glimpse of a bare male form, prone facedown on a massage table within the bedroom, before the woman shuts the door behind her.

Through a foyer on the other side of the living room I sight the unmistakable visage of Rumer Hawke. Wearing gray sweatshirt and sweatpants, he's seated in a half-lotus on a round rug, facing a deeply tanned, impossibly fit man of indeterminate age with a close-cropped beard and bald head, clad only in a pair of runner's shorts. Isabella will be pleased to hear that Rumer, at least, apparently does prepare for his meetings by aligning his chakras.

Dana inspects the fruit salad. Yuko has slipped unobtrusively into Rumer's space and leans down to speak with him. Abruptly, the great man clambers to his feet. I'd forgotten how tall Hawke is. He towers over both his assistant and his trainer as he moves quickly to a desk, snatching up what I realize, with a jolt of excitement, is my screenplay, recognizable by the oversized type (Dana's insistence) of its title on the front. Clutching the script, Rumer strides into the living room as the food help withdraws, their task completed, wheeling a cart past Dana and out the door of the suite.

"What *is* this?" Rumer says. For an instant, I think he's referring to the array of foods spread out on the table before him. Then I see that he's waving the screenplay in the air, and that he's directing his words at Dana Morton. The question is too rhetorical and too sharply put for Dana to answer. She merely stares at him in alarm.

"This isn't the story I bought," says Rumer. His tone is congenially perplexed. He wears the expression of a man who has been handed the wrong coat by a coat-check girl. "This isn't anything remotely like the movie I wanted to make. What the hell were you thinking?"

For one last, hope-crazed moment, I fantasize what Rumer will say next. *This!* he will cry, brandishing a copy of my novel, this *is the movie I'm making*—extending his arm, palm out, to indicate me—*and this is the only man who knows how to write it!*

What happens in the realm of real time and space, however, is not so pretty. "Well," Dana begins, "from the initial discussions we—"

"Dana," Rumer interrupts. "We talked about a romantic *comedy,* not this, this—" Large veins throb on his high-domed forehead. Flecks of spittle appear at the corners of his lips.

"The breathing," cautions his trainer from the next room.

"—this hackneyed"—he takes a breath—"action comedy—*crap!*" Rumer flings the script into an armchair. The draft knows its appropriate behavior, and promptly bounces from the cushion to land facedown on the floor. The quiet smack it makes is the punctuation that ends Rumer's struggle with his affliction. "Christ, Dana," he mutters, becalmed, and shakes his head at her with a look of pity. Then he turns to Yuko. "Are they coming? Did you find them?"

As Yuko gives him a murmured report, Rumer grabs an apple from the table and turns his back on us. Ears ringing, body become sandbag, I look to Dana Morton. Ever without affect, she is walking toward the door of the suite. I follow, and I'm right behind her as she opens it, when the boom of Rumer's voice halts us on the threshold. "Where the hell are *you* going?"

Amazing, really, the resilience of a dream life. I think the question has at last been directed at me. But Rumer is addressing Dana, and I remain as invisible as I've been since I first set foot into the suite. She clears her throat. "I thought——"

"We've got the call list and something like six projects to deal with before they get here," Rumer says, chomping on his apple.

Dana promptly walks back across the room to join her boss. The bedroom door opens, and the man who'd been bearing hot rocks on his back emerges with a towel around his waist. I pause only long enough to let the eyes of the slick-haired Nathan Colt flick briefly over my face with little interest and less recognition. Then I step across the threshold, leaving the door shut behind me, along with my fabulous career.

And I'm back in the lobby suddenly, a swatch of time gone missing as my mind groped to comprehend the incomprehensible, I'm gliding across the pathways of figures inhabiting some other dimension, as I look for the way out. That's when I glimpse a red dress, a cascade of long dark hair, and I turn, redirecting my leaden feet and the full force of my shell-shocked outrage toward the familiar woman seated in the armchair over there, thinking, *you,* my supposed savior, the ostensible instrument of my inspiration, how could you have misled me so cruelly, what was the meaning of all we went through if it's only brought me to *this*?

But she turns toward me just then—a chic-looking stranger, simply someone else who really does belong in this scene. So the invisible man moves on, a walking question who won't find answers here.

Leo will know. He'll have the insight, the penetration to put my devastation into perspective. True, in our last phone call it was hard for him to talk. Still, such a handicap is apt to make the old writer all the more eloquent, his words being so carefully chosen to begin with. Estelle told me of Leo's incessant messaging, the commands on Post-its stuck all over the house. Even if we have to do it in writing, we'll have our conversation.

At a lull in the oncoming traffic I gun the Metropolitan's motor and make the mad turn across Pacific Coast Highway, zooming into his driveway. Pulling up to the bumper of Leo's green Jaguar, I yank my emergency brake against the steep incline and climb from my car. I've got his present in hand, a novel by Kurkov, which I finally found at Small World Books on the Venice boardwalk, only blocks from my place. It's got vodka, murder, and a penguin in it, a peculiarly Slavic combo that ought to amuse him.

I can hear the waves crashing on the beach below as I hurry through the gate. To sit with Leo on the deck, talking into the wind above the foaming surf—about Rumer, Naomi, Isabella—the whole mess of it will become clearer with his help. I ring the bell impatiently, assured by a glance at my watch that I'm right on time. Leo is a stickler for punctuality. The door swings open. Mrs. D stands on the threshold, facing me with a look of startled incomprehension. "Jordan!"

Estelle stands just behind her, peering out. "I'm sorry," I say, "was I supposed to call before—"

"No, it's all right," Estelle says, speaking to the housekeeper as well as to me. Mrs. D moves aside and she steps into the late-afternoon light, pale, eyes red-rimmed.

"If it's a bad time . . ."

"No, dear, I simply forgot that you were coming," Estelle says, her worn face twitching in a semblance of a smile. "But the thing is . . . Leo . . . He's gone, Jordan." She pauses. "He died, just an hour, an hour and a half ago."

"No." I'm unable to say anything else.

Estelle is nodding, and keeps on nodding as she explains that they haven't even called the hospice people yet, let alone an ambulance, she's been in a state, Mrs. D distraught, they're trying to get hold of Leo's brother, and Trish, the stepdaughter, and it's fine that I'm here, of course, she's already done her crying, but things are a bit crazy just this moment, except it's really up to me, if I want to come in. "If you'd like to say good-bye," Estelle says, smiling while a trickle of tears runs down her freckled cheek.

"You mean . . ."

"Yes, he's here," she says. "He's still in the chair where he passed away. Actually, we were about to open a bottle of wine."

Inside, there's a lamp lit by Leo's armchair, the only other light a rosy glow coming through the glass doors over the ocean. Leo sits, his reading glasses dangling from his pocket, his hands crossed in his lap, the dome of his balding head forward. He looks as though he's merely fallen asleep in his chair. For a while I'm preoccupied with Estelle and Mrs. D, a woman I've never hugged before in my life, who smells faintly of apricots and who feels far more frail in our brief embrace than I would have imagined. There's the illusion that we're speaking softly so as not to awaken the man dozing in the armchair before the windows. Then, when Estelle once again urges me to go, to say my good-bye, I have to cross the living room and face the fact that Leo will not be rousing himself.

I set the gift-wrapped book on the couch and sit on the ottoman next to his chair. Leo's stillness brings it home to me, not so much the absence of a rise and fall of the thin breast beneath his button-down and cardigan, but a quality of absolute repose that seems to still the air between us. His skin has a waxen look. His large hands, liver-spotted, slightly swollen, are already yellowing. His head seems so big, hanging down. His lips are closed, the long face shadowed. He emanates weight, heaviness.

"Leo," I say. Whatever tears I have to shed are still suspended, held somewhere in abeyance in my slowed comprehension of what sits before me. This is still Leo, yet not the man I came to see. I have the sensation of looking at a sculpture of my friend, a skillful rendering true to everything of Leo but his essential animation.

"You look good," I whisper, before I even know what I'm saying. I brave a touch, reaching out my hand to lightly, gently clasp him on the knee. Not cold, not warm. *You're not in pain,* was what I meant by my words, and it's true—whatever the struggle, Leo in his new state has a serene, untroubled expression. According to Estelle, who has uncorked the wine and can be heard moving about the kitchen with Mrs. D behind us, he'd made the usual complaints about the terrible food he was being forced to eat, had seated himself to look at the paper, and closed his eyes a moment in fatigue. When Mrs. D approached him a few minutes later with the bowl of soup, he had already breathed his last.

I see now that the stain on Leo's pants cuff, the stickiness on the parquet floor beneath my own right foot, is the remnants of potato-leek. There's a hole in one of his old black socks. I glance up into Leo's closed eyes, imagining a faint smile on the old man's lips. But no, the nothing that I can't get used to stubbornly persists, a benign indifference that's humbling, and in the next moment, maddening.

What am I supposed to learn from this? How am I supposed to understand? I feel my guilt flaring—why did it take me so long to get here?—but honestly, it's infuriating: The words, the words, Leo's gift, it's meant to be my reward, and it's doubly cruel to be deprived, just now.

Only the ceaseless waves, breaking placidly below, the quiet chatting of the women in the kitchen, a soft sigh from Estelle, the clinking of glass. I look to Leo, friend, teacher, man who has the answers, silence radiating from his stolid form like the ultimate Zen koan. Who am I sitting with? Who am I, if I can no longer be the younger friend, the writer protégé, the student and companion to a curmudgeonly sage?

It occurs to me that it takes death to stop the process of projection. Whatever shadows had been cast on the screen of me have vanished, what images I had cast upon the figure of Leo have ceased to move and function. I can only be who I am, and Leo can only be a dead man. I rise from my seat, lean in to press my lips to his unfurrowed brow, and murmur some words of love and farewell.

From across the darkening living room comes the quiet whir and click of Leo's printer. Estelle is retrieving the single sheet that slides out of it as I join her. "There was an e-mail he didn't finish," she says, and holds it out to me. I look down at the page, startled to see my own name.

Jordan:

I'm sorry, but I think we'd be better off waiting for another day.

Though in truth, maybe we've waited for later for too long.

Jordan, there is no later.

All we have

Here it ends, the one sentence suspended forever, and I know how Leo would hate such sloppiness, the lack of punctuation, let alone definitive closure, but I believe I understand how the thought might have finished.

I thank Estelle for printing it out. She's seating herself on the couch, Mrs. D hovering nearby, proffering a glass of wine. I take it from her.

"Sit, Mrs. D," says Estelle, and the housekeeper moves to the chair at my right. We all exchange a glance, then raise our wineglasses, tilting toward each other, then the man in the armchair.

I sip the Beaujolais, swallow. "It's not bad," says Estelle, and I nod. Mrs. D clears her throat. The three of us instinctively look to Leo, who in this household has always been the arbiter of taste.

Light shines from my kitchen window through the tipu tree's leafy branches. It gives a gold cast to the bungalow's facade, makes the shadow-dappled greenery gleam here and there, revealing a stray white blossom. It's a place, half-hidden from view, a cozy corner of Venice-near-the-beach that I'd admire, were I a passerby, and would want to be inside of and envy having. It's small, anything but lavish, but it has its character, this home, and it's mine. More than this, I think, pushing open the gate with its familiar, predictable creak. It's ours.

All we have . . .

The lady of the house is at her stove. I smell her cooking as soon as the door swings open. There is her bag by the easy chair, her sketchpad on the ottoman, her magazines, makeup, a candle lit atop the TV, Nick Drake singing soft and happily melancholic on the stereo. The only thing missing from the scene is Maxi's bark and snuffling from his perch beside the couch.

When I call a hello, Isabella comes quickly to the kitchen door, a spatula in hand. She's wearing the dress I bought for her in Santa Fe, with its Southwestern Native American colors, under an apron she brought with her from Rome, charmingly faded and stained. Her hair's down, long and lustrous, one earring, a painted Mexican bottle cap, tangled in the tendrils of hair about her right ear, a line of tomato-stained flour on her newly tanned cheek. *"Amore,"* she says, and envelops me in a fierce hug, as if I've been gone for days and not mere hours. "You're all right?"

I called her with the news about the end of Leo and the rest of the day's events. She was compassionate, kind, had wanted to know if there was anything she could do.

"I'm okay," I tell her now.

"And Estelle?"

"Remarkable," I say. It's true. Leo's wife exhibited a grace I can't imagine possessing under similar circumstances. Mourning will come, she said when I was leaving. It would be around for a long time, there was no hurry to indulge it now.

All we have . . . I give Isabella's shoulders a squeeze as I step back from her hug. "What do I smell?"

She smiles. "Something you like."

I go to the stove, grab a pot holder, and lift the top of the big pan, releasing a cloud pungent with tomato, garlic, mushrooms, olives, meat. I inhale, transported. This pasta dish is Isabella's invention, my favorite. On another burner, deep green spinach, sautéing in a simple sauce of butter and lemon. A Cabernet on the counter. The colander full of steaming linguine in the sink.

I look to Isabella, who in honor of Leo, of my loss, is being a wife. "It's the first time I cook for us in a while, so it has to be good, eh? It's almost ready. Here." She opens a drawer, produces the corkscrew.

I nod, picking up the bottle. "How did it go at the gallery?"

"Very good. I tell you about when we eat." She hesitates. "I was so tough with you this morning. I hope you'll sorry me."

Forgive is a word she still hasn't mastered. I don't correct her. "Of course I do. And I shouldn't have yelled so loud."

"And Jordan, I'm sorry, but these people, Rumer and the woman, they are idiots, they would only have made a mess of your good work, a mockery! Someone else is going to make your movie, someone who appreciate what you do. We're going to find out this was a good thing to happen." Absorbed in picking flecks of cork off the bottle's lip, I nod, listening to the circular stirring of Isabella's big spoon in the saucepan. "This isn't just a day for sadness," she goes on. "This is new beginnings. God is like that—we know. When he takes away, he also gives."

There's something just a tad overpracticed in her voice. I again have that sensation, as I've had a few times since her return, that Isabella is playing a part. I glance over my shoulder. Isabella, unaware, is gazing into the sauce. I'm startled to recognize on her face the same expression of ancient sadness I glimpsed that afternoon, years ago, when I came to visit her at her old studio. Her eyes have that same tragic cast, the Modigliani planes and angles of her face fixed in a deep, ingrained grief. The sadness I'm seeing now isn't grief for Leo, whom she didn't know so well, or for anything belonging to the present moment. I know, as I knew then, that I am seeing the face that lies beneath all the other faces, the fundamental repose of her soul and character.

Isabella senses my attention and looks up, her expression immediately shifting into a benign and pleasant mask, but it's already slipping, too makeshift to stay in place. Though she manages a tentative smile, the air has gone out of the room.

And now I'm thinking again of another room, the almost-empty white studio I saw when she brought me in there that first time, with only one broken chair inside. Well, I bought her a new chair. I got pillows, a rug, a couch—our home is filled with beautiful things. The two of us have filled a life with so much of what she'd asked for, and still she wanted to leave. She had been sad when she arrived, and after all our moments of love and happiness, she's still sad. Even now, she can't maintain her attempted smile. Bewildered panic sweeps through me like a wind. I thought I was safe on home ground, after the day's disasters, but the ground has shifted. There's a truth rushing toward me from a ways off, one I can't quite recognize yet, and my impulse is to run to meet it.

I take hold of her arms and turn her around to face me. "What?" she asks.

"Isabella," I say. "I want you to pretend it's not me. Pretend you're speaking to your priest, or your mother, or your diary. I'm not going to judge you, I'm not going to argue, I'm going to listen. But I need to know what's been going on with you. I need to know what we're going to do."

"All right . . ." she says, cautious.

"Let's take a walk."

"But the dinner!" Something in my face must have gotten to her. I see her repress her disappointment. *"D'accordo,"* she says. "We can heat it up."

"Good idea. And here's another," I say. "Let's take the bottle."

Out into the night, out of the home that's suddenly grown too small around me, Isabella on my arm, the sound of our footfalls on the pavement unnaturally distinct as we trace the route we've taken, so many times, to walk Maxi before bed. There's no one to be seen or heard on our block, not even the whoosh of a passing car. It's like walking through a ghost town, or a town where ghosts have spellbound all the other living souls in the neighborhood. I doubt even Naomi, were she still at large, would invade this sphere.

I've posed a simple question: What decision has Isabella come to, about our marriage? But it's not a thing I can force out of her, this truth. She is a woman, after all, so there is no straight line that leads from there to here in what she says. First there is what led to the decision, then within that, the different ways to look at the decision, all of this colored by a tangled skein of emotions and complexities of perception, so that I understand, when we're halfway round the block, that I'll have to go round and round the question with her as we walk around the block. But I will keep walking round it, bottle in hand, because I'm a man, so long as I hold on to what is now a wary stillness in the center of me, and I will not, cannot stop walking until the answer to this conundrum is revealed.

Her problems in Rome, yes, her conflicted feelings about me, check, the complications brought on by news of my infidelity, right, what she realized she missed about her life here, versus the pull of what is so good about being home, yes, and then the added turmoil of her brief fling with this boy . . .

"But you ended that."

"Oh, yes, it's over, for me," she says. "But Italian men . . ."

"He's still pursuing you?"

"It's not important."

I feel the tug of another concentric circle, a distraction. Focus. "And are you still angry with me, about being with Naomi?"

She shrugs. "I don't like to think about it."

"This morning, you were so furious."

"You say it's over, and I believe you."

"But that's why you came back, ultimately. Because you thought maybe you were losing me."

"I was worried," she admits.

"Are you glad you did?"

"*Sì.* But it's complicated," says Isabella.

"If I were to ask you now, have you made the right choice—"

"Such an interrogation!"

"I'm sorry, Isabella, I'm just trying to understand. The thing is, you don't seem happy," I say. "Is it because you're upset about what's happened with Rumer? I mean, it's true, now the movie may not even get made. Things could get harder before they get easier."

"I know. But really, I'm not very worried."

"Then . . ." I've been listening to her the way someone pulling in a long rope might listen, trying to gauge the size and shape of what holds on to the other end, and it's as if the rope has gone slack in my hands.

We're back where we began, outside our own gate. A street lamp casts a hostile orange light over the tree at block's end, as if trying to fry the color out of it. I crane my head back. The sky is so clear you can feel there's nothing between you and the stars. But the clarity between the two of us is still elusive. I turn back to my wife. "Look: Just be straight with me. Have you come back for good? Or is this a kind of experiment?"

Isabella purses her lips, considering. "Okay," she says. "With everything that's been going on, with both of us, the kind of day you had, *Madonna*! I didn't think to talk about this now, but maybe after all—"

"Talk to me," I implore her, bottle tucked beneath my arm, my palms clasped and bobbing up and down before me, the gentle beseecher, that gesture I've seen Isabella herself use. "Just tell me the truth."

"You want to know why I came back?" I nod. "Because I had a plan."

"A plan?"

"Yes, I have an idea, a wonderful plan for what we can do together."

"Really." I had a plan, she has a plan. We begin to walk again, and I take another long pull at the bottle. The wine is an antidote to gravity, as if the more I drink, the lighter my body weighs. I hold it out to Isabella. She shakes her head.

"It's what I was thinking," she says, "when I decided not to go to Todi. I had a vision, a very clear picture of all we could be, the two of us. For a better marriage. And since—"

"Wait, that was nearly a week ago. Why didn't you tell me about it then?"

"I was going to! And then I find you still carrying on with this woman, and we were fighting, and things got so confused . . ."

"All right," I say. "So you changed your mind?"

"No, in fact, the more I think, the better it seems to me, this idea. The more sense it makes."

"So tell me."

"Do you want to hear? Because, baby, even tonight, the state you are in—"

"This is absolutely the best time to tell me," I assure her.

"This is what I think," she says. "We can be married, but not really *married.*" She slows her stride. "Why do we have to live the same life we've always lived together? Maybe it's true that I can't be always in

America. So why can't I be in Italy—sometimes with you, and sometimes not? Why must we always stay here at home?"

"Well, I have to make a living."

"But you are a writer! You don't have to live in one place. And I am
an artist, and I *need* to travel. Jordan, when I was in Rome, I went to
dance the tango with these friends of Claudio—an amazing night, they
do the *milonga,* the music so amazing, and the dancers, you would not
believe! Half of my new drawings are from this, the colors, and the bodies, the men are so elegant and these women, Jordan, they would drive
you crazy, you have to see . . . Anyway, I become friendly with a man
who has a gallery and a restaurant in Buenos Aires, so simpatico—he
loves my work, he even bought a drawing, and he makes an invitation,
'Come to Argentina! Any time!' And he can put us up, he has a hotel
there, too, the man is wealthy! And this is not just a dream, this is a real
thing, believe me, I can tell the difference. We even begin to organize a
show, to show my drawings—"

"Sure. 'Come and stay with me in Buenos Aires,'" I say. "Did you
happen to mention you still had a husband?"

"Of course," Isabella says. "He knows I'm married. The invite is for
the two of us, together. And you would love it in that city. So inspiring!
We dance the tango, we go out every night—you'll write two movies in
a week there."

"Uh-huh."

"No, don't be this way, listen to me, *amore.*"

"I'm listening. But a trip to Argentina, this is a plan to make a better
relationship?"

"No, it's just one thing. I'm talking about Buenos Aires, Rome—
didn't you always say you want to spend time in Spain?"

I chuckle. "And I'd like to be in Bali, sure. But Izzy—"

"There's a world out there we could be exploring! And it doesn't
have to be expensive. We can live simply, I have friends in so many places.
We rent out our home here, I sell a few paintings—you'd be amazed how
we can get along. But the traveling is only a part of the idea."

I take a slug of wine. "What's another part?"

"Look, you've been with this woman, but it's something I understand. I'm not saying I don't have feelings, you know how I can be—today I was completely out of control! But when I'm honest with myself, I know that what happened with you is only natural. Just as for me, when I was with this boy in Rome, I won't pretend to you that it wasn't exciting. So why does it have to be, that both of us are denied these things? Because we're married? Who is to tell us what that has to mean?"

"What are you saying?"

"I'm saying that maybe a little more freedom is not a terrible thing. If we love each other, and our love is strong—maybe we don't always have to be everything to each other. If I am attracted to someone, if you want to be with another lover . . . Why does this have to destroy what you and I have together?"

I stare at her. "Did you smoke a little something before?"

Isabella laughs. "No, come on. I'm being serious."

"But Isabella, what if I don't want another lover? When you left, I couldn't imagine being with another woman—I had to imagine one to be with!" I blurt. "She wasn't even a real person."

"Superficial maybe," Isabella says. "But real enough."

You have no idea, I think, recalling what happened the last time I tried to come clean about this, no use trying again, and besides, focus: "The only reason I was with her was . . . was out of desperation. If I have you, why would I want somebody else?"

"Come on, Jordo." She nudges my arm with her fist. "You're a guy, after all. You think I haven't seen the way you look at Carmela?"

"Please. The way she dresses . . . and besides, she's a lesbian."

"Sometimes she's with a man. And she is very, very attractive. You know, one time, even she and I . . ." Isabella wiggles her eyebrows and takes the bottle from me.

"You're joking." She shrugs, drinks. "I'm amazed you never mentioned this."

"I didn't think to talk about it." Isabella wipes her mouth with the back of her hand. "But in truth, there is even this side to me. What if I wanted to be with a woman, for a time? Why does this mean I can't still be with you?"

"Why?" I shake my head. "Are you really asking?"

"Yes, because I see how narrow is this box we've put ourselves in! Jordan, it's like that stamp, the rubber stamp you have, you remember? It says 'Open Everything, Everywhere.' This is a beautiful thought! So is it just something for you to print on top of an envelope you send? Or is it a truth about a way to be living?"

I put a hand to my head for a moment, assuring myself that it's still all there. At my feet, the pavement's littered with flattened soda cans, old newspapers, the splayed junk from an overturned shopping cart. "We said we would have a child," I remind her. "How long are we going to put that off?"

"If we do still want to have children, now is the time for us to explore, to live, while we are young. Because I had tried, you know, to be this thing—the wife who cooks and stays at home, and then we have the babies—but what I realize is I am not this thing! And why am I supposed to be? And why are you the traditional husband, bringing home the food for the table, while I clean the house, and you bring a little *vino* to have with dinner—all that's missing is you smoke a pipe, right? Like American TV from when we were kids."

"And Maxi brings me my slippers while I read the paper."

"Yes, exactly!" Laughing. "This is not you. And this is not me. Jordan, I'm an artist. Do you know what that means?"

"Of course I do."

"But to really be free—this is what is so important! To both of us."

I consider, holding the bottle up in the direction of the streetlight. Almost empty. "So you've really been thinking about this for a while." Isabella nods. "Why didn't you tell me when you got here?"

"*Amore* . . . When I come home, and the place is so clean and nice, and I see how much you want everything to be the way it was, I didn't have the heart yet to begin, *Ciao!* Here is your crazy wife, with her mad idea . . . And the jet lag—and everything that goes on since I come back!"

"It has been a little nutty," I allow.

"Very!" she says. "But finally we're talking, and this is good. Because I want you to see what I'm seeing. The places we could go, the kind of a life that's possible for two people like us to have—two artists, who can think wide, and deep!"

I see the espresso cup steaming on the café table in an unknown city, my journal open on the zinc-top table. And afterward, a walk, deep in reverie, through the trees by a European river—Isabella, strolling to meet me by a sun-soaked marble monument, beret perched jauntily on her head. I'm wearing new shoes and a fashionable suit jacket, driving a vintage foreign car, we've joined a group of fellow writers and artists, belting down cognacs at a smoke-filled bar, where maybe another woman, blond as Isabella is dark, may smile at me, the promise of a provocative interlude—but still, back to Isabella, running hand in hand with her through a station to catch our next train to another country, another adventure . . . It's the life I've read about, had imagined for myself when I was younger, shimmering high and marvelous before me like a cloud-borne castle in the sky.

"Think, *amore,* what it would be like, to write in Buenos Aires, in Rio. Or even Tibet! In the mountains, in a little cabin, we could live like the monks live, so simple . . ."

And suddenly the light dies, like a bulb popping, and I'm back in the night that surrounds us. "Simple," I echo. "You in the temple, and me with a flock of sheep."

She laughs. "Maybe so! Who knows?"

"And if you end up getting involved with a monk, I always have a sheep to sleep with," I muse, and nod. "Yeah, that's a perfect arrangement."

"Jordan," she says, chiding.

I turn on her. "Isabella, who are you talking about?"

"What do you mean?"

"This is not me! You've put me in your fantasy—a delightful, beautiful fantasy—but it's not really me. It's not the real *us.*"

"You just can't think beyond the only life you know," she retorts. "You're not even willing to take the risk—"

"Because I'm not even in this! You've got some imaginary Jordan in this movie. Maybe he looks like me, but it's not me." Now I'm seeing those white shoes she gifted me with, the white socks she sent to the man who should be wearing them. "I'd *like* to be him, sure, this enlightened, romantic, sophisticated writer—"

"If you would open your mind—"

"—but what about the me who drives you crazy? The one who wasn't there for you enough, emotionally, the guy who was off in his head all the time, the guy who was so *dark*! And too inflexible, and too American—"

"Inflexible, yes, that much is true, because even now you can't open up to a new way of thinking, you always say no first, and then—"

"Isabella, this couple you're describing—it's not even *you*! Christ, as if the same woman who was slicing up lingerie with a carving knife this morning is going to suddenly be fine with . . . mistresses from around the world? Like I'll be okay with you and your lesbian girlfriend? What are you saying?!"

"Calm down, Jordan—"

"Calm down? On a day when my career blows up in my face and one of my best friends becomes a corpse, to hear the woman I love tell me that to save our marriage, she wants me to take tango lessons and see other people?"

"Please stop yelling."

"I can't! I can't believe that all the time you've been here, you're not even *here*!" The bottle flies from my hand, breaks with a crash and splatter on the curb across the street. "You're already off on another adventure, running away . . ."

"*Calma, amore*—please—"

Shaking my head, I have hold of her hands, and looking into her frightened face in the shadows, her dark hair framing the pale oval, the stricken gaze that gives her the haunting beauty of a church Madonna, I see it. I know how hard it must be, to live with such a sadness inside, and I see how it keeps her moving, trying on these other ways to be, and my heart aches for her, for her sweet hope, and her child-like energy and imagination. "Listen to me," I say. "Maybe it frightens you, to be alone, but I think your plan—what it's really saying is that you need to have your own life. This picture you're painting . . . It's just for you."

"No." She grips my hands tighter. "If you could be free, in your mind . . ."

"It's your freedom," I say. "I'm not sure I even know what mine is, but Isabella . . ."

"If we love each other, if you really love me . . ."

I keep shaking my head, because I know now I can never fix this, though I once promised her I could. I can make her smile, but it will only last a moment, and chasing that smile will drive us both crazy. And my eyes are filling with tears, because I do love her, but I understand, finally, that my love isn't going to be enough.

Sometime in the night, I wake to the sound of Isabella crying. I put my arms around her and kiss her wet cheeks as she clings to me. It's the beginning of a slow, fervent ritual of tributes, to her lips, their shape and pliant warmth so familiar, that soft, soft inch of skin above the pulse in her neck. Isabella, too, finds the places she's loved so many times, the crook of my arm, the side of my nose. All the long-known pieces of us both receive a last greeting and farewell. After the hours of talking, this is the eloquence we seek. The smallest caresses express whole monologues of memory, so that her hands cupping my butt, fingers slipping into the little fold of flesh beneath the curve of one cheek as only she knows to do, brings the memory of a walk on the streets of Garbatella back to me, the tall prewar tenements with their vine-covered, cracked concrete walls, the color of faded ochre and rust. Nuzzling my chin into the swell of her breast returns the smell of the fresh-baked ciabatta bread we shared, huddling beneath the covers of the fold-out couch in her studio on a freezing winter night, the ancient heater creaking, casting dancing shadows on her paintings and the high ceilings. Past and present melding, now that there is no future—the urgency of my hands tightening beneath her back, a reminder that her flight to Rome has been booked, the feel of her legs wrapping round me as my hips shift within her hips saying, yes, it's true, we've talked out all the other solutions, and as I push the furthest tip of me as deep as I can reach inside her, her ragged breath at my ear, her teeth capturing my earlobe and releasing it is another acknowledgment of this—this is what we're losing, the taste of each other's tongues while our bodies clench and unclench in a kind of exultant despair. As she arches beneath me I see the solemn faces on the ancient broken column heads she showed me, upturned in the mud of the Appian Way, then her own wild grin as she spun and spun the loose wheel of her old Chevy, the day I bought it for her. And the bed rocks, time suspending for one last time, tomorrow with all its promised loneliness evaporated, a tenderness between us that prolongs each rush and retreat, until, bearing down with a fierce, steady rhythm, I'm with her in the café by the station, with its long brass pipe along the counter like a dancer's practice bar, its dark wood walls and the old men and the endless rows of pastries, where she pointed out her favorite, the one she'd always come to gobble down after school, and I had pictured her there, with all the uniformed schoolgirls, lips smeared with white powder sugar—and here is the woman grown, moaning against me while I clutch at her in a final urgency. The sudden rush to release catches us both by surprise, and we watch each other, eyes straining in the darkness as the pleasure that's never been this painful crests and breaks. And already she's crying again, sobbing harder than before, and this time I join her.

I pad into the bathroom for tissues, find none, can't get the toilet paper to rip properly, so I pull and keep pulling. When Isabella sees me reenter the bedroom in the dim light, trailing an endless roll of tissue, she laughs.

We cuddle beneath the covers with wads of the tissue scattered round, tremulous and giddy like two lost children up long past their bed-time.

"Do you remember that night," Isabella asks, "when we stayed with Derek in his mansion?"

"Oh, God," I say. "With that witch's moon. Like a cat's eye."

There had been a Picasso, an original oil painting, hung above our bed. I'd never seen one so close, outside of a museum. I got up in the middle of the night to pee, and when I came back to the bed, I couldn't keep my fingers from running over the old canvas, feeling each hardened brushstroke, tracing the lines, thinking: Picasso, Picasso.

"My silk pajamas," Isabella says.

"Which you left there, though they cost me a fortune, and I never got to see you in them again."

"You know how it is with me. But *Madonna,* that moon! I was a little scary."

I laugh. She means *scared.* "Yes," I say. "You were scary."

I remember Corsica, waking up to walk outside and watch the moon on the black sea, and back inside, seeing Isabella's hair dark on the white pillow. The mixture of contentment and unrest. Things were already failing between us then, already becoming impossible, but I didn't know that yet. She probably did, in that knowing but not really knowing way—she sensed it, I realize now, before we were even married. Just as I'd known that darkness of hers, how it lay underneath all the happiness, the dancing, her constant whirling celebration of life.

What did we do, the two of us? What dream did we make up?

"Who knows?" Isabella says, as though she's been listening to my thoughts. There's this, too—this affinity between us, the moments when we understand each other so well. So why shouldn't we have thought that it was meant to be?

"Who knows," I echo.

"Maxi," she suggests.

"Maxi!"

In the darkness, I can imagine the dog's dark shape, snoring in his little bed in the far corner of the room. I picture the slow rise and fall of his furry stomach.

"We did the best we could," says Isabella.

"You're right," I say. *"Hai reggione."*

7

Resolution

*A reconciliation that reaffirms the primal
importance of the relationship: usually a happy
but bittersweet ending which, while signifying a
serious commitment, has been achieved at the
cost of great personal sacrifice to the protagonist.*

*E*arly in the morning only two mornings later, when so much has been attended to and taken care of but so little has really changed, when it's our last morning together like this, I drift from a dream into the shallows of wakefulness, the sand I'd just imagined I'd been sprawled on now the smooth warmth of the sheets. The dark tidepool is the shadows of the bed, and emerging from it like a pale bluff of stone is the curve of Isabella's naked shoulder, so still and solid that, lying beside her, it's impossible to believe it will disappear, that this ever-familiar monument, the landmark of so many mornings, is about to vanish from my sight.

But though the speed of it surprises me, things have been decided, arrangements made—it's as if time has caromed into the two of us to send us spinning into our separate orbits. I remember what day it is, what it is that has to happen, and I don't want to begin it, not just yet, so I take refuge in that dream, the bits of it still washed up, glimmering, at the edges of my consciousness. We were on the beach, that strip where Isabella had drawn her figures with a stick, the sun hanging low over the coastal mountains. Silhouetted against it in the foam of the tide, a little girl turned on her toes, spindly-legged, hair long and wild. Dancing an impromptu ballet like some netherworld nymph, smiling over her sunburned shoulders at us sitting nearby in the sand, an audience of two. Something uniquely familiar about that face—and I realize that, of course, she's our daughter. I'm about to call her by name, a name caught tantalizingly on the tip of my tongue, when the alarm rings, rude, insistent, and she disappears into the realm of dreams. It's time to go.

The low-flying Boeings . . . driving up the departures ramp . . . the white zone . . . There is a moment, when I've deposited Isabella and her bags in front of the International Terminal and maneuvered into traffic to circle back to the parking structure, when the déjà vu is overpowering. Maybe my life is going to consist of endlessly repetitive trips to LAX. I'll keep picking them up and dropping them off, all my nearest and dearest, in some deranged karmic loop. Now that I'm a working writer only in theory, are the fates telling me I should moonlight as a limo driver?

Back in the terminal, an unexpected absence of conflict: no problems with Isabella's flight, ticket, with overweight baggage. She's only brought two suitcases, since the bulk of her belongings will be shipped or picked up on a return trip later in the year, when she'll manage the serious packing and removal of herself from my home and from my life.

All of what is to come still seems unreal, as unreal as the narcotic, eternal flow of activity inside the terminal. Isabella and I stroll among restaurants that resemble stage flats in their ever-pristine brightness. She takes my hand as we loiter by the duty-free shop windows. We can see each other reflected in the shop windows, a fine couple, close in height, fitting in style. I note that we both still wear our wedding rings.

Little eddies of sadness flow and recede in me. I've already had some practice getting used to being alone doing our time apart, but I've never fully considered what a newly unmarried life might be like. And while my mind dutifully goes through its motions of rationality and control, my body is in rebellion. My stomach, treated one last time to the richness of Isabella's cooking, churns, aggravated, as if it senses the deprivation to come.

Isabella is wistful and subdued. She hangs on to me when we stop by the beginning of the security line. I turn to hug her, afraid that I might lose it, those tears welling again, ready to roll. I think of how you're supposed to do this, the stoic, graceful way it's done in the movies. When we finally pull apart and I see that she's crying, I force a smile. "You can't possibly have any more tears left," I tell her.

"I know."

"You'll only get me started, and that's no good. They'll revoke my license to be a manly man."

She sniffles, smiles. "It just seems so . . . so . . ."

"Horrible," I offer. She shakes her head. "Ridiculous."

She laughs. "*Sì,* all of that. No, I just . . ." She sighs. "I'll miss you."

I nod. *"Anche io,"* I say. "But we'll talk. And it won't be too long before we see each other again."

"I know. But then why are we even . . ." She stops herself, looking at me. "I know. I know what we said, and still . . ." She shakes her head. "We love each other."

I take hold of her hands. "But that doesn't mean we're able to make each other happy."

She nods. *"Sì, io ricordo.* I remember everything. I only wish . . ."

"I know," I say. I wish she'd already found what she needed to find of herself. I wish I hadn't begun to lose some of myself in my dance of trying to fulfill her. We both wish we could have a big fat do–over of our life together, but you don't get those. And the line is moving.

"Maybe after a while we'll begin to feel different about this."

"Maybe," I say.

Her face brightens. "Who knows what can happen?"

All I can do is smile then, because my throat is very tight. I push a curl of her hair from her eyes. "Tell the pilot to drive carefully," I say. "Precious cargo."

"Sì," she says. "And you be good. I call you when I get there."

I nod. *"Ti amo."*

"Ti amo."

I kiss her forehead and step back. She looks at me with a piercing simplicity, her eyes memorizing this last image of me, before I press a packet of tissues into her hand, kiss that hand, and let it go.

I linger, watching Isabella approach the security check, and its demands for belt, earrings, bracelets, ring. It's getting harder to see her. When she emerges at the end of the process, still putting herself back together, she looks for me and waves. We keep the waving up until she gets to the turn-off to the gates. Isabella blows me a kiss, and disappears around the bend.

Alone again, I'm drained, flattened. Suddenly ravenous, I return to the faux-French café and pay a small fortune for a muffin and coffee. I dunk and munch, watching people pass without seeing any of them. This is all I am, will ever be capable of doing. I'll sit in this one spot while the earth completes any number of revolutions round the sun. I'm stuck trying to comprehend the scary, uncanny speed with which all that's been my life has transformed into memory. *When I was married,* I'll say.

Finally I tire of staring into the void, flicking my fingers at an empty paper coffee cup. It takes an enormous effort, but I rise from my chair.

Back on the main floor, traversing the cavernous lobby, I struggle against an invisible but formidable current. It's the force of what lies outside the terminal doors—the drive home to an empty apartment, the expectation of what awaits me: nothing. The specter of loneliness rises up like a colossus in my path, halting me in my tracks. How am I supposed to get around it?

Panic seizes me by the chest. I have to stop walking and take a few deep, shuddering breaths. So much for stoicism—you can wear it like a mask, but the expression of all that's been suppressed beneath it writhes and wriggles, tearing at the surface skin with its sharp edges. Those feelings I don't want to feel are ready to rip me up, like a pack of furies in the wake of this fear. The fear itself has to be halted, but how? My thoughts scurry blindly, then freeze by a sudden opening, tiny feelers quivering.

I veer to the row of public phones. I get out my little address book with the card still jammed against its back cover. On the third ring, Marie picks up. And no, sorry, I've just missed her—in fact, Marie has only this minute arrived home from dropping Naomi Dussart at the airport. She'll be back after the weekend, if I want to leave a message . . .

Meant to be. Has to be meant to be. Yes, it's an unseemly idea, a desperate, cheap-shot distraction, but why else have I been handed such a fortuitous coincidence? According to Marie, Naomi's flight to Telluride is on American at 4:45, which by my watch gives me thirty-two minutes. The answer to my anguish is that close. Saved! Out the doors, adrenaline pumping, I decide to run for it.

I start out at a trot, a jog, but the terminal isn't as close as I remembered it. As I gather speed, zigzagging my way between lost-looking Europeans, airline personnel with their natty coats and carry-ons, I start to laugh. Because really, come on: How many times have I groaned through this predictable climax, in how many romantic comedies?

It slows me down for a moment, the absurdity of what I'm enacting. But I'm not rushing to make someone a marriage proposal, I'm simply accepting an invite for fun on the ski slopes—from a delightful Frenchwoman, young enough to be impressed by me still, her inspirational American teacher, someone who doesn't see me as a sum of disappointments, who will welcome me into her vacation bed. Isn't this the least that the suddenly single man I've become deserves?

Now begins the game of avoiding collisions, a sprint around this pillar, a bypass of that family, a quick feint off the sidewalk and a deft dash alongside traffic to avoid a cluster of Asian tourists. Soon enough comes the obligatory obstacle: an airline worker pushing a long line of baggage carts, blocking my way entirely, just as the terminal sign finally comes into view ahead. I slow, panting but undeterred. Even when I do collide, unavoidably, with an executive whose briefcase clips my knee, a good, sharp, no-fun whack right on the bone, I'm smiling at the ridiculousness of this.

The sliding doors whoosh open. I still have time. What I don't have is a ticket. Amazingly, as though I really am in movie unreality, there's no line at all at the ticket counter. I have no baggage to check, no passport necessary. And though I sweat and twitch and agonize, approaching the metal detectors, I'm finally through them with nearly ten minutes to spare.

I run. I'm down one corridor when I realize I've misread the gates sign, and double back. This side is under construction. I'm moving too fast, not thinking clearly. When I bolt around a pair of pillars that are yellow-taped, meant to block civilian passageway, I make a run for what looks like a shortcut back to the central hallway, only to find that it dead-ends in an authorized personnel–only door, closed and locked. I'm lost in some back-corridor labyrinth, while frustratingly, I can hear the hollowly echoing footfalls and loudspeaker announcements from the other side of the wall. I trot round a corner and then stop short, arrested by the full force of my own foolishness.

What the hell am I doing? How is the person I've been running after ever going to fix my feelings, fill up that dreaded hollow? I stand there catching my breath, and it's as if I'm inhaling little spurts of reality. No, I realize, horrible as it seems, I have to be alone. Feeling whatever it is that I have to feel is the only way I'm truly going to get through this.

And now the first person I've seen since I got waylaid back here appears at the other end of the hall, striding toward me. And I don't suppose I should feel any surprise when I recognize that face.

There's no mistaking her. Dressed as she was that first day she surprised me in my garden, emerald green eyes sparkling at me with the amusement I know so well. Not the real Naomi Dussart, but My Naomi. I walk to meet her as she slows at the corridor's end, standing before a panel of reflective silver that mirrors my approach. And by the time I'm facing her, I know that this moment was my real destination.

"Where were you going?" she asks.

"I dunno," I admit. "I was wanting—"

"To lose yourself in another drama?"

Talking to her again is like being drop-kicked into the bracing air of a higher altitude. "Well, last I heard, I *am* a lost cause."

"Maybe not entirely," she says.

Maybe not. Because she's here, isn't she? And that must mean something. "It's good to see you," I tell her.

"Um-hmm," she says. "Things getting any clearer?"

"Well, I know you didn't show up to help me write a screenplay." She shakes her head. "What have you got against movies, anyway?"

"Nothing," Naomi says. "I simply can't support you doing something that isn't *you*." She sighs. "Don't you think it's time you got started on *your* project?"

"But I don't have a project."

Naomi looks exasperated. "Jordan," she says. "You're carrying it in you."

I stare at her in bewilderment. "Would you . . . Naomi, just this once, could you maybe, possibly, *be specific?*"

"You've been making up a story about what your life is, and revising it as you go along," she says. "And have you ever had control over how it'll work out in the end?"

"I guess not," I admit.

"Try to remember that as you start a new story," she says. "Which you'll have plenty of time to do. Now that you're alone."

"Wait a second. You're already leaving? Again?"

Her smile is playfully mocking. "I seem to remember you asking me to go."

"Yes, but now . . . !"

Naomi shakes her head. "Silly boy." She steps closer to me, looking up into my eyes. "So you want me to stay with you, do you?" she asks softly.

I say, "Yes, please."

She laughs. "You think we'd make a lovely couple?" She moves around me so that she stands beside me, the two of us facing our reflections in the mirrored surface of the wall. I watch her stretch on tiptoe to nuzzle at my ear, hear her husky whisper as she steps behind me. "Think of what you wanted," she murmurs. "Think of what you want . . . and how you might get to it, on your own."

The vibration from her breath in my ear melds with the hum of unseen machinery as her arms steal round my chest, hands caressing me, roving up my neck. There's a whirring of invisible wings as her warm palms press my cheeks, slide up to cover both my eyes, and in the momentary darkness, I think I hear the chiming of distant bells, and a moist wind scented with sand and sea moves through me. Then her hands fall away, I open my eyes, and for an instant, I see that cloak of mirrors I donned in my nightmare, flashing and then shattering, and it's Naomi I see facing me in place of my own reflection, as if she's standing in front of me. The paleness of her skin as the white diaphanous material blows round her is blindingly bright, and in the next instant, the radiance of her is dissolving, body become transparent, the features of her face overlaid on, then merging with mine. As I watch, the whole of her appears to seep into the whole of me, until only her smile is left to hover on my lips, and the last vestige of her eyes' green becomes a tiny gleam in my startled gaze.

I face myself in the mirror, feeling a warmth deep in my gut, like the small blue flame of a pilot light, newly lit. I look frazzled, shell-shocked, though as I continue staring at myself, my deep breaths shallowing, I see calmness steal over my features, with a hint of curiosity. Who is this guy?

Not the face of a failed husband, or a respected teacher. Gone are the shadows of other faces that had been superimposed on my face, the overlays of so many identities born of so many other people's points of view, donned with my own complicity. Missing now are all the roles learned from all of those movies, and in their place . . . someone who's decent enough to look at. Some new lines around the eyes, the beginnings of gray in the hair over my ears, but with no one else to define or pass judgment upon it, the face has some kind of character. Whatever it signifies, it's mine.

What I see is a man still standing. With a ticket in his hand, which could just as well be a ticket to anywhere.

~   ~   ~

The terminal proper is filled with the ebb and flow of human traffic. I move through it renewed, vibrating. So many other people going so many unknown places. I stand in the center of the shiny floor, turning one way and another, eyes caught by the impossible bulk of a student's backpack, the amazing hues of a middle-aged woman's high-heeled shoes. And striding toward me—impossible, but isn't it . . . ?—the tall, thin figure of the black homeless guy who was sitting in the street in front of my place the night I was locked out. Slim and gangly, a briefcase in his hand, ambling from the counters toward the escalators to the gates.

When he passes right by me, I realize, of course, that it can't be my thin man, though the resemblance is uncanny. This man is dressed in a stylish suit, his hair shorter and more kempt. But watching him ascend, I imagine he is the man I met, somehow transported to this wealthier realm.

You're carrying it in you.

I remember Naomi's smile as the thin man in the terminal disappears from sight, and I move to the side of the crowded floor. So what am I carrying? Standing beside an empty bench, I reach into each pocket of shirt, pants, jacket, and lay out all their contents before me. I sit down and survey . . . what?

There is Isabella's lighter, the cell phone, a napkin from Zulu, a small seashell that came from the Adriatic, years ago. Map to a treasure, a code waiting to be deciphered? I read every shard. I fondle the objects before carefully returning each to its proper home. Nothing adds up, at least not yet. But I'm thinking about the time I've spent seeing someone who nobody else could see, and all the times I've been invisible, even to myself. Then, like the glimmer of a tiny candlelight on the dark seawaters, some wisp of a notion of an almost-idea echoes in the recesses of my mind . . .

There's tinny surf music all around me suddenly, a repetitious loop of it. The noise bewilders me until I understand that the cell phone, which has never yet rung, is ringing. I retrieve the slim silver pod from my jacket, flip it open, press the call in, and with keen interest, put it to my ear.

"Jordan Moore," says Dana Morton.

"Dana," I say warily.

"Listen, I know things have gone more than squirrely between us, and the last time was not fun time, so I'll cut right to the chase with you, okay?"

"Okay."

"Rumer's let go of the project. I'm free to run with it, and I can get it set up at Paramount. Mary's an old chum, it'll take one call." She pauses. "Are you in an airport?"

I'm trying to process. "But . . . What about Nathan Colt?"

"Nate cut bait, sweetie. Look, all personal issues aside, you know and I know that we did a good job: This is a green light–able project. And seeing as it's Paramount, your boy Stan ought to be able to get you in the high six figures."

"The high six figures." It sounds more like the name of an alt–rock band than a concept of money I can comprehend, but in the next moment, some sense of the magnitude of what is about to happen finally begins sinking in.

It's the bright metallic-blue body with a black top, I realize, that's the Mini Cooper for me. With a sunroof. I picture it parked outside my gate, shiny new, with the roof open. Closed. Opening again . . .

"We can get your movie made," says Dana. "Talk to Stan. Work out what you need in the deal. And we'll talk later."

I stop playing with the sunroof. Enough is enough, I decide, and if I'm ever going to really go for it, I should go for it now. Can I do this? Am I ready? Am I willing to do what it takes to do it, after all the plans and dreams? Above me the screens flicker, flights appearing and disappearing. "There is no later," I say.

"Excuse me?"

"Some other time, Dana," I tell her, and flip shut the phone. I feel the weight of it in my palm. Then carefully, gingerly, knowing that it's now capable of going off at any moment, I carry it over to a nearby trash can and drop it inside.

I turn my attention to the list of flights posted on the monitors above, step closer to look at all the many destinations. I lift my forefinger in the air, close my eyes, move that finger randomly in a circle . . . stop. And open my eyes again.

I will not go to Anchorage, though assuredly Alaska would be a change of pace. Still, what seems clear and undeniable to me in this moment is that I must go somewhere, and as I'm thinking this, my eye falls on a familiar name, someplace closer to home, a place which, after all, I've so often promised to visit.

The baby cried the whole time the plane taxied down the runway, shrill wails cutting through the rumble and churn of the engines, but now that we're lifting off the ground, he's gone silent, mollified by his mother dangling a red flannel rabbit before his eyes. I watch this scene reflected in my dark window, with my window seat and an empty one to stretch out in, as this flight to New Orleans is only half full.

No, it won't be the same there. But then, what is?

In the resolution of a proper romantic comedy, there's simultaneously a sense of both triumph and defeat. Though the primal importance of a relationship has been reaffirmed, it's often at the cost of some personal sacrifice to the protagonist. And it's true that I'm feeling the exhaustion, the spiritual wear and tear that comes with my having lost so much, in such a short amount of time. But there is a spark of joy at the core of this defeat. I can feel what's been won, stirring in the depths of me.

The baby across the aisle is fascinated, face alight now that he clutches the rabbit in his mini-hands. Before I might have turned away, but tonight I can't stop looking. Just a rabbit to me, but what is it to the baby? A big, soft, warm red thing, all bright, ripe, fuzzy goodness—like a glowing star plucked from the plane's dome of a ceiling, which must seem cathedral high. It's a wonder that this brilliant redness can be held. As for me, I wonder what invisible hand is lifting us, aerodynamics being merely someone else's imaginary logic, all of us passengers enacting a testament to secular faith, telling ourselves another kind of story . . .

I'm doing Naomi's work now, on my own.

Practice, I suppose, for whatever will emerge. And what will it be, this idea, the new work—this life that I'll craft? I really don't know. But to get it started, it only makes sense to go somewhere as unknown as a blank page, leaving behind me for a while this city and its ceaseless fantasies, along with the rest of everything known, all the things I've held and had to let go.

Moments after claiming the rabbit as his, the baby holds it out, a proud offering to his father. Dad sits indifferent, absorbed in a magazine. The kid persists, batting at his arm with the fuzzy rabbit ears, as the plane arcs up into the sky. I watch, as unprepared for what might come next as ever, but intrigued, recognizing persistence and indifference, those two immutable laws of the known universe. Also there is hope, the bright headlights, beaming gold gleams on the dark roads that unfurl far below.

Acknowledgments

Foremost thanks to Bob Dolman, the book's best friend, and to Deena Metzger, who forced me to write it. Gilbert Girion, Nan O'Byrne, and Jimi Hawes talked me through the thing. It's in your hands due to three visionaries who got it, early on: producer Brian Brightly, agent Joe Veltre, and Sally Kim—an extraordinary editor.

I thank all my readers, especially Judith Lewis, Douglas Soesbe, Steven Wolfson, Jennifer Salt, and Carol Flint; thank you, Anna Hailey, for the title. Thanks to Barbara Abercrombie and Bob Adams for a writer's nirvana week in Twin Bridges, Montana, and to the staff of the Immaculate Heart Center in Montecito, California, who often provided the perfect room.

Bless you, Dani Minnick, for the lightbulb at the start and that cheer at the finish. I'm grateful for Ken Johnston's compassion and the Fergus Greer clan's company. Ed Lipnick lives on in these pages, and the spirit of Peter Trias, who brought me to Electric Avenue. Much love is due the über-supportive merry Mernit family.

And of course I thank Claudia Nizza and Minni, without whom . . .

About the Author

*B*illy Mernit is an expatriate New Yorker who currently resides in Venice, California. This is his first novel. Visit him at www.billymernit.com.